D0287260

"Signal 63"

Officer Needs Help!

Harold B. Goldhagen

Llumina Press

ISBN: 1-59526-408-6

Printed in the United States of America by Llumina Press

Library of Congress Control Number: 2006904608

Dedications

This book is dedicated to the men and women who wear the badge of the Atlanta Police Department: past, present, and future.

And, to my two children, Jay Alexander Goldhagen and Kris Goldhagen Silvers, who have grown to be outstanding and successful adults of high moral character.

And, to my wife Betty Jean Bledsoe Goldhagen, who more than anyone made possible my career. Betty carried the burden of home and family, enabling me to work irregular schedules and numerous extra jobs throughout my career. The love and passion I have for her is the same as it was when we first met nearly 50 years ago. I owe it all to her.

Acknowledgment

This book would not have been published without the sharp eye and even sharper mind of my very good friend, Michael Elia, whom I've known for 47 years.

Mike, a retired professional editor of two major book publishers, sacrificed many paid free-lance hours in order to be my personal editor over the past 18 months. Uniquely qualified for this role – not to mention the fact that several times he rode with me in a patrol car over the years – Mike spent a great deal of time and effort putting my manuscript in order.

For years, Mike and I have shared a deep common bond. When Mike first agreed to help me with my book, I knew that he was doing it out of love, friendship and mostly, because I had asked him.

Working closely with Mike has given me a newfound respect for the work that he did on a daily basis during his career. Without question, I am the beneficiary of his enormous talent.

Many years ago, the late Mario Schimeme, a close friend to both Mike and me, told me that to thank a true friend for a kindness is not only unnecessary, but might be insulting. Following Mario's wisdom, I'll just say that I am forever grateful to my pal, Mike Elia.

Table of Contents

"Signal 63"

Officer Needs Help!

"Signal 63"

A motorist gets a reprieve instead of a traffic ticket.

A meal is left unfinished by an officer at a diner counter or restaurant table.

A clandestine meeting between an on-duty officer and his girlfriend in some secluded spot is interrupted.

Officers receiving the call signaling that a fellow officer is in physical danger and needs help, by their next heartbeat, will head to where they can provide that help.

"Signal 63" will initiate all of the above and more in the Atlanta PD.

Throughout police departments and agencies, large and small, it receives the highest priority. It is initiated when the 911 operator is notified that an officer is in physical danger. It is broadcast over police radios, dispatching an immediate response within the broadcast area.

Police departments in different cities have different signal codes, but the message is the same: "Officer down," "Officer needs assistance," "Officer needs help." Most police departments dispatch calls for help using a series of signals and codes, usually a number—not for secrecy, but to expedite the call.

The codes or signals indicated below will generate massive police response in the respective cities, as will a call for help in any police department in any city.

New York City	-	Signal 10-13
Los Angeles	-	Code 999
Miami	-	Signal 10-15
San Francisco	-	Code 406
Chicago	-	Signal 10-1
Denver	-	Unique beeping signal
Milwaukee	-	"Assist an officer" (no number)
Atlanta	-	**Signal 63**

Prologue

My nostrils began to twitch at the scent creeping through the closed windows of my patrol car. Burning wood? Where?

A red-orange glow appeared in the midnight sky just above the tops of the small, rundown frame houses. They were little more than shacks in a poor neighborhood of Atlanta.

Driving toward the glow, turning onto Sampson Street, I saw flames shooting above one of the houses. I keyed the car microphone and shouted, "Signal 33 [fire]. Sampson and Highland!" As soon as the dispatcher acknowledged my call—"OK! Got it"—I raced to the house.

Over the sounds of the fire, I heard the screams of small children. I could not see them, nor could I hear any adult voices, just the high-pitched cries of the young.

I kicked in the front door and hollered, "Where are you? Can you hear me? Come to my voice. Come to my voice." The screams only intensified.

I tried, but could not step into the house. The wall of heat kept me at bay.

I got on the floor as I'd seen firefighters do (where the hell were they now?), bent my head down and tried to crawl past the door. The heat reached to the floor; that way was impassable.

The kids were still screaming; I ran around to the sides and back of the house, where I hoped the heat would be less intense. There was no back door, and the windows had bars across them.

From the time I called in the alarm, not more than a minute had passed, but it seemed much longer. I was cursing and praying the goddamn fire department was on its way.

What's taking them so long? I can't do this by myself! I need help.

The screaming stopped.

When the first fire truck arrived, I was at the front door, in the firemen's faces, trying to hurry them as they unraveled the hoses and donned their gear.

By this time, the house was fully involved.

No more screams; no more crying. The only sounds were those of the house burning.

The firemen found the charred bodies of two little girls, one four years old, and the other, six. No one else was in the house; the adults who lived there were out somewhere.

Never before had I requested to be relieved from my watch. It was 4:00 AM; I had four more hours, but I had to get away.

I heard the screams and the crying in my head.

I had to get home.

I heard the screams and the crying.

My uniform was torn and dirty.

I heard the screams and the crying.

That was more than forty years ago.

Many times I wondered whether I could have tried harder, figured out some way to rescue the little girls.

I still hear the screams.

Introduction

I was a police officer with the City of Atlanta Police Department, starting as a rookie cop in 1962 and retiring as a captain in 1992.

Thirty years. A long run. A few bumps in the road along the way. No other profession could have given me more satisfaction or a greater sense of accomplishment and reward, even during moments of agony and pain.

The Atlanta Police Department, not unlike other major police departments, performs many functions. Over my career, I served in different capacities. The entire time, I was where I wanted to be—on the street—either in uniform, as a detective, or working in special operations. The few times I had to work in an administrative function, I was like a caged bird.

I had the honor and good fortune to serve with some of the most dedicated, competent men and women ever to wear a police uniform. But some embarrassed or disgraced that uniform and the badge pinned to it.

A street cop in a major city gets an education not available in any institution of learning. It's an education gleaned from the losses suffered by a victim, from the pain inflicted by a criminal, from a cop's tedious nights, weekends, holidays, bad weather, boredom, and loneliness—as well as moments of excitement.

There is frustration, lots of it; there is anger, lots of it; and there is stress, lots of it. Not all of the frustration, anger, or stress comes from fighting and dealing with criminals. Most comes from one or more of four sources:

- The city council – The police department is the political football of city hall bureaucrats, whose miles of red tape run a dizzying maze, stifling even the most fundamental, low-level police transaction.

- The courts – "We, the people—" depend on the courts to dispense justice. But the courts regularly barter sentences for guilty pleas, a system of justice that would be the envy of the accused criminal in other places in the world. Justice? Often, it seems to the cops who have risked life, injury, and their future, that justice has little or nothing to do with guilt or innocence, right or wrong, or even truth—especially when the criminals they apprehend are released on technicalities.

- The media – The defenders of the First Amendment and the public's right to know. It's okay to support the public's right to know, but their right to know what? Everything? No. Not information that interferes with police operations; not information that jeopardizes police investigations. This interference goes beyond the intent of the First Amendment. But, the media fulfills its intent in exposing police and city officials involved in criminal, corrupt, or improper conduct.

- The public – Some people are pro-police, some are anti-police; most don't care either way. The public watches police shows on television, so they think they know what police work is all about. But the public is misinformed, to some extent, by the TV shows, and is misled by what police officials and politicians say.

My story takes place in Atlanta, Georgia, but it could be any major US city from New York City to Los Angeles. Cops are cops; people are people; crime is crime. Serving in a major police department is a tough way to make a living under ordinary circumstances. As you will read, my circumstances were anything but ordinary.

I wrote this book to provide a better understanding of what it is like to be a cop, as seen through the eyes of a cop—my eyes.

Harold B. Goldhagen
August 2005

Part One

Patrolman

The Beginning

I was born during a December blizzard, in New York City, in the middle of the Great Depression. I grew up on the streets of four boroughs of the city–Manhattan, Brooklyn, Queens, and the Bronx, but not Staten Island, which lacked a bridge to the rest of New York City at that time. If, as President Lyndon Johnson declared to John Califano, his head of Health, Education, and Welfare, growing up in the streets of Brooklyn served him better in Washington than his Harvard education, then perhaps growing up in the streets of New York City prepared me well for a career as a police officer.

Graduate school was two years in the Merchant Marine, three years driving a truck in New York City delivering typewriters and office machines, and two years in the US Army.

Without the benefit of a placement office, I wandered, one day in 1961, into the personnel department of the City of Atlanta and filled out an application for employment as an Atlanta police officer.

Application and Selection

I made it through the selection process, despite my lack of formal education and a high school diploma. I was on shaky ground with some of the other requirements, also. I had dropped out of high school after tenth grade, at age sixteen. But I had a GED high school equivalency diploma, obtained during my years in the army, surely the smartest thing I did in the army, and the best thing the army did for me.

I took the Atlanta PD written test and passed with a score so high it surprised me. The medical requirements were rigid: 20/20 eyesight, without glasses, normal blood pressure, and minimum height and weight requirements. I had no problem with the first two requirements. I barely made the latter at five feet, eight inches, and one hundred thirty pounds just out of the shower and not yet dry. I was in excellent physical condition and deceptively strong for my size. The agility test was no problem. I could do pushups until the instructor tired of counting.

The background check was more restrictive than it is today.

Today, there are no height or weight requirements. Many other requirements have also lapsed. Forty years ago, an Atlanta police officer was not allowed to drink alcoholic beverages, neither on nor off duty. Worse, a police officer discovered with liquor in his home—his home!—was subject to dismissal. It's so different today! Today, as long as you haven't used drugs within six months of your application for employment as an Atlanta police officer, you can get the job. Back when I applied to the department, one outstanding parking ticket could disqualify an applicant. Once on the job, if you were involved in a serious traffic offense, you were gone—no longer a cop. Today, applicants with misdemeanor records are hired in Atlanta as police officers.

The Background Check and My Army Record

I was twenty-two years old in 1956; the US Army still drafted eligible young men. Had it been a volunteer army, I would not have been a soldier. But, due to the draft, I was an unwilling soldier in the US Army. The Korean War was over; the US was not yet involved in Vietnam. It was a peacetime army. But there was a war between the Army and me! My resistance had no political or ideological basis, as was the case for draft dodgers during the Vietnam War. I just didn't want to be in the army. I didn't have the right attitude to be a soldier. My attitude made those two years hard for me.

The troop train transporting me and sixteen hundred other draftees from Fort Dix, New Jersey arrived at Fort Benning, Georgia sometime around three a.m. It was raining, a hard, driving rain. We were hustled out of the train, through the rain, onto open trucks. The faster the trucks drove, the harder the rain pelted our faces, and the deeper it penetrated our clothing. We arrived, a half hour later, at a group of dismal wooden barracks. We were herded inside and instructed to find a bunk and get some sleep. I was wet through to my underwear. I tried to sleep, not very successfully. But it didn't matter. An hour and a half later, the lights went on throughout the barracks, whistles blew, and the screaming started.

Welcome to the United States-fucking-Army! They probably still have not figured out that that is a stupid fucking way to treat anyone starting any kind of endeavor anywhere—especially the US Army.

I was assigned to Bravo Company, 9th Training Battalion, 30th Regiment, 3rd Infantry Division. For each company, there were drill instructors whose missions in life (and most DIs were career army) were to make men out of misfits and mamma's boys, and they start out assuming that all draftees are misfits or mamma's boys. The drill instructor for my squad was Corporal Ashcraft, a young country boy from North Carolina. Corporal Ashcraft held the power of life and death, it seemed to me, and him, over the squad to which I was assigned.

From the first day, he made clear that he disliked Yankees and Jews. I had to endure his dislike and unwarranted hatred because I was from New York City and a Jew. It was like that between us for sixteen weeks—eight weeks of basic training followed by eight weeks of advanced infantry training.

Corporal Ashcraft, Drill Instructor, let me know, in no uncertain terms, that he was going to break me, announcing it to everyone in Bravo Company.

Army regulations specify that trainees must be given a ten-minute break every fifty minutes. The breaks are critical for one's well being, especially during the hot, humid months of June, July, August, and September. The training was physically exhausting. When breaks came, everyone found a shady spot, sat or flopped there, and did not move for the entire ten minutes.

I didn't get that rest during those minutes. Corporal Ashcraft, Drill Instructor, pulled me to the side at break time and had me perform painful and injurious exercises—wearing my steel helmet, minus the plastic helmet liner and webbing, while I "double-timed" in place. The helmet bounced on the top of my head each time I jumped. He also greatly enjoyed making me duck walk (walking in a squatting position) to his cadence, not allowing me to stand. These exercises caused headaches and leg cramps, but I never gave him the satisfaction of knowing I was hurting in any way. On evenings when it rained, Corporal Ashcraft, Drill Instructor, ordered me to mop the wooden landing outside the barracks and keep mopping until it was dry. When

3

the rain fell all night long, I would be there all night—mopping, mopping, mopping—into the morning.

I never complained. But everyone saw what was going on, even the other drill instructors.

Corporal Ashcraft, Drill Instructor, had the power because he was a drill instructor. But I had a plan. I told him, every chance I had, "Ashcraft, keep it up. When sixteen weeks are over, I'm going to find you. When I do, one of us is not going to walk away!" I smiled when I said it. As his stupid shit continued, I kept smiling.

When training ends, most trainees are shipped to Army posts in the US and around the world. Drill instructors, such as Corporal Ashcraft, Drill Instructor, count on this. However, this time, a few remained at Fort Benning.

I was one of them!

One Saturday, several weeks later, Corporal Ashcraft, Drill Instructor, was getting off duty at noon. I went to Bravo Company and waited for him at his car in the parking lot. He walked into the lot with a few other drill instructors. I walked briskly up to him, without saying a word. When I reached him, I knocked him down. He curled up on the ground, so that it was not a fight between him and me, but a beating! I straddled his chest and slammed his head against the parking lot, over and over, faster and harder. I was in a rage. My fury was fueled by flashbacks of his abuse during the past sixteen weeks–the steel helmet bouncing on my head, causing blistering headaches, the leg cramps that kept me awake nights, and the sleep deprivation on nights when I mopped the entrance to the barracks.

I was so focused on beating Corporal Ashcroft, Drill Instructor, that I was unaware spectators had drawn near to watch. Slowly, I became aware of shouting, and then several pairs of hands grabbing me, pulling me off him. One, a drill instructor, stood me up against one of the cars, and calmly, sternly, said, "Okay, he had that coming. Now, call it even. Get out of here. And don't come back!"

I felt a lot better after that.

But I developed a bad attitude toward anyone with the power to do what he wanted to anyone who did not have power to resist or fight back. I became the guy no one was going to fuck over. My attitude created problems for myself, then and later in life.

I was tried by summary court-martial for one incident and by special court-martial for another.

The summary was over an encounter with a female officer. She was an army nurse; there were not many females in the military in the mid-1950s. I was on the main post in Ft. Benning, Georgia, walking with two of my buddies, when we passed her, in uniform—a lieutenant. My buddies "threw her a highball," meaning they saluted her, as required. I walked past without doing the same. She called to the three of us, "Soldiers, stop!" We stopped, turned toward her; she looked directly at me, "Don't you know you're supposed to salute an officer?" I didn't respond, except to refuse to salute her. She made a note of the name sewn into my fatigues and asked for my unit, which I gave her. When we returned to our unit, about an hour later, the company commander was waiting for me.

He asked whether I was aware that she was an officer. Didn't I know I had to salute officers in uniform? I replied I didn't want to salute female officers. That made him angry enough not to ask why. The captain told me that if I didn't return to the main post, meet with her, apologize, and salute her, he would initiate a summary court-martial, which the company commander had the authority to do. I refused, leaving him to deal with my punishment. "If you refuse, you will chop down trees for thirty days," he said.

"Gimme the ax!"

He did. I chopped down trees, eight hours each day, every whack witnessed by an NCO, as required by army regulations. I wonder if, in today's environmental consciousness, that punishment is still in effect.

A special court-martial is more serious than a summary. I was at a formal guard mount–that's the inspection for formal guard duty at the main post, where the generals and VIPs work and reside. My uniform was clean, pressed, infallibly creased, shoes shined so well they reflected, brass polished, my rifle barrel cleaned and unobstructed–but not according to the eyes of the officer of the day. He looked down the barrel, snapped it back in the required military fashion, and said, "Your rifle does not pass inspection; you are relieved from this guard mount. Return to your barracks, where you will be restricted until further notice."

Back in the barracks, everyone else was somewhere else. I lay on my bunk, wondering what the OD saw in my barrel that would offend the generals and VIPs, when one of my company's NCOs entered. Word of my relief had gotten around; he started to harass and then verbally abuse me about it. From the sight, sound, and smell of him, it was clear he had been drinking. He taunted me, challenging me; I did not like what he was saying to me. If he didn't know from my face, he surely knew when I glared at him and said, "Go fuck yourself!" He invited me into the latrine to "Settle it like men." (As opposed to what? Settling it like children? Like women?) As we entered, I tripped him; he stumbled down the steps toward one of the sinks. I grabbed him by the back of his fatigues, steering his momentum, shoving his face into one of the sinks.

I left him in there, stunned.

I went back to my bunk, grabbed my stuff, shoved it into an AWOL bag– that's what it was called then–and left the US Army.

I was gone for twelve days. AWOL.

Even as I left, I knew I would have to return. But I just had to get away from the army, the rules, the uniforms, the mentality, the culture, the jargon, the careers, the buttons, the salutes, and everything else that made the army what it was.

But no matter how much I hated being in the army, I wasn't a deserter.

I returned on my own, prepared to take what was coming for having been relieved from a formal guard mount, for assaulting a non-commissioned officer, and for being AWOL for twelve days.

At my court-martial, I didn't deny the charges, although I did try to justify the assault on the NCO. At my trial, Master Sergeant Casey asked to address the court. I worked for him, causing him nothing but problems; I figured what he would say would put me in the stockade for sure, maybe even bury me under it. He identified himself as a decorated combat infantry veteran of World War II and the Korean War. He said that if he were ever again in combat, sharing a foxhole with someone, he would want me in that foxhole with him. I was stunned. It felt good to hear someone of his military experience say something like that about me. I was overwhelmed that he said it at my court martial. He must have impressed the panel. My punishment was six months in the stockade, I was demoted two grades in rank and forfeited all pay and allowances for six months. It could have been a lot worse were it not for Master Sergeant Casey.

The next step was for the regimental commander to sign the order transferring me to the stockade. That order was never signed. Sergeant Casey rode to see the regimental commander with me and the MPs. The colonel was ranger qualified and an advocate of the US Army Rangers.

Casey worked out a deal with him, with my consent. I would go to Ranger School. If I completed the entire nine-week course, my six-month sentence would be suspended, and I would not have to spend an extra six months of "bad time" in the army. I would, however, have to make up the twelve days of AWOL. I made it through, I had plenty of motivation.

My army record included many "Article 15s," company punishments for minor infractions, such as out-of-doors in uniform, but without the required hat, or tossing a cigarette to the ground without first field stripping it, or failing to maintain my bunk or locker area according to army SOP. Punishment usually was two hours of extra duty each evening for two weeks, cleaning weapons, clearing weeds, cleaning the mess hall grease trap, and so on.

My Army Record and My APD Oral Interview

Atlanta Police Superintendent J. L. Tuggle conducted my oral interview. He had, right before his eyes, my army records, showing my courts-martial and my discharge form, which showed that I was honorably discharged, but had not received a citation for good conduct. I worried about what to say when he asked me about the courts-martial and the lack of a good conduct medal, but he never asked or mentioned any of it.

What Superintendent Tuggle, a Southern Baptist and religious fanatic, asked was whether I was a good Christian. I replied, "No, I am not a good Christian because I am not a Christian. I am a Jew."

I went home, told my wife Betty that Tuggle had looked at my army record, never asked about it, and then asked if I were a Christian. We didn't say much to each other; we had dinner, and then I tried to fall asleep, without success, because I was thinking about where else to look for my future. I figured the Atlanta Police Department was done with me. I was sure Tuggle hadn't questioned my army record because what he saw gave him no reason to ask about it. The "good Christian" thing was the clincher.

What was Tuggle Thinking?

For the next week, I scanned the want ads, went on interviews, but found no job. Then I received an official-looking envelope in the mail. It was from the Atlanta Police Department. I didn't rush to open it; I figured they were sending their regrets that they could not hire me. Not wanting to face the news, I opened the envelope reluctantly. It was my notice to report to the police academy for training!

For a moment, I wondered what Superintendent Tuggle had thought, but I looked again at the notice and didn't care what he had or hadn't thought. I only cared that I had made the final cut and entered a class of twenty-eight recruits, from a pool of about thirteen hundred applicants.

That was February 1962.

The Police Academy

Police academy training consisted mostly of classroom courses— laws and ordinances, rules and regulations, rules of evidence, traffic direction, report writing, court testimony, radio procedure, how to handle calls, and crime scene procedure. We also had a good deal of hands-on physical training, including calisthenics, which sometimes brought us to the limit of our endurance.

In one exercise, we held a five-pound dumbbell in each hand, arms extended straight out from our sides, parallel to the floor. We had to hold our arms this way until the instructor permitted us to drop them, trembling, aching, and leaden, to our sides. Roy Foster, one of the biggest recruits at six-foot-three, stood next to me. He was struggled, trying to get through the torment, but he just couldn't hold up his left arm. He rested his dumbbell on mine, unnoticed by the instructor, and somehow I found the strength to support the double load. This is how bonds and friendships were formed that last a career.

Self-defense and the mechanics of arrest were harder to endure. We were randomly paired against each other; each pair had to go at it on the mat. The instructor "encouraged" the gladiators to really fight each other. Better to get some bumps and bruises and learn to defend yourself with a fellow recruit in the gym, where you can get prompt medical attention if need be, than be unprepared on the street, where you could be hurt or killed by some thug. The instructor let the fighting get pretty rough, usually stopping it just short of blood. The instructor didn't always achieve that goal! During one session, I paired off against Ken Burnette, who was about my height, but outweighed me by thirty pounds. As things got rough, I attempted to get him in a headlock, and I hit his nose with my arm harder than I intended. Blood spurted from his nose, ending our self-defense training for the day. It was weeks before Burnett's nose mended. I felt shitty about the whole thing; I apologized to him more than he wanted to hear over the next several weeks. Ken was a deeply religious person and very forgiving and understanding. We have been the best of friends since that day.

Officer James Wade Hagin

We spent a week on the pistol range, where recruits learn to shoot the .38 caliber Police Special revolver. We were required to qualify with this weapon to graduate from the academy. The recruit class that previously had gone through the academy for all other training was joining our class for pistol training. The first day on the pistol range, I met Wade Hagin. Wade was shooting in the lane next to mine. I was a respectable shooter and had no trouble qualifying, but I was not as good as Wade. He scored higher than I scored all week, including a perfect score in the final round. Wade won the trophy over sixty other recruits.

We became best friends.

He came from the rural town of Statesboro, in South Georgia. He grew up on his father's farm, picking cotton and tobacco and doing whatever the hell else farmers did back then, and maybe still do. The two of us surely made an odd couple. One, a WASP from South Georgia—quiet, introverted, not much to say, a Huck Finn; the other, a Jewish boy—born and raised in New York City with the gift of gab, outspoken about many things. Water and oil don't mix, but we did. We were bound by our intense desire to be Atlanta policemen. We made a pretty good team in the years to come.

Graduation

After all the training—graduation. At graduation, I was sworn in by Police Chief Herbert T. Jenkins, issued a badge, an ID card, a Smith and Wesson .38 Special service revolver, twelve bullets, a pair of white gloves, and a metal whistle, but not a uniform. I had to buy that myself. I purchased my Atlanta police uniform out of my first month's salary—three hundred and twenty-six dollars. When fully outfitted, I was Patrolman H.B. Goldhagen, badge number 1479, ready to slay the dragon, fight crime, and eradicate the forces of evil. I anticipated my first assignment with hope and the intention to do what I was trained and ready to do.

The operation of the Atlanta Police Department was simple in 1962. Police functions were handled by one or more of four divisions—the uniform, traffic, detective, and administrative divisions. Everything operated under the roof of the police station in downtown Atlanta. The uniform division had the lion's share of personnel, and it was there that rookies were assigned upon graduation from the academy.

Atlanta Police Academy Diploma – 1962

APD recruit class photo – Patrolman H.B. Goldhagen
(rear row center)

My First Assignment

My first assignment saw me headed to the uniform division, morning watch—midnight to 8:00 a.m., the "graveyard" shift—the least desirable watch. When you're new in an organization with a twenty-four-hour, seven-day-a-week operation, expect the worst shift. I was prepared when I was assigned the morning watch, with Tuesdays off–that was back when an Atlanta policeman had a six-day workweek. Six days a week for three hundred and twenty-six bucks a month didn't make me a Fortune 500 junior executive, but that was okay. I was then, and remain now, an optimist. I believed that, in the next thirty years, things would get better.

Reporting for duty that first night, I was a "roustabout." When a cop with a regular assignment had worked his six days and was getting his "rest on the seventh day," a roustabout substituted for him. As a roustabout, I drove a patrol car, drove a paddy wagon, walked a beat, answered phones in the general office, dispatched calls from the radio room, and secured prisoners at the Grady Hospital detention area, among other assignments for which the morning watch was responsible.

We gathered for roll call in a large assembly room in the basement of the police station. The captain and other superior officers of the morning watch conducted roll call.

"Goldhagen, car twelve, with Blore," thundered Captain Beavo Brooks in his gravelly voice. Twelve's beat covered the fringe of the downtown area and extended northwest of the city. Officer C.B. Blore had been around a few years. Something about his demeanor caused me to understand that a rookie cop keeps his eyes and ears open and his mouth shut. During most of the night, we rode in silence, interrupted only by calls dispatched to other units and general chatter on the police radio. I learned real fast that this was his car; he drove it, and he called all the shots. It was not hard to realize that I was with him because I was assigned to be with him. He tolerated me because he had to. Most of the time, he treated me as though I weren't there. It was clear that my presence annoyed him. Midway through a morning watch is 4:00 a.m.—time to eat lunch. During lunch, one cop remains in the patrol car, listening to the radio, while the other cop grabs something to eat in one of the all-night joints somewhere on the beat. Should a call come in, the cop in the car pounds on the horn, the cop in the joint leaves his lunch—and together, they answer the call.

As we pulled up to an all-night greasy spoon on our beat, Blore got out of the patrol car and went inside without uttering a word. Through the window, I saw him sit down and order, and watched as his food was served. I sat in the car, hoping he would finish quickly because I damn sure didn't want to have to blast the horn, disturbing his lunch, to respond to a call. When he returned to the car, he continued the silent treatment as he put the car in gear. He was about to drive away. Before he could, I made my first decision as a cop and partner of another cop. Without comment, I got out of the car, went inside, and ordered a giant grease burger. Had I waited for him to acknowledge that it was his turn to wait in the car while I ate, I would have gone hungry that night.

My hunger and my self-respect satisfied, I returned to the car. We continued our patrol, and soon we were chasing a traffic violator who refused to stop at our signal. As we entered an intersection against a red traffic light, Blore had to hit the brake and swerve to avoid hitting a car coming through the green light. We slid on the pavement, which was still wet from an earlier drizzle, spinning our car three hundred and sixty degrees. The good thing about completing a three hundred and sixty-degree spin is that you end up in the same direction you were heading before the spin. Blore accelerated, continuing forward, managing not to hit anything. We caught up with the violator in the next two blocks. He knew he was caught, so he made no further attempt to flee. Before getting out to arrest him, Blore and I sat in the car momentarily, giggling like a couple of high school freshmen who had gotten away with a prank. That brief moment broke the tension built up earlier that night. The remainder of the watch was uneventful. I had made it through my first night as a real live cop in a big city.

As time went on, I realized that Carl Blore was not a bad guy. It was not that he didn't like me. His attitude toward me was not personal. He was a product of the system—the police culture—a closed society, a society that feels it's "us" against "them." Policemen tend to be suspicious of everyone, including rookie cops. Even though a rookie wears the same uniform and has a badge, there is no difference. About what other cops do, a rookie is expected to "see no evil, hear no evil," and most important, "speak no evil." Among police, there's an unwritten, unspoken code of silence. The rookie must see nothing, so there's nothing about which to talk. He must keep his mouth shut. Until a rookie proves himself, he is kept at a distance by the veteran cops. When they see that the rookie can keep his mouth shut, he is admitted to the inner circle.

It was all about whether the rookie could be a "pimp." A pimp is someone who provides women and arranges for them to perform sexual acts in exchange for money. The same term was used to refer to a policeman who heard, saw, and then told higher ups about other cops' improper conduct, violations of rules and regulations, and other infractions. Not long after my first day, I learned the meaning of "pimp." Pimps were isolated from and ostracized by other cops. That's the way it was when I became a cop. Most fellow officers refused to work with or talk to a pimp—including many superior officers. Nor was this treatment subtle. It was openly hostile and cold. A pimp's on-duty life was miserable; he usually ended up leaving the department.

A police officer who uncovered a "crooked cop," an officer "on the take" or involved in criminal or illegal activity, such as taking bribes or stealing, was commended by other officers and his superiors. Corruption was not condoned, it was not tolerated—not by any rank and file cop, or by superior officers. Back then, there was a distinction between a cop who did not follow the rulebook and a crooked one.

Going to the Crack

"Cracking" has been a tradition with policeman for many years, and might still be. It happens everywhere. New York City policemen call it "cooping." It is usually done in the wee hours of the morning watch. A policeman "going to the crack" goes to a secluded, out-of-the-way spot, hidden from public view, such as wooded areas or industrial parks—or maybe the end of an alley or behind a building. Once there, he removes his gun-belt, shoes, and tie, then snoozes. Things slow at that time of the morning; there's not much activity on the radio. Nevertheless, a policeman in the crack learns how to listen to the radio with one ear.

Policemen go to the crack in groups for various reasons. The main reason is that it is less likely that someone will walk up to your car while you doze and blow your brains out when other patrol cars are around. Also, should you be sleeping so soundly you fail to hear a radio call, someone in the group will most likely hear the call and wake you. Some police officers in the crack get so comfortable they wouldn't hear a lightning bolt hitting the ground a few feet away.

Not every police officer cracks. I've been in the crack with as many as eight other patrol cars and two paddy wagons. Most rookies don't want to spend a couple of hours hidden in the woods or behind a building watching a bunch of veteran cops sleep.

Hollywood Douglas

The first time I went to the crack, I was working a patrol car with Officer JR "Hollywood" Douglas. He was mean. He was well known by most burglars and street thugs. A man would try to mess with him once—never a second time. Even other policemen feared him. He was a walking arsenal. Once I counted three guns (his service revolver, a snub nose, and a derringer), two knives (he kept them hidden in his belt and could have them out and opened, simultaneously, in a split second), a nightstick, a blackjack, brass knuckles, and a metal three-cell flashlight filled with lead (instead of batteries).

One early summer morning, Hollywood and I were in the crack, along with several other patrol cars. Hollywood was resting well. I was awake, listening to the radio, hoping to have to respond to a call so we could leave. I didn't want to be there, but he was the veteran, and in any police partnership, the pair does what the veteran cop says. I sat there, fidgeting with my flashlight, turning the switch on and off. It must have sounded like a pistol being cocked (that's what he told me later) because all of a sudden, he came out of a sound sleep, pulled his pistol, cocked it, and had it under my nose before I could say, "Oh, shit!" He had a look in his eyes, a wild look that froze my blood. After I regained my composure, I said things that people didn't usually say to his face. I was scared, but I was mad, so mad that I didn't care he was a veteran, the Mister Bad-ass veteran. He threw his head back, howled his strange laugh, and that was the end of it. We became friends after that, and shared some heavy policing in later years. But I never again went to the crack in the same car with Hollywood Douglas.

Hollywood was a strange man and an even stranger cop. There was the time we answered a routine call. At the location, Hollywood knocked on the door, a woman answered, and the moment she opened the door, he screamed in her face, turned around, threw his head back, howled that strange laugh, and returned to our car. The woman had no idea why he did it, I had no idea why he did it, and I doubt Hollywood knew why he did it. He did many other weird things. There were complaints about his

14

behavior. They persisted until brass had to do something about him. He was removed from the street, assigned to communications where he dispatched cars to calls. One night, strung out on pills (no secret to any who knew him), he went crazy on the radio, using foul language, disrupting communications, muttering unintelligibly. The watch captain and several superior officers had to go into the radio room and forcibly remove him. He never returned to work.

Signal 80

A month out of the police academy, I learned that police work was not all "cops 'n robbers." Officer WL Reynolds and I were working Car 16 in the southeast part of Atlanta. We received a signal 80—a report of a stray animal—in this case, a mule. We were to be on the lookout for the mule and contain him. It didn't take us long to find him. The mule was in the middle of Moreland Avenue, one of the city's main thoroughfares. I grew up far from the outdoors, in the big city of New York, where I had never seen a mule in the street—I had never seen a mule. I knew that a mule wasn't the same as a horse, but I didn't know what the difference was. I didn't know whether to shoot him, ride him, or just leave him be and get the hell out of there. Reynolds knew what to do. He took the mule by the bridle, led him to the curb, and tied him to a telephone pole.

We called for a paddy wagon. It was too small to transport the mule. We came up with another idea. We called for a station house prisoner to come out to where we were. We told him to lead the mule, walking him by the bridle. We trailed slowly behind, our emergency lights flashing, all the way to the Atlanta zoo. It took us an hour. Once there, we couldn't find anyone to accept the mule from us. Repeated calls to zoo officials were received with refusals to come out and indignation about being awakened in middle of the night. Having a mule on our hands and not knowing what to do with him was not their problem.

We came up with still another idea—we'd take the mule to the city prison farm. The farm was a good distance away. With the prisoner still leading the mule, setting the pace, Reynolds and I followed in the patrol car. We got to the farm as dawn broke, beating rush hour traffic. Success at last. We dumped ol' flop ears at the farm, called for the paddy wagon to retrieve the prisoner, whom we think, endeared himself to the mule. Then Reynolds and I headed for the nearest bacon, eggs,

15

and coffee, where we mused that we had spent the entire watch "watching" the rear end of a mule.

Later that day, I saw our mule staring back at me from the human interest page of the newspaper. Ol' flop ears got his picture in the paper, and Reynolds and I were merely mentioned for our eight hours of baby-sitting.

Taking a Leak

Commercial burglaries occur mainly when the business is closed, locked up for the night, and everyone is gone. One of the morning watch's priorities is answering calls of possible burglaries in progress, hopefully catching the burglar in the act. Back in the 1960's, it was legal to shoot a fleeing felon. Not many felons tried to run. When a burglar was caught in the act, the standard operating procedure was to render to him a good ass kicking.

My first encounter with a burglar came about a month after my first day on the job. I was working a car with Officer KE Crowe. The first part of the watch was routine. We answered a few calls, made several traffic stops, arrested a drunk driver or two, and enjoying the culinary delights of the all-night pancake house. At about 4:00 a.m., checking our beat for burglaries, we both had to make a pit stop. We pulled in behind a closed supermarket. As we stood beside the car taking a leak, I noticed someone peering at us through the cracked-open back door of the supermarket. Still peeing, I casually made a comment to Crowe about not being able to piss in private, even in the middle of the night. He asked why I said that. I told him. He zipped up immediately and instructed me to watch the back door and shoot anyone attempting to flee. He jumped in the car, called for backup, and drove around to cover the front.

As other units arrived, we found the back door had been forced open. Groceries and meat were stacked up just inside the door, ready to be transported. We searched the store for a long time but could not find anyone. There were about a dozen policemen searching with Crowe and me. Captain Clyde Hamby and Sergeant Jack Eaves arrived. We searched for another twenty minutes, but still could not find anyone in the store.

The captain, a no-nonsense tough guy with a growl in his voice and a cigar clamped in his teeth, wanted to know who saw the burglar. All eyes were on me as he "questioned my powers of observation," suggesting that perhaps I suffered from the overactive imagination of a new cop on the beat. It was obvious there had been an attempted burglary, but it was just as obvious that the burglar was gone. I stuck to what I saw and insisted that the burglar had not left through the back door, the only way out, or I would have stopped him. The captain ordered the search to continue.

I hoped we would find the burglar. Not only did I fear the captain's wrath, I did not want to lose my credibility. I wanted the other cops to accept me as one of their own. Eventually, we found the burglar hiding in a far corner of the ceiling. He had hidden himself in such a way that the probing flashlight beams did not fall on him. He descended from his perch–well, was pulled from his perch, and stood defiantly among the dirty, sweaty, pissed-off cops, boasting that he made more money in a night of burglarizing than any cop earned in a month. His remarks made us mad because it was true. He bragged that he would be out of jail on bond before we got off duty, and that made us even madder because we knew it was likely to be true, too. The remarks were more than enough for our grizzly ol' captain to smack the burglar in the chops and knock him down. Captain Hamby turned and left without a word, Sergeant Eaves at his heels. Three policemen grabbed the burglar and finished what the captain had started. When they were through, the message was clear to the burglar—"Don't get caught burglarizing by the Atlanta police." After witnessing my first police-administered ass kicking, I was glad I was not a criminal, especially not one caught by the police.

Through the Little Rear Window!

I had an uncle who was a milkman. I was very close to Uncle Lou; he was like a second father. He lived in an apartment a few blocks from my family, in the Bronx. His milk route was in Staten Island, an underground commute via the subway, over water on the Staten Island ferry (there was no bridge at that time), and then on rural-like roads, on a bus, to the Borden's Milk Company barn. He left his apartment at 3:30 a.m. and arrived at the barn at 5:30 a.m. When I was a young man, out for the "evening," I'd return home just before Uncle Lou left for work. I'd drive to his apartment building and double-park at the entrance, waiting to drive him to the ferry at the lower tip of Manhattan. On bitter cold mornings, he would step into the warmth of my car—"Ah, delicious," was all he said, but it was enough to express his appreciation.

When I left for the army, he lost his ride to the ferry. On the ferry, he'd write notes and letters on the blank side of his Borden order book pages. "Harold, button your buttons. Shine those shoes. Keep your locker straightened. Make your bunk better." I received one of those terse messages from Uncle Lou every day during basic training at Fort Benning, GA. After basic training, he wrote complete letters, which came in the mail several times each week.

My first hands-on experience with a violent person came one night while working a Southside car with Officer JA Phoebus. We answered a signal 44/47—44 indicated a robbery, 47 meant a person was injured. Arriving at the location, we found a milkman with a bloody head sitting in his truck. We called for an ambulance. While waiting for it to arrive, the milkman told us what had happened.

After leaving the barn with a truckload of milk and other dairy products, the milkman stopped to prepare his load for the pre-dawn delivery on a desolate city street, as he had done each morning for the past several years. Someone jumped into the truck and began beating him in the head with a brick. The assailant threatened to kill him. The milkman managed to jump out of the truck. As he fled, the assailant got behind the wheel of the truck, shouting that he was going to run the milkman over, but he could not release the brakes. The milkman ran to a nearby city sanitation facility, where workers called the police.

When the milkman returned to the truck to meet us, whoever had attacked him was gone; missing from the truck was the milkman's canvas bag, containing his money, papers, and identification.

We called for robbery detectives to meet us at Grady Hospital, where we turned the milkman and the investigation over to them. Phoebus and I returned to our beat. Two hours later, as dawn broke, we went to breakfast at a diner on our beat. As we were eating at the counter, the short-order cook pointed out a guy sitting at the closed service station across the street. He told us the same guy had been in the diner earlier, behaving strangely. We finished breakfast and drove across the street to the service station. I got out of the patrol car to check on the guy. He had a canvas bag. I looked inside and found the items described by the milkman. Without any difficulty, I put the guy in the back seat of our patrol car. Atlanta PD patrol cars in those days, more than forty years ago, were two-door cars without a screen between the front and back seats. Phoebus was driving. I got on the radio and cancelled the lookout we had placed earlier for the guy who attacked the milkman. I advised the robbery detectives that we had the perpetrator in custody and that they should meet us at the station.

On the way, our suspect (even forty years ago, our training required us to use words like "suspect," "alleged," and the ambiguous, "perpetrator," no matter how hard the evidence), who was not handcuffed, repeatedly muttered things like, "I have done a bad thing, and now I have to pay for it." He rolled down the little half-window in the back of the patrol car, and dove out, headfirst. I could not believe he fit! He hit the pavement and rolled many times before he stopped. Phoebus hit the brakes. I jumped out before the car came to a stop. The guy got up and ran down a side street; I pursued, thirty feet behind.

I drew my revolver, demanding he stop, or I would shoot. He stopped, spun around, facing me, hands in the air above his head, shouting, "I'm Puerto Rican, and I don't go to jail." When I got near enough, he dropped his hands and surprised me with a hard right to my head, knocking me down. He was still swinging at me when I got up. In self-defense and anger, I replied with several blows to his head with my revolver, the only thing I had with me when I jumped out of the car. My nightstick and flashlight were still in the car. When Phoebus got to us, we got the assailant under control, although he continued to flail and struggle to get free. I ran back to our car and called for another car. When I got back, I had to jump in again because Phoebus was exhausted.

Within a couple of minutes, several patrol cars arrived. With the help of arriving cops, we were able to handcuff him. Among them was Hollywood Douglas, who attacked him with his lead-filled three-cell flashlight. Hollywood said he was going to, "Teach this nigger he can't jump the police," and proceeded to thump his head with the "flashlight." Despite the blows to his head, our wild man screamed repeatedly that he was not a nigger; he was a Puerto Rican. He and Hollywood kept up the debate for several minutes. Hollywood must have decided that he'd won the debate because he turned to me and said, "Puerto Rican, shit! He's a goddamn nigger. Nobody but a nigger could be hit on the head that many times and still want to argue!" He threw his head back, howled his strange laugh, got in his car, and left.

I suffered bruises and scrapes—Phoebus, the same, but he also had a broken finger. Our wild man needed quite a few stitches to close the gashes in his head. He was also severely skinned and scraped. Images of Uncle Lou flashed across my eyes, and I felt some satisfaction at the extent of the robber's injuries. But I still can't figure how the hell he managed to get out so fast through the little rear window.

WR Dickson

The night I worked with Officer WR Dickson was different from the nights I worked with other veteran police officers. Dickson was different. Throughout the night, I was included in whatever decisions were made. *We* decided when and where to eat, *we* decided where and when to stop for a coffee break, and *we* decided whether to go to the crack. For the first time, I felt I was a full half of a partnership. It didn't matter to Dickson that I was a rookie. What mattered was that I was a person who wanted to be a cop. Dickson did not make me feel inadequate or subservient—feelings imposed by other cops to make sure you knew you were a rookie. Whatever I felt about myself as a rookie came from within me, not from Dickson. I was smart enough to follow his lead in the important matters during the night. Nothing much noteworthy occurred, but even routine stuff was enough to let me know that the chemistry was right between us. For the first time in my young career, I truly enjoyed working with another police officer. He had a genuine warmth and goodness. It was clear he cared about other's feelings.

The following night, we were assigned to work together again. I felt good about that. I felt very good. It was another uneventful night, but it was a good night because we were getting to know each other. You get to know someone pretty well, riding in a car together for sixteen hours. I sensed a friendship developing. His regular partner was sick and was to be out for several days. The third night, I arrived at the assembly room, where all the cops mill around before roll call, engaging in war stories, trying to out-bullshit each other. Dickson found me and told me that he had peeked at the assignment sheet; we were working together again. He seemed as pleased as I was. We flipped a coin to determine who would buy breakfast. I won. Things were going good, or so it seemed.

The assignments at roll call did not coincide with those Dickson had seen on the sheet. A new rookie, a guy named Warhurst, was assigned to car 19 with Dickson. I was assigned to walk one of the beats downtown. This last minute change came about because Warhurst needed experience in a patrol car. Dickson and I looked at each other, shrugged, and said, "Next time."

When I arrived at my beat, I pulled the callbox to report to the police operator. She babbled words that sounded like she was saying, "Dickson is dead!"

Dead?

Dickson and Warhurst were on their way to their beat when a drunk driver ran a stop sign and broadsided them on the driver's side. Dickson was thrown from the patrol car and crushed under the drunk driver's car. Warhurst sustained a broken arm and other injuries.

The callbox hung from a wall of skewed bricks on a building at Broad and Mitchell Streets; it was, at that time, a rundown section of downtown Atlanta. I heard the operator's words, "Dickson is dead—killed—about twenty minutes ago—" but my brain hadn't yet reacted.

She kept talking. I said nothing.

Dickson and I were going to be partners again tonight. He was going to buy breakfast. I saw him smile, heard his voice—not more than an hour ago. The disappointment I felt at not working together gave way to disbelief.

I suppose I was in shock. I had never experienced it before. I didn't know for sure. To this day I still am not sure what shock feels like. But I know what I felt that night.

I hung up, put the phone back, and just stood there, looking at the box. Then I looked away and continued the watch I had started not more than a half hour ago.

A long way to go that night—a long way to go.

That was my first experience of having a policeman killed in the line of duty. There have been far too many during my career. I attended Dickson's funeral. It devastated me. Attending funerals has never gotten any easier.

Surviving a Rookie Mistake

"To err is human," and cops are human. When anyone screws up or makes a mistake, he or she causes inconvenience or extra work for others, and is embarrassed at the least. When a new cop screws up, it is usually referred to as a rookie mistake. It is embarrassing for sure, and sometimes causes more laughter than inconvenience or extra work, but there have been instances in which screwing up is fatal—the rookie cop's last mistake.

Officer Roy Foster and I, just a couple of months out of the academy, were working a car together one night. Two rookies working together were like the "blind leading the blind." During the first several hours, we were busy, mostly answering disturbance calls in the inner city ghetto area our beat covered. Things slowed some at five a.m., when we received a silent burglar alarm at a liquor store at the corner of Boulevard and Houston Street.

When we arrived, Foster went to the door to look in, and I stood in front of a large plate glass window, peering into the darkness of the store. I saw nothing in the darkness of the large room at the front of the store. A small light in the back room provided just enough illumination to help me make out a figure where I hadn't looked initially. There, in the middle of the store, was a guy pointing a shotgun at me. I dived for the sidewalk and the protection of a two-foot-high glass-blocked wall just below the window. As I hit the ground, he fired, and blew out the window where I had been standing a moment before. Shattered glass scattered over me as I hugged the ground. Several parked cars across the street were damaged by the blast. Foster returned fire, and so did I.

We called for backup. After that initial shotgun blast, all was quiet within the store. A short time later, Foster and I, with several other officers, entered the store. On the floor of the back room was a guy with a gunshot wound to the head. He was dead. Beside him was a 12-gauge shotgun that had been hit by one of our bullets, which jammed the pump mechanism.

He had cut a hole in the roof so he could drop down into the store, bypassing the audible alarm. But when he opened the door to the back room, he set off the silent alarm, to which we responded. The shotgun belonged to the store and was loaded with .00 buckshot, which could destroy the human body.

I've passed that liquor store several hundred times since; each time, I relive the dumb rookie mistake I made that night. I was lucky—it wasn't my last mistake.

On-the-Job Training

Working as a roustabout can be the best on-the-job training. You work with a variety of veteran officers, benefiting from their years of experience. The smart rookie picks up and retains the best from the veterans, and hopefully recognizes and discards that which is not their best. Unfortunately, the bad habits and apathy of veteran cops are not among the best that rookie cops can emulate. Veterans like to provide rookies with advice, the most common being, "Forget all that shit they told you at academy, this is the real world," and, "You'll never get in trouble doing nothing." The message in the latter is never to do more than you have to, don't go the extra mile, be mechanical, without compassion, and never get involved.

I am hardheaded sometimes. I didn't heed either lesson well, especially the latter. My stubbornness has caused me pain over the years.

The Real World?

Police officers see life at its most basic level. Every day, they see the violence, the tragedy, the despair, and the horror of life. After a while, the world a policeman sees becomes the "real world." When he tries to explain what goes on in his real world, citizens, due to ignorance or personal agendas, don't believe him. Citizens not only disbelieve, they argue that it is not the way the policeman says it is. The policeman becomes frustrated, cynicism evolves, and the policeman becomes estranged from "normal society." He seeks the company of other policemen, who "understand" how things are and who know what's going on. He becomes a member of the police subculture and begins to regard everyone else as an asshole.

What effect does this transformation have on the policeman's wife? What role does she play in the topsy-turvy world he has chosen? When divorce rates are ranked by occupation, police officers are in the top three. Suicide, alcoholism, and stress are also prevalent. In recent years, the ugliness and devastation of drug abuse has become an acute concern.

How does the policeman's wife cope with the anxieties of these afflictions, anxieties that push and pull her in different directions? She is isolated from their non-cop friends as her husband withdraws further into the closed circle of other cops. She is cut off from a normal social life. Policemen spend their first several years working nights. Only when they start working daytime shifts and get weekends off can they resume normal social lives with their wives and non-cop friends. Some cops never get back to their normal social lives. The lucky wives are the ones whose husbands get evenings and weekends and are able to do things with their family and friends.

My wife, Betty, has not been lucky in that regard. I have been blessed to have her as my wife. Betty and I were married two years before I became a policeman. When we married, she was young, sweet, innocent, and gorgeous, from Cleveland, Tennessee, a small town in the foothills of the Smoky Mountains. God endowed Betty with a figure that would make a Playboy playmate envious. More than that, God gifted her with an intelligence, disposition, and personality that wonderfully affected everyone in her presence. Everyone liked Betty. She was quality.

That quality endured. She was forced to bear the burden of many things because I was either at work, appearing in court, sleeping, or working extra jobs. During my first five years at the department, I was assigned to the morning watch and had Tuesdays and Wednesdays off. (About a year after I was on the job, we were given two days off, a helluva lot better than only one day off each week.) Betty passed up evening parties, dinners, and informal get-togethers because I was working. I missed daytime cookouts, picnics, and the kids' ball games because I was sleeping. The lonely nights, the sick children, the bumps, the bruises, and broken arms, Betty had to deal with it all by herself.

Policemen who work at night have many opportunities with women. Maybe it's the uniform, or the authority it represents, that attracts women. Most policemen's wives cannot handle this knowing women are there for their husbands to take if they want. Many wives insist their husbands work the day watch. It's not easy to get on that shift. Police brass is neither sympathetic nor responsive to wives who are alone at night or jealous of other women. Wives start nagging and in many cases, the marriage ends in divorce.

Betty handled the inconveniences, the doubts, and the fears throughout my police career. I knew, without her ever telling me, when she was worried for my safety. She never made a big deal about the times I returned home hurt or disturbed about something that happened during the night. There were times she told me that she preferred I not be a policeman. She always felt I had the ability to be something else. She wanted me to have a job without the danger of police work, a job that would allow a normal relationship between a man and his family, a job that would provide better than a policeman's job. What set Betty apart from most of the other cops' wives was that she said what she said, and that was it. She didn't nag. She never nagged.

One of the things Betty liked most about me was my sense of humor. After six years as a policeman, I lost it; my sense of humor was gone. I became extremely cynical. Sometimes what I regretted most about being a policeman is not the other things I mentioned, but that Betty lost my sense of humor.

It has been written that policemen are a special breed. But not much has been written about the truth—that any woman who marries a cop, puts up with all the crap that she has to endure, and stays married to him, is the most special breed of all.

When my son Alex and daughter Kris were young, I missed a lot of their ball games, cheerleading, and other childhood activities, but they made me feel like we were a complete family, that I was a full-time father. That made me feel good, although I knew my job made me a part-time father. Working the morning watch, when the courts are not open, meant I had to appear in court during the day, and besides my police job, I worked extra jobs, second jobs, so I could afford for Alex and Kris do some of the things their friends were doing. Working two jobs always made me so damn tired.

Alex and Kris always understood. More than that, I had their respect. As they grew into teenagers and young adults, they never did anything that might cause me embarrassment. They were kids, but they were mature enough to realize their actions would be a reflection on me.

Roustabout Assignments

I spent my rookie year as a roustabout, working every beat in the city of Atlanta, including walking beats. At that time, a cop walked a beat alone. When he needed assistance, he had to get to a call box. A cop on a walking beat who needed assistance often had to depend on a citizen to call to the police operator. Today, when you see Atlanta policemen walking a beat, they are usually in pairs and carrying hand radios for instant communication.

Roustabouts were subjected to unwanted assignments from time to time. For instance, working the police detention ward at Grady Hospital was about as much fun as painting a house. One of the worst assignments for a young patrolman was working in the general office. It included answering the telephone and typing reports for officers in the field as they dictated from a call box, among other clerical duties.

Wade Hagin made the mistake of admitting he could type when he first arrived in police uniform. He was thus scheduled to work the general office a couple of times every two weeks. He was usually Mister Hyde, a mild-mannered, laid-back, easy-going young man with a pleasant personality and a friendly word for everyone when he worked any other assignment. But he turned into Dr. Jekyll, a red-faced, grumpy, scowling grouch of a man with a chip on his shoulder the moment the captain announced at roll call, "Hagin, general office!"

I never had to work the general office, perhaps because when I was asked if I could type, I confessed that I didn't know a typewriter from a Sherman tank.

There is the spontaneous, unintended humor that sometimes emerges from casual conversation, like the night I was assigned to car 17 with Officer JJ Cooke. He was a big guy, ten or fifteen years older than I; he spoke slowly and softly—just a "good ol' country boy."

We had just left the police station after roll call, on our way to 17's beat, when, in an attempt to break the ice between us, Cooke asked if I had any "druthers." I replied I had two—one older, one younger. He looked at me, as if to say, "What the hell are you talking about?" which prompted me to look back at him like, "What the hell, didn't I answer your question?" I soon learned it was a common Southern colloquialism, meaning would I "druther (rather) do this," or would I "druther (rather) do that."

For the next few seconds, the only sound inside the patrol car was the chatter from the police radio. We regarded each other as if the other was a being from a different planet. I was from planet New York City, where we ask if someone "would rather do this" or "rather do that." Cooke's planet was the South, where "what are your 'druthers?'" meant exactly the same thing. It could have been a scene in the film, "My Cousin Vinny."

That exchange found its way throughout the ranks of the morning watch. But it went beyond; for a long time I was asked by cops about "my druthers."

Whistler's Mother and Mary Magdalene

There are special one-time work details. One was when two famous, priceless paintings, "Whistler's Mother" and "Penitent Saint Mary Magdalene," were brought from Paris on loan for display at the

Atlanta Arts Center. Ten Atlanta policemen were detailed to guard the paintings twenty-four hours a day, seven days a week, for two months. Wade and I were the chosen guardians in the wee hours of the morning watch. The paintings had to be within sight of at least one of us at all times. From time to time, one of us could break to use the bathroom, stretch our legs, breathe fresh air from an open window, but we could not leave the building. We had to brown bag it if we wanted to eat lunch.

My appreciation for fine arts was woefully lacking. We looked at those paintings for two months, and I wondered why people wanted so much to see them. Not me. I was more appreciative of the art in the Playboy magazines we thumbed through to pass the time. We had a small transistor radio and got to know the Top Twenty so well, we could have sung them, if we'd had voices to sing. We sat in straight-back chairs, a little table between us. We played cards a lot. I still owe Wade a little over thirty million dollars.

My First Regular Car

Roustabout work is okay. You get to know the city and the cops who work with you. After a while, you become an asset, rather than a liability, to the watch commander. He'll assign you anywhere because he's sure you'll be familiar with it. That kind of trust makes you feel good about yourself. But there comes a time when you would like to have a regular car. It creates a sense of belonging, of having arrived. Your car gives you an identity. You know where and with whom you are going to work each night.

Officer AW Gilman had to choose a new partner when his regular partner was transferred to the traffic division. When the sergeant informed me that Gilman had asked for me, and that he would approve it if I were interested, I jumped at it. What a boost to my ego—being chosen over all the other young roustabouts on the morning watch.

Car 32 covered a beat just west of the downtown area—all black, low income, high crime. We were sandwiched between the area covered by car 12, with Wade Hagin and Carl Blore on one side, and the area covered by car 31, starring "Hollywood" Douglas and his partner, Rex Merritt, a big, beefy, tobacco-chewin', good ol' boy from South Georgia. AW Gilman was not the typical morning watch cop. Gilman never went to the crack. Car 32 rolled all night long, except when its occupants were answering calls, stopping traffic violators, or eating. If one of the other cars in our district did not answer the radio when they received a call, we knew where to find them. We would run by the crack, revive our comatose heroes, and continue about our business. Most of the time, we let them sleep, took the call, and handled it ourselves. Gillman was a worker, and that suited me fine.

It was hard to get close to Gilman. We were partners on the job, but never socialized off duty. I never knew much about his private life, and he never asked about mine. He did give me a beautiful German shepherd dog. He had two; they fought all of the time. He couldn't keep both, and he wanted a good home for Gus, a dropout from the Atlanta police K-9 corps. He was not well suited for police work because he was too headstrong. Gus would not respond to commands with predictability, so none of the K-9 officers would work him on the street.

I learned a lot during the time I worked with Gilman. We caught a hell of a lot of burglars together, more than I've caught in all the time since working with him.

One-Man Cars!

One day, sometime in 1963, the Atlanta Police Administration made an announcement that sent shock waves throughout the entire department. One-man cars! Every Atlanta patrol car was to have one officer assigned to it, day or night, high crime area, or not. Chief Herbert T. Jenkins ruled the APD with an iron fist, with little, if any, interference. Chief Jenkins was convinced that one-man cars would provide Atlanta with double the coverage with the same number of police officers. Of course, the city would have to double the size of its fleet of patrol cars and provide maintenance for twice as many cars.

This mandate generated a serious concern for the safety of Atlanta's finest. Everyone raised hell about it—the cops, the cop's wives, the media, the civic groups, but to no avail. Two-man patrol cars in Atlanta became a thing of the past, the end of an era, the end of the Goldhagen/Gilman partnership, and the end of a regular car for me. Gilman, the senior man, remained in car 32; I went back to roustabout.

This was the first of many changes to alter the course of history in the Atlanta Police Department in the years to come.

And It's Goin' Good!

Police work in the big city has been described as hours of boredom interrupted by moments of terror, but there is also the humor that comes with police work. All cops have favorite stories that let us laugh together, the laughter usually at someone else's expense. My best stories were stories that made others laugh, even though the laughter was at my expense. Some of the stories I told about myself were damned embarrassing.

One of my most embarrassing moments occurred in 1963. I was working a car in the Morningside/Ansley Park area one night, well aware that on that beat, a certain barbecue restaurant was a regular target for burglars. I made sure to check this place several times during the night. Sometime between four and five o'clock in the morning, I made a routine check, and I noticed a glow from within. I stopped the car, got out, and upon closer inspection, saw flames bursting out of the restaurant's chimney! I hurried back to the car and called the fire department. Back then, the entire Atlanta Police Department was on one citywide radio frequency. There was a direct hook up from the patrol cars to the fire department dispatcher. Subsequent to reaching the dispatcher, all radio transmissions could be monitored in every patrol car in the city.

I became excited after notifying the fire department of the location of the fire. To impress upon the dispatcher the urgency of the situation, I added, "And it's going good—" The captain started my way, as did the lieutenant and a couple of sergeants, all of whom heard me on their radios. Eight patrol cars also heard me and were on the way.

Having made my call, I jumped out of my car and ran towards the building to assess the situation further. When I got closer to the building and looked through the window, I came close to going into shock. To my horror, I saw an employee cleaning the barbeque pit. Each time he scraped the grease from the grill into the hot coals an enormous flame roared towards the ceiling and shot out the chimney.

I had screwed up with a capital S. I ran back to my car for the second time, this time a little faster; I could hear the fire and police sirens screaming, coming closer. I got on the radio and tried to cancel the fire department, but they came, anyway, half a dozen fire engines, pumpers, ladder trucks, and the battalion chief's car. I tried to stop them from unraveling and hooking up the hoses. They flicked me aside as they started their attack on the building with axes and poles. They stopped, freezing in their tracks when they looked in and saw the cook firing up the grill.

It seemed like half the goddamn police department had arrived. Everyone realized what had happened, and were all glad they were not me. The fire department battalion chief wanted to know who belonged to the voice of car 34. He had choice words for me. I took it. I didn't say a word. I was embarrassed and humiliated. All these firemen, legitimately asleep, responded to a false alarm because of me. Worse, most of the cops who responded came from out of the crack. I'm not so sure the police captain and other superior officers weren't also "resting comfortably" somewhere.

As the captain left, he muttered that the police department was falling apart, going to hell—because they hired dumb-asses like me. For the next several years, I was stuck with the nickname "Smokey."

Racial Segregation and Integration

In the early sixties, racial segregation was a way of life in the Deep South. It was mandated by state law and affected every facet of society, including the police department.

The civil rights movement, which had been around for years, and for the most part had gone unnoticed, got a major boost from the United States Supreme Court in 1954, when the court ruled that racial segregation in the public schools was unconstitutional. It was the landmark decision of Brown v. The Board of Education of Topeka. The implementation of that ruling was left to the individual states. School systems throughout the southern states took no action, in spite of the decision. The court failed to make provisions for enforcement; therefore, the ruling was virtually ignored.

A short time later, an incident occurred that would improve the course of integration in the United States in the years to come. State law or city ordinances racially segregated all public facilities in the South, including the public schools, public transportation, hotels, restaurants, hospitals (including ambulances). Segregation extended to restrooms and drinking fountains.

In Montgomery, Alabama, the city bus system was segregated, as were most other southern public transportation systems. Whites were seated front to rear, and Negroes were seated from rear to front. Accordingly, as the bus filled, the driver, who was white, would announce, "Niggers to the rear." Anyone who did not comply was subject to arrest.

One evening, in 1955, a Negro woman, Rosa Parks, was a passenger on a Montgomery city bus. She was on her way home, tired after a day's work. The bus became crowded, and she was ordered to give up her seat to a white man. She refused, the police were called, and she was arrested. This single act of defiance by a tired Negro woman was the beginning of the civil rights movement in earnest.

The Montgomery Improvement Association, the local Negro civil rights organization, got involved. After several meetings, they decided to call for Montgomery's Negroes to boycott the buses of the Montgomery transit system. The majority of the riders on the buses in Montgomery were Negro. The Montgomery Improvement Association felt that the loss in revenue suffered by the transit system would force the city to integrate the buses. The Negroes of Montgomery drove themselves back and forth to work, participated in organized car pools, or simply ensured themselves time to walk, even when tired after work.

The city resisted, and the stalemate was on.

The bus boycott lasted over a year, and during that time, the Montgomery Improvement Association and the National Association for the Advancement of Colored People appealed the conviction of Rosa Parks to the United States Supreme Court. Rosa Parks prevailed, and racial segregation on the buses of the Montgomery transit system was history. Emerging from the leadership of the MIA, as its president, was Martin Luther King, Jr. The civil rights movement was off and running.

The Movement, as it became known, spread throughout the southern states. The lunch counter "sit-ins," which began in 1960 in Greensboro, NC, soon became a common occurrence in other southern cities. The Freedom Riders of 1961 were a major ingredient of the Movement. The integration of the public schools in Little Rock, Arkansas needed the aid of federal troops.

Dozens, and then hundreds, of incidents occurred throughout the South. In 1960, Rich's, Atlanta's largest department store, was the target of a sit-in demonstration by Negro students from the Atlanta university system, a complex of black colleges near downtown Atlanta. Scores of demonstrators were arrested. Later that same year, Police Chief Herbert T. Jenkins was credited with avoiding bloodshed when a large number of Negro students from Atlanta University converged on the state capitol in a protest march, with a list of grievances for the governor. State officials had announced that the demonstrators would not be permitted on capitol grounds. The state capitol was surrounded with five hundred state troopers armed with shotguns and tear gas.

Chief Jenkins stood in the way of the column of marchers, confronting them across the street from the capitol. After a strong conversation with their leader, Lonnie King (a student leader, not related to Martin Luther King), Jenkins persuaded him to return the protesters to the college. The day ended without violence, and the city of Atlanta dodged a bullet.

Atlanta, however, did not escape the turmoil and chaos of the sixties; things turned violent and ugly. It was a volatile time for blacks and Southern whites. From both sides, there was resentment, mistrust, fear, and hatred. Some members, black and white, of Atlanta's community, took a moderate and rational view. Influential people from the political and business sectors joined with emerging leaders, religious groups, and the Atlanta media. They understood that the inevitable was imminent. Radical reform was in the air; changes were coming that would alter the course of socioeconomics in Atlanta.

Chief Jenkins was a reformer, an innovator, "a man ahead of his time." Of the many changes and reforms implemented since becoming police chief in 1947, the most controversial was his vision of Negro policemen in Atlanta. There were Negro policemen in some northern cities, but Negroes in police uniforms in the South? Hard to imagine.

In 1948, the first eight Negro police officers were working their beats on the streets in Atlanta, Georgia. Chief Jenkins had pulled it off with the support of Atlanta Mayor, William B. Hartsfield, despite considerable objections from Atlanta's white community. Jenkins and Hartsfield orchestrated a compromise with a very nervous, unsure white community. Jenkins, Hartsfield, and the leaders of the white community in Atlanta agreed upon the following conditions:

1) Negro policemen would have no authority or arrest powers over white citizens.
2) Negro policemen would only work in Negro areas.
3) Negro policemen would be headquartered in and work out of the Negro YMCA.
4) Negro policemen would be led by a white commanding officer.
5) Negro policemen would be completely segregated from white policemen.
6) Negro policemen were not permitted to wear uniforms or carry their equipment when off duty, as the white policemen were allowed to do.

Not a giant leap forward, but, "A long journey starts with the first step."

Years later, in 1962, when I became a policeman, the Negro policemen were no longer operating out of the Negro YMCA; they were operating out of the building that housed the rest of the Atlanta Police Department. Negro policeman were still segregated from the whites; they had to use separate locker rooms, restrooms, and roll call facilities. But there were about thirty-five Negro policemen in 1962, and they were commanded by a Negro sergeant, then the only Negro superior officer on the APD. Their watch, referred to as the six p.m. watch, operated from six p.m. to two a.m.

They still only worked in Negro areas in 1962, but that year, they were given arrest power and authority over whites. This caused resentment from white citizens that spilled over to the white policemen. The Negro policeman was tolerated by his white counterpart, but was considered and treated as inferior. The most glaring example was in the patrol cars assigned to black policemen. A patrol car in a big city police department is good for about one year. It is driven seven days a week, twenty-four hours a day. Most of it is stop and go city driving, with a lot of idling. Police officers put many hard, abusive miles, from either need or carelessness, on their patrol cars. When the patrol cars were taken off the line and replaced with new cars, the old, worn-out cars were assigned to the six p.m. watch.

I heard no complaints about anything from the Negro policemen. I sure heard plenty of negative comments from the white cops about the Negro cops. The white cops considered the Negro cops subservient and didn't have much to do with them.

It didn't take me long to see the inequities, but my need for acceptance by my peer group suppressed my sense of fairness. I chose not to speak out because I did not want to be known as the big-mouthed Jew from New York who came to Atlanta and tried to tell the APD what was fair and what wasn't. Moreover, if the Negro cops were happy, why should I care about the inequities inflicted on them? That was how I felt in the beginning, during my first years as a cop in Atlanta. Later, my attitude changed drastically.

I have been referring to blacks as "Negroes" but in the early sixties, the acceptable term in Atlanta for a black person was "colored." Facilities were marked "white" or "colored." I could not believe that Grady Hospital had separate emergency rooms, the "White Clinic," and the "Colored Clinic." Police report forms had race and sex designations listed: WM, WF, CM, CF. The term Negro didn't become official in the Atlanta Police Department until the late sixties.

Civil rights within the APD boiled down to the essentials the individual policeman, white or colored, had to do every day on the job. Crimes were committed, calls had to be answered, and auto accidents had to be handled, among the many other duties in any policeman's daily routine.

Although the attitudes of some white policemen were changing, most agreed and were satisfied with segregation. They saw nothing wrong with it and were comfortable with their perceived superiority over the colored. Most of Atlanta's white policemen at that time were born and raised in the South. Racial segregation was a way of life, the way things were; they saw nothing wrong with it, and no reason to change it. They saw only their side of segregation, rarely anything that might cause them to feel otherwise.

As the civil rights movement gained momentum and found its way into Atlanta, our vocabulary expanded to include terminology such as civil rights, protest marches, demonstrations, sit-ins, and militant Negroes. Newly organized groups allied themselves with the already familiar National Association for the Advancement of Colored People (NAACP), groups such as the Southern Christian Leadership Conference (SCLC), the Congress of Racial Equality (CORE), and the Student Nonviolent Coordinating Committee (SNCC).

When any of these groups organized protests, or when citizens assembled in any one of the hundreds of spontaneous, unorganized protests, the police called to be the front line were on the side of white society. There were confrontations; scuffles broke out. Often there was violence. Arrests were made. People on both sides were injured. Most white policeman believed, "These militant niggers from up north are coming to Atlanta and stirring up our niggers." Frustration turned into resentment, resentment turned into hatred, and hatred seethed from both sides.

What of Atlanta's Negro policemen during all this? They were in the forefront of the confrontations, alongside their white counterparts. They were police officers; they had chosen to be police officers. They had taken an oath to uphold and defend the laws of the State of Georgia and the City of Atlanta. They knew that the ultimate goal of the civil rights movement was the end of racial segregation and the beginning of freedom and equality for all. They also knew that laws were being broken while trying to accomplish it. The white policemen had no inner conflict, but the Negro policemen did. This moral issue ate at his guts.

For the white policeman, the issue was clear: Negroes were the enemy, especially the young militants imported from other parts of the country. These troublemakers caused Atlanta to explode into race riots in the mid and late sixties, and built a division between the races of Atlanta's policemen.

You Oughta Be a Goddamn Actor

Bird-dogging is an expression used by vice squad detectives when a young, unknown policeman is put out as bait for prostitutes. My ex-partner, AW Gilman, now a vice detective, and his partner, Detective GB Shepherd, asked me to bird-dog for them one night when I was still a new cop.

Millie, a well-known and elusive prostitute bragged that they would never bust her. She was too smart and cautious for any cop; she knew all the tricks—the tricks of her trade, the tricks of the vice detectives, and the tricks she serviced. But she didn't know me.

I met up with Millie in a downtown club, and after some conversation, convinced her I was down from New York on business. That wasn't hard to sell because my "New Yorkeze" still sounded valid. We agreed she would meet me at my motel; I had a room registered in my name at the Heart of Atlanta Motel, complete with my luggage, clothes, toilet articles, and a briefcase. The briefcase contained papers and items that I figured would look like the real thing. After all, how likely was it that she'd realize they were homework problems for a math course I took at night back when I was briefly in New York? I figured my slide rule on the desk would clinch my authenticity.

She said she would come to my hotel room after meeting someone for an early breakfast. The breakfast date was with Gilman and Shepherd, who had spoken to her earlier that evening. Millie hurried through her breakfast. They asked her why the rush. She replied that she had a date. They cautioned her that her date might be a cop, and she could take her first fall. She laughed and told them, "There's no way this guy is a cop, he's just some jerk from New York!" Gilman and Shepherd, biting their tongues, kept straight faces.

They got to my motel room before she did, alerting me that she was on her way. They gave me one of their business cards with a message scribbled on the back. "Millie, this will introduce Officer H.B. Goldhagen APD. Look in the closet. Gilman and Shepherd." They got in the closet just as she knocked on the door. To make the arrest, I had to get her to quote her price for sex. She was cautious and did not want to talk money just yet.

"Come on baby, take off your clothes, and we'll get into bed and talk about it." She peeled off her clothes and quickly was on the bed, naked. I had taken off my shirt, tie, and shoes, stalling for her to say what I needed her to say. She urged, "Come on, baby, hurry up. Don't you like what you see?" I told her I did, but insisted that I needed to know how much what I was looking at was going to cost me. Finally, she said, "Fifty dollars." (With that, we had her. Well, we didn't "have her," but we "had her.")

I told her that I liked what I saw so much that I wanted to keep in touch with her for subsequent trips to Atlanta. I reached into my pocket and handed her the card, which she assumed was my business card. When she read it, she came off the bed and went bonkers. APD's heroic vice detectives fell out of the closet laughing, tears in their eyes, trying to steal breaths through gasps of laughter. She was pissed. The three of us stood there, looking at her nakedness. Her hands on her hips, she indignantly said, "Well, the least you could do is turn around, and let a lady get dressed."

Later on, after things settled down, Millie joined us in a good laugh. Gilman and Shepherd had made a believer out of her. She was charged with soliciting for prostitution and given a "copy of charges." Then the four of us went for a cup of coffee. Millie still couldn't believe that she had been busted. As we parted, she told me, "I'll tell you one thing. You're in the wrong profession. You oughta be a goddamn actor."

Those Who Could Not Accept Change

In 1964, racial integration came to the Atlanta Police Department. No more all-Negro six p.m. watches. White cops and Negro cops shared the same facilities—locker rooms, restrooms, assembly room, and patrol cars. Negro police officers were in the downtown and midtown areas, as well as the affluent, north side Buckhead section. And there were several white and Negro cops working as partners.

But integration still had a long way to go—it hadn't reached the social atmosphere of the assembly room in the basement of police headquarters. Prior to roll call, Negro cops gathered on one side of the room, white cops collected apart from the Negroes on the other side. There was integration, the policy, but there was segregation, the social phenomenon that resulted from that policy. Worse, there was hostility in the air, from one side of the room to the other.

Before the integration of the APD, cops used to arrive early for roll call, to chat among each other, kid around, and tell war stories (often exaggerated for the sake of the humor it would evoke). After integration there was none of this.

On one of the first nights of the new policy, roll call for the evening watch assigned a Negro police officer to work with white officer, RL Braswell. Immediately after roll call, Braswell stomped into the watch commander's office, explaining that he wasn't feeling well and needed a sick day. The captain allowed him to go home.

There were many white Atlanta police officers like Ray Braswell—products of the South, born and raised under racial segregation, they were experiencing difficulty adjusting to integration. Some realized that working with Negro cops was inevitable, so they made adjustments within themselves to accept integration, change their attitudes about it, and get along. Others could not accept integration. To get away from it, they left the APD. Some went to mostly white suburban police departments, some to security jobs with large companies, where there were no Negroes to integrate yet. Others, like Ray Braswell, would not change because they could not change. Nor did they leave. They remained. There were those within the system who preferred they not remain. It wasn't always clear who the antagonist was and who the protagonist. Friction and turmoil resulted for years to come.

A Good Day

The morning watch commanders knew many cops went to the crack in the wee hours. A perk was devised to keep the cops on the streets, looking for burglars, instead of snuggling in the crack or hanging out in donut shops. When a burglar was caught and arrested by an officer on his own initiative, not in response to a call, a "good day" was awarded to that officer, an unofficial day off that the watch commander had the power to give. It was a strong incentive, a motivator to catch burglars.

At the time, my brother Mike, was in Atlanta for a few days on business. He was due to catch a flight back to New York early in the morning. I got permission from Sergeant Adams, my supervisor, to have Mike ride with me so I could drive him to the airport. I was working a Southside car; it would only take a short time to get my brother to the airport.

The night was uneventful. I answered a few calls and stopped a few traffic violators. Mike was not impressed. About four a.m., while checking the beat, I noticed something that didn't look right at a closed gas station. The interior lights were out, but I knew the lights were always left on. When I drove around to the rear, I saw that a window was broken out in one of the overhead doors.

Suddenly, two burglars ran from the building. I jumped out of the car, caught one, brought him back to the car, and shoved him into the back seat. My brother was in the front seat, the burglar in the back seat, and there was no screen between them. I told Mike I was going to check the building. As I left, I handed him my nightstick and said, "Sergeant, if he tries to get out or gives you any shit, shoot him!"

I went around the building and peeked back at the car from the darkness, watching Mike. He was shifting around nervously. I was gone for only a few minutes, and Mike was relieved when I returned. He said it was the happiest he'd ever felt seeing my face coming toward him.

Several patrol cars soon arrived, including Sergeant Adams. Mike had to get to the airport, but I couldn't take him because I had lots of paperwork to do. Sergeant Adams got another patrol car to take Mike to catch his flight. At the end of the watch, Sergeant Adams told me that the captain had given me a "good day." As I walked away, he yelled, "And tell your brother that he got a good day, too!"

May I Borrow Your Pen?

Most policemen, at one time or another, have to deal with a motorist who gets angry while the policeman is writing out a ticket for a traffic violation. "Why don't you catch a real criminal, like a robber, or a rapist, or a murderer, instead of wasting time stopping me for going through a yellow light?"

Sometimes routine traffic stops can be refreshingly humorous, like the time I stopped a large black woman during morning rush hour. She must have weighed three hundred pounds, most of it resting on the accelerator. She was moving pretty fast through the streets in downtown Atlanta. I clocked her doing 50 mph in a 25 mph zone. When I told her why I had stopped her, she insisted, "My 'thermometer' said I just doin' twenty-five." I assured her that my thermometer said she was doing fifty.

Another time, I stopped a woman for running a red light. Not too far into writing her the ticket, my pen went dry. I asked if she had a pen, and I could borrow it to complete the ticket. "You mean to tell me you're going to give me a ticket written with my own pen?" She was incredulous about that, and hesitated reaching for her pen. I made her understand that either she lent me her pen, or she would be delayed while I waited for another patrol car to bring me one. She chose to lend me her pen. She was a good sport; we both got a chuckle from the irony of the situation.

When a traffic violator is stopped and vents his anger by verbally abusing the cop who stopped him, the best course for the officer is to be calm, cool, and maintain his professional bearing. To stand there and argue or answer his tirades with clever retorts does no good. Just tell him why you stopped him, write the ticket, and leave. On one of my occasional bad days, I was writing a traffic ticket for this loud, obnoxious asshole. He was trying to impress upon me that he was a taxpayer and paid my salary. As I handed him his citation, I pointed my finger in his face, looked him dead in the eye with my most contemptible look, "So you're the cheap son-of-a-bitch I've been looking for!"

I never heard anything more about it; I got away with it. I would not get away with a comment like that today, not with Internal Affairs going around, drumming up business. They would have made me pay for what I said to that tax-paying, traffic-violating asshole.

The Guy Who Knows Everybody

The traffic violator that really pisses me off is the influential, well-connected, big shot who knows everyone in the right places. He comes bounding out of his car, throwing names around, starting with the names of police officials, judges of the courts, and ending with half the politicians at city hall.

One night, in the wee hours, I was cruising down Ponce-de-Leon Avenue. There was only one other car in sight, about fifty yards ahead of me, going in the same direction as I. We were both doing the speed limit, when suddenly this third car appeared from a tavern parking lot. It just missed broad-siding the car ahead of me, then crossed six traffic lanes, jumped the opposite curb, and came to an abrupt halt after crashing through the plate glass window of a store front.

When I got to the car and opened the door to check for injuries, I found the driver, the sole occupant. He looked at me, glassy-eyed, and as he opened his mouth to speak, the alcohol fumes were so thick I probably could have ignited them. He wasn't injured, but was surely "blitzed." When he realized he was being arrested and charged with driving under the influence, among other traffic charges, he started reciting his list of influential names—the who's who of Atlanta's judicial system. As I put him in the paddy wagon, he warned that I'd regret arresting him.

One week later, I was given a "routine transfer" to a beat on the southside. The new beat covered an area with one of the highest crime rates in Atlanta. I never regretted arresting him; I never regret arresting assholes like him. But I often wondered what the final disposition of that asshole's arrest in court was. After my initial court appearance, his case was reset, and I was never notified to appear again. Justice at work, you think? Or do assholes that do things as harmful, and possibly worse, as this one did have asshole friends in such high places that they can get away with anything?

To Protect and Serve is the motto of police departments in small towns and big cities everywhere in the US. It's stenciled clearly on the sides or rear of most patrol cars. It's clear to policemen what "To Protect" means; policemen are trained to recognize when and how to protect. Not so clear is when, how, and to what extent "To Serve." There's little or no discretion when it comes "To Protect." There is a lot of individual discretion when it comes "To Serve."

Here's what I mean:

Just after midnight, on a miserable March night, with unrelenting rain falling like pellets, I drove up behind a car stopped on LaVista Road, north of Cheshire Bridge Road. It was parked with the lights on, half in the lane of traffic, the other half on a very narrow shoulder. The left rear tire was flat. There were two young women sitting in the car. They didn't know what to do about the flat tire.

I called for a wrecker to change the tire, or at least get them off the road before a drunk driver came along and ran into them. I was advised by the police dispatcher that all wreckers were tied up, handling the numerous accidents caused by the rain. The only rain gear I had in my car was a short rain jacket. I made my decision "To Serve." I put the women in my patrol car, then rummaged around in their trunk until I found the jack and lug wrench. Luckily, their spare tire was inflated. I proceeded to change the tire with the flashing blue lights of my patrol car keeping the traffic off me, the headlights allowing me to see what I was doing. Passing cars splashed me with dirty water from the road.

The two women sat in the patrol car the entire time. As soon as they saw the spare tire was on, and the trunk lid closed, they jumped out of mine, ran back to their car, and without a word drove off, leaving me standing in the middle of the street, wet through to my skin, filthy from the splashing. I would have appreciated an acknowledgment that I had served "Above and beyond." I got no "Thank you," no "Goodnight," not even, "So long, sucker." Nothing. Not a word. I was pissed. I went to the precinct, cleaned up, and dried off as best I could. I had no change of clothes, so I was a mess for the rest of the watch.

I kept an eye out for that car for the longest time. It's just as well that I never saw those young women again; I probably would have gotten myself into trouble. If faced with the same situation, would I do the same thing? Probably not. There are always people, like those two ungrateful women, who ruin things for others.

Don't Even Sweat

There came a time when the brass decided to have two patrol cars cover the downtown area. Wade Hagin had been working the one car, and when the second car was added, it was offered to me. I suppose I had done my penance for arresting that drunk driver, and had learned my lesson to never again arrest an influential asshole with asshole friends in high places. I was given a chance at a better assignment. I jumped at it, and things were looking up again.

As time went on, Wade and I became inseparable, to the extent that we might as well have been a two-man car. Whenever I got a call, he would back me up, and vice versa. One night, we arrested a couple of burglars that had broken into one of the local automobile dealerships— Boomershine Pontiac.

When we pulled up, we got out of our cars to check the building. I went down the dark alley on one side of the building, and saw a guy walking away, as if on a stroll. I stopped him, put him up against an overhead door with small windows, which I could peer through without releasing him. I saw a head move on the other side of the windows. I tapped on the glass with my pistol. The face, surprised, looked at me, wide-eyed, opened-mouth. I said, very calmly, "Don't even sweat!" I

41

held him at bay with my gun pointed less than twelve inches from his face. Other cars arrived, and Wade, along with the other cops, went inside. Wade cuffed the guy, who seemed relieved to no longer be staring down the barrel of my gun. The guy I had in the alley was the second burglar. Several days later, I received a package from Blackie, a personal friend and transplanted New Yorker, in the mail. Inside the package was a cardboard "drive-out" license tag with the dealership slogan, "I got mine at Boomershine."

Bars, Drunks, and Brawls

Certain calls had to be answered repeatedly in and around the downtown area. When we worked that area, Wade Hagin and I answered those calls. It was no different for any cop working that area. We responded to calls from the joints, the bars, the taverns, and the clubs in a relatively small area of downtown. The Plantation Club, The Bar Ranch, The Covered Wagon, York's Poolroom, Carl's Club, Ruby Flocks, Al's Friendly Tavern, The Bottom of the Barrel, and The Zebra Lounge are gone now, but not the unpleasant memories—memories that nevertheless reflect what we did almost every night while we worked there. The cops who remember these places are the cops wearing a string of hash marks on their sleeve.

A signal 29, denoting drunk and disorderly conduct or a fight in progress, meant "fix bayonets" to the cops answering a call to one of those locations. The call could have been for anything from a drunk bothering everyone, to ten or twenty drunks engaged in a barroom brawl. It was usually more like the latter, which resulted in "stick time." In those days, there wasn't an internal investigation every time a cop put a knot on the head of an unrelenting drunk. But that was then, now is now.

"Do you know who I am?"

One October night in 1964, during the presidential campaign, I was patrolling my beat when I was flagged down by the doorman of the Dinkler Plaza Hotel. Then, the Dinkler Plaza was *the* hotel in Atlanta. There was a disturbance of some sort inside. When I went in, I saw a group of people on the far side of the lobby. It seemed they were arguing. One guy was louder than the rest. As I made my way toward them, the hotel's night manager saw me coming and broke away from them, intercepting me before I reached them. He assured me there was no trouble; one of the guests had had too much to drink, and the others were going to put him to bed. That was fine with me. I turned to leave, and on my way out, I heard the loud voice shout, "Hey, you little son-of-a-bitch." I turned toward the shouting, which continued, "Yeah, I'm talking to you, you no-good cop bastard."

The hotel manager apologized for his drunken guest and implored me to let his associates handle him. I started to leave for the second time when that jerk caught up with me at the door to tell me it was a good thing I was leaving because he was about to kick my ass. With that, I took him outside and put him, not too gently, into my patrol car.

While waiting for the wagon, I did the paperwork that accompanies an arrest. Mr. Big Shot tried to impress me with being President Lyndon Johnson's state campaign manager. I assured him I would not hold it against him. He couldn't believe he was going to jail. When I placed him in the wagon, he warned me that if I went through with the arrest, he would have people in high places deal with me. When the case came up in court, I was excused and told I was not needed. The case was heard in the judge's chambers. The disposition was a thirty-day suspended sentence.

About a week later, I was given a "routine transfer," walking Cheshire Bridge Road from one end to the other, a distance of about one mile. Back then, that street was the boondocks, just a few small businesses scattered along its length and one all-night eatery. There was a call box at each end of Cheshire Bridge. I was instructed to pull the box (open the metal telephone box mounted on the side of a building or telephone pole and lift the receiver connecting one to the APD switchboard) on one end, and in the following hour, to pull the box at the other end. I was to alternate boxes the entire watch. I was not to get in any patrol car. Other cops were not to pick me up, not even to let me sit in their car for a few minutes to warm up. That was one long, lonely, cold winter. Did I have any regrets for arresting that drunken asshole, no matter who he was? No regrets. None. The following spring, when the cars got busy, I was reassigned to roustabout in the cars. I was just a victim of a politician's wrath for a while.

The real victim was the night manager of the Dinkler Plaza Hotel. He lost his job. The general manager called from Denver the next morning to fire him over the telephone. Mr. Big Shot was Pope McIntire, a lawyer who was indeed President Johnson's campaign manager for the state of Georgia. Mr. Big Shot drunken tirade, made me suffer a cold winter walking a beat, but worse, he got the night manager of the hotel fired. Mr. Big Shot could not have done it by himself; he did it with friends in high places.

The Krispy Kreme Driver Tried to Help

One morning, about seven a.m., just an hour before I got off duty, I was patrolling Peachtree Street in the heart of downtown, when I saw a drunk harassing people at a bus stop. I pulled the car around the corner, out of the way of rush hour traffic, and walked back to the bus stop. I took the guy by the belt and led him back to the car. Suddenly, he broke loose. He was not quite as drunk as he appeared. We went at it, and by this time, I had my blackjack out, the strap wrapped around my wrist. He grabbed the blackjack and jerked it so violently that the strap broke. Now, he had my blackjack, and I had what was left of the strap. We continued to fight; I wrestled him toward the patrol car. I got the door open, and we fell in across the front seat, me on top of him. I grabbed the radio microphone and called for assistance. (The only radio we had back then was in the car.) We continued to fight, spilling over the front seat into the back seat. (There were still no screens in the patrol cars.) This time he was on top, working on my head with my own blackjack. I tried to keep him close so he couldn't rear back to take full swings. A crowd of people gathered around the car, and one guy, a driver for a Krispy Kreme Donut truck, stuck his hand inside the patrol car, trying to help me. He was hit so hard with the blackjack—a blow intended for me—that it broke his wrist. A couple of patrol cars arrived, snatched the drunk out of my car, did a little dance on him, and threw him into a wagon.

I was more embarrassed than hurt. I took some kidding, made my report, and went home. When I got home, Betty could see that I had been "tattooed." She spent part of the morning counting the lumps on my head. That was the last time I carried a blackjack.

Detective

Time for a Change

F ive years on the morning watch. Five years going to work when my friends, neighbors, and most importantly, my family, were asleep. Five years coming home and going to sleep when they were going to work, to school. Five years upside down from everyone else.

I took the next detective test, passed, and was placed on the eligibility list. Six weeks later, my name came up. I was issued a gold detective's badge. I was ordered to report to the Fugitive Squad in the Detective Division.

It was delightful to work in the sunshine, with a regular partner, out of uniform. No calls to answer, no family fights to break up, no wrestling drunks, no automobile accidents to handle, no waiting for two or three hours to go to court after working all night. Most delightful was sleeping at home at night.

The Fugitive Squad

The function of the fugitive squad is to locate and apprehend any person within the City of Atlanta wanted by the APD or any other law enforcement agency anywhere in the US.

The work of a fugitive detective is different from the work of a homicide detective. A fugitive detective has to locate and apprehend people who have already been identified as having committed a crime, but have fled confinement. No analysis is needed, there are no clues to look for, no high-tech crime lab, no crime scene. A fugitive detective doesn't need any of that. A fugitive detective relies on someone to reveal where the fugitive can be found. A fugitive detective needs an informant. The most effective detectives, fugitive, homicide, or any other squad are those with the greatest number of knowledgeable, reliable informants.

It takes time to develop a network of reliable informants. They are street people—prostitutes, pimps, low-level drug dealers, thieves and their fences. A fugitive detective must figure out how to get informants to provide the information needed to locate and apprehend the fugitive.

The simplest way is to pay informants for their information. The FBI and other law enforcement agencies regularly pay their informants. Not the Atlanta Police Department. The APD does not pay money for information.

One common way of obtaining information is by trading with anyone recently apprehended for a crime. The detective offers the perpetrator the opportunity to provide useful information about where to locate a fugitive, in exchange for the detective's assurance that he will ask the district attorney to offer a plea bargain. A plea bargain is survival, the best possible survival, for the perpetrator.

Revenge also motivates recently apprehended criminals to provide information. Sometimes, one partner in a joint crime screws the other out of his share of the proceeds. Jealousy is another motivator. It is not unusual for a wife or girlfriend to surrender her husband or boyfriend after learning that he has been cheating. A detective has to earn the trust of those who might provide information about a fugitive. Once that trust is lost, by not keeping up his end of deal, the flow of information dries up.

"Five dollars is missing."

I was a new fugitive detective, without informants. Detectives with informants get phone calls from them. The only time the phone rang for me was when Betty requested I pick up milk and bread on my way home. The partners I worked with were veteran detectives with regular informants. Over time, I developed my own network of informants who provided information as reliable as the information from the veterans' networks.

Sometimes things happen when you least expect them. One night, I was working fugitive evening watch without a partner, cruising downtown, when I heard a lookout on an armed robbery of a nearby liquor store. Not more than a few moments had passed after hearing that lookout, when my eyes fixed on one guy in the crowd crossing the street in front of me as I stopped for a traffic light. He matched the lookout I had just heard. Maybe it was his body language. He was walking faster than others in the crowd were, looking over his shoulder in the direction of the robbery, and he matched the description—gender, color, height, size, and clothing. I was convinced he was the one who committed the robbery.

He was walking against the direction I was driving. I decided to circle the block quickly and quietly, instead of leaving the car, and the radio, to follow him on foot. As I expected, there he was, walking toward me at the next intersection. I decided to take no action because of the crowd. I circled the block again. And there he was again. Even though I never looked at him directly, I was sure he hadn't noticed me.

I did not report my actions to "radio" (police jargon for the radio dispatcher) because I was concerned that backup would respond with blue lights and sirens, causing my suspect to disappear into the crowded downtown streets. The lookout advised that he was armed with a revolver. I circled the next block, timing my arrival to meet him at the next intersection. And there he was, no longer as furtive as the first time I saw him, probably because he had distanced himself from the scene of his crime. He was strolling casually, directly toward me. My timing was perfect. Just as he stepped off the curb, I drove as close to the curb as I could without jumping it, and stopped in front of him, causing him to bump into the side of my car. He seemed confused as to what had just happened, and that moment of confusion gave me enough time to jump out, run around the car, and come up behind him, announcing, "I'm a police officer. Put your hands on the car."

Because I was behind him, he did not see that I had my revolver out. He responded immediately, putting his hands on the car. In the next moment, he moved a hand from the car towards his waist. Before he reached his waist, I jammed the barrel of my gun into his back. He froze, not a muscle twitched at that point. I reached around and pulled a loaded .38 caliber pistol from the waist of his pants.

I cuffed him and searched him. In his pocket was a brown paper bag containing several hundred dollars. I did not count it. I called the robbery detectives. When they arrived, I turned everything over to them.

Later that night at the station, about to go off duty, the robbery detectives told me they returned the stolen money to the liquor store owner, the victim of the armed robbery. He complained that it wasn't all there—five dollars was missing. He wanted them to talk to me about it.

I was pissed. Damn, was I pissed! That ungrateful son-of-a-bitch! I caught the bastard who stole his money; I caught him within minutes of the holdup. I could have been shot recovering his goddamn money. I couldn't believe that son-of-a-bitch thought I would steal five dollars out of several hundred or whatever the goddamned amount. I would not have taken any amount out of thousands of dollars of stolen money, surely not five fuckin' dollars!

I'm sure the robbery detectives hadn't taken it. They were as incredulous as I was about the accusation. What happened to it? Maybe the thief dropped a five-dollar bill. Maybe the liquor store owner miscounted the amount taken. The more I thought about the accusation, the madder I got. Maybe things like this are what cause cops and detectives to ride around as if they were wearing blinders.

Atlanta, the 1960s, and Riots

In the summer of 1966, the civil rights movement exploded across the United States. In most major cities, some incident or confrontation between Negro youths and the police sparked a disturbance, which grew into burning, looting, and general lawlessness. In the resulting riots, entire sections of cities were burned or destroyed, and worse, there were many deaths and injuries.

The lid blew off Atlanta in the Summerhill section, a high-crime, poverty-stricken Negro area a few blocks from Atlanta Stadium. Two auto theft detectives, both white, were attempting to arrest a young Negro in a car reported as stolen. They had stopped him at Capitol Avenue and Ormond Street. During the attempt to apprehend him, the car thief was shot and killed. Hearing the shots, a crowd began to gather and grew larger and larger as word spread that a black youth had been killed by white policemen.

Stokely Carmichael, the leader of the Student Nonviolent Coordinating Committee, went to black communities from city to city, rallying blacks against whites, through any means, including violence. It just happened that Carmichael was in Atlanta that day, and within an hour, was inciting the crowd with cries of "black power" and "white devil." The chants turned the crowd from curiosity seekers into an angry mob of over a thousand Negroes. The detectives put out a call for help, a signal 63. As police responded, the mob threw rocks and bottles at them, the responding units themselves put out a help call. More and more police arrived. More and more rocks and bottles were thrown. Police cars were overturned. Hand-to-hand fighting between police and Negroes ensued.

When Atlanta mayor Ivan Allen Jr. arrived, he tried to talk to the mob, to reason with them, to restore some semblance of order. He stood on the hood of his car, but the mob rocked it back and forth so violently that he gave up trying to appeal to them and left the area. About one hundred Georgia state troopers were called and held in reserve, assembled at Atlanta Stadium. They were ready to respond, but were never deployed. After using tear gas and shooting shotguns in the air, Atlanta police eventually managed to gain control. The mob, no longer raging, was still a crowd, remaining, perhaps, to see what might happen next. No one was killed, but dozens were injured and scores arrested.

All available Atlanta policemen, detectives included, were pressed into service during the crisis. The police department was under emergency operation. Off days and vacations were cancelled, and everyone went on twelve-hour shifts, either midnight to noon or noon to midnight, seven days a week.

My twelve-hour shift started at noon. We patrolled on foot in groups of four, each of us armed with a shotgun, service revolver, nightstick, helmet, and gas mask (some masks were useless because they had been in the supply room, unused, for such a long time that the seals simply deteriorated). Things had calmed down after that first day; only scattered incidents, involving small groups of snarling youths and antagonized policemen, flared up now and then. The small groups were immediately arrested and taken to jail, which smothered the spark that could incite a mob.

On the second day, the mayor and police chief rode through the area, assessing the situation. Shortly afterward, the police chief ordered that all shotguns were to be turned in and out of sight. We felt naked without them. Everyone was pissed off and grumbling. But it became clear that heavy firepower was not needed. Four days after the riots started, the crowd dispersed, police were pulled out of the area, and the crisis was over.

Within a week, there was a bigger riot just east of downtown in another depressed Negro area. A white couple in a car stopped for a traffic light on Boulevard, at Angier Avenue. There, they were harassed and threatened by a group of Negro teenagers. When they approached the car, the white guy pulled a pistol and fired into the group. They sped away in their car. One Negro teenager lay dead.

When police arrived, they were met by shots, fired from the crowd gathered around the dead teenager. Police Sergeant Morris Spears went down with a head wound. A signal 63/50/4 (officer needs help/person shot/ambulance on the way) went out. When the responding cops arrived, they were mad that one of them had been shot. The mob was mad because a Negro had been killed by a white guy. The situation became increasingly violent and out of control.

There was greater damage during this riot. Police cars, as well as civilian cars, were overturned and burned; buildings were damaged, some of them burned to shells; stores were looted. Again, twelve-hour shifts were imposed, off days were cancelled, four-man patrols were instituted, and we were decked out in shotguns, helmets, and the rest of the riot gear. This time, I had the midnight to noon shift. Five days after the start of the riot, order had been restored. Many arrests were made, and both police and rioters sustained injuries. Except for the teenager, no one else was killed. After a short convalesce, Sergeant Spears returned to work.

As the weather cooled off towards the end of 1966, so did the racial tension, which had hung in the air, like a heavy fog. Stokely Carmichael was still in Atlanta, and so also was H. Rap Brown, another black militant whose presence had been felt in several riot-torn cities up north. Both advocated violent revolution, and did their best to accomplish it. Both promoted "Black Power" in the Negro communities. H. Rap Brown expressed it thusly, "Violence is as American as cherry pie." Carmichael wasn't quite as poetic, chanting, "Burn, baby, burn," while American cities went up in flames.

When spring arrived, an uneasy calm remained. There was major rioting in other US cities. In Atlanta, if a white policemen attempted to arrest a Negro for a crime, large or small, there were riots. The Atlanta police dreaded the long, hot summer coming, while SNCC, with Stokely and Rap looked forward to it.

In June 1967, anxieties focused on Dixie Hills. At the center of this community (west of downtown) was a city housing project of approximately six hundred units. The problems in Dixie Hills were typical of most public housing projects—too much garbage, infrequent pick-ups, faulty plumbing, no air conditioning, rats and roaches, and a high crime rate. People in the community were victims of their own neighbors.

The Dixie Hills community included hundreds of single-family homes that surrounded the housing project. At the center of all this was a small strip-shop plaza, comprised of a grocery store, cleaners, and several other storefront businesses. The teenagers and young adults, having nothing to do and nowhere to go, hung out at this plaza.

One night, three of those hanging out were arrested in the shopping plaza on minor charges. Forty to fifty people gathered during the arrests, not in violence, but expressing enough verbal anger to cause officers concern. Nothing developed that night.

The following night, a small contingent of Atlanta police officers, under the command of Captain EH Little, was assigned to Dixie Hills. A command post was set up in the shopping plaza. Stokely Carmichael showed up with other SNCC members. It didn't take long for a crowd to develop in Dixie Hills. The people were right there, on their porches, leaning out their windows, hanging around the plaza, within steps and minutes of forming a crowd. That happened even faster when someone like Stokely Carmichael was around. He and the other SNCC members tried to incite the crowd, shouting over and over and louder and louder, "It's never going to change," "The black man will always be murdered by the white devils," and "You gotta do it like they did in other cities, burn, baby, burn." He was like a preacher, his frenzy instilling the same in his congregation. Captain Little ordered Carmichael to leave. He refused and was promptly arrested. There was a murmur of resentment from the crowd, some taunting the police verbally, but nothing more. Most of the people drifted home, and the rest of the night passed without incident.

On the third night, Stokely, out on bond, fired up the crowd at a church meeting in Dixie Hills. During those years, a church was the black community's place to meet to discuss civil rights issues, such as segregation, poor living conditions, and police brutality. After Stokely motivated the congregation in the church, they gathered around the plaza to see what the police would do next. Stokely was not with them, he had left Dixie Hills, I guessed, not wanting to be in the middle of a riot.

Motivated, Stokely's congregation taunted the police fervently that night. Suddenly, an alarm started ringing outside one of the stores in the plaza. Someone from the crowd had climbed up and begun hitting the bell with a stick. One of the Negro officers ordered him down. A number of men from the crowd confronted the police officer, protesting his attempt to arrest the bell ringer. Scuffles broke out between police officers and protesters. The scuffles escalated to a melee. After one of the protesters was shot in the leg by a police officer, the melee elevated to a riot. The volcano had blown its top.

I was working the evening watch, riding alone that night, when I heard Captain Little's voice requesting "every car in the city." The twenty or so policemen at the plaza were surrounded by more than a thousand angry, rioting Negroes. A signal 63 was given for every patrol car, detective car, paddy wagon, and motorcycle in the city to go to Dixie Hills. That was the only time in my career I heard a call for every police vehicle in the city to respond. Flashing blue lights stretched out on Interstate 20 as far as I could see.

I turned into the street that led to the plaza; there was a motorcycle cop immediately in front of me. People lined up on the right side of this street pelted police vehicles with rocks and bricks as they went by. The motorcycle cop, physically exposed to the missiles, was vulnerable. I pulled up on his right side, shielding him with my car, and we rode the gauntlet together. We made it to the plaza unharmed, but the windows on the right side of my car, plus the back windshield, were shattered.

The shopping plaza was a combat zone. The urban rioters' arsenal— rocks, bricks, bottles, cement blocks, anything that could be hurled and harm—was thrown at us. From out of the darkness, Molotov cocktails flared, and we heard gunshots. Neither the cocktails nor the gunshots injured any of us. I was in my business suit, armed with a five-shot, snub-nosed, .38 caliber revolver—no extra ammunition, no helmet, no nightstick, or shotgun. I didn't know what the hell I was doing there.

Cops and police brass continued to pour into the plaza. One captain would give an order to do something; a few moments later, another captain would give an entirely different order, followed by a lieutenant telling us to do something else. If the situation weren't so dangerous, it could have been a scene in a Three Stooges comedy. Clearly, we didn't have our shit together.

Someone in brass decided there should be cops on the roof. Once there, they could prevent the rioters from getting to the roof to hurl things down onto the police. Officer RL Braswell, always the first to respond, climbed onto the roof of a paddy wagon that was backed up to the building. He was about to climb further onto the roof when a television network news team (all the media people, local and national, were there) lit him up with a floodlight to get him on camera.

I yelled at them to turn off the damned light. The cameraman responded, shutting it off. The reporter in charge of the news team began informing me of a lot of First Amendment shit. I informed him that if he turned on the light and lit up another policeman again, I would break the light, kick his ass, and put him in jail. The threat impressed him; he left the light off. (I saw that same reporter a short while later, holding a handkerchief to his bleeding leg. He had been hit with a broken bottle and had to go to the hospital for stitches.)

The captains and lieutenants were on the radio, requesting riot equipment from downtown. The APD had acquired a Brinks armored truck some years before. It had been used through the years for one thing or another, as the need dictated. In the mid-sixties, it was kept downtown at police headquarters, stocked with riot gear—mainly helmets, riot batons, and gas masks. Different people were charged with the responsibility of bringing the "riot truck," as it came to be known, and its equipment, to where it was needed. Lieutenant Herman Copeland, a forty-year veteran who mainly hung around the station, handled the riot truck on the evening watch.

Missiles from out of the darkness bombarded us. When we heard the thud of a brick or rock making contact, we looked around to see who was hit. One of the cops clutched his head, blood trickling from between his fingers. Where was the riot truck with the goddamn helmets? Superior officers were on the radio, pleading with downtown; downtown assured them the helmets were in the truck and on the way.

Things at headquarters were frantic. Lieutenant Copeland was in the building somewhere, but where? When he was located, he couldn't remember where he had left the keys to the truck. When he found the keys, the truck wouldn't start because the battery was dead, probably from lack of use. That meant finding jumper cables; where were they? Every moment that passed during Copeland's charade at headquarters meant it was likely another policeman's head was bleeding. The one thing in our favor was that the gas tank was full. Lieutenant Copeland finally headed west on I-20, towards Dixie Hills. He was running "code 3" (blue lights and siren), but it was an old truck and Lieutenant Copeland, older than the truck, couldn't exceed 45 mph. When we finally saw it, the truck looked to us like the cavalry.

Lieutenant Copeland swung that beautiful 1947 International Harvester armored truck into the plaza parking lot, and we swarmed around it. I stood at the rear of the truck, where many policemen grabbed the doors and flung them open.

A lawn mower and a rake—that's all there was inside. A fuckin' lawn mower and a goddamn rake! What happened to the helmets? How the hell did a lawn mower and a rake get in there?

One of the captains cut short his furious words to call headquarters, barking orders to whomever was on the other end to get into the supply room, get the helmets and riot sticks, load them into a paddy wagon, and get them to the plaza as fast as possible. It was an hour, but they arrived, helping us to survive the night with only a few more cuts, bumps, and bruises.

The frenzy of the mob began to wane. The rioters may have gotten tired of hurling things at us. It didn't matter to us why they stopped. They stopped, and slowly began to drift away from the riot scene.

The beginning of the next night, the fourth night, was calm; police and the crowd faced each other, quietly waiting to react to whatever might happen. The police all wore helmets, most were equipped with riot gear, and some were issued shotguns. There were about two hundred of us. Police blocked streets leading into the Dixie Hills community. Only residents and people authorized by police were allowed to enter.

The standoff continued without incident until a Molotov cocktail landed among a group of policemen. Police responded immediately, attacking the crowd with their riot sticks. Most of the crowd ran off; those who remained struggled against the riot sticks. Suddenly, the unmistakable sound of a shotgun blast was heard over the noise of the crowd. A Negro man in his fifties, sitting on his porch across from the plaza, was struck in the head and died instantly; three others near him, one of them a child, were wounded by pellets from the blast. The crowd scattered. The night was over.

No policeman admitted firing the shotgun. Some insisted it wasn't fired by one of them, but by someone from the darkness of the plaza or beyond. Because there are no ballistic comparisons of shotguns, the only thing known for sure was that the pellets were similar to the ammunition issued to police, and the same type of shotgun fired them. That death remains unsolved to this day. I've always believed, and still do, that it was fired by a policeman.

The mayor declared a state of emergency, and a curfew was imposed at Dixie Hills. At the plaza, tensions abated over the next few days, and more and more cops were pulled from riot duty. It was over except for scattered incidents, which were snuffed out immediately.

Atlanta was lucky. In many cities, such as Los Angeles, New York, Newark, Detroit, and Washington, DC, the death toll was high, and property damage well into hundreds of millions of dollars.

Homicide

"Goldhagen, there's only one way to work homicide in this city, and that's my way." Without telling me to sit down, that was what Lieutenant WK Perry, commander of the homicide squad, said to me the moment I entered the room. "Forget about all that glamorous bullshit. It's hard work and long hours. It's hair, blood, and eyeballs. It's walking through someone's bloody brains after they've been blown out of the poor bastard's head. It's the sight and stench of a rotting or burned corpse. If I tell you to do something one way and you think you know a better way, forget it—because you don't."

Looking at me with piercing blue eyes from a face carved of granite, he challenged me. "If you can't live with that and a lot more, you might as well go back to fugitive, or wherever the hell you came from." Our eyes locked, I took a deep breath, and told him I was ready to go to work.

Several weeks earlier, homicide had had an opening for a detective. Other squads were notified of the opening and invited to recommend likely candidates. When such an opening occurred, it was an opportunity for lieutenants either to get rid of dead wood or recommend an apt and deserving candidate who might regard homicide as the most interesting, exciting, and desirable assignment. Lieutenant Ed Samples, the fugitive squad commander, brought me in and introduced me to Lieutenant Perry. (I never knew which option motivated Lt. Samples).

Samples turned and left. Perry didn't get up from behind his desk. I was not asked to sit down; we didn't shake hands. Perry looked me in the eye and proceeded with his welcome aboard speech.

In 1966, the homicide squad handled everything from victims of a bloody nose to murder, as well as rape and other sex crimes. My first assignments paired me with different veteran homicide detectives until I demonstrated that I knew what the hell I was doing.

Most of the homicides were "smoking guns," where the victim and the perpetrator knew each other—the victim was killed by a family member or neighbor or friend or business associate. These homicides were easy for a detective to clear because the perpetrator was usually still on the scene, the gun, knife, or whatever weapon, "smoking" still in his or her hand when the police arrived. Sometimes the perpetrator fled before the police arrived, but his or her identity was known. It was just a matter of time before an arrest was made. For those kinds of homicides, the detective's work was mostly paperwork—procedural stuff—making sure that the reports of the crime were complete, the witness statements accurately recorded, and all the evidence was collected, identified, and analyzed. The homicides that challenge a detective are the "who-done-it" homicides—that is when a detective has real work to do.

Although a homicide detective works a regular shift—the same hours, usually for a month—that doesn't mean he goes home at the end of his watch, not if a homicide has occurred on his watch. No matter what the clock says, he must work the crime scene. Working the crime scene means supervising the technicians as they search the immediate area for evidence, such as spent shells or fingerprints, take measurements that could reflect where the victim was in relation to the perpetrator, and photograph the victim and immediate area. Working the crime scene means the detective makes notes and renders sketches, both of which are needed so he can start work before the results of the technicians become available to him. Working the crime scene also means canvassing the area, collecting anything that might serve as evidence, talking to people who might provide useful information, taking witness statements, and interrogating suspects, if any are available.

That is why working homicide means lost sleep, missed dinners, and screwed-up social or family plans. It's the same for the homicide detective whether the crime is murder or rape, except that most rapes are of the "who-done-it," stranger-to-stranger type. Although in a rape, there is always at least one witness—the victim.

The Goliaths Abuse David

Working alone one Wednesday morning, I received a call to meet a patrol car in the West End section on a signal 49 (investigate a rape). When I arrived, the police officer turned over to me a twenty-four-year-old white female and her two-year-old son. Although she had a phone in her home, and there were phone booths on the street where she lived, she had called the police from a phone booth at an intersection several blocks away to report she had been raped. After getting from the patrolman the information I needed, I drove the victim to be examined at Grady Hospital—the trauma one center for the Atlanta police. The official report of examinations usually followed several days later. After she was examined, I took her to the homicide squad room, where she told me what happened.

She said she was divorced, living with her young son in an apartment on Lawton Street. (Where whites were moving out of their apartments, and Negroes were moving into them; at the time, the apartments were about a fifty-fifty mix, racially.) She told me her apartment had two levels, the bedrooms upstairs, the living room, dining room, and kitchen downstairs.

She and her child were upstairs in the bedroom, asleep. At about three a.m., she was awakened by a Negro man straddling her stomach. He had one hand over her mouth, the other held a knife to her neck. He warned her, "Be quiet, or I'll cut your goddamn throat." She said she nodded her head, and as soon as he took his hand away from her mouth, she assured him that she would not scream, and then pleaded, "Please, don't hurt me."

He told her to take off her nightgown and remove her panties. She said she hesitated, and he placed the knife under her nose and threatened, "If you don't do exactly what I say, when I say it, I'm going to cut your kid's head off!" Although she was afraid to move, she removed her nightgown and panties and lay passively while he raped her. After she thought he was finished, he said to her, "If you don't act nicer to me and show how much you enjoy being with me, I'll kill the child." And he raped her again.

Terrified, she decided she would do whatever she needed to satisfy him. She was willing to do anything to keep him from getting angry with her and hurting her baby. When he demanded that she "Suck my dick," she did it. He asked if she had ever been "Fucked by a Negro man" before. She replied, "No," but thought it would please and maybe satisfy him if she admitted he was the best she'd ever had. She said he put his mouth on hers, and she went along with his passionate kisses. He told her to turn over, and he entered her anally. She was hurting and crying, but convinced him that her cries were the sounds of passion.

He remained until dawn, and he said that he would like to come back in a few days. She agreed that he could return on Saturday night at eight o'clock. She said it was like "making a date" for him to return. They went arm-in-arm downstairs to the kitchen, where he had a glass of water. He warned her not to call the police and said he would hang around down the street to see if any police cars came near her apartment. If he saw any police, he would come back to get the kid. She said she told him he didn't have to worry about that. They embraced and kissed goodbye, as if they had been lovers. He left through the back door.

She said she locked the door, ran upstairs, grabbed her son, and went back down to the living room, huddling with him on the couch for a couple of hours, afraid to move. At about ten a.m., she got dressed, and, terrified, with her son went out of the building, looking over her shoulder as she walked five blocks to the telephone where she called the police. Her story was taken down by a typist and signed as her written statement,

I went to her apartment on Lawton Street, and had the crime scene technicians, meet me. The scene was processed, examining the bed linens and towels for blood, semen, and hair. The fingerprints lifted from the drinking glass on the kitchen counter were as clear as if he had voluntarily given his prints as required for a security job.

Later that afternoon, I relayed to Lieutenant Perry all of what the woman had told me. Homicide detectives in the squad room heard what I reported and razzed, criticized, and insulted me. "Listen, Goldhagen, that woman didn't have a mark on her. No white woman would let a nigger rape her and do all those other things to her without being half-dead from resisting." They went further, thinking they were instructing me. "Any decent white woman would die, rather than to go through all that with a nigger. She probably invited him over, and when he left, she was afraid the neighbors might have seen him leaving and made up the whole story to cover her ass." Their final insult was, "Goldie, you can't be so goddamn naïve and believe these fairy tales every time some woman sheds a tear and claims she got raped." There they were, the Goliaths who knew everything, and there I was—without a slingshot.

They left the squad room, probably feeling they had smartened up a new homicide detective. Lieutenant Perry and I were alone in the squad room, and he asked me what I thought. I tell him that not only did I believe her story—I thought the rapist was dumb enough to keep the date on Saturday. I told him I wanted to be inside her apartment, waiting for him. He agreed and told me to contact my victim and arrange it. It made me feel good about myself when he said he would be there with me.

I met Lieutenant Perry at the homicide office at six o'clock on Saturday evening. I called the victim to let her know we were leaving the office. We would be in plain clothes and would knock on her back door. While I was on the phone with her, Lieutenant Perry checked out a shotgun from the vault to take with us.

Twenty minutes later, we arrived at her back door and knocked. She opened the door, and she was hysterical. We observed in her apartment a white male—her ex-husband. He had come to be with her on Saturday. He had been guzzling beer, probably all day, and was shit-faced drunk.

It turned out that the rapist had arrived early and knocked on her front door, moments after I spoke to her on the phone to let her know we were on our way. She peeked out of the window, saw it was he, and decided to stall and not answer. Her ex-husband flung open the door, expecting to play the role of hero. The rapist backed into the front yard, pulled out a knife, and challenged him. "Come on out and get a piece of me, if you want to, you white mother-fucker!" The would-be hero slammed shut the door and locked it. The rapist walked off.

I was so pissed at the drunken nitwit that I told him what I thought of him and all of his ancestors. I threatened to put him in jail if he opened his mouth and uttered so much as one syllable. The lieutenant and I remained for ten to fifteen minutes, chatting with her, reassuring her that she would not be without our help. She calmed down, and I asked her to call me if she saw the perpetrator again, and that whether or not she did, I would be in touch with her. Lieutenant Perry and I left, and as we got into the car, an uneasy feeling came over me. I suggested we park down the street, wait, and watch for a while. We were not in a detective car, which criminals and eight-year-old kids recognize as police cars. We were in an inconspicuous undercover car.

We were not sitting there for more than fifteen minutes when we saw a Negro male walk up the street. He fit the victim's description of him in every detail. We stopped him, identified ourselves, and when I searched him, I found a five-dollar bill, two one-dollar bills, eight quarters, and a pocketknife, similar to the one the victim had described. We put him in the car, without cuffing him, and drove back to the victim's apartment.

The victim saw us and approached our car, and when she saw our passenger, she lost control, screaming and yelling hysterically, "That's him! That's him!" The ex-husband got brave again and told the Negro in our custody what he would do if he could have him alone for five minutes. (I considered that it would be one way to get the drunk out of

59

our way. I could put them in the car together and let him get his drunken ass kicked!)

After the victim regained control, she told us that her next-door neighbor, a seventy-nine-year-old, invalid, white woman had just called to say she had been raped and robbed. We went to see the neighbor, bringing with us our prisoner. The woman looked at him and cried out, "That's him!" She screamed, "He tried to kill me! Take him away from me!" Sobbing, she told us that he had broken in her front door and raped her while she lay on the living room couch. He then robbed her of eight dollars—a five-dollar bill, two one-dollar bills, and eight quarters. Bingo!

Lieutenant Perry told me to take the rapist—we had him on two counts of rape, in addition to aggravated sodomy and armed robbery— out of the old woman's living room and into the kitchen. As soon as we got to the kitchen, he bolted for the back door. I made a dive for him, grabbing him around his shoulders, and then felt myself stabbed. He had a boning knife, with a thin, six-inch blade, and a thick, wooden handle—the kind of knife used in butcher shops. Where or how he got it didn't matter while he was trying to plunge it into my chest. I was able to grab his wrist with my right hand and stop him from driving the knife home. I could not reach my gun, and I could not let go of his wrist; we were in a life and death dance in that small kitchen, breaking everything in it.

Reacting to the sounds he heard, Lieutenant Perry appeared in the doorway, racking the shotgun we had brought with us. Hearing that sound, I had two worries. One, this crazy son-of-a-bitch was trying to make me wear the boning knife. Two, the lieutenant was about to try to shoot him off me, likely getting a part of me, as well.

Reaching into the adrenal reservoir everyone has for life or death situations, I managed an all-or-nothing surge of energy—enough to push myself away from the rapist. We separated. I fell back against the wall. He was left standing in the middle of the kitchen. He was about to lunge for me when Lieutenant Perry hit him with a blast of .00 buckshot. The rapist went down, but came up on one knee and swiped at me again. I drew my revolver, and I was going to shoot him, but Perry hit him with a second blast. He never moved again.

I was treated for the stab wound to my chest. It was not deep, so I did not have to be admitted to the hospital, but I did have to buy a new shirt. We were never able to determine how he got the boning knife. The old woman said it did not belong to her. He probably had it somewhere on his person. I probably missed it when I searched him and was satisfied to have found the pocketknife. I should not have been satisfied. I should have searched further, more thoroughly. It was the kind of mistake a rookie policeman might make.

We pulled the deceased rapist's records. His prints matched those taken from the glass in the first victim's kitchen. He was thirty-five years old and had a lengthy rap sheet. He had been arrested for murder, rape, robbery, aggravated assault, burglary, and assorted misdemeanors. He had spent time in the state mental hospital. What the hell was he doing out, walking around, free as a bird?

The homicide detectives who had abused me when I reported the rape to Lieutenant Perry never congratulated me or apologized. They never even mentioned it—not in my presence. The Goliaths, who thought they knew everything, were felled by the slingshot of my persistent belief in a woman who did whatever she had to do to protect her child from harm.

An Offer I Could Refuse—and Did

In the early 1960s, there was only one other policeman in the Atlanta Police Department who was a Jew. He was Superintendent Fred Beerman, who worked in the office of the chief of police. Beerman started with the City of Atlanta in the mid 1940s as a civilian clerk. Police Chief Herbert Jenkins assigned Beerman to the chief's office, recognizing his brilliant mind and enormous talent in financial matters. He was later appointed to the rank of superintendent and placed in charge of the fiscal division. All purchasing and inventory control of equipment, bill payments, and other financial matters passed through his office. He was the keeper of the books. Superintendent Fred Beerman retired not long after I joined the Atlanta Police Department. He was hardly seen by the rank and file cops, the street cops, whereas I interacted with them every working day, from my first day as a rookie, later as a young patrolman, and then as a detective—the only Jew among the non-Jewish cops.

For a white Southern boy, being accepted into the police culture of "us vs. them" was difficult, time consuming, and emotionally exhausting. For me, a New York Jew, it was even harder, longer, and more draining.

The Atlanta Police Department at that time lacked diversity. It was almost entirely white, except for the very few "colored." There were no Latinos, no Asians, no women, no Jews. I was different, an anomaly.

I heard all the words and remarks—"Jew boy," "Hebe," "kike," "Abie," "sheeny," "mockie," "matzo ball," "kosher." Most were not trying to be offensive, or malicious, but funny and amusing, not realizing how hurtful the words were. I showed no anger. I did not challenge them. I took it all and kept smiling. I wanted so much to fit in, to be accepted.

I wanted so much to be accepted that I became just like the other cops, using offensive or malicious words towards blacks. I felt I was accepted when I started saying, "nigger," "jungle bunny," "coon," "boy," "burr-head," "blue gum"—even though I still regularly heard "Jew boy," "Abie," and all the rest of the amusing references to Jews.

The cases that were the start of my work in homicide in 1966 were being prepared for trial in 1967. During those preparations, I had lots of contact with the Fulton County District Attorney's office. Lewis Slaton was the district attorney, supervising a dozen or so assistant DAs. The number one ADA was Paul Ginsburg, a Jew.

One day, I was in Paul Ginsburg's office discussing a murder I had handled. He got up, closed his door, sat back at his desk, and made me a proposition. Move away from Douglasville, where I was living at the time—twenty-five miles west of Atlanta, more rural than suburban back then—and relocate to the Morningside area of Atlanta, where there was a large Jewish population. He offered to help me find a house I could afford. Join the synagogue and become active in the Jewish community. Do all that, and he and other powerful people would see to it that I made captain within a year. Guaranteed. Within one year.

I couldn't believe what I was hearing. Advance from detective to captain in one jump? That had never happened in the history of the APD. Back then, promotions were made for a variety of reasons, mostly the wrong reasons, but only one rank at a time. I told Mr. Ginsburg I would have to think about it and talk it over with my wife, and I would get back to him.

Betty and I discussed it at length and agreed that there were no free rides. You don't get something for nothing. There would be strings attached, and I didn't want to be obligated to anyone. I didn't want any obligations outside those required of me as a policeman. I didn't want to be beholden to anyone outside the ranks of the APD. I didn't know what favors might be asked of me, and I didn't want to be in anyone's "pocket." Most importantly, whatever advancements I might achieve during my career, I wanted to accomplish on my own, without "help" from anyone.

A week later, when I gave Mr. Ginsberg my decision, he expressed his disappointment and emphasized the golden opportunity I was passing up.

I was certainly tempted, but I held firm. The matter was never discussed again; it was as if his offer had never occurred.

I mentioned it to only a few close, trusted friends. Each of them said they would have taken the deal without hesitation. Of course, I was the only Jew, so no one else got the offer. I did make captain towards the end of my career, and I did it on my own. I owed nothing to anyone, and I had the respect of most of those who knew me.

Any regrets about not taking the offer? I did second-guess myself over the years when I saw others, due to politics, nepotism, race, or gender, advance more quickly through the ranks than I, but no—no regrets.

I Lied!

Hosea Williams was a black civil rights activist and high-ranking member of the Southern Christian Leadership Conference (SCLC) in Atlanta. He was an obnoxious, aggressive, offensive bully—and a racist. He was always first to plunge into any controversy with a black and white racial issue, especially when it involved the police. It seemed controversy was the purpose of his existence.

Officer RD Marshall was a white Atlanta policeman with a long record of complaints for brutality. He was a beefy, cigar smoking, tobacco chewing, redneck bully—and a racist. Atlanta's black community viewed Marshall much as Birmingham's black community viewed Bull Conner.

One Sunday afternoon in 1967, while was assigned to homicide, I happened to be in the police detention area of Grady Hospital when I heard a disturbance in the corridor. I looked out and saw Officer Marshall with Hosea Williams in tow. Marshall had him by the arms, pulling and pushing Hosea, and Hosea, although not resisting, was walking very reluctantly. They were shouting in each other's faces.

Inside the detention area, I saw Marshall push Hosea into one of the holding rooms, follow him inside and slap him twice, knocking Hosea down. Marshall then came out of the room and locked the door. Marshall had arrested Hosea for a disturbance out on the ambulance ramp. I was in the detention area the entire time and was still there when the wagon picked Hosea Williams up to transport him to the city jail. There were accusations by Hosea Williams and denials by

Marshall, which resulted in a big investigation. I was in the middle, the star witness in the investigation.

Hosea said he was brutally beaten by Marshall. He said that Marshall threw him into the room, punched him in the face and stomach, and rabbit-punched him. He said he suffered blows from Marshall at least a half dozen times. He said when he was on the floor, Marshall had repeatedly kicked and stomped him. Hosea's accusations were an exaggeration and distortion of the two open-handed slaps across the face.

Marshall said that when they got to the detention area, he put Hosea in the holding room, then closed and locked the door. He said he never struck him. That wasn't the truth, either.

What did I do? I rationalized. I did not like either one for what they were; they were both bullies. I disliked Hosea more because he was a thorn in the sides of the police, and because he was a racial agitator. The black community wanted Marshall's badge. I didn't believe that losing his badge fit the crime of the two slaps. If I told the truth, the black community would get Marshall fired.

I supported RD Marshall's denial. The "code of silence" is a powerful force among police officers. You don't "rat out" another cop. I made my statement to Internal Affairs and thought that was the end of it. It wasn't.

The incident got into the newspaper and TV news. Hosea led demonstrations outside the police station. Things grew into a formal hearing before the Public Safety Committee of the city council, previously known as the Police Committee of the Board of Alderman. The hearing was like a court trial, with attorneys representing both sides. The one difference was that witnesses were not under oath. That took a lot of pressure off me, because I had never committed perjury and never would. I was the key witness. When it came time to tell the truth, I lied! I said that Marshall had never struck Hosea. My testimony swayed the committee, and Officer RD Marshall dodged another brutality complaint, all of which were probably true.

Hosea Williams had lied about the extent and severity of the beating. RD Marshall lied about not slapping him. I lied because of peer pressure. I wanted to be one of the boys, not be a "rat," or a "pimp." The more I thought about Hosea's lies, the more intensely I disliked racial agitators.

In later years, I regretted the decision to lie. With this telling, I feel relieved that it is off my chest. Had I been under oath, I would not have lied. If I had to do it all over again, I would not lie.

Returning Fugitives

A refreshing break in routine for a homicide detective was traveling to another city to pick up a fugitive wanted in Atlanta. It was considered a perk among detectives, simply because it was a big deal—getting on a plane, spending a night, having dinner and breakfast in another city.

A person might be picked up for a minor crime or stopped by the police for a traffic violation. In either case, local police check his or her name through the National Crime Information Center (NCIC). If the detainee is a fugitive from another state, that information is reported to the local police, who hold him and notify the jurisdiction he fled.

I took three trips to retrieve fugitives, all murder suspects. Two detectives were usually sent to return a prisoner. I had been working alone on all three cases, so when the time came to return the fugitives, the lieutenant assigned another homicide detective to go with me.

Detective Fred Russell

The first trip was to New York City, where my murder suspect had fled. He eventually got into an altercation and was picked up by the NYPD. When they learned he was wanted for murder in Atlanta, they called and spoke with homicide Lieutenant JE Helms for confirmation. The fugitive was held by the NYPD for us to pick up. Following the call from the NYPD, Lieutenant Helms called me at home, where I was enjoying a day off. He said there was no need for me to come in; he had assigned Detective ND Lauth to go with me, and Lauth would make all the necessary arrangements. He would have all the paper work, plus our tickets, and would meet me at the Atlanta airport the following day for a noon flight. That was okay with me; Lauth was a bright guy, had been around, and was someone I felt I could work well with.

But there was a last minute change. When I arrived at the airport, there stood Detective Fred Russell. I was dismayed because I was looking forward to working with Lauth. It wasn't that I didn't like Russell, or that he wasn't a nice guy. It was just that Fred Russell was not the partner to have going into the hustle and bustle of New York City to transport a murder suspect. Detective Fred Russell was a short, rotund, older man, not fleet of foot.

Once airborne, I learned that the arrangements Lauth would have made, Fred had not. The only thing he knew was that we were to be in New York City's municipal court at nine a.m. the next morning for an extradition hearing. He said we would meet with the detectives in court when the case was called. Fred didn't even get their names. All he knew was that they worked out of the "fifth squad detectives." I surmised that would be the Fifth Precinct, in lower Manhattan.

Then the really bad news—he had not arranged for anyone to meet us at the airport. Police courtesy dictates that police officers arriving on official business are met at the airport and provided transportation while in the city. This courtesy is universal and practiced everywhere.

As soon as we land at New York's LaGuardia Airport, I go to the pay phone and start calling. I explain my mission and that I am not sure who I should be talking to. I get rude replies, quick transfers, and lost connections. After going through a fist full of coins, I am finally connected to the Fifth Detective Squad, where I am again treated with rudeness for my inability to identify to whom I should be talking. Finally, someone gets the idea that I should speak to Detective Smith. He gets on the phone. "Yeah, me and my partner, Detective Brown, are handling your boy." The way he spoke to me was not the way I would have talked to a policeman from another city. He sounded like he was jerking me around, as if he was about to give me the brush-off. I tell him we just got off a plane, and needed transportation from LaGuardia. He told me that Brown was off, and that he was about to go off-duty. When I asked if someone else could pick us up, he said, "We don't got no fuckin' cars. We share one car with some other guys." He went on to say, "Anyways, you wouldn't want to ride in that piece of shit. It's filthy inside, all rusted out, and draggin' a fuckin' fender."

I got the message; there was no need to say anything further. I told him we'd see him in court in the morning and hung up. I was really pissed at Fred Russell. There was a Holiday Inn not far from the airport. I got on the phone, made the reservations, and Fred and I grabbed the shuttle van, went to the motel, and checked in.

My mother and father still lived in New York, in Queens, not far from LaGuardia. We were invited for dinner. We had a delicious meal of chopped liver, matzo ball soup, beef brisket, and potato kugel. We wolfed down our food. Fred didn't eat the chopped liver. Fred was kind of a novelty to my parents; he talked about his favorite meal—baked ham, collard greens, black-eyed peas, corn bread, and sweet tea. My mother made a concoction she called iced tea, which I could tell didn't thrill Fred, but he drank it, anyway. Fred charmed my parents with his gracious southern gentlemanliness.

The next morning, we took the shuttle, which left us at a subway station, where we caught a train to Manhattan. I had to reacquaint myself with the New York Subway System. It had been more than ten years since I had ridden the subway on a regular basis. I tried to impress upon Fred the dynamics of the subway during rush hour. "Fred, you've got to keep up; stay with me. If we get separated, we'll probably never hear from you again." We made it into midtown Manhattan and had to change at Grand Central Station. I found myself pulling and pushing him; he seemed to be moving in slow motion, gawking at everything. Fred and I were like Abbot and Costello.

At the municipal court, we found the right courtroom and hooked up with Smith and Brown. The hearing went okay, and the judge turned the prisoner over to us. A court clerk called my name and told me I had a telephone call. I went into a small office to take the call. Ruben Garland was on the other end.

Ruben Garland was a defense attorney in Atlanta. He was flamboyant, played by his own rules, and was probably the best criminal attorney of his time. He was representing our prisoner. Garland said he was staying at a hotel in midtown Manhattan and wanted us to stop by and talk to him. We first had to find someplace to park our prisoner for the day. It was about ten a.m., and our return flight wasn't until eight p.m. We had ten hours to kill and didn't want to drag our prisoner with us around New York City.

I told Smith and Brown of our dilemma and asked if they could hold on to him for a few hours. They said they couldn't because he was now in our custody. "But," Smith said, "We could sneak him down to the basement and chain him to a fuckin' pipe." I replied, "Thanks, but no thanks," and asked, "What about the city jail adjacent to the courthouse?" He made a call and we were in. The four of us deposited him in the "Tombs," the common but unofficial name for the New York City jail. We had to pick him up by four p.m. If not, we wouldn't be able to get him out until the next day.

Fred and I went to the hotel and met with Ruben Garland in his suite. He told us he was about to call room service and offered us lunch. I declined for both of us, and Fred looked at me in disagreement, but said nothing. Garland was disappointed we didn't have his client with us. He told us he wanted us to stop by so he could confer with his client. I told him he could have conferred with his client in court this morning. I let him know he was at the city jail if he wanted to confer.

I interrupted our chat with Garland because I had to go to the bathroom. As I got up to go, I noticed that Garland had put a fifty-dollar bill on the coffee table. When I returned to the living room, I didn't see the fifty. Fred and I left shortly after and stopped at a deli to grab hot pastramis on rye. Fred had no problem eating that! One of the things I miss about New York City is the availability of all kinds of authentic ethnic food.

We head back downtown, towards the city jail. Fred lobbied hard for us to bring Garland's client by the hotel on the way to the airport. When we checked our guy out of the "Tombs," it was only three p.m. We had five hours to kill before our flight. We couldn't wander around the city with him for that length of time, so we went back to Garland's hotel. After they talked for a couple of hours, the three of us left and took a taxi to the airport.

Those were the days when airline travel was not restricted by the federal laws that were later passed, but the airlines discouraged transporting prisoners. Fred Russell and I were short white guys. We were dressed in business suits. Our prisoner was a black male, over six feet tall, dressed raggedly, and he looked nasty.

An Eastern Airlines gate agent who had been giving us the eye, called a supervisor, who then called me over to the side and wanted to know who we were. I identified myself and confirmed that we were returning a prisoner to Atlanta. He called the captain from the plane, and we had a three-way conference. The captain wanted to know if we were armed, and I told him we were. It was up to him whether we flew on his plane or not. I thought he was about to tell us to go Greyhound, when he said, "Okay."

He wanted us to board first, and be seated in the last seats in the rear. I told the captain that we'd let our prisoner use the restroom before the passengers boarded, and once he was seated, he'd stay in his seat until we landed in Atlanta. I told him that a patrol car would be waiting on the tarmac at the gate, and we'd take him down the aircraft's rear stairway. All of that satisfied the captain; in a short time, we were airborne. The flight was uneventful; we returned our prisoner, safe and sound, to the Atlanta City Jail.

Fred and I never discussed the fifty-dollar bill Garland put on the table, or why it wasn't there when I returned from the bathroom. I never took another trip with Fred Russell.

Horton in First Class; I'm in the Back

The second trip to New York City was also to return a prisoner. This time, homicide Detective, M.E. Horton, was assigned to go with me. I made all the arrangements. It was a day trip, up and back the same day. There was no court hearing. Two NYPD detectives from a Brooklyn precinct met us at LaGuardia Airport. We took custody of our prisoner in Brooklyn, and within a few hours, were back at the airport to return to Atlanta.

There were no problems boarding this time. We took the prisoner to the restroom before takeoff and were seated in the rear of the plane. When the plane was in the air and leveled off, one of the flight attendants came to the rear and gave Horton a loud hello and a big hug. I was unaware they had been dating, on and off, and he hadn't known she was working that flight. She told us there were available empty seats in first class, and invited us to move forward, but we knew the airline would not want us to take our prisoner to first class. Horton was excited about the opportunity to sit in first class and chat with his date. I told him I would remain in back with the prisoner while he went forward and made plans for a date later that evening. It was an unexciting flight for me, but not for Horton. There was a patrol car on the tarmac, waiting for our prisoner and us.

A Twin-engine Prop Plane Is Not a Perk

The Pennsylvania State Police picked up one of my murder suspects. They held him at the State Police Barracks in Carlisle, PA, about forty miles from Harrisburg, the state capitol. Homicide Detective H.F. Pharr was assigned to go with me to pick up the prisoner. I got along okay with Pharr, but he was a little rough around the edges. He had no social graces, was sort of a redneck, and not well traveled. I made arrangements with the Pennsylvania State Police to have someone meet us at the Harrisburg airport. This was a trip up and back in the same day.

The two major airlines flying out of Atlanta were Eastern and Delta, and neither had direct service to Harrisburg. I shopped around, and the best I could do was take an Eastern flight to Philadelphia, and from there, a commuter flight to Harrisburg. Pharr's partner at the time, Detective Lee New, said it was a good thing I made the travel arrangements, because if it had been up to Pharr, we would have flown to Savannah, then taken a bus to Harrisburg.

The first leg of the trip was on a big, smooth-flying jet. The second leg, on a two-engine propeller commuter flight, bounced us in our seats—up and down, forward and backward, left and right—for almost an hour, all the way to Harrisburg. Pharr said he was not getting back on that plane or any plane like it. A Pennsylvania state trooper was waiting for us when we landed in the dinky airport in Harrisburg. He was "squared away"—six feet tall, trim, in a neatly pressed uniform, all creases precisely where they should be, brass shining, leather polished, looking like a Marine Corps recruiting poster. Because of our flight, we had green, sickly complexions. Pharr's suit, which didn't fit him well, looked even worse from the rumbling during the flight. The trooper, as a representative of the PA state troopers, looked good. Pharr and I, as representatives of the Atlanta PD, didn't, and that was embarrassing for me. Pharr didn't seem to notice.

When we arrived at the Carlisle barracks, the sergeant I spoke to on the phone was expecting us; he was in charge of the barracks. He took us to an authentic German restaurant for lunch, in the middle of Pennsylvania Dutch country. Pharr didn't know a wiener schnitzel from a bologna sandwich. We both ate and enjoyed.

We returned to the barracks, did the paperwork, and were driven to the airport to return to Atlanta. Our prisoner balked when he saw the plane we were about to board. Pharr balked, too. He and the prisoner wanted to return to Atlanta by bus. I stood firm enough to persuade them to board the plane. It was a white-knuckle flight for the three of us; we were relieved when the plane rolled onto terra firma toward the gate. The second leg to Atlanta was uneventful.

After we dropped our prisoner off at the city jail, Pharr was officially relieved of his assignment. He said that was the last trip he would ever take with me. And that was ok with me.

Detective Larry Peaden

I had been on the homicide squad only six months, yet I'd had five partners during that short time, my break-in period. My first regular partner was Detective Larry Peaden. He had been in the squad for about a year. I saw him around, but didn't know anything about him. Not long after starting to work with him, I discovered that he was unlike other detectives.

His best asset was his photographic memory. He never forgot a face, or the name that belonged to it. When he worked a crime scene, he was haphazard, running helter-skelter in different directions. All his actions appeared disconnected.

When we arrived at the scene of a homicide or rape, he went through it like a chain saw. He was like the "Road Runner," zipping here and there, changing directions. He never seemed to take notes, was satisfied that he'd gotten everything we needed, and was ready to go not long after arriving on the scene.

That wasn't how I worked a scene. I plodded, slowly, methodically, writing, sketching, taking inventory, not wanting to miss anything— any possibly significant detail, no matter how small.

Back at the office, when we put together our notes to make a joint report, I would see that he hadn't missed a thing. Many times, I was awed to find that despite his race through a scene, he had picked up a detail or two that I had missed in my slow, systematic search.

Peaden was a pleasant, friendly guy; he had a terrific personality and a sense of humor. That was one side of him. The other side was dark and mean. I got to see both. Larry Peaden had the worst, most vicious, violent temper I've ever seen. When we apprehended someone, whom we knew, from descriptions and evidence, had committed a heinous crime, such as a rape, during which the victim was subjected to degradation and injury beyond the rape itself, Peaden, with his powerful hands, would grab the suspect by the throat and choke him into unconsciousness.

Peaden had no more love for blacks than most of the white Atlanta policemen, but what made him worse was his temper. His uncontrollable rages kept us on the edge of disaster, as the civil rights of criminals became more and more of an issue.

"They planted the gun on him."

One rainy afternoon, my cousin, Mel Goldberg, was down from New York, visiting as a guest. I thought it would interest my cousin to see me in my role as a homicide detective, so I invited him to spend the day with Peaden and me. We were called to the scene of a police shooting. From the chatter on our radio, we understood that a suspect had been shot and killed by a pair of auto theft detectives—in the back seat of their car. The uniformed sergeant who requested our response urged us to hurry.

The freeway and surface streets were wet from the rain. We raced from the east side to the west side of Atlanta, a long distance on slick pavement without emergency lights or siren (detective cars back then were not outfitted with emergency equipment, just a horn like in any ordinary automobile), Detective Larry Peaden pounding on the steering wheel of our swerving, skidding car. We slid through traffic intersections and around corners, without regard to stop signs or red lights. We jumped curbs and took short cuts through parking lots. In our wake were shocked, angry, confused motorists; my cousin Mel got the ride of his life.

We arrived at the scene where the incident occurred—a situation similar to the one that had sparked the riots in Summerhill a year before. There was a crowd of Negroes, and many cops. The auto theft Detectives, DT Johnson and WH Everett, related the circumstances of the shooting. A uniformed policeman had apprehended a Negro male wanted for car theft. The policeman called for an auto theft car to meet him at his location so he could turn over his prisoner. Johnson and Everett arrived, searched the prisoner, and then, without handcuffing him, placed him in the back seat of their detective car.

They drove through the area, looking for the car he admitted stealing. He told the detectives he would show them where he had left the car. "I left it around here somewhere, but I can't remember exactly. Just go up and down these streets; I'll spot it." After cruising unsuccessfully for a time, their prisoner complained he was getting cold and asked if he could put on the jacket he had been carrying when the policeman picked him up. It was a heavy winter jacket.

The jacket was draped across the back of the front seat between the two detectives, the collar end towards the prisoner in the rear, the pockets towards the front. Johnson was driving. Everett turned and grabbed the jacket, feeling the pockets for contents as he handed it to the prisoner. The jacket was not fully out of Everett's grasp when the prisoner reached into one of the pockets and pulled out a pistol. Everett reached over the front seat to grab the pistol from the prisoner's hand. The prisoner brought up his foot, reared back, and kicked Everett in the chest, knocking him onto the front floorboard. The prisoner reached over the front seat, his pistol aimed at Everett. Johnson drew his revolver, driving erratically, turned, and fired two shots at the prisoner, who slumped over in the back seat, dead.

The crowd, seeing him in the back seat, dead, blood oozing from the gunshot wounds, was growing ugly. Ordinarily, the scene of a crime is blocked off. Photographs are taken, evidence is gathered, and witnesses are identified for later statements. The medical examiner and undertaker also do their work at the scene. But the crowd was too reminiscent of the situation at Summerhill for normal procedure. The field supervisors, responsible for the uniformed patrolmen, with input from Peaden and me, decided to get the hell out of there, before things got like they were at Summerhill. We would process the shooting elsewhere. We instructed Johnson and Everett to drive their dead passenger to the police station.

In the detectives' parking lot at the station, we saw that the dead prisoner had fallen over during the ride and was now in a clump on the rear floorboard. To photograph him, as required for a homicide, Peaden and I propped him back up in the seat, assured by Johnson and Everett that that was his position after he was shot. ID photographed him, Peaden and I completed our paperwork, and we were done for the day.

The next day, the victim's mother came to the homicide office and insisted that her son had not had a gun. She accused Detectives Everett and Johnson of planting the gun on her son after shooting him. Unconvinced, I traced the dead auto thief's weapon to a gun shop in downtown Atlanta. It was purchased about a year before he tried to shoot Everett. The purchaser? The dead auto thief's mother.

The medical examiner complained that he should have been called to the scene, as required by law. The body should not have been moved until he arrived and approved the move. Because of his complaint, an informal investigation was held. We had to justify our decisions and actions. The outcome of the investigation was that our actions were proper and prudent, given the circumstances. Maybe we should have called the medical examiner, and left him there to deal with the crowd. People don't understand situations like that.

The shooting was declared justified by the DA's office, and then a grand jury, and Peaden and I managed to slip through the cracks and get by with our unorthodox processing of the crime scene.

Mel was with Peaden and me the entire time. He was particularly astonished at the way we moved the dead body to be photographed in the exact position he was in after he was shot and killed. Every year or so, whenever Mel and I visit, he likes to talk about the wild ride that Peaden took us on.

Driving a Taxi: A Bare Living at High Risk of Life

Pieces of a jigsaw puzzle—that's what homicide detectives have to work with following a murder, rape, kidnapping, shooting, or stabbing.

They find as many pieces as they can and fit them together to form a picture. How did it happen? When did it happen? Who was there?

It was about seven a.m. Larry Peaden and I were about to finish our shift on the morning watch. A call came in. The body of a cab driver had been discovered lying on a dirt street. He had been shot in the head. Homicide was needed immediately on the scene. No one from the day watch had come in to the squad room yet, so we responded.

The abandoned taxi was on the same street, two hundred feet from its driver's body. The ignition switch was still in the "on" position; the taxi was in "D"—drive gear. The moneybox was on the front seat, with nothing in it. The driver's pants pockets were turned out. Robbery was clearly the motive. The cab was last heard from several hours earlier at the Greyhound bus station in downtown.

We started processing the crime scene, a laborious, unglamorous task. The ID section was there with their crime scene techs; the medical examiner arrived, followed by several other detectives, to assist us with the canvassing. A few uniforms were detailed to help preserve the integrity of the crime scene. Everything was photographed, sketched, measured, and inventoried. The interior of the taxi was dusted for prints, the neighborhood canvassed for witnesses who might have seen or heard anything.

It was late that afternoon when we completed the paperwork. I went home, slouching from fatigue, had a quick dinner, and flopped into bed hoping to get some deep, restful sleep. We were due back for our normal midnight to eight a.m. morning watch shift.

In the weeks that followed, we tracked down leads from the crime scene. As there were not many, we contacted our usual informants. From either source, there was nothing. We soon hit a dead end; everything went cold. In the meantime, other crimes were being committed, and we were assigned our share of those crimes. In the movies, on television shows, the homicide detective lives with one case, just one—that's all he does until he gets the bad guy. In real life, a homicide detective works simultaneously on a dozen or more cases; back then, we might work on any number of violent crimes—murder, rape, aggravated assault. Today, there is a squad for homicide, a squad for sex crimes, and a squad for aggravated assault. Three separate squads considerably lessen the burden on the detectives.

Our break in the cab driver murder came a month later. Two policemen in Griffin, a small town forty miles south of Atlanta, caught a prowler siphoning gas from a parked car in the middle of the night. During the arrest, they discovered that the car he had been driving was reported stolen during an armed robbery in Atlanta. The Griffin police officer found a .25 caliber automatic pistol on the suspect. Atlanta robbery detectives went to Griffin to bring the suspect back to Atlanta.

The robbery victim identified the suspect as the robber who had taken his money and car at gunpoint. Because the gun used in the cab driver killing was a .25 caliber automatic, the robber's gun was sent to the state crime lab. Meanwhile, his fingerprints were compared to prints lifted from the murdered driver's taxi. A single print found on the portable, plug-in spotlight lying on the front seat of the taxi matched the robber's print, and the crime lab's ballistics report concluded that the bullet that killed the cab driver was fired from the gun found on the robber caught siphoning gas in Griffin.

We confronted him with the print match and the ballistics results. He confessed and implicated a sixteen-year old juvenile as his accomplice. He stated that he and his partner had needed money, so they decided to rob the cab driver. They hopped in a taxi downtown, during the early morning hours, directing the driver to an address on the lonely dirt street on the fringe of downtown.

When they arrived, he told us he grabbed the driver around the neck, put the gun to his head, and demanded money. He said the driver resisted, and the gun went off. They took the money they found in the cash box on the front seat. They went through the dead driver's pants pockets and found no money; they threw the driver out of the cab, onto the street, and attempted to drive away in the taxi. After driving about two hundred feet, they stalled the taxi, the engine apparently flooded as they tried anxiously to get away. They left the taxi and walked away.

They killed the taxi driver and robbed him of six dollars and his wristwatch. Had they looked in the driver's shirt pocket, they would have found thirteen more dollars.

They were tried and convicted.

"Thirty, or forty, or fifty times..."

After completing an evening's work on the swing shift (four p.m. to midnight) where they were both employed, a Korean woman and her American boyfriend drove in her car to Grant Park, where they parked at a dark, lonely spot. It was just after midnight. They sat in the car, talking.

Four young, Negro men appeared at the car, demanding that the woman open the locked doors. She panicked, pounding her foot on the gas pedal; the car stuttered and stalled. One of the men pointed a pistol at the woman and threatened to shoot her through the window if the doors were not opened. Trapped, threatened with death, the couple unlocked the doors.

They were taken out of the car and separated. Two of the men took her to a nearby pavilion where they stripped her, raped her, and forced her to commit fellatio on them. Her boyfriend was robbed of whatever money and valuables he had and was beaten by the other two men. When the first pair was done with the woman, they switched places with the other two. The woman was raped and sodomized twice more. The boyfriend, although he offered no resistance, continued to be roughed up.

The woman was ordered to get her torn underwear and clothes back on. She and her boyfriend were then forced onto the rear floorboards of her car and ordered not to get up; they would be shot if they tried. The abductors got into the car—two in the front seats, two in the rear, and drove around for a while. Although the couple obeyed instructions, neither making a sound nor moving a muscle, the boyfriend was pistol-whipped several times, and the woman painfully pressed to the floorboard by the feet of two in the seat above her.

The driver pulled the car alongside the curb and the abductors took their victims into an abandoned house on Pullium Street, not far from Atlanta Stadium. There were no lights in the house; besides trash and garbage, the only other thing in the house was a torn, filthy mattress on the floor. The woman was stripped of whatever was left of her clothes and again raped by each of the abductors.

Her boyfriend was forced to take off his pants and lie face down on the floor next to the mattress. He was kicked, punched, and slapped repeatedly. They were going to "teach this white mother-fucker a lesson." They made him stretch his arms, hands, and fingers out over his head, flat on the floor. His tormentors, with a large machete, took turns chopping at the floor to see who could come closest to his fingers. The machete blows were struck with such force that chunks of wood were chopped out of the floor. If he flinched, they threatened, "We'll shove something up your ass."

The couple's ordeal continued and worsened over the next four hours. New faces, more people, were standing over them. The word had spread to the thugs in the neighborhood. Anyone who wanted some Chinese pussy could get it in the abandoned house on Pullium Street. And they came, not only for pussy—the newcomers forced themselves into every opening of her body, sometimes more than one at a time.

One rapist screamed at her to be more physically active for him. She either didn't understand, or was too worn out, or just didn't care anymore, to engage herself as he wanted. She was slapped, punched, kicked, choked; two men twisted her arms and legs at the same time. As she endured what was happening to her, she became increasingly exhausted, leaving her with less energy for terror. When she didn't respond, he became enraged, and put a knife blade under one of her toenails. The boyfriend tried to explain that she didn't know enough English to understand what he wanted her to do. The other thugs beat him, and told him not to say anything, unless they asked him a question.

Exhausted and afraid, they slowly realized it was quiet; there was no one around them. They were alone in the room. They gathered up what clothing they could find, hurriedly put it on, went to the door, and looked outside. Nothing. They saw no one. As best they could, they started to run. They hadn't gotten far beyond the front door when the abductors and rapists came at them from where they had been hiding and waiting, behind trees, behind shrubs, and in dark corners in the house. Like a cat with a mouse, the rapists played with their victims. The couple was restrained and dragged back into the house, where they suffered more of the same for another hour.

Again, there was quiet; they were alone. They saw no one as they got up. This time, they didn't think about their clothes. He took her hand, told her to run with him—to run, and keep running—no matter what. They got to the sidewalk, ran up the sidewalk, almost to the corner, when the abductors and rapists showed themselves and started toward them. There was an all-night gas station a block away; the couple, followed by their attackers, headed for it. What part of her body the boyfriend could not hold in his arms to carry, he dragged as he ran, both yelling, screaming as loud as they could. Their screams attracted the attention of a passing car and several people at the gas station. They kept running. The attackers stopped chasing; like rats sensing harm, they scurried back to their sewers.

The bleeding and badly beaten victims were taken inside the gas station and wrapped in blankets. The gas station attendant called for an ambulance and the police. The victims explained to the responding police officer what had happened, although it was not hard for him to figure out. Because of the nature of the crime, he requested a homicide unit to meet him at Grady Hospital, which was where the ambulance would transport the victims.

I received the call at about five a.m. Larry Peaden and I were working the morning watch, but he had taken the night off. I first saw the victims at the hospital emergency entrance as they were taken out of the ambulance on gurneys and wheeled inside. As they were prepared for medical treatment, I spoke with them briefly. From what they could tell me, and from the information I had from the officer who answered the call, I put together an overview of what had happened.

On my way out of the room, I looked back at the battered little Oriental woman, and asked quietly from the door, "How many men raped you?" She replied that she didn't know how many men, but she said that she had been raped, "thirty, forty, fifty times." She wasn't sure.

"Hey partner," I apologized into the telephone to a sleepy Detective Larry Peaden. "I hate to wake you so early, but I've got a hell of a mess on my hands. I need your help." I gave him a brief rundown; he said he would meet me as soon as he could get dressed and drive in.

Forty minutes later, we were in the abandoned house on Pullium Street, where we recovered the victim's clothes beside the roach-infested mattress. On the floor next to the mattress were fresh chunks of wood and gashes in the floor, as though hacked out—probably by the machete. The woman's car was located about a mile away by another team of detectives. The car and the house were processed for evidence; many fingerprints were lifted in both places, many fingerprints besides those of the victims.

There was so much to be done. Although the clock read eight a.m., the end of our watch, we had to continue working. The house was photographed, measured, and sketched. What little evidence there was—used syringes, used condoms, chips from the wood floor, bits of torn clothing—was collected and inventoried. There were many fingerprints lifted, probably useless as evidence, but we took them, nevertheless. We also took the filthy, nasty mattress. Peaden and I, along several other detectives, canvassed the immediate area of the vacant house for possible witnesses. No one saw or heard anything. We went to the Grant Park crime scene, and processed it. Not much evidence there.

After the victims had been examined, treated, and released from the hospital, Peaden and I brought them to the homicide office for their written statements. It was a slow process. They were physically injured and emotionally traumatized. Taking the statement from the Korean woman was difficult. She didn't speak English very well, we didn't speak Korean, and there were details we needed to get down as clearly and precisely as possible. Fortunately, she was as persistent as we were in recording it all as it happened. We learned her handbag, her wallet and money, her driver's license and other ID, her wristwatch, and other jewelry were taken from her, and it was very well described in the statement. From him they took his wallet, his money, his driver's license and other ID, his watch, and his ring. We completed our incident report—a form in which the information is conveyed in a standard format—checked off the boxes and filled in the blanks, with only information that describes what happened. (This report is for the public, and is available to the media and anyone else.) Then we worked on supplemental reports, narratives written by the investigating detectives that describe everything and anything that might help solve the crime and prosecute the criminals. It is a long, tedious document, not available to anyone outside the police department and district attorney's office, as it represents an ongoing investigation. Completing those forms was the hard part; not nearly as hard for us was tagging and inventorying the evidence and briefing the lieutenant. We did all we could do for that day.

I hadn't eaten anything, not a crumb of nourishment, or a morsel of junk food, since four a.m. It was now five p.m. I got home an hour later, ate supper, and fell into bed, exhausted. What sleep I was going to get had to be restful sleep because I was not going to be in bed for long. I was due back in at midnight, only six hours later. That's when the hard work would begin—the heavy lifting—identifying and arresting those who had viciously, brutally, raped the woman "thirty or forty or fifty times."

We started our search in what we figured was the most likely place—the vicinity of the house on Pullium Street. The rapists seemed to know exactly where they wanted to take their victims and where they could easily get others to join in, probably enhancing their popularity. Because they were familiar with the area, we thought it likely that there were those familiar with them, their habits, their activities—those not involved in the rape, who might be willing or made to be willing to help us in our investigation.

We concentrated on the neighborhoods of Summerhill, Peoplestown, and Mechanicsville, applying pressure to get the identities we needed. We asked the watch commander to have beat cars (a patrol car assigned to a specific sector) park outside beer joints and dives (beer joints so unsavory they are patronized only by neighborhood hangers-on), and take off after anyone driving away from one of them, stopping them to see if they had been drinking and were fit to drive. Peaden and I visited these joints every few days, letting it be known that until we had possible identities the DUI enforcement would continue.

We asked the vice-lieutenant to shut down "liquor houses" (places with no license to sell beer, whiskey, or moonshine) in those neighborhoods. Peaden and I visited with the owners of these houses, making clear to them that once we had names, their operation could return to normal, which meant the police would go back to ignoring them. Vice detectives swept the streets of prostitutes, causing a downturn in the financial well-being of their pimps.

In addition to those specific targets, beat cars randomly and regularly cleared street corners of "homeboys"—neighborhood groups hanging out on corners.

Vice detectives, burglary detectives, fugitive detectives, narcotics detectives, robbery detectives, larceny detectives, auto theft detectives, and other homicide detectives, all helped, calling in markers from informants (favors allowed for insignificant infractions in return for later information helpful to investigations), asking for names for Peaden and me to follow up on. Life in the underbelly of the 'hood was disrupted and very uncomfortable.

An informant who wanted "things to go back to normal," expressed that one night to Patrol Officer JW Caldwell, who worked a beat car in Peoplestown. He told Caldwell he had a name; Caldwell came, unannounced, to Peaden and me, with that name.

Every policeman, as well as civilians—ID techs, radio dispatchers, telephone operators, and clerks—were working this case. It was a joint effort. Peaden and I never forgot that a patrolman walked in with our first lead.

We needed an arrest warrant for the suspect and a search warrant for his premises. To get that, Officer Caldwell provided an affidavit testifying to the reliability of his informant in past investigations and to the suspect's arrest record for similar violent crimes. He lived in close proximity to the scene of the crime, and his profile matched the description of the age and race as provided by both victims of the abduction, aggravated assault, and rape.

The judge issued both warrants. We executed them before dawn, rudely awaking our first suspect from a sound sleep. Searching his bedroom, we found the Korean woman's wallet, her driver's license, and several items bearing her ID—a slam-dunk on our first suspect. We arrested him and returned to the station, where he was fingerprinted and photographed.

Next, Peaden and I took him into an interrogation room. We wanted the names of the others. The US Supreme Court was on our side at that time. The landmark Miranda and Escabedo cases had not yet been decided. It was not necessary for police to advise a suspect of his rights before questioning him.

We confronted him with her wallet—he said a friend found it on the street and gave it to him. We insisted he tell us who else was involved in the rape—he denied knowing what we were talking about. We were still questioning him, trying to get him to say something we could use, when we received a call from the ID section confirming that his prints matched some of the prints lifted from the inside of the Korean woman's car.

I took the call and told Detective Larry Peaden what I had learned from the ID techs. Before I had put the phone down on the receiver, Peaden had his powerful hands around the suspect's throat, squeezing, choking him nearly unconscious. Thinking him unconscious, I delivered several blows with a telephone book to his head, meant to revive him. (Blows from a telephone book hurt, but leave no marks.) We asked again for him to admit his part in the rape and give us the names of the others. Again, he denied it. Again, Peaden's hands wrapped themselves around his throat. Again, the telephone book connected with his head. After the second round, his memory started working. He remembered the names of the other three of the first four rapists. He gave us a written statement, detailing what occurred that night—starting in Grant Park and continuing in the abandoned house on Pullium Street—and his involvement in what happened.

Was it right, what Peaden and I did to get his admission of guilt and the names of the others? If we hadn't done what we did, we would not have gotten him, or the others. But we got him, and we got them.

With the names of the other three, we got arrest and search warrants, located and arrested them, searched their premises, and found other items—the boyfriend's wallet and ID, his watch, his very distinctive ring, and the rest of the raped woman's jewelry—which the suspects had distributed among themselves.

We took each, separately, back to the station, where Peaden and I continued our "choke 'n' phonebook" question and answer sessions until we had the answers we knew to be the truth, based on the evidence we had recovered, their fingerprints from the woman's car, and statements incriminating each other.

Now we wanted the names of the others who had raped the woman and assaulted her and her boyfriend. The four suspects we had arrested provided some of those names; other sources provided additional names. Once word got out to the boys in the 'hood that we had four suspects of the abduction and rape in custody, confidential, anonymous phone calls were received by Peaden, me, and other detectives, from persons asking to meet us at a desolate location in the middle of the night. Now that the first four suspects were in custody and providing names, informants felt this was a good time to pay off their "markers," delivering to their detectives the names of other suspects. Other names came during meetings with, or phone calls from, petty thieves, local hoods, owners of the beer joints and liquor houses, pimps, and prostitutes, all wanting things to return to normal. They all wanted to give us names, names they probably knew before and were reluctant to reveal, but now were willing to provide so as to appear helpful in the eyes of the police.

As we learned names, we checked each and found that most had criminal records. The fingerprints each matched fingerprints found in the house, but that meant nothing; they could have left their fingerprints there when shooting up, fucking some woman, or just hanging out of the rain. What was helpful was that the ones with criminal records had mug shots on file, which could be used to identify suspects in a photo lineup. These IDs enabled us to positively identify many of them in a physical lineup.

With respect to the original four suspects, we had positive fingerprint matches and recovered from them stolen items matching descriptions given by the victims. Each suspect implicated the others and none of the four could come up with alibis for the date and time of the abduction. Police pressure was so great in the neighborhood, their friends feared implicating themselves by fabricating an alibi, and their girlfriends would not alibi boyfriends who had fucked another woman.

There was a separate photo lineup, where each victim independently positively identified each suspect, then were positively identified in separate physical lineups as well.

We received names for approximately twenty suspects, but the victims could positively identify only five, in addition to the original four. Our guts, our instincts, our experience as detectives, our common sense, dictated they were guilty, or had participated in the rapes in some way, but there was not enough for the DA to indict them. We had to let them walk, thinking they could again get away with the same kind of crime. They escaped punishment, didn't they?

But we did have nine of the bastards. The district attorney backed off one because he was sixteen, the evidence against him was weak, and because someone was needed to testify against the eight others. The DA let the juvenile make a deal—his testimony against the other eight, in return for trial in juvenile court for punitive action. He slipped through the cracks of the judicial system. Yeah, we know about the law and the judicial system. But he was allowed to slip through the cracks.

Each of the eight wanted, and got, separate trials. The trials went on and on. The original four were convicted and sentenced to death. (At that time, kidnapping, rape, and armed robbery were capital crimes.) Two were given life sentences. Two decided they did not want to risk a trial; they each pleaded guilty in return for twenty years in prison. The death sentences of the four were later commuted to life in prison.

The victims were terrific witnesses, the woman, especially. That small Korean woman, frightened, bewildered, bewildered by our complex judicial process, told her story in broken English. Everyone tried to shoot holes in it. She first told the horror story to me, then to a very skeptical Detective Larry Peaden. Each time we arrested one of the animals who raped her, she had to tell it again in municipal court, where she was subjected to more skepticism. Next, she had to face a grand jury of twenty-five people and convince them of the truth of what happened to her and her boyfriend.

In meetings and interviews with Peaden and me in our cramped squad room, she heard snide remarks made by some homicide detectives—detectives whose attitudes about women and rape belonged to another culture in another place and time.

She was really roughed up during her testimony in each of the trials. On the witness stand, she was subjected to hours of cross-examination and grilling by a battery of defense attorneys. At each of the six trials (two defendants took pleas instead of going to trial), defense attorneys tried to get the jury to see her either as a brainless, provocative woman, who should have known better than to be in the park in the middle of the night, or as a whore who got what she deserved. She could withstand the bullying by the defense attorneys for one reason. She knew what she knew. She never wavered from the details of what had happened to her.

Why does the victim of a violent crime not only suffer the crime, but also what happens afterward in the criminal justice system?

Why?

Why Didn't He Shoot?

People in police custody who require medical attention are brought to the police detention area in Grady Memorial Hospital and held there. The detention area is not a desirable assignment. It gets hectic, at times resembling an Army MASH unit in a combat zone. Prisoners complain of ailments—actual or imagined—knowing they will be taken to the hospital, where they seize any opportunity to escape. A surprising number of prisoners succeed in escaping while being transported or while in the hospital's detention area.

Officer Ray Braswell, working the evening watch as a roustabout, was assigned to Grady Detention one busy weekend night. Braswell and the other officers working the detention area were busy taking prisoners back and forth to the emergency clinic, a distance down the long corridor of about fifty yards.

One prisoner, a young Negro in his twenties, had been in jail for several days, awaiting trial on a burglary charge. He had been to the hospital several times. Each time, doctors failed to find anything medically or physically wrong with him. Braswell and the other cops were not stupid; they recognize the prisoner's ploy. He was brought into the detention area, where he had to wait to see a doctor. Gunshots, stab wounds, broken bones, heart attacks, and such get priority. It looked like a long wait. He lay face down on a rolling stretcher with handcuffs on each wrist attached to the stretcher. He was locked inside a holding room with several other prisoners.

Braswell entered the room to get the prisoner who was next in line for the emergency clinic. He checked the handcuffs on the young Negro burglar, and then turned his back to get the prisoner about to be treated. In those few seconds, the burglar broke both pairs of handcuffs, reached out, and took Braswell's gun out of his holster. Another officer working the detention area stepped out of one of the holding rooms; Braswell hollered that the prisoner had his gun. The cop was older, nearing retirement, and was unable to react quickly to Braswell's warning. Taking the older cop's gun, the prisoner now had two.

Officer JA Sizemore, who was working a patrol car and had picked up an injured drunk, entered the detention area. Braswell shouted to Sizemore, warning him about the armed prisoner. Sizemore pushed the drunk into the gunman and ran down the corridor towards the ambulance exit. He explained later that there were people in the corridor; it was not a good place, not a good time, for a gun battle. A better place would be on the ambulance ramp at the end of the corridor, the quickest way out of the hospital. He cleared everyone out of the way and waited for the gunman to exit.

The armed prisoner slowly backed out of the detention area, a gun in each hand—one pointed at Braswell, the other at the older cop. Braswell was anticipating the moment the prisoner would run. When he did, Braswell jumped him from behind, pinning his arms to his sides. But the prisoner was strong and agile; he brook loose from Braswell's grasp, whirled around, and aimed both guns at Braswell's stomach. But he did not fire either gun.

Braswell's lucky day!

Instead, the armed prisoner backed away from Braswell, ran down the corridor, fired several random shots into the ambulance driver's lounge—without hitting anyone—and continued through the exit to the ambulance ramp, where Sizemore and his gun were waiting for him.

Sizemore fired a couple of rounds, but missed. The prisoner returned fire, and didn't. Sizemore went down, shot in the side. Officer TD McMillan was coming up the ramp, unaware of what was going on, but fully aware in an instant, when he saw the exchange of gunfire. McMillan fired once and hit the armed prisoner in the heart, killing him instantly.

Sizemore was carried into the emergency room wearing a chest tube, a device inserted whenever the chest cavity is punctured, to prevent the lungs from filling with blood, resulting in death. The doctors declared that the only reason he was alive was that he was in the hospital when he was shot. If he had been shot anywhere else in the city, he would have been DOA when his ambulance pulled up to the hospital.

When the body of the prisoner was examined, both handcuffs were found still attached securely to each wrist, a broken length of chain dangling from each. The other halves of both pairs of handcuffs were still locked and attached to the stretcher.

I saw Ray Braswell later that night in the homicide office. He was preparing his written statement about the incident. He felt really bad, and looked it. He blamed himself that Sizemore was shot. He said it was the worst night of his life. When I saw Ray Braswell cry, I wondered what would have become of him had Sizemore not survived the shooting.

Two questions linger, unanswered, since that incident in 1968:

How the hell did the prisoner break not one, but both pairs of handcuffs?

And why didn't he shoot Braswell?

The Fingerprint in Blood on the Plastic ID Card

Wade Hagin received his gold detective badge at about the same time I received mine. He was assigned to burglary, where he worked for about two years. He was then transferred into the homicide squad; we became partners. We lived across the street from each other; we were best friends, as close as brothers.

Only one pair of homicide detectives worked the morning watch. Wade and I volunteered for it. The twenty other homicide detectives let us have it, gladly. We were responsible for following up sex crimes and crimes that drew blood between midnight and eight a.m. in the city of Atlanta. We enjoyed our work, we were good at what we did, and we had the track record to prove it. People throughout the Atlanta department and even the public began to notice "Hagin and Goldhagen."

Wade and I had just spent several hours at Grady Hospital, sorting out some of the carnage that had occurred in the city on that hot, summer Saturday night/ Sunday morning. We received a signal 50/48 (person shot/person dead) call at about five a.m. to meet uniformed officers at Heygood Street and Linam Avenue, in the high-crime black area in the shadow of Atlanta Stadium.

On the floor of a ransacked apartment in the rundown frame house was the body of a young Negro woman. She was dressed in a short nightgown that was open down the front; she was nude from the waist down. We observed what appeared to be a gunshot wound to her forehead.

On the floor under and around her body, was a large amount of blood, what seemed to us to be an unusually large amount. On the bed was a broom; the handle was smeared with blood, from the tip of the handle to about eighteen inches below the tip. On the floor next to the body were matches that had been ignited and spent. The matches prompted us to examine the body closer, and we noticed that some of her pubic hair had been singed.

We called for the Atlanta police ID section and the medical examiner to meet us at the scene—standard procedure. We also requested the Georgia State crime lab to respond, which was not standard procedure, because of the bizarre nature of what we found.

The bed was in one corner of the room, against a wall. Above the head of the bed was a window, opened from the top. In the corner, behind the bed, we discovered a plastic Grady Hospital card (similar to a credit card) belonging to the dead woman. It was lodged in a crack, hidden from view, between the wall and the floor molding. The smooth plastic surface of the card was smeared with blood; within the field of blood, we saw a perfectly clear fingerprint.

After surveying the scene of the horrible crime, we questioned the neighbor who reported it. The neighbor told us that he was awakened earlier in the night by his wife's screaming that someone was in their bedroom, touching her. He said he grabbed his shotgun, fired, and saw a figure jump through an open window in his living room. He didn't think he had hit the intruder because he was gone so fast.

He called the police, they arrived, found no suspect in the area, got what information they needed for their report, and left. The neighbor said he and his wife could not get back to sleep, not only because of the anxiety of what had just happened, but also because of the incessant crying of a baby nearby. They followed the crying to the wide-open front door of the neighbor's house. They continued into the house, following the baby's cries. On the bed, amidst all the blood, was the baby; on the floor beside the bed was the body of the dead woman. They took the baby back to their house and called the police again. Their first call had been articulated with anger and fear about the intruder. This call was with horror.

The autopsy confirmed that the gunshot wound to the head was the cause of death. The excessive amounts of blood were a result of hemorrhaging caused by the broom handle having been forced far into the victim's vagina and rectum. The medical examiner recovered a bullet from the head of the victim. We now had a bullet that could be used in a ballistics comparison and a bloody fingerprint.

As the day watch came on duty, we requested another team of homicide detectives to assist us. Several hours later, all of the preliminary investigation was completed. We were discussing the case, Wade and I comparing notes, for the benefit of the newly assigned detectives to work with us. One, Louis Graham, offered what might have been a remote coincidence, "It looks like something Joel Tiller would do!" But for Wade and me, that comment reenergized us. Graham had our attention; he went on to explain that he had worked a case several months back. Someone entered a house, burglarized it, and then began fondling the woman asleep in her bedroom. She woke, screamed, and then the intruder jumped out of the same window he had entered. Neighbors chased him, caught him, and restrained him until police arrived. Graham responded to the request for a detective, arrested the intruder, Joel Tiller, and placed him in the city jail.

Later that night, the correction officers at the city jail learned that Joel Tiller had not yet reached his seventeenth birthday. He was a juvenile. According to Georgia state law, a juvenile cannot be housed in a city jail; therefore, he was transferred to the Fulton County Juvenile Facility. Here's a strange coincidence: Wade and I transported him to the juvenile facility back then, as a favor for Graham, who was going off duty at midnight. We remembered it well, because that was the night Martin Luther King, Jr. was assassinated in Memphis.

If Tiller was at the jail long enough, he might have been fingerprinted as an adult offender before it was learned that he was a juvenile. Georgia law prohibited the fingerprinting or photographing of juvenile offenders, except when authorized by a juvenile court judge. It seemed like a long shot, but we tried it. It paid dividends. We found Tiller's fingerprints in the record file—each of Tiller's ten fingers. All we needed was one—the one that matched the fingerprint in blood on the hospital card found in the victim's bedroom. The ID technician compared the file prints with the print on the hospital card.

Positive!

We had "Joel Tiller," written in the victim's blood!

We drew up two warrants—an arrest warrant for Tiller and a search warrant for the gun. It was Sunday morning, but we found a judge to sign the warrants.

We went to where Tiller lived with his mother. Both were home. We explained why we were there and proceeded to search the house. They had a couple of small dogs running around, and there was dog shit all over the place, which made it smell like a kennel that had never been cleaned. Wade and I, with Graham and his partner, and the police officers who accompanied us, were close to getting sick to our stomachs from the stench. Fortunately, the search didn't last long. We started in Joel's bedroom. I found the gun in the third drawer of his dresser, under some clothes.

Wade and I drove Joel and his mother downtown to the homicide office for an interview. Graham and his partner took the gun to the state crime lab for the ballistics test—it was positive. The bullet that killed the victim, and was removed from her head, was fired from the gun we recovered from Joel's dresser drawer.

Joel Tiller never denied his guilt. He admitted the crime and freely talked about it. He said he had been out late, walking around, when he heard "a voice" tell him to burglarize a place. He said he looked through the window of a small house where there was a light. He saw a woman and a baby asleep in a bed under the window. The window was open from the top. He climbed through the window, down onto the bed. He got off the bed without waking either of them. He rummaged around, trying to find something to steal. He couldn't find anything he wanted and decided to leave. He had a gun in his belt in the front of his pants. As he stepped from the bed to the window, the woman woke and grabbed his foot. He pulled his gun, turned around, and shot her. He jumped out of the window, ran across the street to an old burned-out building, and hid there in case the police came.

After awhile, satisfied that no one was going to come, he went back to the house, and climbed in the window a second time. When we asked why he went back, he replied, "I wanted to see where I shot her." She was lying on the floor with her legs half on the bed. The baby was still asleep. He tried to get her to talk to him, but she didn't respond. He started to prod her with the broom handle, and when she didn't respond, he got mad. He said he didn't remember forcing the broom handle into her body. He also said he didn't remember singeing her pubic hair. He found her purse on the bed, which he had missed the first time. He dumped out the contents, not finding anything he wanted, and then left the apartment—this time through the front door.

He said he walked around the corner and spotted a house with an open window. He climbed through the window and looked in the bedroom, where he saw a man and a woman sleeping. As he touched the woman, running his hand over her back, down to her ass, she woke terrified, screaming at him. He ran and jumped back through the open window. He was about to leap off the porch when someone shot at him from inside the house. He ran a few blocks until he was sure no one was chasing him, then walked the rest of the way home and went to bed. When asked about the gun, he replied that he had stolen it from a car some time ago.

Joel Tiller was tried as an adult in superior court, where he was convicted and sentenced to life in prison. I've never been satisfied in my mind whether Joel Tiller had severe mental problems and was not responsible for his actions, or whether he was a cold-blooded killer, leading anyone who would listen to believe his bullshit about hearing voices, and not remembering certain things. It didn't matter what I thought, one way, or the other. What mattered is that anyone was a potential victim of Joel Tiller, as long as he was free to stalk the dark, lonely streets.

Hymns in the Trauma Room

From the frequent "smoking gun" domestic homicide, to the puzzling, time-consuming, stranger-to-stranger, "who-done-it" killing, from brutal rapes to senseless violence, from the tragic, to the bizarre, to the comical, there was never a dull moment during the morning watch. Hagin and Goldhagen were always there, ready for it during the late 1960s, through the early 1970s. Homicide detectives spend a large part of their shift at the Grady Hospital emergency room. We developed a good working relationship with most of the doctors and nurses; we got to know them, individually and professionally, and they got to know us. Most of the doctors were young interns, and there were always new faces, due to frequent turnover among the doctors. The nurses do not turnover (not in the emergency room) at all, or not nearly as frequently. Because they are more permanent, nurses can be a source of information, a valuable asset to a homicide detective. Most of the doctors and nurses are helpful in this regard; they try to cooperate with our investigations, but every now and then, a doctor or nurse can be a pompous asshole. Most detectives learn how to get around assholes—the medical variety or any other kind. There are times when detectives and emergency room staff help each other, maybe only in small ways. On several occasions, we've held down the victim of a gunshot or stab wound so the doctors could insert a chest tube.

One night, we received a "person shot" call to Grady emergency. When we arrived, the cop who initially responded told us it looked like one of the many street corner shootings of the Negro ghetto area, where all the neighborhood thugs hang out. After the shooting, everybody left. When the cops got to the scene, all they found was the guy lying in the middle of the street, bleeding.

We entered the trauma room where the victim was being attended. He'd been shot three times—twice in his chest, once in his stomach. The doctor looked at us and gave us the nod, the signal that he needed us to hold him down so the doctor could insert a chest tube. A chest tube is a life-saving measure that must be done as soon as the chest cavity is punctured. It can be extremely painful. As soon as the patrolman, Wade, and I grabbed him, the doctor sliced him and jammed a chest tube through his rib cage. The shooting victim fought, screamed, and cursed, but the tube saved his life.

After he settled down and we could question him, the first thing we asked was, "Who shot you?" Despite his pain, he coyly replied, "Who me?" We asked our question again, and he replied, "I don't know, man." He was playing with us, and we knew why. He was going to settle the score himself when he was released from the hospital, and he didn't want any help from us. Well, if he didn't give a shit about prosecuting whoever shot him, why should we give a shit? But we do—not for him, for ourselves. If this shit-head died, we would have a homicide on our hands. If he lived, and didn't talk to us, we would be stuck with an unresolved aggravated assault. If he got out of the hospital and got his revenge by killing the shooter without revealing to us his identity—that could result in an unsolved homicide. He knew who shot him, and we were determined to find out his name.

The doctor was in the trauma room with us the entire time; he heard our conversation. We'd had many dealings with that doctor; he liked working with us, and we liked working with him. The doctor and I exchanged glances that communicated we were on the same frequency about what to do next.

I asked the doctor in a theatrical, official voice, if the patient was going to die. Instead of replying directly (he was ethically bound not to lie), he asked if I would join him in singing a hymn. He asked if I knew "Rock of Ages." Being Jewish, I don't know many Christian hymns. But I thought I'd heard that hymn in a movie once, so I figured I could fake it. I informed the patient that he was going to die with a lie on his lips, and that meant he would go straight to Hell. Then I gave him the bad news. I told him the guy who shot him would get away with it, laugh his ass off, and probably piss on his grave.

The doctor began to sing "Rock of Ages." I mumbled, words slowly hanging on notes, anticipating the doctor's next words and notes. Wade, the uniform cop, and the nurses turned solemnly away from us, so as not to show their grins. When their shoulders shuddered, I knew they were laughing. They marched out of the trauma room. Hearing something unusual in the trauma room, ER staff stuck their heads in the door, regarding us with incredulous looks.

Our victim survived his gunshot wounds; none of the three hit a vital organ. He eventually gave the name of the shooter. Wade and I got a warrant, located him, and arrested him for aggravated assault. The victim declined to prosecute. The shooter and victim walked. Wade and I didn't lose any sleep over it. The only thing that concerns us when thugs shoot, stab, and cut each other is that we clear our reports.

In this case, I also got the satisfaction of knowing that I would never have to sing in a church choir!

Overtime Hours—No Overtime Pay

Wade and I worked the midnight to eight a.m. homicide morning watch for a longer period than was required or expected. We liked it. And as long as we weren't complaining about anything associated with the morning watch, the other homicide detectives were delighted for us to keep working it. All the morning watch uniform brass got to know us; they appreciated our quick response when they needed us. The Grady Hospital ER doctors and nurses saw us so often that some of them began to regard us as part of their staff.

The morning watch might seem like a time when not much happened, a time to kick back, cool it, and just pass the hours until the shift ended. It wasn't like that at all. We were almost always busy. Sure, there were pockets of down time, but most of the time we were either busy or very busy. Some nights things got hectic, and there were nights beyond hectic—crazy.

On most summer, weekend nights, we were needed at Grady as soon as we walked into the squad room to report for duty. Once we got to Grady, shootings or stabbings would arrive from different directions, stacking up in the emergency room. There would be so many that by the time we were able to leave the hospital, it was daylight. It didn't matter that our shift was about to end; we had to return to the office to reduce to offense reports and supplements all the notes we had taken at the hospital. Evidence had to be inventoried and tagged, in addition to whatever other details were needed to put together a case file representing each incident covered in the hospital that night. That was drudgery, but it was the easy part. The hard part was the legwork, investigating each case. After all that, we sometimes got to drag ourselves home in the mid to late afternoon.

One night, we were at Grady when we got a call from the police dispatcher requesting homicide detectives at opposite sides of the city. At one end, a shootout between two brothers, resulting in the death of one. At the other, a cab driver was found shot and killed behind the wheel of his taxi. Wade went to Forest Park Road to handle the brothers' homicide. I headed for Bankhead Highway to the scene of the cab driver homicide.

The homicide Wade went to handle was straightforward. The perpetrators were known, and known to each other—fighting over a woman. They challenged each other to a duel, agreed to meet in the middle of the street, a la "high noon." One brother ended up in the morgue, the other at Grady Hospital in ICU. Nevertheless, the crime scene had to be processed, evidence inventoried and tagged, witnesses located and their statements taken, offense report and supplement written, and so on. Wade was going to be tied up for the rest of the night and into mid morning.

When I arrived at the scene of the homicide I was to handle, I observed a taxicab in the parking lot of a gas station. The driver was slumped towards the passenger side of the front seat, a gunshot wound to the back of his head.

The witnesses at the gas station said they saw the taxi turn suddenly into the lot and stop abruptly. Two white males got out of the taxi, said they thought the driver was sick, then walked away, and disappeared.

The taxi dispatcher told me the driver had picked up a fare near the downtown Greyhound bus station. The dispatcher said the driver's last words on the radio were, "Rolling to Hightower." The gas station was located at Bankhead Highway and Hightower Road. This was what homicide detectives refer to, colloquially, as a "whodunit." No known perpetrator; a general description is all a homicide detective has to start with. When the homicide is a "whodunit," the crime scene must be processed intensely, and everything else must be done just as meticulously.

When the day watch reported, several other homicide detectives came to the scene to assist me. When they arrived, I was able to break away, go home, get a real lunch, and rest briefly. Later that day, Detective DL Pike found a gun in the weeds alongside a building, not far from the gas station. The gun was a cheap .22 caliber Rohm RG-10 revolver, commonly known as a "Saturday Night Special."

I dragged myself out of bed and went to the office, where the gun was turned over to me. I brought the gun and the bullet taken from the victim's head to the Georgia State Crime Lab. I traced the gun to a pawnshop in downtown Atlanta. It was purchased on the day of the homicide by a white male who had been released the day before from the Georgia State Prison at Ware County, in South Georgia.

I was so damned tired, I was losing track of time; even the days were running together. When had I slept last? Most of the legwork had to be done during business hours. Detectives on the day watch were helping quite a bit, but it was my case, and there were things I had to do myself.

From the pawnshop's records, I obtained the name of the purchaser—Roy Willbanks—and ran it through the State Pardons and Parole Board for recent releases. That's how I learned of his release from prison and that he lived in Rome, Georgia. After getting a warrant, the Rome police located Willbanks, arrested him, and turned him over to us.

He confessed as soon as we got him downtown to the homicide squad room. Willbanks said he hadn't known his accomplice, the other white male witnesses saw leaving the taxi, prior to the incident. They met in a bar and struck up a conversation. They both had "done time," and decided to buy a gun with the few bucks they had between them and go out and rob someone.

He said their intention was to get a taxi to take them to a place they knew to be dark and secluded, so they could rob the driver. Willbanks was in the back seat, behind the driver, holding the gun to the driver's head, when the driver swerved off the street and bounced into a gas station. He said the gun went off accidentally. Willbanks and his accomplice jumped out of the taxi and walked away. After a block or two, the two split up, and Willbanks threw the gun behind a building. The bullet that killed the cab driver was fired from that gun. His fingerprints were on it, and his fingerprints were lifted from the interior of the taxi.

Several other homicide detectives working on this case learned that on the night of the murder, hours before, the men had picked up two women at a cafeteria and gone back to their room with them at a local flophouse. When the detectives located the women, they admitted that they had been with two guys, but had never seen them before or since.

Eight months later, a telephone call was received at the homicide office from a woman who said that her husband had told her he was in a taxi when the driver was killed. Detectives went to her house; she named her husband, Howard Haney. She said he had beaten her up a few days ago and left. She didn't know where he was.

Haney's mug shot, in a photo lineup with others, was shown to Willbanks, who said he was the guy with him in the cab at the time of the murder. The two women also identified Haney from his photo. We went looking for him. He wasn't hard to find; he couldn't stay away from the downtown beer joints.

Other cases required us to work straight through—thirty-six, sometimes forty-eight hours. Back in the 1960s, there was no overtime, no comp time. When you worked homicide, you were expected to work beyond the end of your shift, and you were not to expect to be paid for working those hours.

"Luck is the Residue of Design."

Some detectives are more successful than others are. Here's my list of what makes a successful detective:

- Aptitude, or the competence to do detective work
- The intelligence to use aptitude fully and efficiently
- Conscientiousness, willingness to continue, go further, and be alert in face of exhaustion, rather than satisfied with doing no more than has to be done
- Informants—trusted, reliable, resourceful informants
- And luck, lots of it

It was about two a.m. when Wade and I received a signal 49 (rape) to Grady Hospital. When we arrived, the victim was being examined and treated. While waiting for her to be released, we learned from the responding officer that the rape occurred in the victim's car, in a parking lot downtown. We told him to impound the car, and then we notified ID section to process it.

The victim, a white female in her mid-thirties, worked as a waitress at a restaurant in the Hyatt Regency Hotel. She had gotten off at closing and walked to her car parked in the lot at (what was then) Ivy and Harris Streets. As she opened the door, she was grabbed from behind, and then felt a knife at her throat. She was told not to scream, to get into the back seat. Her attacker got in with her. He told her to take off her clothes and that he would cut her throat if she resisted. He raped her, then opened the car door, jumped out, and ran. She put her clothes on, went to a pay phone at the corner of the parking lot, and called the police.

She described her attacker as a young Negro teenager and gave us a very good description. Her car had front bucket seats with chrome strips down the sides of the seats. She informed us that there had only been a couple of people inside her car during the last month. We took the victim's fingerprints and the prints of the others she said had been in her car. ID was able to eliminate all the fingerprints but one, found on the chrome strip on the side of one of the bucket seats.

Now all we needed was a suspect. We did all the things that could be done in this type of case. We checked the fingerprint database and the MO files—modus operandi, the method of operation—to see if we could identify any known offenders of this crime. Because he was more than likely a juvenile, neither fingerprints nor mug shots would be on file. We cruised the area around the Hyatt and the parking lot during the same hours as the rape; we leaned on informants; we canvassed for a possible witness. Nothing!

Exactly one month after the rape, we were cruising downtown, going north on Peachtree Street at Harris, during the same hours the rape had occurred, when I glanced down Harris Street and saw someone walking a block away, on Ivy Street. We circled the block once, stopped the car, and observed a young Negro male, simply standing there, aimlessly, on the corner. He was wearing the same clothes the rape victim had described. I got out of the car. Speaking to him, I learned that he was a sixteen-year-old juvenile. We knew he would have no prints on file. We needed fingerprints! I had an envelope with some mug shots in my jacket pocket. I took out one mug shot and talked to him to divert his attention while I wiped it clean on the tail of my jacket behind my back. I held picture by the edges and handed it to the teenager, asking if he recognized the guy in the picture. He looked at it and said he didn't know him. I asked him to turn it over to look at the name on the back. He turned it over several times, satisfying me that he had left all his prints on it. I retrieved it from him, holding it again by the edges, and carefully put it back in the envelope.

He had a knife in his pocket that looked like the one she described. It exceeded the legal length, a violation of the Atlanta city knife ordinance. We also had him on a curfew violation. Either violation was enough to take him to the homicide office. Which we did.

I immediately dropped off the mug shot to ID, asking that the prints be checked against the print lifted from the car in our rape case. I gave the ID tech the case number, told him we would be in the homicide office, and asked him to call as soon as he had the results. Within fifteen minutes, the phone rang. It was the ID tech. One of the prints from the mug shot matched the print lifted from the victim's car. We knew we had him, but we had to make it legal. Getting the rapist's fingerprints the way I did was good enough for us, but it would not be good enough for the courts.

Georgia state law provides that a juvenile cannot be fingerprinted or photographed without the authorization of a juvenile court judge. Wade called Juvenile Court judge, Richard Langford, at home. It was three a.m. Wade woke the judge. He told the judge whom we had, why we had him, and how we got him, but did not tell him about the fingerprints on the mug shot. Juvenile court judges are very strict. If the judge had felt we had done something we should not have done, he would have gotten pissed off, and it could have cost us the case. Wade gave the judge justification for having the juvenile printed and photographed. Wade explained that the juvenile was at same location, at the same time, wearing the same clothes, and had in his possession the same type of knife used in the crime, answered the physical description, and had no justifiable reason for being there at that time of night. Wade told the judge we picked up the juvenile on both a curfew violation and a knife violation. He told the judge we had a print lifted from the crime scene and needed to print the juvenile to see if there was a match. Wade told the judge that we also needed to show the victim a photo lineup that included the juvenile.

Judge Langford gave his permission to print and photograph the juvenile. We charged him, and after all the paper work was complete, we dropped him off at the Fulton County Juvenile Detention Center. We treated ourselves to breakfast, not a particularly special breakfast, but the most satisfying breakfast we'd had in a long time. The next night, we went by the Hyatt Hotel restaurant, where the victim picked the suspect out of a photo lineup.

Luck! Was it really luck? Was it good luck that we weren't killing time, sitting in a donut shop or IHOP somewhere, every night at that time? Was it luck, or was it that we liked our work and cruised that same area, over and over, night after night, for a month?

When I think something is due to luck, I think of what Branch Rickey, the general manager of the Brooklyn Dodgers once said. "Luck is the residue of design!" I suppose that was his way of saying that sometimes you create your own luck. In 1947, Branch Rickey gave Jackie Robinson the opportunity to be the first black professional baseball player in major league baseball, and he turned out to be a superstar.

Homicide Detectives H. B. Goldhagen (left) and J.W. Hagin (right) at Grady Memorial Hospital Detention area.

Detectives Hagin (left) and Goldhagen in a briefing with morning watch Homicide Lieutenant B. J. Stecher (center).

"Hagin and Goldhagen"

Part Two:

Detective,
Continued

For the homicide detective in a major city, murders, rapes, kidnappings, shootings, and stabbings are what they do every day, all day. It's their business. For most, it's business as usual. For me, that attitude was beginning to turn upside down. Where I was once passionate about investigating and solving these crimes and dispassionate about the perpetrators, I was beginning to feel contempt for the scumbags who committed the crimes and worse—my contempt was beginning to show. Early in my career, all that mattered to me was nailing the perpetrator, white or black. If the perpetrator was black, what mattered was that he was the perpetrator—not that he was black. Over time, what changed for me was that black perpetrators were black. Race was distorting the equation.

The population in Atlanta was shifting rapidly in the late sixties. Whatever the proportion of blacks, it seemed larger than it really was. If blacks made up, say, forty percent of the population, it seemed like twice that. Remember, I was seeing from the perspective of a homicide detective. Crime was continuing to increase, but there was no increase in police resources. Negroes were committing most of the crime, their victims mostly Negroes. In my investigations of violent crimes, I became increasingly aware of the difference between black victims of black criminals and white victims of black criminals. White victims were subjected to racial hatred as well as the crime, but that was okay, according to many psychologists, sociologists, politicians, religious leaders, liberals, and those in the media. They offered excuses for the "angry young black man" and his viciousness towards white victims.

That wasn't okay to me. I saw Negro criminals commit violent crimes against Negro victims and white victims, but it was more than violent crime against white victims—there was deliberate abuse, intentional degradation, determined humiliation. I saw it clearly, especially in cases where a Negro male had raped a white woman.

I began to see things in terms of black and white—no grays—only black and white. Black was wrong, bad; white was right, good. I became obsessed with the distinction, especially when I discerned a black thug. One form of human life I loathed, despised, detested—from long ago—was a bully, anyone who got fun out of beating up on people.

My attitude stemmed from my experience as a young boy. My family was one of only two Jewish families in the predominantly German neighborhood of the Ridgewood section of Brooklyn. My brother, Mike, two years older, and I went to same grammar school. That was during World War II.

Most of our classmates' parents were born in Germany. "Overseas," how Europe was commonly referred to at the time, the war was between the Nazis, who were Germans, and the Americans. From what many of my classmates heard in their homes, the war in Ridgewood was between the Germans and the Jews. That's how it seemed to my brother and me as nine and seven-year-old kids in the early 1940s.

Jew baiting became a popular sport in school; Mike and I were the targets. The German bullies waited for us outside the school; when they saw us appear at the door, they shouted, "Get the Jew boys and cut their eyes out! When Germany wins the war, Hitler will come to America to get rid of all the Jew bastards!" Many afternoons, Mike and I ran a gauntlet of verbal threats and physical blows, fleeing from school to home.

Physically, I was a little guy, but I was very fast. I got away from the German bullies most of the time, but there were times I didn't. I got my lumps. But each time I didn't get away fast enough, at least one of the bullies got a few lumps, too. The bully who got hurt the last time wasn't quite as aggressive the next time. It didn't take long to figure out that the only way to deal with a bully was to stand up to him. Be prepared to hit him as soon as he hit you. Better still—hit him before he hit you. Still better, let him know that you would hit him if he even looked like he was thinking about hitting you!

Thirty-five years later, I was no Jewish kid subject to bullying; I was a white cop witnessing bullying by black criminals in Atlanta. There was also bullying by black activists, politicians, even religious leaders, who were increasingly influential.

101

Most immediate, as a police officer, was the pressure in my socio-economic environment from the Negro police officer. Tired of playing subservient roles to his white counterparts, he started demanding what he had been deprived of, simply because he was black. The Negro policemen in Atlanta wanted to ride a motorcycle; he wanted the opportunity to be a detective, be promoted in rank, maybe someday be chief of the APD. Why not chief? Because he was black. That's why. Not in 1968.

Nevertheless, changes in the racial makeup of the Atlanta Police Department were inevitable despite stiff resistance and open hostility from white policemen. The APD had become a racially divided police department.

Personally, I felt physically threatened on the street, in uniform or out, by black thugs; I felt that my advancement in my career was threatened by Negro policemen. I reacted strongly. The white Jewish kid became a racist. More and more, we heard, "Black is beautiful!" I didn't see it—not through the thickness of "black power."

Too Old for Denver, Not Too Old for Englewood

Late in 1968, I considered a change in career. The Atlanta Police Department was getting blacker and blacker; whites were proportionally fewer and fewer. I was resentful and bitter. I knew I wanted out, but out to where, to do what? Sell shoes in a department store? Sit at a desk all day in an office? Tighten bolts on an assembly line?

No! I was a cop, and I was determined to remain a cop.

Wade had just returned from a vacation in Denver, Colorado. Most of the people he saw on the streets, day or night, were white—very few Negroes. That was the opposite of what we saw in Atlanta every day and night.

It was enough to prompt Wade and me to submit applications for employment with the Denver PD. Within a week, we were on a plane headed for Colorado. We applied and tested for the Denver Police Department, and since we were there, we decided to look into jobs with other police departments in the Denver metro area. I was over the age limit for the DPD—a few months over. I was disappointed that they would not waive their age requirement, especially since they would have gotten a cop with years of experience. We returned to Atlanta feeling dejected, wondering what to do.

102

A month later, the police chief and assistant chief of the Englewood, Colorado Police Department came to Atlanta to meet with Wade and me. We had submitted applications for employment with the Englewood PD while we were in Denver. The Englewood PD had the same age limit as the Denver PD, but Englewood was flexible; they wanted us for a specific purpose, so they waived the age limit. They had a proposition; come to Englewood, on special assignment, in an undercover capacity, to investigate a year-old unsolved murder. Whether we were successful or not—of course, they wanted us to solve the case, or at least see if our results coincided with theirs—we could become regular members of the police department, starting at the bottom, working our way up through the ranks. They implied that because of our experience, we would move upward at an accelerated pace. It was not an easy decision for Wade and me to make. We weighed the pros and cons. What clarified the decision was looking at it in black and white. We had to get away.

With my possessions stuffed into a U-Haul-It, trailing behind my car, and Wade's in a U-Haul-It behind his car, the Hagin and Goldhagen wagon train headed to Englewood, Colorado!

"Spies? Wade and me? Spies?"

After settling in the house the Englewood PD had rented for us—Goldhagens in the upstairs apartment, Hagins downstairs—we went to work. Few people knew who we were or what we were doing. The district attorney's office briefed us thoroughly on the case, and then we were given the year-old case file of an Englewood teen-ager whose nude body was found lying in a ditch. She had been raped and strangled. The prime suspect had been arrested and charged with her rape and murder, but had been released due to insufficient evidence. He was still the prime suspect, but no one could prove it.

The suspect, Marvin Smith, was a student at The University of Colorado, Denver Center. Wade and I enrolled as students, with the knowledge and consent of a university official. The idea was to take several classes with Smith, get friendly with him, and see where it might take us. One of the classes was a political science course taught by a radical professor of the "new left." Our cover was blown when the professor got wind of our subterfuge from another faculty member. The professor denied us entry to his class. This was early in 1969, at the height of campus unrest at colleges across the country.

The February 10, 1969 edition of the college newspaper, "The Colorado Daily," blared the headline "Cops Drop Plan to Spy," followed by a front-page story. The plan had to be scrubbed; we had to start at the beginning.

We knew from experience that it was going to be difficult working a cold, year-old homicide without informants, where the prime suspect has already dodged a bullet and knows he's being looked at again. We were not allowed to interview Smith. We did what we could—re-interviewing others in the case and trying to come up with new angles and a fresh approach. After a couple of months, the answer was always the same—Marvin Smith did it! The original investigators had it right, as far as we could determine. Wade was convinced. I agreed that Smith probably did it, but I wasn't one hundred percent sure. I had a nagging feeling that the killer was someone just passing through, not connected with the victim or Englewood, Colorado. In my mind, it was just a chance meeting with tragic results. It remains an unsolved homicide.

"What did you expect them to call you?"

Most of the Englewood policemen had seen us in and out of the police station and at the district attorney's office during that investigation. No one had explained who we were, why we were there, or what we were doing. In any working atmosphere, when people don't know what is going on, paranoia sets in, and rumors start flying. The speculation about us ranged from investigators from the DA's office, conducting an internal investigation and trying to nail Englewood cops, to a couple of hotshot homicide detectives trying to take over. We even heard talk that we were federal agents.

When we reported for duty to the patrol division in uniform, it seemed as if the entire Englewood PD was cold and unfriendly. It took a couple of months to convince them why we had come and how we got to be in their PD, a couple of cops, just like them. After a while, they became less suspicious, the barriers came down, and most warmed up to us.

I handled calls and situations differently from what they were accustomed to in Englewood, CO. One day, I received a call to a gas station, with instructions to see the attendant. When I pulled up, I saw a Negro in a gas station uniform. I didn't like him as soon as I saw him. I blamed every Negro that breathed for my having to leave Atlanta. I sat in the car and looked at him, making no attempt to get out. When he finally walked over to me, I asked if he had called and what he wanted.

He said three white guys had been at the station and giving him a hard time about something. He said as they were leaving, they called him "a goddamn nigger." He wanted to give me a description of their car and the tag number. I looked at him, saying with my face, "You got to be shitting me!" There was a long pause, each regarding the other, he not knowing what to say. I knew exactly what to say next, and I said it in my most sarcastic voice. "What the fuck did you expect them to call you, a goddamn Eskimo?"

Later that day, after he had filed a complaint on me, I was called to the police station. Sergeant Penny asked if I said what he said I said. I replied that I had indeed said what he said I said. To be sure he got it exactly; I repeated to the sergeant, "What the fuck did you expect them to call you, a goddamn Eskimo?" Adding this time, "Or a goddamn Chinaman?" His jaw dropped open, him not believing what he heard. He stared at me, shaking his head; he was still standing there when I nonchalantly walked out of the station, got into my patrol car, and drove off. I never heard anything more about it, perhaps because some members of the Englewood Police Department thought I was crazy.

I Was Safe Inside with the Shooter, Not Safe Outside with the Cops

One evening, later that month, an incident caused the other officers to become still more concerned about my behavior. The police were called, yet again, to a residential neighborhood where two neighbors had been feuding for a while. From his front yard, one neighbor shot the other with a rifle. The victim, not badly wounded, was transported by ambulance to the hospital. The shooter went back into his house.

When I arrived at the scene, there were five patrol cars parked in front of the house. After I learn what happened, I left the other cops and ran to the corner of the house. As I made my way to the front porch, I looked back towards the street, where I saw eight uniformed Englewood policemen crouching safely behind their patrol cars, their guns drawn and aimed in my direction.   Seeing the guns, looking like they were aimed at me, I got scared. I ran, as fast as I could, across the front of the house, up the steps, onto the porch. I peeked quickly through the window nearest me and saw the shooter sitting passively in a chair, just inside the front door. Not seeing the rifle in his hands, I rushed through the door and grabbed him. Sergeant Ron Frazier followed right behind me. The shooter quietly admitted that the rifle was in the bedroom.

Before Frazier or I had a chance to retrieve it, one of the patrolmen, Bill Belt, seeing that we had apprehended the shooter, left his position behind his patrol car, ran past us into the bedroom, grabbed the rifle, and strutted out of the house like a winning athlete, his hands carrying his trophy over his head.

What I did was not a common event for a police officer in Englewood. They made a big deal of it. I did it, not out of bravery or stupidity. It was instinctive from experience in many similar situations in Atlanta. I reacted by going towards the problem, not away from it. I knew from looking in the window that he didn't have the rifle in his hands; what I was concerned about were all those guns the officers in the street were pointing in my direction. It was not hard to figure that inside the house was a safer place for me than on the porch, vulnerable an overreacting cop flinching at a sound or shadow and squeezing the trigger of his gun. After that incident, the Englewood cops gave me a respect I hadn't noticed from them before.

"They don't never win!"

Police everywhere have their "regulars"—calls that come from the same people, at the same location, for the same reason, over and over again. The police, recognize these regular calls, yet respond every time. "Here we go again!"

One regular was a family disturbance that occurred almost every Sunday in the fall or winter. The husband drank all day Sunday and was drunk before the end of the day, when he beat up his wife. Every time he beat her, she would slip away to a phone and call the police, who responded, arrested him, and took him to jail, but by the time his case got to court, she would drop the charges, and he would go home. This was their routine, so it also was police routine most Sundays.

Then there was a Sunday when things started out as usual—the familiar call, at the same time, that we should respond to the familiar location. When we arrived, the scene was not as usual. When she opened the door to let us in, she was red, puffy, disheveled, beaten up. We were prepared, as usual, to have to fight him and drag him out of the house. Not this time. We found him lying in the bed, bloody and unconscious. The ambulance took him to the hospital; we brought her to the police station, where she told us what had happened.

She explained that her husband was a fanatic Broncos fan. The Denver Broncos football team in 1969 was bad, as bad as the Atlanta

Falcons, and I knew how bad the Falcons were. She said he watched the Broncos game on TV every Sunday. When they lost the game, his mood turned dark and ugly. He brooded about the loss while continuing to drink. Anything she said, no matter how well intentioned, no matter how insignificant, would cause him to explode, and would beat her. It was a repeat performance, almost every week during the football season.

After the game this Sunday, he beat her, and then passed out on the bed in a drunken stupor. She had had enough. She seized the opportunity with a baseball bat, breaking many of his bones. That was clear enough to us and the EMTs. What other damage she had done with the bat, the MDs in the emergency room would soon discover.

She explained that she was tired of getting beaten up every time the Denver Broncos lost a football game. She looked at us, tears filling her eyes, wanting us—someone, anyone—to sympathize. "And you know what? Those goddamn Broncos, they don't never win."

Time to Go Home

We had been in Colorado for almost a year, and things didn't feel right. Nothing seemed to fit. Wade and I kept telling each other, and ourselves, that we needed time to adjust to the slower pace and the different ways things were done. We slowly realized we were not going to be able to adjust, no matter how much time we gave ourselves.

A big problem for us was the inactivity. Nothing much ever happened, and when something did, it was not a big deal, but everyone made a goddamn big deal out of it. The other problem was the liberal attitude that prevailed—in the courts, among city officials, in police administration policy, and in how the public felt about things, especially the media.

We became increasingly unhappy. We escaped our problems in Atlanta and ran into different problems in Colorado. The police in Colorado had a disdain for Mexicans, their largest minority. The cops referred to the Chicanos in derogatory terms, such as spics, wetbacks, beaners, and taco eaters. There was a lot of friction and animosity. Would we replace one bias for another? There was no sense in running; there was no place to go. There was no "greener grass" anywhere for us.

There were three clear, simple choices for us:

Sell shoes in a store somewhere and be miserable.

Stay in Colorado with the Englewood Police Department and be miserable.

Return to the Atlanta Police Department and be miserable.
After little debate, we chose the last; it was time to go home.

The "hippie" phenomenon peaked in Atlanta between 1969 and 1971. Its beginning was more than two decades earlier, in New York City's Greenwich Village, then the popular gathering place for intellectuals and artists—the "Bohemians." From there it spread to San Francisco's North Beach area. From both coasts, the emerging cult heroes became "Pied Pipers" to a generation of white middle-class youth.

This new generation reached puberty during the Eisenhower administration, a time when young people were expected to follow the moral and religious values followed by their parents. From both coasts, gurus urged the new generation to see what they were looking at when they regarded the preceding generation. What they saw was hypocrisy, deceit, indifference, and resignation.

The young became restless. Their heroes, Allen Ginsberg, Jack Kerouac, and William Burroughs, fanned the embers of that restlessness. James Dean, both as himself and as his character in *Rebel without a Cause*, became a model for young people's behavior.

Author Norman Mailer saw what was occurring and where it was going. In *The White Negro*, he wrote of things to come—and they came. He was right on target. He referred to "hipsters"—the increasing numbers of young people flocking to join the "counter culture." It wasn't long before they became known as "hippies."

Hippies were looking for a cause, a reason to protest—to be heard. They admired the Negro and his struggle for civil rights. They sympathized with and supported it, but it was not their fight—they could not identify with it. They needed their own fight.

In May of 1960, the House Un-American Activities Committee in San Francisco held hearings investigating the identities of possible Communists in the higher education institutions. Several hundred University of California students from the Berkeley campus, across the bay, jammed into city hall. When ordered to leave, they refused. Using tactics learned from the Negroes during the civil rights sit-ins, they simply sat down, and did not move. The police had to use fire hoses and night sticks to clear them away. With this, hippies everywhere found their cause—an oppressive government that denied citizens of their civil liberties. The battleground was to be the college campus. In

1964, the campus at Berkeley exploded with student unrest and protest, setting off a chain reaction of violence at colleges throughout the United States.

Meanwhile, the United States had gotten involved in a war in Vietnam, unpopular with many. The war generated mixed feelings in the American public. The US military was comprised of draftees; it was not yet a volunteer army. As the war in Vietnam escalated, resistance to the draft grew. Draft cards and American flags were burned. "Hell, no, we won't go!" was echoed on campuses across the country. The "campus radical" was born, and members of the "New Left," Students for a Democratic Society (SDS), took the lead. Their Marxist rhetoric soon turned to violence.

A more radical group was formed—the Youth International Party. Members of YIP were called "yippies." Their purpose was to organize thousands of students, from colleges across the country, to go to Chicago to disrupt the Democratic National Convention in 1968.

Chicago's mayor, Richard Daley, warned that lawlessness would be dealt with severely. The riots in the streets outside of the convention amphitheatre were covered live on television and received worldwide attention. The media declared the violence "a police riot." Chicago cops took the rap.

Missing from the glaring newspaper headlines—"Chicago Police Riot"—and the TV coverage of police beating the shit out of everyone as they arrested them, were the hundreds of incidents that occurred between police and demonstrators in Grant and Lincoln parks in the days prior.

The world did not see the yippies, hippies, protesters, and demonstrators as they used cans of aerosol hairspray as flamethrowers to burn the cops. Nor did they see all of the objects thrown at police, including piles of human feces and jars of urine. There were no pictures of policemen with globs of spittle dripping off their faces.

It all culminated on the last night of the convention, outside the amphitheatre. Did the cops overreact? Were they angry? Mad? Seething? Who was at fault? There was enough blame to go around on all sides. Over six hundred arrests were made and almost two hundred policemen injured.

Riot gear for police officers in 1968 usually consisted of a "Class A" uniform, a blue plastic helmet, an elongated nightstick, and gas masks. This was paltry protection, compared to riot duty police officer's gear in 2005, which included fatigue uniforms, steel toe boots, Kevlar helmets with face shields, bulletproof vests, shin, knee and elbow protection, riot sticks, gas masks, pepper spray, sap gloves, and ballistic shields.

The leaders of the riots were arrested and charged with conspiracy to cross state lines with intent to incite a riot. They were indicted and brought to trial. Jerry Rubin, Abbie Hoffman, Dave Dellinger, Tom Hayden, Rennie Davis, John Froines, and Lee Weiner became known as the "Chicago Seven." Black Panther Party leader Bobby Seale, also arrested in the melee, was added to the group, which became known as the "Chicago Eight." Froines and Weiner were acquitted. The other six were convicted, but when they appealed, their convictions were overturned on a technicality.

A militant group split off from the SDS, calling themselves The Weathermen, after a line in a Bob Dylan song—"You don't need a weatherman to know which way the wind blows." They engaged in violent criminal acts, including armed robbery and police assault. They bombed and burned selected buildings. They formed an alliance with the Black Panther Party, and were strong supporters of Fidel Castro, Che Guevara, and the Viet Cong. The Weathermen were so extreme and violent that both the SDS and the Black Panther Party eventually broke away from them. Later called the "Weather Underground, they ended up criminals, hunted by the FBI. Several blew themselves up when a homemade bomb went off in their New York townhouse.

Campus violence ended in May 1970, almost ten years after it started, with the tragedy at Kent State University, in Ohio. The demonstrations had gotten out of hand, and local police were unable to handle them. The Ohio National Guard was called in. For several days, there were skirmishes, burnings, rocks, bottles, tear gas, threats, and antagonism from both sides. A troop of sixteen guardsmen fired into the crowd. After the smoke had cleared, four students were dead, nine wounded.

That was May 4, 1970—the day I returned to Atlanta reinstated by the police department, ready to resume my duties as one of Atlanta's finest.

I Did the Only Thing I Could—I Challenged Him

Once again, I had to start at the bottom. It didn't matter that I was more experienced, capable, knowledgeable, productive, and successful.

Atlanta's civil service laws required that all police officers joining the department enter with the rank of patrolman. This also applied to reinstatements, excepting appointments at the rank of deputy chief and chief. Since I wasn't being reinstated at either rank, I was reinstated in the Atlanta PD as a patrolman, a wiser, older roustabout, this time on the evening watch.

I was back on familiar ground; it felt good. I would have to work a patrol car until the next detective test; I was confident I would pass and be reassigned to homicide, where I felt I belonged.

The evening watch, patrol division, is the most active watch, especially on Friday and Saturday nights, when things get dangerous for a patrolman working a one-man car.

I was assigned to a car in the northwest side of the city one Friday night. My beat included Perry Homes, the largest low-income, high-crime, Negro housing project in Atlanta. It was so busy on that particular night that whenever a patrol car "pulled back into service"—police radio jargon advising the dispatcher that the previous call had been handled and the unit was again available to receive calls. The radio dispatcher advised cars on that night to "stand by to copy,"—more jargon meaning "get ready to write down calls coming in because there were going to be more than one, all needing responses at the same time. The dispatcher assigned priority to each call, something the patrolman himself could easily determine—calls reporting stolen bicycles fell below a call for a shooting. On summer weekend nights, every police officer, including superior officers, hustled their asses trying to answer all calls—even the stolen bicycle calls. With every officer working a one-man car and responding to calls, every one was vulnerable, due to lack of backup. The critical basis for the one-man car concept does not exist—there is no back up available.

I received a call at about nine o'clock, just after dusk. "Car 21, at Kerry Drive and Kerry Place, signal 24/69, shotgun." (Demented person/ person armed with shotgun.) It was in the middle of Perry Homes. Every policeman knew that a call in the project had the potential to get out of hand. Just hearing those signals coming over the radio got my juices flowing. I knew I had to prepare for things to go bad, and that I would have to handle it alone, without backup. On calls like this one, it was standard to send more than one car. But because every officer was responding to other calls, there were none available.

I came around the corner, and there it was. Was my adrenalin pumping? Sure. Were my senses on high alert? Of course. Was I prepared to take flight for safety? Definitely. Would I? No. I had to do what I was there to do.

About a hundred people were standing there, away from one guy, who was off by himself, holding the shotgun, previously leveled at the crowd. When he saw my car pull up, his attention shifted from them to me. Several people ran over and told me they were the ones who had called the police.

As I got out of the car, in the best position to go for my gun, I knew better than to even gesture toward it because I'd be dog meat before it cleared the holster. Instead, I took the biggest gamble of my life. I stared at him from a distance of about thirty feet, the expression on my face stern and committed. Loudly and clearly, so that everyone in the crowd could hear, I said, "Put down that shotgun, and I'll whip your ass!"

The gamble was that it wouldn't piss him off and cause him to pull the trigger. The gamble was that he would respond to the challenge thrown at him by a little white policeman to beat the shit out of him. He was a big guy, a fierce-looking big guy. Did I really want to risk trying to whip his ass? No. But a physical confrontation was not my goal. The shotgun motivated my challenge.

He took the bait, flung his shotgun to the ground, and charged me like a water buffalo. The crowd grabbed him before he reached me and proceeded to kick his ass. Whew! They were pissed at him for terrorizing them before I arrived. I thought they were going to kill the bastard. After they subdued him, I offered my handcuffs to restrain him further. Someone put the cuffs on him. When the paddy wagon arrived, a number of people picked him up and heaved him inside for his ride to the hospital.

From the moment I arrived until he was taken away, I never had to lay a hand on him. The crowd did it for me. It was the first time that the residents of a Negro housing project and I were on the same side. It wasn't until later, replaying the situation in my mind, as I usually do afterward, that I realized that the crowd had been my backup.

"Who the fuck is this guy?"

"Any car near the Greyhound Bus Station, signal 63/50/4!" (Officer needs help/person shot/ambulance on the way.) When a signal 63 comes over the radio, every cop that hears it springs into motion and heads in the direction specified. The motorist being issued a traffic ticket gets a reprieve. Coffee or hot meals are left. The clandestine meeting with a girlfriend is interrupted. Policemen don't waste time when the life of a fellow officer is in danger. Between one heartbeat and the next, the officer is on his way. Every cop racing toward the location has one hope at the forefront of his mind—that the "person shot" is the bad guy, not the cop. On this night, it wasn't the bad guy.

I had recently transferred to the morning watch. It was shortly before five a.m., and I was working on the western edge of the city, the furthest distance from downtown, when the call came in. The Greyhound bus station was in the center of downtown. I was too far away to be of any immediate help, but my reflexes steered me toward the bus station anyway, adrenalin pumping.

As I made my way in on Bankhead Highway, a curvy main thoroughfare dotted with traffic lights, the radio broadcast the excited voices of the cops who had arrived at the scene. "Give that ambulance a rush call; we've got an officer shot!" Usually, when the first patrol cars arrive at a scene, they are sufficient to handle the situation, there is no need for additional cars. But in a signal 63, cars keep responding. When I heard, "Let those cars come on, we're receiving gunfire," I realized something big was happening at the bus station. That was confirmed when I heard, "We need tear gas!"

I flipped on my blue lights and siren, running a full-blown code 3 (emergency call, immediate response, haul ass). There was hardly any traffic, but I was slowed by a light rain, which made the streets slick. From what I heard, it seemed that someone was barricaded in the baggage room and shooting at the cops, but no one was sure who or how many. As the confusion seemed to worsen, the faster and more recklessly I drove, taking wet curves curb to curb.

The ambulance that was to transport the wounded officer to the hospital arrived, and the officer was put into it, but the ambulance could not be restarted. Another ambulance was dispatched. I heard one voice, desperately, sadly, trying to interject that the downed officer looked "signal 48" (person dead). When the ambulance returned to Grady Memorial Hospital, Atlanta Police Officer, Donald D. Baty, was DOA.

I arrived at the bus station, the brakes and tires of my car hot, smoking, and stinking, about fifteen to twenty minutes after the original call came in. Patrol cars, detective cars, private cars, buses, and taxis were snarled in a hopeless traffic jam. Patrol cars were in the middle of the street, on the sidewalks—doors open, engines running, blue lights flashing—some with their sirens still screaming. I drove within two blocks of the bus station, left my car, and proceeded on foot to join the cops who had left those cars. As I ran past patrol cars, I turned off sirens and closed doors.

I was the last cop to arrive.

An eerie quiet hung over the interior of the bus station. There was the unmistakable odor of gunpowder, and a thick layer of smoke, making halos around the ceiling lights, much as in an indoor pistol range. Although the shooting was over, civilians were still huddled behind and beneath whatever they had found for cover when the shooting started. Most of the policemen were standing around, taking aimless steps, the kind of thing that demonstrates the collective shock that happens after these kinds of incidents.

"What the hell happened?" I asked of no one in particular, trying to get someone to fill me in.

Officer DD Baty had been assigned to a foot beat at the Greyhound and Trailways Bus Stations downtown. The bus station was a high priority assignment; there was a constant need for police presence. Bus stations nationwide, likely worldwide, attract the underbelly of society—thieves, pickpockets, derelicts, winos, pimps, prostitutes, runaways, nickel-and-dime drug pushers, street thugs—especially during the nighttime hours. They all preyed on unsuspecting travelers.

Here's what I was told:

Wordell Brock had been released from the United States Air Force on a Section Eight—a mentally incompetent discharge. He arrived from Alabama on a Greyhound bus; he had a layover of several hours in Atlanta before boarding the bus to his final destination somewhere in Kentucky. Shortly before five a.m., someone reported to Officer DD Baty that a Negro on the street outside the bus station had just robbed him. The robbery victim pointed to Wordell Brock in the passenger waiting room, identifying him as the robber.

Officer Baty walked up to Wordell Brock, and after a few words, Brock stepped back, pulled a gun, and fired several times, point-blank. Witnesses later described how Officer Baty, on the way down, drew his revolver and fired several rounds, none of which hit Brock. Officer Baty fell to the floor, shot three times.

Someone called the police, and the signal 63/50/4 was broadcast. Wordell Brock ran into the baggage room and shot at the first cop that entered the bus station. That drew fire from the cops as they poured into the bus station. The word spread fast that the guy barricaded in the baggage room had just shot Baty. Policemen shot wildly into the baggage room. They emptied their revolvers, reloaded, and emptied them again.

Every recruit who goes through the academy is instructed in firearms discipline—there must be justification for firing a weapon; fire only with concern for the safety of the public, only a specific, justified target. There was no firearms discipline in that bus station. The police were out of control.

Most of the people fled the bus station when Brock shot Baty. Those who didn't, or weren't able, to flee crawled under benches or hid behind obstacles. Two people dove for safety nearest where they were when they heard shots fired in the passenger waiting room—the baggage room. One of those taking cover was the operator of the shoeshine stand, the other was a passenger who had arrived earlier on a Greyhound Bus. Both were Negroes.

Homicide detectives LF New and HF Pharr, who were responsible for handling whatever it was that had occurred, were among the last to arrive at the bus station. They made their way through the army of pissed-off, out-of-control cops. When they reached the baggage room, they saw some policemen shooting at a dead Negro. New saw a cop beating the shit out of the shoeshine operator. Not only was the cop beating up on the wrong guy, he was beating up on a guy who had already been shot in the arm and leg. New called an ambulance to take the shoeshine operator to the hospital.

The other Negro in the baggage room was dead, shot and killed by police bullets. As cops came into the baggage room, they pumped more rounds into his dead body. A gun was found on the dead body. But there were two problems. That gun had not been fired–the state crime lab confirmed that later, and the dead Negro was not Wordell Brock. Witnesses confirmed later that the dead Negro was not who shot the police officer.

I learned all this from questioning different police officers who had been present when things were happening. I was in the baggage room, trying to put those bits and pieces into a clearer picture of who did what to whom.

There were about twenty policemen in the baggage room, moving in slow motion, their conversation whispered. Some cops were trying to stifle the sniffling that came with the tears that ran down their cheeks. Their anger had been displaced by shock. There was calm now; there was quiet.

I stood in the corner of the baggage room, quietly talking to Officer RM Rambler, who I had known during my earlier time in the Atlanta PD. I was trying to get more information about what happened. As we spoke, I noticed movement among the luggage in the bins beside me. I looked and saw a Negro male behind some luggage, lying down in the baggage bins. I turned to Rambler, pointing down. "Who the fuck is this guy?"

Rambler didn't reply; instead, he dove past me, towards the guy lying in the luggage. When Rambler straightened, he was holding a revolver he had snatched from the guy in the bin. My brain clicked into gear. This guy was the cop killer, not the guy laying dead a few feet away.

I pulled Wordell Brock out of the bin, straightened him up, and smashed my gun into his face. Word traveled like a lightning bolt through the baggage room and into the rest of the bus station. Before I could hit him again, the nearest bunch of cops went out control again, taking him away from me. On the way from the baggage room to a paddy wagon outside the bus station, he was repeatedly dropped, dragged, punched, and kicked by a mob dressed in police uniforms.

Several people tried to protest the way Wordell Brock was violently removed from the bus station. They were shoved aside. Out on the street, in front of the bus station, one Negro in his mid-twenties attempted to protest to two Negro cops. They threw the protestor across the hood of a parked car, beat him, rolled him onto the ground, and left him there, unmoving. No one paid any attention.

After the wagon left with the cop killer, superior officers gained control of their cops and sent most back to their beats. Detectives New and Pharr remained at the bus station to sort out things, make their reports, interview witnesses, and collect evidence—including Wordell's gun, Baty's gun, and the dead man's gun. Then they had to go to the office to take written statements, and do everything else that was needed to communicate the morning's events.

Top police brass were concerned about how to explain why the police shot and killed the unknown man. Their anxiety was gone the following day, when someone reported he had been robbed near the bus station the night before. The robbery victim was taken to the morgue, where he identified the dead guy as the robber. Brass breathed a collective sigh of relief. The dead guy was listed in the official record as a "felon, killed by police." Nobody raised any hell about it. So that was that. Case closed. Wordell Brock was declared insane and never brought to trial. He was sent to a mental hospital.

There was a big funeral for Baty. As for every Atlanta police officer killed in the line of duty, there is a brass plate, with his name, the date he was killed, and the manner in which he was killed in a display case, alongside the brass plaques of other officers killed in the line of duty, in the lobby of the police headquarters building.

The shoeshine operator never sued the city of Atlanta for his injuries, as far I know. New spoke to him at the hospital; he said that he felt no anger towards the police for shooting and beating him, he understood the feelings and actions of the police. He was glad we got the one who killed the officer.

Every police officer, no matter what rank, goes through an annual in-service training curriculum, with respect to firearms discipline and justification for shooting his or her weapon. The incident at the bus station is the basis for this new training.

The False Alarm That Wasn't

Most policemen work their entire careers without ever firing their service weapons in the line of duty. The only time they draw their guns is either to qualify annually on the pistol range, or to remove the rust from the working parts. Cops' guns have been found so rusty that they were inoperable. Cops carry, in their holsters, guns that could not be fired, even if necessary.

Officer Ray Braswell was a cop who was always in the middle of the action and needed to have his gun ready for use. Murray's Liquor Store, at the corner of Pryor Street and Ridge Avenue, was in one of the worst high-crime areas of Atlanta. Armed robbers held up the place during business hours; burglars broke in at night, taking with them all they could carry.

A special police holdup/burglar alarm was installed and connected to the communications section at police headquarters. When activated, it sent a silent signal, dispatching a patrol car immediately to the scene. Store personnel only activated the alarm during an actual armed robbery. There were prerequisites for how responding officers should act upon arrival. Sounded good, but the system worked only when it was applied properly. It didn't work when: the alarm was inadvertently activated; there was a power failure; or someone signaled anything other than an armed robbery. There were so many "signal 65s" (silent alarm) from the liquor store that the cops working the area became accustomed to them; they grew complacent because most were false alarms.

One evening, Officer Ray Braswell received a signal 65 to Murray's Liquor Store. Braswell had been regularly working the beat car that included Pryor and Ridge. He was familiar with the occasional hold-ups at Murray's, as well as the frequent false alarms. Officer WL Boyd, a black cop who worked the car covering the adjoining beat, had also answered many calls from Murray's that had turned out to be false alarms.

Boyd responded as backup whenever a call from Murray's was given to another car. He heard Braswell get the call and advised that he was only a couple of blocks away and would arrive as backup. Braswell let Boyd know that he was on the other end of the beat and that it would take him a few minutes to get there. Boyd understood what Braswell really meant. "A few minutes" in police-speak means more than a few minutes.

Boyd arrived first at the liquor store, parked at the front door, and walked in, intending to admonish the manager to be more goddamn careful with the goddamn alarm button. Instead, two armed robbers greeted him, relieved him of his service revolver, cuffed him with his own handcuffs, and took him to a back room and locked him inside. They asked the manager if it was his Cadillac parked outside. He replied yes, then they demanded his keys to the car.

Braswell pulled into the liquor store parking lot, saw Boyd's patrol car, and waited for Boyd to exit from Murray's giving the high sign, unspoken language that "everything's ok; just another false alarm." Braswell had been waiting for Boyd only a few seconds when he saw a Cadillac with a Negro male at the wheel drive off the lot. If Boyd had come to the door and waived him off, Braswell would have known that everything was okay. But unbeknownst to those in the store, the store manager's car had just been stolen. The Cadillac looked suspiciously to Braswell like the store manager's Cadillac.

Boyd did not come to the door. The Cadillac became unimportant. Braswell got out of his car to see why Boyd had not signaled him.

Braswell hadn't taken a step from his car when one of the robbers took his first step out of the store, gun in hand, expecting to find his cohort in the Cadillac, ready to go. He didn't see the Cadillac; he did see Braswell. They surprised each other. The gunman shot at Braswell, who dove behind his car. The bullet missed him, smashing through the windshield. Braswell's car was left of the store's front entrance—the driver's side door, his shield from the robber. The robber, unable to go anywhere where he would not be vulnerable, took a few steps toward the passenger side of Braswell's car. From their positions, only the width of the patrol car separating them, they were at point-blank range. Braswell jumped up, vulnerable, shooting over his car, and then ducking down. The robber did the same. This was repeated between them several times. Braswell began to figure out the robber's rhythm. Braswell coolly stretched his arms across the hood of the car, his revolver cocked and pointed at the spot just vacated by the robber. When the robber next popped his head up, Braswell shot one round into his face. Braswell jumped onto the hood of the car and fired two more times into the robber as he slumped toward the ground dead, his gun still in his hand.

Hearing the distant sirens of patrol cars, Braswell figured they were responding to a signal 36/63/25 (robbery in progress/ officer needs help/ shots fired). He ran into the liquor store to check on Boyd. Inside were the store manager, an employee, and the very scared, very embarrassed, very grateful, Officer WL Boyd.

The manager's Cadillac was found a short time later, a few blocks away. That robber was never identified and never apprehended. On the dead robber was the $6,000 taken in the robbery. Still in the safe, overlooked by the robbers, was $100,000 in cash, as was usual every Friday—for cashing paychecks.

Identification found on the dead robber represented him as Raymond Hunter, age thirty. His fingerprints were sent to the FBI, in Washington. It turned out that Mr. Hunter was really Wordell Ellis, wanted in Houston, Texas for killing a Houston police officer during an armed robbery. The Houston police learned from the FBI that Mr. Ellis, the cop-killer, was shot and killed by Atlanta police officer Ray Braswell. Not long afterward, Ray Braswell received a giant Valentine's Day card from the Houston PD, bearing the message, "Ain't Love Grand," and signed by eighty Houston police officers.

There's no way a municipality can pay a cop like Braswell to do what he did. But eighty other cops can send him a Valentine.

Why do Ray Braswell and others like him stay in this job? It's often dangerous and almost always thankless. Why? Not for the money. For the excitement? To help make our city a better place to live? For the opportunity to defuse a bully? Some guys become cops, hang around for a few years, and then leave after realizing either that police work is not what they expected, or that they don't want to put up with all the crap that goes with it.

The rest of us stick around and become career police officers. It's a bumpy road, with lots of ups and downs. We make friends and develop enemies along the way. We sometimes squabble with our friends and fight with our enemies. We get clannish, separating ourselves politically, racially, individually, and in other ways, as well. None of that matters if you hurt one of us. If you do, you will have a ferocious, blue tidal wave come crashing down on your ass.

A Quick, Smart Burst of Light Was Enough

One night, as Officer Ed Hanson drove his paddy wagon, he saw a Negro male sitting in the middle of the intersection of DeKalb Avenue and Sutherland Terrace. Henson stopped, got out of the wagon, and figured the man to be drunk, nuts, or both. He put him in the wagon and started for the station—another routine arrest of another drunk—happens all the time.

The prisoner demanded Officer Hanson's attention. He turned, still driving the wagon and saw the barrel of a gun pointed at him from the cage door separating the driver's compartment from the prisoner's area. The "drunk" ordered Hanson to open the cage door. Hanson complied, quickly opening the driver's door so he could bail out of the wagon. Leaving the rolling vehicle, Hanson rolled on the ground and was shot at twice—both shots missing him. The gunman drove off in the wagon, leaving Hanson on the ground.

Hanson flagged down a passing car, jumped into the car, and instructed the driver to follow the wagon. At DeKalb and Arizona Avenues, the wagon went through a field and across railroad tracks. Stopped in a field of overgrown weeds, it appeared that the wagon wasn't going any further. Hanson got out of the car and instructed the driver to go to a telephone, call the police, and specify where and what had happened, where he was, and that he needed assistance. As Hanson waited in the weeds near the railroad tracks, the gunman spotted Hanson and tried to run him down with the wagon. Hanson fired, his bullet shattering the windshield. The wagon got stuck on the tracks, and the gunman jumped out and fled into the weeds.

The driver of the car, as instructed, called the police. Immediately, over the radio, was heard, "Any car near DeKalb and Arizona, signal 63." Every patrol car within several miles responded. A police officer needed help, so many police responded, adrenalin pumping. Officer ER Richards was the first to arrive. He walked through the waist-high weeds in darkness so thick he didn't realize he was within reach of someone else. Richards did not see him until he was close enough to reach out and touch him. He ordered the man to turn around and face him—a big mistake. The man turned and fired, hitting Richards once in the stomach. Richards returned fire, and they both went down.

Among the cops swarming into the area was Officer Ray Braswell. No one could see Richards, who was down and out of sight among the dark weeds. He was badly wounded, calling for someone to help him. No one responded to his calls; there was also a gunman out there in the weeds. Richards continued to cry out, begging for help. Still, there was no response from any of the cops.

Braswell could not listen to more of Richards' cries for help. He charged into the darkness towards Richards' voice. Just before reaching him, he heard a noise off to the side. Braswell switched on his flashlight for a quick burst of light. There was the gunman on the ground, his gun pointed towards Braswell's flashlight beam. Ray Braswell shot into the darkness where the gunman had been illuminated by Braswell's flashlight and didn't stop firing until he had emptied his gun. There was no noise from the gunman; he never moved again. He didn't get off a shot; he was dead.

Officer ER Richards survived. He returned to work after a long convalescence, but was never the same. He took a disability pension shortly after.

Why do some of us keep doing it?

Who the hell knows. I don't know why I kept doing it. But I did.

Susan E. Doty

When the results of the detective test were posted, Wade and I had placed within the top five of those who took the test. We were assigned back to homicide, our natural habitat. We went to work, as fresh as if we had been on a long vacation.

Occasionally, a brutal or bizarre crime will attract the media. As they report it, and people talk about it, it is driven further into public awareness. I've worked both cases that were buried in the back pages, and those that made the headlines of the Atlanta Journal-Constitution and local TV news. One case that became a media event, commanding front page headlines and the lead story for the local TV news for days and remained news for weeks, began in the simplest possible way.

Wade and I arrived for work one Friday afternoon in December 1970, and Homicide Lieutenant, JE Helms, met us in the squad room. He handed us a report of a missing woman. "Look into this," he said.

The woman's boyfriend had just filed the missing person's report, and he was still in the office. We spoke with him, getting her name (Susan Doty), her age (twenty-five years old). She was a single, white female, she lived in an apartment on Roswell Road in Sandy Springs, a suburb just North of Atlanta, and she had gone to work the previous day (a Thursday) and was to meet a female friend that evening for a birthday celebration at a downtown hotel. She never showed up at the birthday party, nor did she phone the friend to say she wasn't going to be there.

The boyfriend became concerned when she didn't come home that night. He spent all day Friday looking for her, checking the metro area hospitals, as well as searching for her in places she frequented. The boyfriend called friends and acquaintances, but no one had seen her or heard from her. Failing in all that, he went to police headquarters to report her missing.

Wade and I accompanied the boyfriend to Ms. Doty's apartment on Roswell Road. The apartment didn't yield any clues as to her whereabouts, or any reason for her disappearance. What we did observe was corroborated by what we were told later by people who knew her—she was a very orderly, disciplined, and structured person. She was not careless or flighty. She never acted on impulse or did anything on a whim. She was dependable and punctual. If she said she would do something or be somewhere, you could be sure she would do it or be there. There were no loose ends in her daily life; everything was neatly wrapped and in it's place.

The apartment was a reflection of Susan Doty. Not only was it immaculate, everything in it fit. It was orderly, as if planned by an interior designer, but the apartment was not clinical or sterile; it had warmth. The clothes in the closet were sorted and grouped, each in their proper place, hangers spaced equally apart. The shoes stood in pairs on the closet floor, toes and heels lined up precisely, none of the shoes flopped to their side. In the bathroom medicine cabinet, everything was grouped properly and spaced evenly, the labels facing outward to be read quickly and easily. Everything in the apartment was in precise order.

Susan Doty was an honor graduate of the highly respected Vanderbilt University and employed by The Girl Scouts of America as the southeastern sales representative. Her accounts were retail outlets for Girl Scout clothing. She had recently completed a course in securities at Emory University in Atlanta, and planned to sell securities part-time. On the day of her disappearance that Thursday, she'd had lunch with one of her customers, a buyer at the Sears department store in the Buckhead section of Atlanta. Susan and the buyer, a woman, returned to the store after lunch. Then, at about two p.m., their business completed, Susan Doty said goodbye to the buyer, who later gave us a written statement that she saw Susan go out the door and walk through the parking lot, in the direction of her car. The buyer was the last person to see Susan and her car. Susan and her car vanished.

A petite, 5'3", blue-eyed blond, Susan Doty was last seen by her boyfriend leaving her apartment that Thursday morning. Susan was dressed in a brown, long-sleeve jumper, a brown V-neck blouse, a camel-colored coat, a brown print scarf, and brown shoes, carrying a small, brown handbag. In her statement, the Sears buyer described the same outfit. We searched her apartment for articles comprising the outfit she wore; all were missing. Wade and I surmised that this was an indication that she had not returned home to change clothes; she was probably still wearing them.

By the end of our tour of duty that Friday, our preliminary investigation led Wade and I to believe it would be out of character for her to disappear or leave town without a word. The situation didn't look good for Susan Doty. Susan was the "needle in a haystack" of nearly two million people in the Atlanta metropolitan area; a larger haystack taking into account the state of Georgia, and larger still the US. Wade and I knew we had to find that needle, fast—before it was too late. We sensed foul play.

The veteran homicide detectives felt a wave of déjà vu. In 1965, another young woman, Mary Shotwell Little, disappeared from a shopping center parking lot in the Buckhead section. Ms. Little was never heard from again, and her body was never found. Her car was recovered the following day, in the same shopping center, where it was searched for, but not found on the day of her disappearance. In her car were still the groceries she had bought before her disappearance. The seats were smeared with blood, and a few articles of her clothing were found in it. The Atlanta Police Department committed all of its resources to trying to locate her, establish a motive, and come up with a suspect. Everything led to a dead end. More man-hours were spent on the Mary Shotwell Little case than on any other case in APD history. The file is voluminous; it remains an unsolved missing person report.

Wade and I conferred with our bosses, Homicide Lieutenants JE Helms and CJ Strickland. Collectively, we decided to ask the media for extensive coverage, showing Susan Doty's photo and a photo of an exact replica of her car, a 1968 Pontiac Le Mans, dark green with a black vinyl top—Georgia tag number 1-13766. Both photos appeared on TV and in the newspapers.

The strategy got results. On Sunday night, I was working alone (Wade had taken the night off). I received a call from the manager of a jewelry store in suburban Cobb County, which adjoins Atlanta, providing us with our first lead.

The manager told us that on Friday, the day after the disappearance, a young white male came to the store to buy three pieces of jewelry worth $391.00. To pay for the jewelry, the guy used a credit card issued to Susan E. Doty; he produced his driver's license for identification. The manager made the routine call to the bank that issued Susan Doty's card. The bank denied authorization for the charge. The guy then produced another credit card issued in Susan E. Doty's name. When the manager questioned him about the cards, the guy replied that he and Ms. Doty were married several days before. Without calling the second card's bank for authorization, the manager would not allow the credit charge. The guy took back his driver's license, Susan Doty's two credit cards, and walked out of the store.

About thirty minutes after I received the call from the manager from his home, Lieutenants Helms and Strickland and I were at the store, where he agreed to meet us. The manager told us he saw the story of the missing girl, Susan Doty, on TV. He remembered her name from the two credit cards the guy tried to use on Friday. More important to us, he remembered the name on the driver's license—Larry Davis. He was sure the driver's license belonged to the guy who produced it because his picture was on it. The credit card purchase slip had been completed before the bank denied authorization; after the guy left the store, the manager tossed the credit purchase slip into his wastebasket.

We checked the large dumpster that served the small shopping plaza in which the jewelry store was located. It had not been emptied. I climbed in, suit and all—I was outranked; low man goes into the dumpster—and started sifting through the mess. Lucky for me there were no restaurants in the plaza; most of the contents were dry trash. As I poked around in the darkness, aided only by our flashlights, I thought about all of the vermin in there with me. Every now and then, I caught a putrid whiff of something that was more than discarded papers. After a short time, I found two sacks of trash from the jewelry store.

Back inside the store, we dumped the contents on the floor, and a few minutes later, there it was—the credit card purchase slip. Imprinted on it was the name of Susan E. Doty and the signature of Larry Ronald Davis.

Returning to police headquarters, we checked through ID and found a criminal record for Larry Ronald Davis—white male, age twenty-seven. It gave a home address in Conyers, a small town about twenty-five miles east of Atlanta. He was no longer living at that address, and current whereabouts were unknown. He was an ex-convict, having served time for kidnapping, auto theft, and escape. He was wanted for armed robbery.

On Monday morning, we met with the jewelry store manager and showed him six mug shots of white males, all the same age, having the same physical characteristics as Larry Ronald Davis. He looked through the mug shots, pulled one out, and turned it toward us. "That's him." It was Larry Ronald Davis' mug shot.

Later that Monday, we received information from the Citizens and Southern Bank that on Friday, one of their branches had cashed a check of Susan Doty's for $950.00. The endorsement signature later proved to be a forgery. The third party endorsement was by Larry Ronald Davis.

The news media gave the story top coverage on TV and in the newspapers, running Davis' picture and informing the public that he was wanted for robbery and was a suspect in the disappearance of Susan Doty. This prompted a frantic call from a woman urging us to meet with her and her husband in their Cobb County apartment. She didn't want to discuss it on the telephone, but she said she had very important information concerning Larry Ronald Davis.

Sitting in their apartment a short time later, they told Wade and me that their friend, Betty Jean Smith, who was living with them, was Davis' girlfriend. On Saturday afternoon, Davis had come to the apartment and told "BJ" to pack her things; they were going away. He was driving a dark green Pontiac Le Mans, borrowed, he said, from his uncle. It had a U-haul luggage carrier mounted on the roof. They were last seen leaving the couple's Cobb County apartment, driving the car, loaded down with all their clothes and personal belongings.

The couple was very concerned about the safety of Betty Jean Smith. They said Davis had been staying with them, and they felt very uneasy in his presence. They were convinced BJ was not even aware of the Doty disappearance, but should she learn of it and confront him, he might harm her.

On Tuesday, piecing together all that we knew up to this point, Wade and I felt that the chances of finding Susan Doty alive were very slim. We concentrated our efforts on finding her body. Knowing that Davis frequented the Cobb County area, we started at the Buckhead Sears Store and followed the four-lane highway where it crosses the Chattahoochee River at the Atlanta-Cobb County line, and began searching the wooded area.

Meanwhile, Reverend WW Willoughby started the day Tuesday by leaving his car at the garage for routine maintenance and driving a loaner. He had several appointments that would take him across the Metro-Atlanta area. He stopped into a Douglas County drugstore for lunch, where he read about Susan Doty in the Atlanta paper. After lunch, in Cobb County, the loaner car broke down. The reverend called his garage from a nearby service station and decided to walk the half mile back to the car and wait for the service truck.

As he walked along the left side of Windy Hill Road, facing traffic, he noticed a checkbook lying on the grass. He picked it up and looked inside. When he read the name on the checks, "Susan E. Doty," he hurried back to the service station to call the Atlanta police.

That was about the time Wade and I were poking around in the woods along the river. We received a signal 39 (meet a person) at the service station at Interstate 75 and Windy Hill Road. We were only a couple of miles down the road when we got the call. Within five minutes, we were talking with Reverend Willoughby, who showed us the checkbook and how he came to find it.

We returned with him to where he found the checkbook. Nearby, I picked up a small, brown paper bag with the name "Susan E. Doty" written on it eight times, as if someone was practicing her signature. We also found an empty Smith and Wesson gun box that had contained a .38 caliber snub-nose revolver. The sales slip was still in it, purchased with Susan Doty's credit card.

I went back to the service station, telephoned Lieutenant Strickland, advised him of where we were and what we had discovered, and asked him to send more detectives to help us search. We had a strong feeling that she was very close. Since we were out of our jurisdiction, the lieutenant called Cobb County Police, asking them to send detectives to help.

Soon, two Cobb County officers arrived, Assistant Chief Bennett and Detective Lieutenant Harold Davis. After giving them a quick briefing, we split into pairs and started searching. Chief Bennett and I took one side of the road, Wade and Lieutenant Davis searched the other side. Chief Bennett and I recovered a car owner's manual, Susan Doty's license tag receipt, and an insurance card, among other articles normally kept in a car's glove compartment. We continued searching, making a wider swath into the wooded area alongside the road.

Wade eventually found her. Her body was buried under a pile of leaves, beneath a barbed-wire fence, about twenty-five feet from the road. The only visible signs of her body were the heel of one shoe and the back of her head.

The scene filled up with Atlanta and Cobb detectives, Cobb uniformed officers, forensic people from the state crime lab, news media, and the medical examiner. The news was out; Susan Doty's body had been found on Windy Hill Road. Curiosity seekers surrounded the roped-off crime scene. Cobb police closed Windy Hill road to traffic. Still, the curiosity seekers came to see what they could not get close enough to see.

I watched the crime lab people brush away the leaves, revealing her body. She was lying face down, dressed in the outfit she was last seen wearing. Her panties and pantyhose were pulled down to her knees. Her hands, feet, and knees were tied to each other with white cord. It appeared that Larry Ronald Davis had raped her before he robbed and killed her.

They turned her over; her eyes were open and seemed to be looking at me. I could not shake the feeling that she wanted to say, "What took you so long? If only you'd found me sooner, he wouldn't have killed me!"

I was merely a spectator within the confines of the crime scene; I was so close to her; I could see her so clearly. She looked like she had been dead for no more than a day. I felt bad, guilty.

I felt I had failed. I was angry with myself and angry with my partner; we hadn't found her in time to save her from being murdered. I was angry with Larry Ronald Davis—for killing her, for tying her hands so goddamn tightly that one hand was swollen and discolored, for the agony she must have suffered when the circulation in that hand had been cut off. I became obsessed with the need to arrest Davis. I wanted to handcuff that fuckin' bastard as tightly as I could, until he cried and begged for the handcuffs to be loosened, and then I would tighten the cuffs further, telling him that what I was doing to him was not as bad as what he'd done to Susan Doty. I was not supposed to feel that way, not want to do that, but as a human being who had seen how Susan Doty was killed, I would have done it without a second thought,

My anger was displaced by frustration when Lieutenant Strickland called Wade and me together with Cobb County police officials, instructing us, "Turn everything you have over to them, it's their case now!"

We didn't like that, but there was nothing we could do. It could not be determined where she was murdered. Because her body was found in Cobb County, everything was in their jurisdiction. In legal terms, the "venue" for the prosecution would be in Cobb County.

After the processing of the crime scene was completed, the undertaker removed her body. The news media shut down and the crowd dwindled, and then disappeared. Cobb police re-opened Windy Hill Road to normal traffic. Wade and I lingered for a few more minutes where the leaves were brushed off Susan Doty's body, each with our own thoughts, contemplating the events of the past six days. We got into our car and headed back to Atlanta.

Overall, it had been a shitty day.

A few days later, we got the autopsy report from the Cobb County coroner. The cause of death was suffocation. The time of death was sometime on Friday (she was last seen alive at two p.m. Friday). The body had not started to decompose due to the low temperatures and the insulation of the leaves covering her. These conditions preserved her body from the time of death until we found her on Tuesday. Apparently, she was killed at about the same time we were assigned to the case. This helped us somewhat with our guilt and the feelings that we could have prevented her death. The autopsy report confirmed she had been raped.

We had already placed a nationwide lookout for Larry Ronald Davis; teletypes were sent to every law enforcement agency in the

United States. His details were entered into the NCIC (National Crime Information Center) computer. Everything was done, all of the legwork—the nuts and bolts stuff. We turned over the entire case to Cobb County. All they had to do was to sit back and wait for the fuck to surface.

Meanwhile, other murders, rapes, and aggravated assaults were occurring in the city. We were assigned our share. For Wade and me, the Susan Doty case was officially history; it was Cobb County's responsibility. But personally, I could not turn my mind away from the case. I was haunted by the look in Susan Doty's eyes when she was turned over.

I fantasized that I would find Davis, even though I was sure he had left the state. During down time, while working other cases, Wade and I looked for Susan Doty's car, checking shopping center parking lots, apartment complex parking lots, desolate areas—everywhere we went, we looked for a 1968 Pontiac LeMans, dark green, black vinyl top, with the license tag, Georgia 1-13766.

To this day, there are six sets of numbers etched in my brain, besides the birthdays of my wife and children. Numbers I'll never forget. My birthday, my social security number, my wedding anniversary, my US Army serial number, my original Atlanta PD badge number, and Susan Doty's car tag number, 1-13766. I knew my chances of ever seeing that last six-digit number were slim to none.

A month had passed when Lieutenant Strickland received a telephone call from a detective in San Antonio, Texas. "Did we want Larry Ronald Davis for murder?" No, they didn't have him, but his girlfriend, Betty Jean Smith, was at the San Antonio Police Department, making inquiries about Davis—if he was wanted, and if so, why. That was the beginning of the end for Larry Ronald Davis.

Betty Jean Smith and Larry Ronald Davis left Cobb County on the Saturday after Susan Doty was murdered. They left Georgia, driving Susan's LeMans across Alabama, Mississippi, Louisiana, Texas, crossing into Mexico. They spent a few days in Matamoros, Mexico, then re-entered Texas, going as far west as San Antonio. They rented an apartment in a duplex, where they stayed for a few weeks. One night, while washing clothes at a laundromat, Betty Jean decided to call the couple she had been living with back in Georgia. She was stunned to learn that Davis was the subject of a nationwide manhunt. When she returned to the apartment, she confronted him with the accusation; he denied it, reminding her that her friend in Atlanta didn't like him, and suggesting she was trying to make trouble, driving a wedge between Betty Jean and him.

Betty Jean Smith thought about the past month that she and Davis had been on the move. She wanted to believe Davis, but she was beginning to suspect that he was a liar, a thief, and God knew what else. Then it hit her. The name on the credit cards Davis had been using since they left Georgia was "Susan Doty." The next morning, after Davis had left the apartment, Betty Jean went to police headquarters in San Antonio, which prompted the phone call to Lieutenant Strickland in Atlanta. Betty Jean never returned to the apartment. She flew back to Atlanta that evening.

When Larry Ronald Davis got home that night, San Antonio police and the FBI were waiting for him. He pulled into the driveway in Susan Doty's car, and although he had a loaded revolver in his possession, he surrendered without resistance.

Atlanta Police Superintendent of Detectives Clinton Chafin laid it out for me. "Cobb police are going to fly to San Antonio and return Davis in Susan Doty's car. Either you or Hagin can go with them, but not both of you. Let me know which of you will go." Cobb County picked up the tab for one of the Atlanta detectives. The City of Atlanta would not spend another dime; the case belonged to Cobb County. We both wanted very badly to go. Wade and I flipped a coin. He won the toss.

Two one-way Atlanta, Georgia to San Antonio, Texas airline tickets were purchased for Atlanta Detective, J.W. Hagin, and Cobb County Police Lieutenant, Harold Davis. Cobb County Sheriff, Kermit Sanders, flew out a couple of days later and joined them for the drive back. For what little Sheriff Sanders contributed to the case, Wade thought I should have occupied that fourth seat in the car. No one knew more about that case than Wade and I, and I was a good interviewer, especially scumbags like Davis.

Larry Ronald Davis waived extradition proceedings (the legal process required in transferring the custody of an arrested subject from one state to another) and was turned over to the three from Georgia. Susan Doty's car bore a Texas tag, which Davis admitting stealing. He directed Wade and Lt. Davis to a gas station, and to the field behind the station, where Wade recovered the bent Georgia license tag that belonged on Susan Doty's car. Wade restored the Georgia license on the LeMans, and the four started the long drive home.

Sunday was my day off, and I was at home when the phone rang. It was Wade. They were in Alabama, expecting to arrive at the Cobb County Jail within the hour. It was a cold, rainy, dreary January day, a day you're usually glad to be home, warm and dry. The weather was the farthest thing from my mind an hour later, as I stood in the cold rain at the entrance to the jail. They drove past me and stopped inside. That's when I first saw Georgia tag number 1-13766. I had thought about that car and tag number every day, many times each day, for over a month. And there it was. I didn't have to imagine it now; I was looking at it.

Wade pulled me aside to give me a quick run down. During the two-day drive back to Atlanta, Davis had talked freely, bragging about how he charmed the ladies, proud of his ability to use people for his purposes. But he became evasive when asked about Susan Doty. He said he was a heroin addict and claimed he did not know what Wade was talking about when Wade asked about Susan Doty. From time to time, Wade would ask, in one way or another, about Susan Doty. Davis clammed up at the mention of her name. Wade thought they would have learned about Susan Doty if I had been on the drive with them.

I wanted an opportunity to talk to Davis before he was processed into the Cobb County jail. Sheriff Sanders gave me the okay to question Davis. Sanders provided an office; present were Wade; Lieutenant Harold Davis, Cobb County; GBI (Georgia Bureau of Investigation) agent, Roy Jones (he had been working on the Doty case with Cobb County); Larry Ronald Davis—and me.

I was seated behind a desk, conducting the interview. The others sat silently against the walls around the room. From the start, Davis was cocky, talking freely about other things, but not saying anything in response to my questions about Susan Doty. I told him to get up from the chair, stand up, and look at what I wanted to show him. He stood up.

"These are pictures of Susan Doty, taken on the day we found her," I told him as I spread a dozen 8"x10" color photos across the desk. He glanced at them, and then quickly looked away.

"So what, it doesn't prove a fuckin' goddamn thing," he sneered. He kept glancing at one photo in particular. It was the photo of Susan Doty after the crime lab technicians rolled her onto her back, her eyes lifelessly staring into the camera. That look seemed to captivate him, the same look that caused me anguish when I first saw her.

He tried not looking at her; he turned his head away, looked back at the photo, away, back, away, back. He stood with his arms folded across his chest, each hand clutching the other arm, rocking slowly back and forth on his feet. He started scratching his arms, still rocking, but looking away less—staring at the photo of her. He said nothing, but continued rocking, raking his arms, fingernails digging into his skin, deep enough to draw blood. Tears welled in his eyes; a solitary tear rolled down his cheek. Larry Ronald Davis was crying.

At that emotional and critical moment, when time seemed to stop, when the only sound in the room, besides the floor creaking as Davis rocked, was five hearts pounding, that's when Agent Roy Jones interrupted for no fucking reason. He asked Davis, "Now, Ronnie, how in the world did you manage to throw that pocketbook that far? It must have been fifty feet in from the path."

What the fuck Jones was talking about? What the fuck did finding that pocketbook have to do with Davis admitting he killed Susan Doty? (Jones was referring to Susan Doty's pocketbook, which he found during his search of a Cobb County dump; the only way Davis could have gotten it there was to toss it from a distance.) Nothing about the pocketbook was relevant to the interrogation. To bring it up at that moment was worse than stupid; it was a meaningless interruption that gave Davis the opportunity to regain his composure.

I had interviewed more than three hundred suspects and witnesses and developed a keen sense of when they were about to turn the corner from avoiding the truth to revealing it. Davis' rocking, his clutching his arms, digging his nails in, his tears, his fixation on the photograph, it all meant he was about to spill his guts. He wanted to talk about it; he needed to talk about what he'd done to Susan Doty. Jones cut Davis off from that moment and wasn't smart enough to realize it. Davis was smart enough to take the opportunity to recover, and never become trapped in the moment again.

I gathered up the photos from the desk, angry, then enraged and disappointed, then frustrated, depressed, and disgusted. I looked at Detective Wade Hagin, and a stunned expression came to his face when I asked, "Are you ready to go?" He nodded his head; we walked out of the room without a word to anyone.

I haven't seen or spoken to Larry Ronald Davis since we left that room. Davis never provided the few crucial missing pieces that revealed how, why, and where he killed Susan Doty.

When the case was about to go to trial, those of us familiar with the facts were sure it was a death penalty case. The district attorney announced he was going for the death penalty. It was expected to be a media event. In his initial appearance, Davis stunned the court when he entered guilty pleas to all five charges—murder, rape, kidnapping, robbery, and auto theft. If accepted by the judge, the maximum sentence would be life in prison. According to Georgia law, the death penalty can be imposed only upon the recommendation of a jury. The judge and district attorney were not going to let Davis off the hook. They wanted to "try him and fry him."

Susan's parents were in the courtroom. They pleaded with the court to extend mercy to the defendant. After several private meetings with the Dotys, the judge and district attorney agreed to abide by the wishes of Susan's parents. Cobb County Superior Court Judge Luther Hames made the following comments to a crowded and hushed courtroom, which included the entire twenty-three member grand jury:

"The greatest single, pressing need of our community, state, and nation today, is the right of our people to be secure in their persons and property.

"The paramount duties of government, written as a basic premise in the preamble of our Constitution and cited and followed by our highest courts since our earliest days, are the protection of life, limb, and property of our citizens.

"Every person has a right to walk the streets in safety. No one should be able to deprive any citizen of this right. Your wife, your husband, son, or daughter ought to be safe in attending church, shopping in a supermarket, filling station, or a bank.

"Even more sacred is the home, and likewise, more perilous is an attack on members of a family in the sanctity of the home. In the past, we have conducted several trials in which decent women, mothers, have not only been raped in their own homes, but have had visited upon them the most perverse, sadistic, and violent treatment.

"It has been said that it is the proud boast of the Anglo-Saxon that a man's home is his castle, protected by the omnipresent and omnipotent, although invisible, spirit of the law—protection in a land where the people are truly free, more invincible than armed men on a granite wall.

"I charge you that it is our great shame that this is an empty statement and a vain boast when we cannot give our people assurance that their person or property will not be violated when they use the streets or occupy their homes.

"Several crimes against the person authorize the imposition of capital punishment. I have no quarrel with those who, because of conscientious scruples, will not accept this penalty as one of the punishments provided by law.

"The punishment of criminal offenses is a matter that addresses itself to the wisdom of the legislature, and not to the courts. The courts are only concerned with whether the standards of law are met, factually. Since 1964, there has been no execution in the State of Georgia.

"This has occurred due to the fact that the executive department of the state government has not seen fit to carry out the mandate of the legislature and the verdicts of juries and sentences of the courts; in fact, there has been an executive repeal of the acts of the General Assembly and a reversal of the verdicts of the juries by such action.

"This same area has also seen long delay occasioned by successive appeals, and this, along with the failure of the executive department to follow the law, has caused the practice to grow up that life sentences with a possibility of parole at the end of seven years are negotiated and pleas of guilty entered as a matter of course.

"Thus, the prosecution is emasculated, the certainty of punishment is deferred, and those whose crimes are of such heinous nature that all of society is offended, are able to escape.

"Society demands that crime shall be punished and criminals warned, and the false humanity that starts and shudders when the axe of justice is ready to strike is a dangerous element for the peace of society.

"We have had too much of this mercy. It is not true mercy. It only looks to the criminal, but we must insist upon mercy to society, upon justice to the poor woman whose blood cries out against her murderers. That criminals go unpunished is a disgrace to our civilization, and we have reaped the fruits of it in the frequency in which bloody deeds occur.

"Anyone who would underestimate or ignore the crime problem should be roused from his complacency by the fact that the average man or woman today is in greater danger than ever before of becoming the victim of a serious crime.

"It has been said that the hottest places in hell are reserved for those who maintain positions of neutrality in moments of great crisis.

"We are now in the midst of a criminal crisis. The time has come to choose sides. Those who don't join the fight to preserve law and order may, in time, be witness to its destruction."

Looking at Davis, Judge Hames continued, "Contrary to my desires, against my conscience, and swayed only by the request of the parents of Susan Doty, I have decided to accept the guilty plea.

"I have no power under the law to pronounce anything more severe than life imprisonment. I hereby sentence you to a life sentence on each of the four charges, whereby life imprisonment is the maximum allowable—these sentences to be served consecutively."

In the Cobb County jail, shortly after being sentenced to four life terms, the media interviewed Larry Ronald Davis. His only concern was getting out of prison after serving seven years, at which time he would be eligible for parole.

"I'm not sorry for anything I did," Davis told reporters. "Man, when the heat is on you, you have to do what you have to do. I sure came out of this thing in damn good shape, didn't I? You know, I can be back on the streets in just seven years. I have a television set in my cell. I've seen those TV newsmen talking about me. Damn! People must think I'm really weird. I'm not the bad guy they think I am. Haven't you ever felt like killing someone? There's just one little motion between thinking it and doing it. That's all, man; there's a little murder in everyone. Look at old Luther over there. Think of all the people he's sentenced to death. He still manages to sleep at night, and believe me, I'll sleep, too."

Asked by a reporter if the situation were the same and he had to relive it, would the girl still be dead?

"Hell, I don't know. It would be about 50-50, I guess. I would do exactly the same thing again. I was backed up and had to get loose."

He told a vague story while in jail awaiting trial—of tying and gagging Susan Doty and putting her in the trunk to keep her quiet, and when he checked on her several hours later, she was dead. When questioned, he said, "Yeah, I told them that. That was my court story— what I was going to tell in court. That's not the way it really happened, but I'm afraid if I tell you how it happened, it might hurt my chances for parole. I would have let her live if—" Davis stopped short. When prodded by reporters to continue, he said, "Oh, man, you're trying to trick me to get me to tell you about the killing again. I don't want to hurt my chances for parole. I don't like it in here, you know? That was the only thing I could have done at the time. I have a very strong sense of preservation. You gotta look out for number one first, you know?

"I left that morning with the intention of stealing a car; that was all. Then all this happened. If there had been any possible way to let her go, I would have let her go. I didn't want to kill anybody, but things just worked out that way; I didn't have any choice. All I can think about or that I'm concerned about right now is getting that parole in seven years. By that time, old Lester Maddox will be back in (the governor's) office and he's pretty good about letting prisoners out. People will have had enough of that Jimmy Carter by then. With my luck, old Luther Hames will be a member of the pardons and parole board when my case comes up for review," David laughed. "I guess I'm a little sorry that girl is dead. I didn't start out for her to die. Her kicking off like that sure didn't help me, either."

Superior Court Judge Luther Hames and Cobb County District Attorney Ben Smith, both sent strong recommendations to the Georgia State Pardons and Parole Board that Larry Ronald Davis never be considered for parole. A member of the pardons and parole board stated, "There is a legal possibility that this man might someday be paroled. But don't make any bets on it."

Susan Doty was a young woman with everything to live for. She was bright, successful, attractive, and well liked by all who knew her. She was planning to be married. Her future looked rosy, but a psychopathic killer cut that future short. Susan Doty was at the wrong place, at the wrong time. As for Larry Ronald Davis, the world would be a better place if he had never been born.

Since his confinement, Larry Ronald Davis has served thirty-three years, and is still serving the first of his life sentences. He has never been considered for parole. Since the day I walked out of the interview room in the Cobb Country jail, I never again saw GBI agent, Roy Jones, and I don't want to.

Hearing, Not Listening

Sometimes we hear, but we don't listen to what we are hearing. There are subtleties and nuances we miss when we are not listening to what we are hearing. And sometimes, someone may be trying to say something in a roundabout, evasive way, and we miss it—something that could have a significant bearing on the content of what we are hearing.

Wade and I were guilty of not listening to what we were hearing one Saturday afternoon. We were working evening watch homicide, and had just reported for duty when the front desk of the detective department called us; there was a guy who wanted to speak to a homicide detective. We were about to leave for Grady Hospital on an aggravated assault case, so we allowed ourselves a few brief moments to talk to this guy on our way out.

He told us that as he was leaving his rooming house on Cherokee Avenue, near Grant Park, he noticed a man lying in the hallway, and it looked like there might be something wrong with him. When we asked why he didn't call the police from there, he said he was on the way to work and didn't have time. But on the way to work, he thought about it more, and wanted to let someone know. He was going past police headquarters and decided to stop to report what he saw.

He gave us the address of the rooming house. We called communications and requested they dispatch a patrol car to that location on a signal 47 (person down). We were running late and didn't want to be any later, so we did what we thought we should, and tried to get rid of him. He gave us his name, Pierre Renaud, and said he was a chef at a French restaurant on Peachtree Road in Buckhead. We politely thanked him for stopping in, left for Grady Hospital, and promptly forgot about it.

At the hospital a short time later, we received a call from our boss, Homicide Lieutenant Helms. The patrol officer had called in and advised that the man at the rooming house was dead and had been shot several times. Lieutenant Helms told us to disregard the aggravated assault case at Grady, he'd send another team, and instructed us to go to Cherokee Avenue to handle the homicide.

Talking to residents of the rooming house, we learned that the victim did not reside there; he was a regular visitor of a woman resident, and they had been dating "on and off." We also learned that Pierre (the chef) and the woman resident were dating "off and on," as well.

After processing the scene, we went to the Buckhead restaurant to have a talk with Monsieur Renaud. Every table in the restaurant was occupied, and there were people waiting to be seated. It was a busy Saturday night at what apparently was a fine restaurant. We located the owner, identified ourselves, and stated our business. The owner told us we'd have to wait to talk to Pierre. It was a full house: he couldn't pull Pierre out of the kitchen.

We advised the owner that we had to speak to Mr. Renaud now. The owner became irate as Wade and I marched past him toward the kitchen. We lead Pierre to a rear hallway, and before we uttered the first syllable advising him of his rights, he blurted that he shot the victim. He showed us the hallway wall, a hole as though a fist had punched through it, and told us that was where he hid the pistol he used to shoot the victim. He said he carried it with him at all times, but at work, he left it in that hole, resting on a brace just out of sight. We recovered the pistol, put cuffs on Mr. Renaud, and took him out the back door.

The owner witnessed all this, irate, not concerned that his chef had just killed a man. When we got Mr. Renaud to the homicide office, we formally advised him of his rights. He signed a waiver that he had been advised of his rights and made a written confession. It was as we figured: he, the dead man, and the woman were involved in a love triangle. He was leaving for work, saw the visitor coming down the hallway from the woman's room, and got so angry he shot him. We asked why he was carrying the pistol. He said he carried it because it made him feel safe, out so late at night after the restaurant closed. His defense was that when he saw the woman's other lover, he shot him in a fit of jealous rage. The courts recognize this as "hot blood," to distinguish from premeditated murder. The Georgia State Crime Lab test-fired his pistol, confirming that the bullets taken from the body of the victim had been fired from that gun.

It didn't take Wade and me long to realize that when Pierre had come looking for a homicide detective; he'd wanted to turn himself in. Wade and I were hearing him, but we were not listening. We were fortunate that after we gave Pierre the brush-off at the station, he didn't have second thoughts about confessing and hop a plane for Paris.

We often wonder who is doing the cooking at the Georgia State Prison, where Pierre Renaud is serving his time.

Willie "Chain Gang" Williams

They had been out on their first date this balmy, April, Saturday evening. They had eaten dinner out and returned to her apartment on Coronet Way in northwest Atlanta for dessert. He was on the couch in the living room; she was brewing coffee in the kitchen. It was about nine o'clock. As he watched her from the living room, he thought he was lucky to have met this pretty, twenty-three-year-old blond girl. She had a pleasant personality and a terrific figure.

The kitchen door led to the parking lot. Someone knocked. She opened the door; there stood a Negro male in his early twenties, a gun pointed in her face. He ordered her back into the kitchen and followed her, closing the door behind him. Seeing her date on the couch in the living room, the intruder threatened to shoot him if he moved.

The intruder, Larry Glass, stood in the hallway, where he could cover the white boy in the living room, and see the bedroom where he had told the woman to go and take off her clothes. She undressed, down to her bra and panties, and paused, but Glass pointed the gun at her. "The rest of it, too, bitch." She stood naked in the bedroom doorway as a second Negro male advanced through the kitchen door. He looked younger, in his teens.

She was ordered into the living room to parade naked in front of her date. "Oh, look at this; ain't she something?" Glass leered to his young companion. He probed at the terrified woman's body, looking at her date, "What about this, you honky mother-fucker? This is what you ain't gonna get tonight!" Glass then told the teenager to let the others in. The kitchen door opened again, and two more Negro males in their twenties entered. Willie "Chain Gang" Williams was one.

The woman was taken back into the bedroom and told to lie on the bed. They forced her date onto the floor of the walk-in closet in the hallway, told him to lie on his stomach, then hog-tied and gagged him. They kept roughing him up, slapping, punching, and kicking him. Willie "Chain Gang" Williams did most of it, saying, "This is what you deserve, you white mother-fucker, for all the years of hell I've been through."

In the bedroom, they raped the woman, forcing her to commit sodomy with each of them. Although all four committed illegal acts on both victims, Larry "Pie Face" Glass and Willie "Chain Gang" Williams, seemed to be the leaders. They brutalized their victims more than the other two did. They hurt, terrified, tormented, degraded, and humiliated their captives.

After Glass raped her, he sat on her chest and forced himself into her mouth. "You like this, don't you? Show me you like it. Stick it down your throat!" When it was "Chain Gang's turn, he raped her.

"You like this, bitch? You never had a black dick in you before." He grabbed her head, jammed himself into her mouth, and ejaculated. She was gagging, but he would not release his grip on her head. She thought she was going to suffocate. He was filthy, giving off a foul odor. The stench made her nauseous; she felt she was going to vomit.

Each man raped the woman on the bed, and the other three beat her date in the closet, then they ransacked the apartment, picking out and stacking things they intended to take with them when they left. They gathered nearly everything she owned. They emptied her closets and drawers of her clothes and jewelry. The television, stereo, and small appliances were placed on the floor at the kitchen door. They even stripped the walls of pictures and a wall clock.

"Pie Face" and "Chain Gang" were in the closet, arguing over which of them was going to kill the boyfriend. Both wanted to do it. "Chain Gang" presented the stronger argument, telling Glass, "I'm gonna do it man, cause the only thing I like better than fuckin' white girls is killin' white boys!"

Hog-tied and helpless, the condemned man was convinced he was about to die. With the gag in his mouth, he couldn't even plead for his life. They hadn't yet agreed on who was to be the executioner, when the two in the bedroom asked what to do with the woman.

Before deciding her fate, "Pie Face" and "Chain Gang" went to the bedroom to get one more piece of her. She was now bleeding from her vagina. "Pie Face" told her, "This pussy is so good, we might have to take you with us." She knew if they took her, she would never get away alive. She was afraid that "Chain Gang" would shoot her before they left. "Pie Face" began to tie her up with some pantyhose. One of them found her car keys and asked if they were to the Mustang parked outside. She nodded yes, and was left hog-tied and gagged on the bed.

Both victims, each hog-tied and gagged, one in the bedroom, the other in the closet heard them as they carried out most of her belongings, loading them into their car and hers. They heard the cars drive off.

Not moving until he was sure they were gone, the date worked himself free of his bonds. Still in the closet, he listened, and then peered out cautiously to be sure they were gone. He went into the bedroom and removed her gag. She started screaming hysterically. Unable to untie the pantyhose, he went into the kitchen, got a knife, and cut her loose.

He called the police; she called her father. The patrolman arrived, realized what had happened, and called for a Homicide car. Wade and I got the call.

We went to work, canvassing the area for witnesses, searching inside and outside for evidence, and did all the preliminary stuff that must be done at a crime scene. ID went over the scene, taking photographs, lifting fingerprints and collecting hair, semen, and blood samples. The victims were transported to Grady Hospital where they both received medical treatment.

They furnished us with very good descriptions of the four rapists. We immediately broadcast "lookouts" with those descriptions, as well as the description and tag number of her car. They described to us the gun, which we figured was a black .22 caliber revolver.

Later, at the homicide office, the woman's date gave a detailed, written statement of what happened. Still traumatized and upset, the woman was not able to provide us with the details we needed. She provided those details in her statement the following day. Her parents took her to their home; her date returned to his apartment. It was almost dawn by the time Wade and I finished the paperwork. (We had been working the evening watch). We called it a night and went home.

The victim's car was found a couple of days later, abandoned in the street several miles from the Coronet Way apartment. Many prints were lifted. After eliminating the prints from the list of people that had been in the car in recent weeks, we were left with prints not accounted for. Our next step was to find those whose prints matched those from the car.

Two months earlier, in February, a Negro male had walked into a small "Mom and Pop" grocery store on Simpson Road in northwest Atlanta and asked the owner, Ms. Iber Wood, a Negro female, forty-seven years old, for change in return for two one-dollar bills.

As she opened the cash register, he shot her in the mouth. Although wounded severely, she reached for the revolver hidden behind the counter, attempting to shoot back. She never got off a shot; he fired twice more at close range. The assailant fled, someone heard the shots, found her, and called the police.

Wade and I responded; we spoke with Ms. Wood at Grady. She could not furnish us with any details except for a vague description of her assailant. She was responsive and alert, although she had difficulty talking due to the gunshot wound to her mouth. Her vital signs were good, and the prognosis, according to the doctors, was favorable.

She explained that when she opened the cash register, he shot her because he was going to rob her, which made the case attempted robbery, not an aggravated assault. It was an aggravated assault, but when robbery is the motive for the assault, the jurisdiction falls with the robbery squad, not the homicide squad, so we turned the investigation over to the robbery detectives.

The following day, while at the grand jury on other cases, Wade and I learned that Ms. Iber Wood had died. Her death made it a homicide, and therefore, our case. All we had for evidence was a couple of .22 caliber bullets taken from her body, a vague description of her killer, and robbery as the possible motive.

The following month, sixty-year-old Bernard Rosenfeld was involved in a one-car traffic accident one afternoon on Marietta Street, near downtown Atlanta. A witness reported that he saw Rosenfeld's car jump the curb, knock down a fire alarm box and a bus stop sign, travel another 200 feet back in the street, and jump the curb again, knocking down parking meters and crashing into the front of a building. Mr. Rosenfeld arrived by ambulance at Grady Hospital where he was pronounced DOA.

Rosenfeld was the owner of a steel supply company located on Jones Avenue, near Marietta Street. His office was closed for business that Saturday, but Mr. Rosenfeld was there, alone, finishing some paperwork. He locked up about two p.m., went to his car in the parking lot, and left. He drove around the corner onto Marietta Street, where he crashed into the building.

An autopsy was performed to determine the cause of death and the reason for the accident. No one expected the autopsy finding: a bullet entered Rosenfeld's chest just below his collarbone, piercing his heart. He had been shot.

Homicide Detectives RW Watson and WF Perkins were assigned to the case. Mr. Rosenfeld was known to keep fifty dollars in cash on him at all times. He had less than a dollar in change in his possession when he arrived at the hospital. All Watson and Perkins had to go on was a .22 caliber bullet recovered from the body, and robbery as a possible motive.

In the fall of the previous year, the nude body of a twenty-three-year-old white female, Susan Kathryn Herald, was found in a wooded area in the northwest section of Atlanta. She had been shot twice in the head and once in the buttocks with a .22 caliber revolver. It appeared as though her body had been dumped where it was discovered. The autopsy revealed that she had been repeatedly raped. The only physical evidence was three .22 caliber slugs recovered from her body. No suspects, no witnesses, no leads.

"I'm gonna break up that marriage"

Wade and I handled our share of cases, and like every other homicide team, we worked multiple cases simultaneously. Wade and I, the only team working the morning watch, returned to the squad room near the end of our shift to complete each night's paperwork.

Orville Gaines, the police beat reporter for the *Atlanta Journal*, made the homicide squad room his first stop of the day, starting at six a.m. He got all the gory details of the nightly blood bath as we made our reports. Because of this reporter's eagerness, and perhaps because more of the gore happened at night, "Hagin and Goldhagen" got a lot of press coverage. The overload of publicity did not sit well with Superintendent of Detectives Clinton Chafin. Whether it was grumbling from our colleagues, or that he just didn't like reading our names in the newspaper so much, he wanted to put a stop to it.

"I'm going to break up that marriage," announced Chafin to Lieutenant BJ Stecher, as he put the newspaper down on his desk. Break us up he did. In a few days, Wade was working with Detective WF Perkins; my new partner was Detective WR "Woody" King.

Woody King "made his bones" as a vice detective for a couple of years before transferring to homicide. I wasn't happy about losing Wade as a partner. We had been through so much together that we were like brothers. But it was done, and I had a new partner—Woody King, who would have been my choice over all the other homicide detectives.

Atlanta had begun to crack down on the city's massage parlors, which were really fronts for prostitution. Woody, acting as a customer, getting the evidence, did more than any one else to get rid of the blight of massage parlors.

My attitude changed after the "break up." When Wade and I were partners, whenever a call came in for a homicide car, one of us would grab for the radio and respond. Now, still seething and smoldering, I was not so quick to answer, and discouraged King, telling him, "The more you do, the less you're appreciated. They don't give a shit, so let someone else do it. Fuck them!" It took some time for me to get over the change.

The Break in the "Unrelated" Rapes and Murders

In May, about a month after the rape of the woman on Coronet Way, Wade and Detective WF Perkins responded to a signal 49/44 (rape/robbery), at a residence in an upscale area of Atlanta. That case provided us with the first break in what appeared to be an unrelated series of brutal rapes and murders.

A white female, in her late thirty's, early forties, was home alone one afternoon. The front door bell rang. When she opened the door, three Negro males pushed their way in. One had gun and threatened to shoot her if she resisted. They slapped her around and dragged her through the house, looking for money, jewelry, anything of value.

The leader of the trio, the one with the gun, told the other two to "look around for stuff." He was going to "take this rich bitch in the bedroom and show her that black is beautiful." With the gun to her head, her life threatened, she was raped and sodomized. Then he told the other two that they could "fuck the white whore" if they wanted. They each raped and sodomized her.

Her two teenage children were due home soon. She said she prayed the three Negroes would find what they wanted, take it, and leave. That's what happened. Finished with her, taking what loot they found, they loaded up her 1964 Oldsmobile, and drove off with it. Her children arrived home shortly after the rapists left. She felt her prayers had been answered.

Detectives Hagin and Perkins did all of the preliminary procedures, which included placing a lookout for three Negro males in the victim's stolen Oldsmobile. Later that night, at the homicide office, they were finishing the paperwork, getting ready to go off-duty, when the phone rang. It was a deputy sheriff from Douglas County, a suburb twenty miles west of Atlanta. They had found the Oldsmobile wanted in the rape and robbery earlier in the day; they were searching for the occupants in the woods near where the car was abandoned. Hagin and Perkins didn't go home; they ran out the door to Douglas County. When they arrived, the Douglas County Sheriff briefed them.

Douglasville Police Officer, Walter Spinks, saw a car run a stop sign. He stopped the car, and while walking toward it, observed that four Negro males occupied it. He asked the driver for his license. Instead of his license, the driver produced his gun and shot at Officer Spinks four times. Spinks went down, and the Oldsmobile sped away. A passing motorist witnessed all this and determined to help, followed the fleeing car, hoping to get sight of the tag number. The car turned off the main road onto a dead-end side street. As the car slid to a stop, each of the doors was thrown open, and the four occupants bailed out and ran into the woods. The Douglas County Sheriff's Department received calls that a policeman was shot and complaints of a disturbance at the end of the dead-end street.

Sirens interrupted the quiet of the crickets and frogs in the woods. Flashing blue lights lit up the darkness as police cars from several jurisdictions swarmed into the area. It was sealed off, and the search began. Officer Spinks was taken to the hospital, seriously wounded, but alive. Douglas County police checked the license tag on the abandoned car, and it came up stolen from Atlanta, wanted in connection with a rape investigation. It was a massive, multi-jurisdictional manhunt—two hundred law enforcement officers and six bloodhounds.

I was off duty that night, at my home in Douglas County, when I received a phone call informing me of what was going on and where. I arrived at the scene and flashed my ID, which permitted me to enter the sealed, restricted areas. In the dark confusion, I didn't see Wade or Perkins. I spotted Douglas County Sheriff Earl Lee, who I knew previously from cases we had worked together. I stayed with him while I was there. When he was called away, I returned home.

Ordinarily, I would never have left. This was what my job was all about, the work I loved doing. But it was only weeks after "my marriage with Wade" was broken up by Chief of Detectives Chafin. I was still angry, still wondering why the hell I should break my ass working so hard when a boss could punish you for doing a good job.

Three of the suspects were discovered, each huddled, trying to appear part of the wooded background. Each had the look of the condemned on his sweating black face. They expected someone would produce a rope, that they would be lynched, like in the old days. This wasn't Atlanta; this area was still rural, and one of their police officers had just been shot. No one knew if the officer was alive or dead. The cops surrounding them looked like they were about to inflict some bad shit on their prisoners.

Each quickly assessed his situation, independently arriving at the same conclusion—survival. They were anxious to give up the shooter. They said that the one who had not yet been found was the shooter, the leader of their gang. They knew him as "Chain Gang"; there were six in their gang, and he took them out in packs of three or four to rob people.

The three suspects were taken to jail for more detailed questioning later. "Chain Gang" was still missing. The search for him continued throughout the night. The cops did not grumble, did not bitch; they made no complaints. This search was for the man who shot one of one of them. Every cop wanted to be the one to find the shooter.

Listening to what the three suspects had to say, it became apparent that in their attempt to save their own asses, they were revealing that they had been involved in a lot more than this case.

As dawn broke, the sheriff's department received a telephone call from a man who lived within the search area. He was excited and said there was someone lying on the ground at the side of his house. The search was over; Willie "Chain Gang" Williams was found with a gunshot would to the head, his own .22 caliber revolver lay on the ground next to him. It was assumed he shot himself as the noose tightened and the search area shrank.

He died the following day at the hospital, never regaining consciousness. The bullet taken from his head was fired from the gun found next to him.

The next day, the three suspects admitted to participating in "a whole bunch" of violent crimes with "Chain Gang," their leader. They furnished us with the identities of the other gang members, one known to them as "Pie Face." They told of the grocery store lady and the steel company man, each shot by "Chain Gang" in the act of robbing them. They told us of about fifteen armed robberies that the six of them had committed under the leadership of "Chain Gang."

They specifically told of the time "Chain Gang," "Pie Face," Willie Morris, and Freddy Caldwell went into an apartment on Coronet Way, raped a blond girl, and beat up her boyfriend. And of the day before, when they went into a rich white lady's house and raped and robbed her, stole her car, and got caught in the woods. They told us of several other rape-robberies.

Willie "Chain Gang" Williams and his five followers had been on a violent crime spree, committing murder, rape, robbery, aggravated assault, and kidnapping.

One month prior to his death, Williams was stopped for a DUI; he was arrested and jailed. He had a .22 caliber revolver, which was taken from him and placed in evidence by the traffic officer, not to be returned because Williams was a convicted felon. That revolver was not the same revolver Williams used to shoot himself. Both of Williams' revolvers were sent to the state crime lab to be checked by ballistics. One was used to murder Ms. Iber Woods; the other was the murder weapon in the Bernard Rosenfeld killing.

The bullets recovered from Susan Kathryn Herald did not match either revolver. That case remains an unsolved homicide. The Herald case (although it was not assigned to me), has always bothered me. If Williams had two .22 caliber revolvers, why couldn't he have had a third? The Herald case had Williams written all over it—everything but the signature.

Douglasville Police Officer Walter Spinks survived, and after a long convalescence, he returned to duty. The bullets removed from him matched the gun found beside Williams' body.

All of those thugs had criminal records for one felony or another. Wade and I collected mug shots of them and took them to the woman who was raped in her apartment on Coronet Way. She immediately picked out Williams, Glass, Caldwell, and Morris, as the four who attacked and raped her. The prints lifted from the interior of her car and apartment matched the prints of these four.

Caldwell and Morris were in custody; Williams was dead. We still wanted "Pie Face." We learned where he was hiding, and that he usually got to sleep between four a.m. and five a.m., the best time for us to arrest him.

The arrest warrant for Larry Glass was signed, and arrangements were made for King and me, with Detectives WR Watson and GF Eskew, to meet in the homicide office at three a.m. We drifted in, bleary-eyed, from either being up late, or getting up too early. We got ourselves organized, and were ready a half hour later.

That's when Homicide Lieutenant CJ Strickland showed up. His sudden appearance surprised us; he never came to the office in the middle of the night. I was further stunned when he instructed the other three detectives to make the arrest and ordered me to remain in the office with him.

Curious, to say the least, I asked Strickland, "What's up? What's going on here? Pie Face is my case. Why am I not going with the others to make the arrest?"

He didn't respond. He tried to make small talk. I would not engage in it. I tried repeatedly to get him to tell me why he held me back. He still would not respond; he just sat there, staring into my face with a knowing smirk. I wondered, "What the fuck did he think he knew?" I paced the floor; he just sat. I interrupted my pacing to look at him, saying nothing. He looked back at me with a constant expression.

This went on for not quite an hour, until the other detectives returned with Larry "Pie Face" Glass. Lt. Strickland, my goddamn immediate superior, had denied me the goddamn opportunity of awakening Larry Glass with the barrel of my gun stuck in his ear.

Still pissed, angry, furious, I helped complete the paperwork. Lt. Strickland, without saying a word, got up and left. After we deposited Pie Face at the city jail, the four of us went for coffee. It was over coffee that I learned why Strickland had prevented me from going with them.

There had been talk that "Chain Gang" Williams was not the kind of thug who would commit suicide; it was highly unlikely for him to kill himself over going to prison. Prison had been a way of life for him, a second home. Because I was observed in the area of the search, because I was off duty, it was thought I might have had something to do with Williams' death. Lieutenant Strickland had actually done the right thing—he protected me from myself.

Larry "Pie Face" Glass and the rest of the gang were tried, convicted, and sentenced to life in prison.

The One Case We Didn't Clear

Because only two homicide detectives worked the morning watch, and Wade and I happened to be the two, we were involved in more cases than any other pair of homicide detectives during the long time we worked together. Homicide Detectives Hagin and Goldhagen were well known to the media, the public, and throughout the APD. Perhaps attention focused on us not only because of our activity in so many cases, but because we solved every homicide case assigned to us— every homicide case but one.

Most homicide cases are cleared by arrest, which means the perpetrator has been identified by the detectives and arrested. Homicide cases that are "solved" are those where the perpetrator has been identified but not apprehended, because he or she has not been located or is a fugitive. Hence, homicide cases can be "solved," but not "cleared by arrest."

You don't have to be Sherlock Holmes to figure out "who did it." Most homicides are not stranger-to-stranger. A family member, a friend, a neighbor, or a co-worker usually commits homicides— someone personally connected to the victim. Find the connections, determine which is the most logical trail, follow it closely, and the case is closed. You don't have to be Sherlock Holmes, but it may take a lot of work to find the connections and determine which trail to follow.

Things didn't evolve that way the night a call came in from a row of apartments on Holly Street. Local residents saw two boys break out the window of one of the apartments. Thinking they might be burglars, one of the residents fired a gun into the air, and the boys ran. After the suspects fled, the residents approached the apartment and noticed a strong odor coming through the broken window. They looked in and saw a man lying on a bed with what appeared to be blood around the area of his head. They called police.

Wade and I responded. We observed the body of a black male, lying face down on the bed, an apparent gunshot wound to his left temple. The medical examiner estimated that the man had been dead for three days. Papers on the body identified the victim as Robert Humphrey, a black male, forty years old, a/k/a "Baby Ray." He was a drug dealer, known by the APD Narcotics and Intelligence Units to be highly connected in the ranks of organized crime. He had a six-page rap sheet with arrests for various violent crimes, plus several arrests for drug trafficking.

Except for the window broken out by the boys, there was no sign of forced entry, and no sign of a struggle. Add that evidence to the gunshot wound to the temple, and our arithmetic equaled an execution.

The neighbors said they didn't know much about the victim; he kept mostly to himself. They showed us a motorcycle, parked in an alcove of the apartment building, and said belonged to him. It was chained to a pipe and had no license tag. The tank between the seat and the handlebars was locked. We forced it open and found two plastic zip lock bags filled with white powder. The Georgia State Crime Lab later determined that one of the bags contained almost pure heroin, worth about $200,000; the other bag contained quinine, a substance used to cut heroin for street sales.

Pinned to a calendar in the Holly Street kitchen was a printed notice:

"Brothers and Sisters:

Narcs and police are beginning the long, hot summer of busts.

If you see the narcs or police hassling or busting anyone, get the badge number, name, description, etc., and bring them to the Community Crisis Center.

Street Dealers:

The narcs are watching you. Go underground. Dealing in the streets will get you busted."

Humphrey was known to carry large sums of money. The last time he was arrested, the narcotics detectives found $32,000 in cash on him. There was no money in the apartment. Robbery might have been the motive, but more than likely it was a mob hit.

We worked it like any other homicide, but never did solve it. "Baby Ray" spoiled our perfect homicide clearance record. Every homicide assigned to Hagin and Goldhagen before "Baby Ray," and since, was cleared by the farm boy from South Georgia and the little Jewish kid from Brooklyn.

"I'm not chasing him up here!"

During the late 1960s, an architectural skyline was developed in downtown Atlanta. The crown jewel of the Peachtree corridor was the new Hyatt Regency Hotel. Designed by John Portman, the twenty-eight-story building had an interior atrium the same height. People came downtown just to walk through the front doors, look up, and gawk. On the roof was the "Polaris Lounge," a circular lounge that turned 360 degrees, very slowly. It was covered with blue Plexiglas that shown brightly night and day. It looked like a flying saucer to some, and stood out like a beacon to others.

During the 1970s, the building boom was on, and everywhere you looked a new structure was going up. It might not have been impressive in New York City, but it was looking good for Atlanta, Georgia. Huge buildings were sprouting, each taller than the previous one. Forty stories, fifty stories, up to seventy-story skyscrapers! The Polaris Lounge was being surrounded and swallowed. In time, the taller buildings would obscure the distinctive blue dome. One of the skyscrapers being built was the Equitable Building, forty stories high.

One night, while working the evening watch, I received a call for a homicide unit to meet a patrol car at Grady Hospital on a signal 47 (person injured). When I walked into the trauma room of the emergency clinic, the medical staff was working frantically on a black male with massive head and face injuries. He was unconscious, unable to communicate. He had been found in an empty parking lot, not far from downtown. He was on the ground behind a car, the trunk lid open—blood over the rear of the car and on the ground close to the car. The doctors were not optimistic that he would be able to talk, but I stood by, hoping.

I learned later that the victim was a construction worker, working downtown at the Equitable Building. I didn't want to poke around there until I learned more about him, what he was doing, and how he had been discovered there. Within a few days, he came out of his coma, was able to talk, and provided me with the following details:

Sometimes in the evenings, when he and his co-workers got off work, some of them would buy beer, go to an empty parking lot, drink, and shoot dice. The evening he was found, after work and gambling, most had gone from the lot, but he and two others remained. The two had a beef with him about something that happened earlier, during the gambling. He was at the rear of his car, and while opening his trunk lid, the argument got heated. One word led to another, and a fight started. One guy grabbed a jack handle from the open trunk and hit him in the face, knocking him down. They began beating him, nearly killing him. They left him lying there. He later identified both by name.

I was working by myself that morning, so I asked Homicide Detective, BL Neikirk, to go with me to the construction site to make the arrests; I had obtained the arrest warrants earlier.

At the Equitable Building construction site, we informed the construction superintendent why we were there and who we were looking for. He checked and confirmed that our suspects were indeed working at that time. The bad news was that one of them was working on the thirty-second floor, and the other was on the thirty-third. Neikirk and I put on hard hats and carried rolled-up blue prints. We were dressed in suits and didn't want to create suspicion before we approached them.

The building had been topped out to its full height, and the floors poured, but all the sides were open—just the superstructure of steel beams. The only way up was in an open cage lift on the outside of the building. Now, I don't consider myself a coward, far from it, but the moment that lift left ground level, my knees got weak. (I had trained for the Atlanta Fire Department at one time, before the APD, and could not complete the Fire Academy because I had a fear of heights.) At the thirty-second floor, I got off the lift, and Neikirk continued up to the next floor. A foreman got off with me and pointed out one of the suspects.

Upon approaching him, I identified myself and told him he was under arrest. My legs were like rubber. I thought to myself, "If he runs, he gets away. I'm not chasing him up here!" I was convinced that if I moved suddenly, just the slightest bit of motion, I would fall off that building. Fortunately, he did not resist, and we both went to the edge of the building to wait for the lift. I was trying to appear cool, calm, as if I did this shit every day, although I felt dizzy from the height. The wind whistling through the beams worsened my anguish. I was relieved when the lift came, even though it meant plunging toward the ground at what seemed supersonic speed. In the meantime, Neikirk had apprehended the other suspect, and the arrests were made without incident.

I've often been asked why we didn't have a couple of uniforms go up with us. I guess it was the way we did things back then. The same kind of arrest today would have brought out the SWAT Team.

I Passed the Test—Reverse Discrimination Failed Me

The promotional system in the Atlanta Police Department has been murky, vague, ambiguous, occasionally a farce, and at least once, scandalous. Herbert Jenkins' twenty-five-year reign as police chief, mostly under Mayor William B. Hartsfield and Mayor Ivan Allen, Jr., was a virtual dictatorship. Promotion to each level in the rank structure was given by a selection committee and promotional board comprised of one person—Chief Herbert T. Jenkins.

Politicians, business leaders, and others of influence would, on occasion, lobby for a family member, close friend, or protégé. These practices led to and fostered favoritism, cronyism, nepotism, and of course, racism. (The only blacks promoted were "good niggers that stayed in their place and didn't cause any trouble.") A cop without a mentor to lobby for his promotion got lost, buried in the ranks for his entire career, no matter how much he deserved promotion. (In New York police jargon, a person of higher rank who can work his influence for promotions, favored assignments, and off days is known as a "rabbi." Raised as a Jew in New York City, I found this use of "rabbi" curious, but never understood its origin.)

In 1970, Mayor Sam Massell, Jr., a white Jewish liberal, took the reins of city government. At the time, there were quite a few vacancies in the police department for the rank of sergeant. The mayor ordered a promotional test given to fill those vacancies. This time promised to be different—a competitive written test with promotions based on those results. The only prerequisite for the test was a minimum of five years service in the APD.

Several hundred applicants took the test; the results showed that thirty-four had made a passing grade. These thirty-four were placed on a list with the highest grade ranked number one, in descending order, according to grade scored. I was twenty-second; Wade Hagin was fourteenth.

Twenty-nine sergeant vacancies were to be filled through this promotional process. Chief Jenkins, who was still APD chief under Mayor Massell, sent the list to the mayor's office with the recommendation that the first twenty-nine on the list be promoted.

It seemed fair and simple enough. But it wasn't what it seemed. The mayor was committed to a 50/50 racial policy in the police department. All day-to-day operations, including assignments, off-days, and promotions had to be broken down on a 50/50 white/black basis.

Of the thirty-four applicants on the list, only five were black. It didn't take a genius to figure out what was going to happen—and it was not going to be good for me. The mayor rejected the list and sent it back to Chief Jenkins with instructions to make it racially equal.

Chief Jenkins met with his assistant chiefs to solve the problem. The chief made minor adjustments, adding a few blacks to the list, and resubmitted it to the Mayor, who promptly rejected it. This happened several times; each time the chief made additional minor adjustments, and each time it was rejected and returned with the same instructions— "It doesn't matter where they come from, but it will be racially balanced."

Finally, in June of 1971, nine months after the announcement of the original promotional list, the order was cut and promotions made. Twenty-nine new sergeants were promoted, fifteen white, fourteen black— effectively, the fifty-fifty racial balance had been achieved. In its wake were eighteen bitterly disappointed, pissed-off white cops, who had been dropped from the original list of thirty-four. I was one of them.

Those who were not part of the original thirty-four, but were nevertheless promoted either failed the test or didn't even bother to take it. These black policemen got promoted simply because they were black. Among the "minor adjustments" to the list were a few whites who were the well-connected beneficiaries of the good 'ol boy mentality, hence they managed to slither onto the list, bumping those who were higher on it.

Wade Hagin survived the cuts and was promoted to sergeant. He took his uniform out of mothballs and was assigned to the field. I remained a homicide detective. Louis Graham, a black homicide detective that took the test and failed it, but was promoted, remained in homicide, and became my sergeant. The 50/50 racial split stuck in my throat for a very long time. This was my first experience with the rationale that justified reverse discrimination—*affirmative action*. Mayor Sam Massell, the great liberal, crowed over his racially fair administration.

Except for eighteen frustrated white policemen, no one seemed to give a damn that failures were promoted instead of those who passed the test. Back then, no one went into court to challenge those actions. We just took it on the chin, complained and bitched to each other about the bastards who did this to us, and the public, and then went on about our work.

The promotional system returned to what it was before—you were "selected" for promotion—a system devoid of the hypocrisy of competitive exams, where test results were tailored so candidates who didn't score high enough could be promoted anyway.

This is not the end of the story. It gets bigger, worse, and more scandalous. More on that later.

The Age of Aquarius

The midtown section of Atlanta was a solid, tidy place; it was out of reach of the hustle and bustle of downtown, and its neat, clean, tree-lined streets made it feel like you were in a small town. There were older houses, well kept, and small businesses, well respected. Most families grew up and spent a lifetime in their homes in the midtown area. Many of the larger houses had been converted into boarding houses, where a cross-section of the city's working class lived. It was still a quiet, simple, pretty section of Atlanta.

Missing were the sounds and presence of young children. They had gone with the "white flight" during the sixties and early seventies—middle-class whites leaving Midtown for the expanding suburbs that surrounded Atlanta.

In 1968, a club/coffee house/hang-out, the Catacombs, opened in Midtown and ended its tranquility. The Catacombs came to life without much fanfare. It was located in the basement of an old house on Fourteenth and Peachtree Streets, smack in the middle of Midtown. It immediately began attracting the hippies that were trickling into Atlanta. The guru of these flower children was "Mother David." The hippies came, and with them, the counter-culture arrived in Atlanta.

They came to Midtown from all over, first by the dozens, then by the hundreds, and finally the thousands, arriving like locusts in a wheat field. The stretch of Peachtree Street from Third to Fourteenth Streets became known as "the Strip." The Strip was to Atlanta as Haight-Ashbury was to San Francisco and Greenwich Village was to New York City, and it was not unlike what was happening in other large cities across the country.

This increasing multitude looked strange to "the establishment," to "society." To the hippies, society sucked! They didn't care what the establishment thought about them; they were opposed to the establishment. To them, the war in Vietnam was wrong, and because they believed it was wrong, they felt they could express their opposition in any way that got attention and satisfied them—lawlessness, disregard for the rights and beliefs of others, drugs, and sexual freedom. "Make love, not war!" They protested what they thought they knew about, but they didn't know about themselves. They didn't realize they were outrageous, repulsive, obnoxious, antagonistic, and unbelievably filthy— some stunk like sewers.

The average policeman was working class, had little college education, if any, and was conservative, patriotic, and law-abiding. And like most policemen at that time, I had no tolerance for what we referred to as "that invading army of shit-eating maggots," who challenged our authority and mocked our laws and time-honored values. The police and the hippies were natural enemies.

Most of these "creatures" were on the streets in the Midtown area, congregating on the Strip, day and night. Their numbers never seemed to dwindle. The "pigs" and the "maggots" confronted each other, all day and all night long. There were hundreds of standoffs, most unreported.

The population of the Strip was comprised of runaways, drug dealers, bikers, bold young blacks, rednecks, street thugs, homosexuals, spectators, and police. Runaways, male and female, from all over the US, came to Atlanta and found their way to "the Strip." They were children, vulnerable on the harsh and cruel streets anywhere. They were raped, robbed, beaten, forced into prostitution; most became drug-craving zombies.

Illegal drugs flowed freely. Pushers could always be found with a supply that could "feed the multitudes." If you wanted some, the "Candy Man" had it, from marijuana to mind-altering hallucinogenics that harmed themselves and others. Drugs were smoked, swallowed, injected, snorted, and sniffed. "Turn on, tune out, get high; the older generation is going to blow up the whole goddamn world, anyhow, so fuck it, man!"

There were the bikers; in particular, "the Outlaws" motorcycle gang, which was to the East Coast what the Hell's Angels were to California. They roared in on their big Harley choppers; they bullied, intimidated, robbed, raped, and committed several murders.

Young blacks from metro-Atlanta came to the Strip in search of white hippie girls eager to share free love with anyone. At that time, blacks looking for sex from white girls still offended the sensibilities of white males, not the hippies so much as the bikers, the rednecks, and the cops—one of the causes of violence on the Strip.

Rednecks from the surrounding rural areas lined the fairway nightly to gawk at and mock the freaks. Farm boys and mountain men looked on in wide-eyed amazement, spitting tobacco juice, uttering an occasional "Golle-e-e-e!" or "Shazam!"

Street thugs, whether black, white, or red-necked, roamed the streets of Midtown, seizing any opportunity to prey upon the weakest of the hippies. The increasing homosexual population of the city lived mostly around Midtown. They were a large portion of the Midtown population, so much so, that the cops regularly asked whether "Atlanta had more faggots or maggots?"

The spectators were primarily tourists and conventioneers from big cities, like Chicago, New York City, Los Angeles, and Middle America—such as Nebraska, Kansas, and Iowa. They cruised the Strip, gawking from the safety of their vehicles—a stream of slow-moving rental cars, pickup trucks, BMWs, station wagons, and dented, rusted VW bugs. Atlanta's suburbanites had to come and look.

As the population on the Strip grew, illegal activities and incidents requiring police action increased. At first, there was one lone foot patrolman assigned to Peachtree and Tenth Streets, but before long, he needed a partner. They worked the foot beat until they were unable to maintain order on their own. Two more cops were added, but soon, the number of people roaming the Strip, and the illegal activities that came with their numbers overwhelmed them.

A stronger, more visible police presence was needed. The City of Atlanta rented an abandoned business on Peachtree Street, south of Tenth Street. A store-front police precinct was established in the center of the Strip. Because of its location, the cops named it, the "Pig Pen." The name was painted in huge letters across the windows, as was a giant caricature of Porky Pig in an Atlanta police uniform.

It was genius, a psychological victory over our antagonists. However, many cops didn't view it as genius; they saw it as insulting and demeaning. As one cop put it, "paint a pair of captain's bars on that pig, and see how fast it disappears!" Nevertheless, the APD pig remained, looking out over the flower children, who could not believe we would call ourselves the same name that enraged us when they used it. The Pig Pen was staffed with a lieutenant, two sergeants, and sixty-one patrolmen, more at night than during the day. If you liked action, you wanted this assignment.

Staff Photo—Marion Crowe

OFFICER GORDON GARNER III SURVEYS HIPPIE SURROUNDINGS AT 'PIG PEN' PRECINCT
Policemen Now Having Second Thoughts About Sign Painted on Their Window

The "Pig Pen" police precinct on the "Strip"

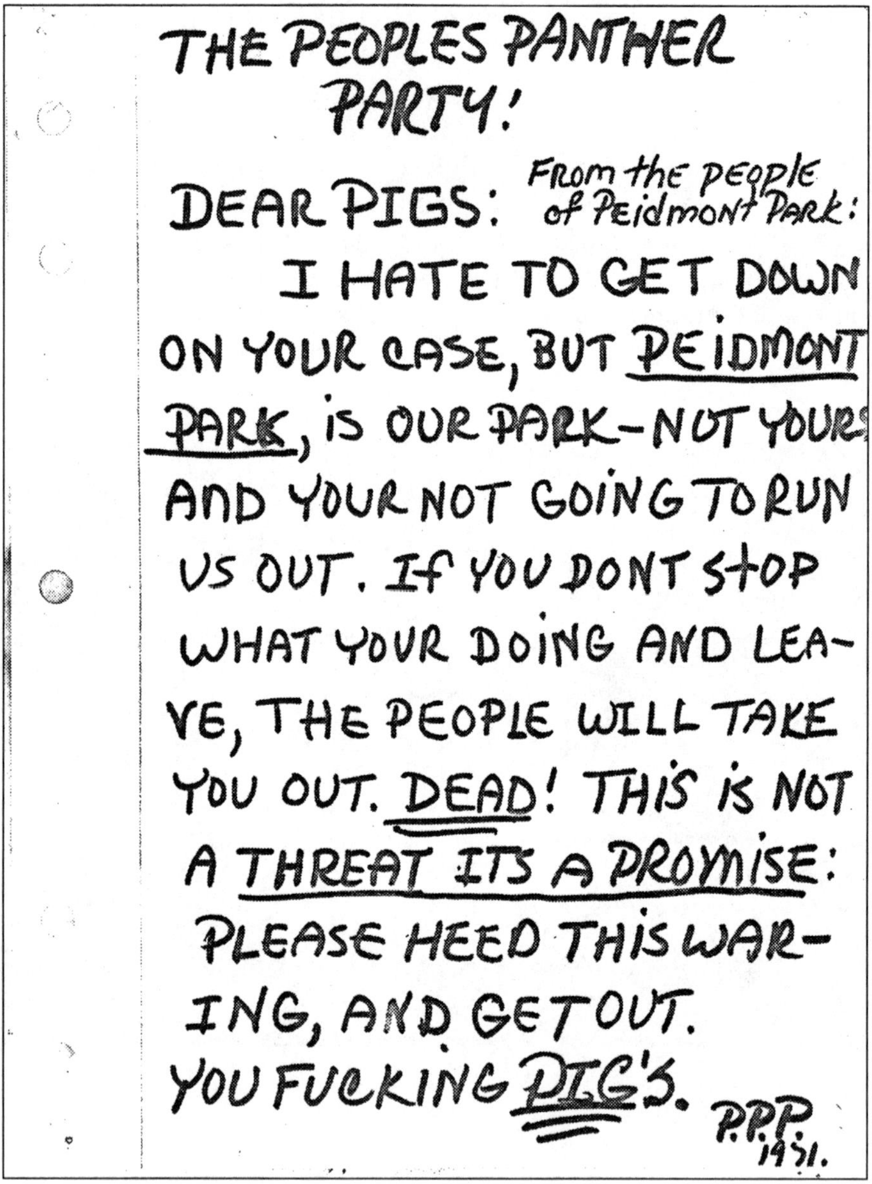

THE PEOPLES PANTHER
PARTY!

DEAR PIGS: From the people of Peidmont Park:

I HATE TO GET DOWN
ON YOUR CASE, BUT PEIDMONT
PARK, IS OUR PARK - NOT YOURS
AND YOUR NOT GOING TO RUN
US OUT. If YOU DONT stop
WHAT YOUR DOING AND LEA-
VE, THE PEOPLE WILL TAKE
YOU OUT. DEAD! THIS IS NOT
A THREAT ITS A PROMISE:
PLEASE HEED THIS WAR-
ING, AND GET OUT.
YOU FUCKING PIG'S.

P.P.P.
1971.

Warning to police to stay out of Piedmont Park

"Police Presence—A Dangerous Atmosphere?"

Piedmont Park, the largest of the city parks, is located in the center of Midtown, just two blocks from the Strip. It became the meeting place, the campground, the hangout for the maggots, the members of the counterculture. No longer did average people feel comfortable on its green spaces. Families no longer used the park's facilities. The tennis courts, the swimming pool, the walkways surrounding the lake, dotted with swings, all went unused; families feared the people who now inhabited the park. Piedmont Park became crime-ridden and drug-infested.

The word came from city hall, "Stay out of Piedmont Park, day, or night, unless you get a call." We couldn't believe it. The police had been ordered to stay out of a public place. Knowing what was going on in the park, this order was hard to accept and harder to understand.

We were told that police presence in the park fostered a dangerous atmosphere—Police presence fostered a dangerous atmosphere?—and might be blamed for violence if it erupted.

One October evening, in 1971, Officers Leon Jones and LR Winn wandered into Piedmont Park. Both were assigned to the crime prevention section, and neither were regular street cops, so they did not get the word on the police ban. They parked their patrol car, and as they walked in uniform among the thousand or so park dwellers, they were generally ignored. The inhabitants knew that cops were not allowed in the park, so drugs flowed freely, and other illegal activities continued. It made no difference that two cops were in the park.

Jones and Winn saw a teenage girl stick a hypodermic needle into a guy's arm, withdraw it, fill it up again, and inject a second guy. Hardly believing what they had just witnessed, Jones and Winn grabbed all three. The ensuing scene must have been like that in the film of Rudyard Kipling's *Gunga Din*, when a British soldier serving in Colonial India found himself separated from his company, inside the sacred temple packed with several thousand armed, English-hating, Hindu fanatics. The soldier stepped into the multitude and brazenly announced that everyone had to follow him because they were all under arrest.

"The pigs are making a bust," someone in the crowd shouted as rocks, bottles, anything, were thrown at the two policemen. Gunshots were fired from the crowd. Officer Leon Jones went down, seriously wounded with a bullet in his stomach. Winn dragged him behind a tree, returned fire, then called for assistance and an ambulance.

"Any car near Piedmont Park, signal 63/50/4" (officer needs help/person shot/ambulance on the way), announced the dispatcher, his voice louder than normal. "Be advised to check area around the pavilion. We have information that one officer is shot, and a second officer is still under fire!"

I was close to the park when the call came in and on the scene soon after hearing the call. Seeing that Jones was being attended, I turned my attention to the hundreds of maggots fleeing the park. I was among the first to arrive. We were outnumbered, but we were pissed. We started kicking ass. The maggots were scared. A cop had just been shot, and they wanted to get the hell out of that park. The ones we caught were given an accelerated course in police brutality. As more cops poured into the park, the tide of battle turned. We beat them with nightsticks, flashlights, pistols, slapjacks. Some we beat so badly they could not move; we left them lying in the bushes. The walking wounded hobbled as fast as they could to get out of the park and away from "the pigs that went crazy."

The following day, Lieutenant Gary Shepherd was summoned to Chief Jenkins' office. Lieutenant Shepherd was in charge of a squad of about forty motorcycle cops. Chief Jenkins' instructions to Lieutenant Shepherd were clear: take back Piedmont Park and clean it up. The pressure was on and the mayor had done an about face. It had taken the shooting of a policeman, and the bad press the police department suffered for keeping policemen out of the park, to change that policy.

It wasn't Lt. Shepherd's first encounter with Atlanta's counterculture. One night, almost a year prior to the Piedmont Park confrontation, I was damn glad to see Lieutenant Shepherd and his "motormen." Wade and I were working homicide on the evening watch, passing by the Strip, when we saw Sergeant Harriman, assigned to the Pig Pen, standing at Peachtree and Tenth Streets. We stopped our car to say, "Hi, Sergeant, how are you doing?" Then we saw, only a few steps behind the sergeant, a policeman fighting with some guy, both going to the ground.

Wade and I jumped out of the car and helped get the guy under control. He was stoned and on a bad trip from whatever he had taken. In a matter of a few seconds, rocks and bottles were thrown at me, Wade, and the other policeman. I looked up and saw that several hundred people had gathered and were about to close in on us. "The pigs are making a bust. Let's kill the mother-fuckin' pigs!"

I crawled back to the car and got to the radio. The dispatcher put out a signal 63 (officer needs help). Lieutenant Shepherd and approximately thirty of his motorcycle cops were only a few blocks away. A cop who needs help loves to hear the roar of police motorcycles, causing offenders to grow increasingly fearful. Shepherd and his men roared in and quickly took control. Vehicular traffic was diverted from Peachtree and Tenth Streets, pedestrians were cleared—a few pedestrian asses were kicked to help them move on. Lieutenant Shepherd approached us as we struggled with the guy who started it all, trying to get him under control. Sergeant Harriman kept telling us not to hurt him. Shepherd looked at the sergeant, not believing what he was hearing, and said, "Don't hurt him—shit!" then promptly hit the guy several times with his nightstick. The guy stopped fighting immediately, and the threat was over.

Almost a year after that altercation, twenty-four hours after Jones was shot, the police ban on Piedmont Park was lifted. Later that evening, at about nine o'clock, Lieutenant Gary Shepherd and his motorcycle cops roared up to the pavilion in Piedmont Park. Shepherd mounted the pavilion steps, and using a bullhorn, announced, "My name is Lieutenant GB Shepherd. Piedmont Park has just changed its name to Shepherd Park, and I want everyone out of my park in forty-five minutes. Those who do not leave will be subject to an ass-whipping and arrest!"

Cops from the Pig Pen and other precincts waited as the remaining minutes of the deadline ticked off. Shepherd repeated the new deadline every five minutes. Some of the crowd left, but the hard-core stuck around, determined to call Shepherd's bluff. After all, he could not violate their civil rights. Could he?

When time was up, Shepherd turned to the cops and gave the order to "Clear the park." For the second night in a row, policemen had the opportunity to release pent-up frustration. When we were done, everything was quiet, except for an occasional moan from the injured.

The next night, at about the same time, Shepherd and his motorcycle squad rolled into the park again. The few inhabitants scurried away. The park was quiet and peaceful for first time in three years.

Officer GE Marshall, a veteran policeman, was also a horseman; he agreed to be assigned to Piedmont Park, to patrol it on a horse that had been donated to the city. Officer Marshall and his horse were the forerunners of the current twenty-horse mounted patrol stabled in Piedmont Park.

Chief Jenkins saw the need for a highly mobile group of well-trained, handpicked police officers to respond, at a moment's notice, with superior force, to any hot spot in the city. Lieutenant Gary Shepherd was given that assignment, and half his motorcycle squad formed the nucleus of this special new group—the Atlanta Police SWAT Team was born.

Officer Leon Jones survived his gunshot wounds, and after a long medical leave (called "injured off" in police parlance), returned to duty and resumed his career.

The Black Liberation Army

James Richard Greene, a cop in the APD, was quiet, pleasant, and unassuming. He was planning to be married, and was in the process of building a new home. James Richard Greene was twenty-six years old and had been an Atlanta police officer for almost five years. He was murdered because he wore a blue uniform and carried a badge. He was assassinated because he was a cop who was in the wrong place at the wrong time. Officer Greene was assigned to the morning watch, driving a paddy wagon on Atlanta's south side. He last stood roll call on a rainy, miserable November night in 1971.

Regardless of our profession, whether we are cops, librarians, or astronauts, we leave for work, do our jobs, and never think about whether we are going to see the light of the next day. Nor did Greene think about that as he left police headquarters, driving his wagon towards his beat.

"Mayday, mayday, mayday!" screamed a strange voice over the police radio. "Policeman shot; need an ambulance." That was not the way a policeman would put in a help call. The dispatcher got a location from the excited caller. The call was broadcast, and every cop in the city froze when they heard it. "Any car near Boulevard and Memorial Drive, signal 63/50/4!" broadcast the dispatcher, giving out that chilling combination of numbers, the foremost attention-getter to come over the police radio.

I was working the morning watch, the only homicide detective on duty. I went directly to Grady Hospital, arriving in time to hear the sirens as the ambulance carrying the wounded officer and the two escorting patrol cars pulled into the emergency entrance.

Greene was taken from the ambulance and rushed into the emergency room. He had been shot in the head, neck, and shoulder. I ran alongside the stretcher, hoping to get any information from him. "Greene, it's me, Goldhagen. Who shot you? How many were there? Were they black or white?" I was talking to deaf ears. His eyes were open, but he couldn't see me. He was gurgling, making an awful rattling sound; maybe he was trying to answer me. I would never know. No more sounds came from him. There was only quiet. The doctors tried to bring him back to life, but Officer James Richard Greene was dead.

I left the hospital and went to Boulevard and Memorial Drive, the scene of the murder. It was raining, as it had been since early evening. There was a police paddy wagon parked at the corner Gulf gas station, which had been closed for the night. The station was sealed off, and there were about a dozen cops milling around. I spoke with Lieutenant SL Salvant, the district superior officer. As we spoke, I saw tears in his eyes; he choked on some of the words. I tried not to notice.

ID was processing the scene, taking photographs, dusting for prints, and collecting evidence. Two slugs were found, one on the floor of the driver's compartment of the wagon, the other on the ground outside the passenger's side. Greene's service revolver, holster, and gun belt were missing. Gone also was his badge; it appeared to have been ripped from his shirt. An empty paper sack, napkins from a nearby fast food restaurant, and a Coca-Cola container were found on the floor of the wagon, in the driver's compartment.

My immediate thought was that someone had just walked up to the wagon and shot him without warning. The scene had all the earmarks of an assassination. What made that less than a definite speculation was the report by Detectives Byrd and Peppers, who had passed that Gulf station moments before Greene was found shot. They said they saw a patrol car parked beside the wagon. All police officers on duty at that time were asked to identify themselves if they were at that location. No one came forward.

Rumors started flying. I heard everything from a romantic triangle, to a burglary ring, to a drug deal gone sour. The media didn't help when, later that day, the front-page headline of the *Atlanta Journal* proclaimed, "Mystery Police Car Sought in Killing of Atlanta Officer."

This was my case, and I had one god-awful mess on my hands. Everyone had a theory and was eager to share it with me. One theory was as good as another, and I could not ignore any of them. There was not much to go on, except theory and speculation. The only thing we knew for sure was that a police officer had been killed, shot three times with two different guns (a third bullet was recovered from the Greene's head). None of the bullets were fired from his service revolver, which was missing, along with his holster, gun belt, and badge. Later that same day, when the commotion had settled down, I was collecting my thoughts and began to put the pieces of the puzzle together.

Officer JR Greene left police headquarters shortly after the midnight roll call and drove to his beat. He did not receive any calls. At 1:20 a.m., he stopped at Grandma's Biscuits, a fast food restaurant located at Hill Street and Interstate- 20. He purchased a take-out order of two sausage biscuits and a Coke, and then drove a half-dozen blocks to Boulevard and Memorial Drive, SE. He pulled into the Gulf service station, which was closed for the night, and parked under the overhang between the building and the gas pumps. He sat in his wagon, out of the rain, and ate his snack.

Officer JD Faucett, working car 41 was en route to meet Greene at the Gulf station, which was a popular meeting place for morning watch cops in that district. Faucett never met Greene, because at 1:15 a.m., he received a robbery call to an all night gas station located on Memorial Drive, a quarter-mile from the Gulf station. Faucett answered the call, confirmed that it had been an armed robbery, and radioed for robbery detectives to meet him. Detectives WH Byrd and BF Peppers, assigned to morning watch robbery, responded.

Sergeant BG Hodnett, one of the district supervisors, had instructed one of his cars to meet him at Boulevard and Memorial. When Sergeant Hodnett arrived and noticed the paddy wagon parked in the Gulf station, he radioed the car that was to meet him and changed the location to a couple of blocks away. Hodnett didn't want three police vehicles parked together at the same place.

At about 1:50 a.m., a private security guard stopped at the traffic light at the intersection of Boulevard and Memorial Drive. He looked at the Gulf station, and through the heavy rain, noticed a police paddy wagon with the lights on and the door open. He thought there might be a burglar in the station and that the officer might need assistance. The guard pulled into the station, and when he approached the wagon, he found Greene slumped under the steering wheel, bleeding badly and gasping for breath. He grabbed the radio microphone in the wagon and started shouting, "Mayday, mayday, mayday," the international distress signal, said he needed an ambulance for a wounded policeman, and gave his location. Sergeant Hodnett heard the help call, and from two blocks away, was the first car to arrive. He confirmed that an officer had been shot and requested a rush on the ambulance.

Detectives Byrd and Peppers, after completing their robbery call, were stopped for the traffic light at Boulevard and Memorial, about a minute behind the security guard. They, too, looked through the rain and saw the paddy wagon. They said they were sure they saw a patrol car parked next to the wagon. What they saw, in fact, was the security guard's car, which through the rainy darkness, was easily mistaken for an Atlanta patrol car. Byrd and Peppers had traveled a few blocks after that when they heard the help call, and rushed back.

Putting together what I had learned added up to no more than I had to go on earlier—a dead policeman, three bullets (fired from two different guns), the officer's missing badge, service revolver, and holster—no suspects, no witnesses, no motive. Out there was a cop killer or killers who we wanted badly. Number one priority.

About a month before Greene was killed, an armed robbery took place at the Fulton National Bank in the West End section of Atlanta. Bank robberies were not uncommon in the city, but what made this one unusual was that the robbers were four black males and a black female, all wearing military fatigues, each carrying an automatic weapon.

In the weeks preceding the robbery at the Fulton National Bank, other armed robberies had occurred in Atlanta and adjacent DeKalb County, apparently by these same robbers. Police began to suspect the group to be an organized paramilitary operation.

A week after Greene's murder, three would-be robbers planned to hold up a convenience store in the part of the City of Atlanta that lies within DeKalb County (this part of Atlanta has dual Atlanta-DeKalb County police jurisdiction). The three sat in their car in the parking lot waiting, as customers came and went, for the right time to enter and hold up the store. Before they could, one of the customers or store employees noticed them and called the police. A one-man Atlanta patrol car responded to a signal 54 (suspicious person). As he got out of his car and walked towards them, one of the occupants ordered the others to "off the motherfucker."

Because of the dual jurisdiction, the DeKalb police also got the call. A two-man DeKalb unit pulled up to the car with the would-be robbers and assassins, just as the lone Atlanta patrolman was walking across the lot. The three police officers told the suspects to get out of the car.

They searched the vehicle, found their weapons, arrested the three, and took them to the DeKalb County Jail. (The Atlanta policeman never knew just how close he came to being shot.)

One month and five days after the suspects were arrested, they knocked a hole in the back wall of the DeKalb County Jail and escaped. Their headquarters were located in a small frame house on a quiet residential street in the Kirkwood area of Atlanta, which also lies in DeKalb County. Atlanta and DeKalb police detectives and FBI agents poured over the house. It appeared to have been hastily abandoned, but everything was still there—the tools of the urban guerrilla: boxes of ammunition, military clothing, communist and revolutionary literature, survival gear, first-aid material, hundreds of credit cards and IDs, instructions and material for making bombs, maps, diagrams, and the gang's plans for robbing various businesses and banks, such as the West End branch of the Fulton National Bank. They even had a sand box to simulate a model of the site of the robbery.

A large container filled with a heavy liquid was on the floor in the center of the living room. Everyone froze in their tracks when a detective opened a trunk and found it loaded with TNT. They also found a box containing sticks of dynamite attached to a timing device, which was wired to the back door. Suspecting a booby-trap, everyone got out of the house and waited for the ATF bomb squad, who, after a quick survey, immediately ordered the entire block evacuated. Luckily, the timing device had jammed when it was set, and the malfunction had gone unnoticed by the gang in their haste to get the hell out of there after their escape from the jail. They knew we would be right behind them, and they had left us a surprise. The booby trap almost worked. Alongside the dynamite and the TNT was a large amount of nitroglycerin in a container on the living room floor. An Atlanta detective sergeant, who told me, "I thought someone had pissed in a jug, and I didn't want one of us to knock it over," had moved it.   The blast would have ruined the day for about a dozen law enforcement officers, plus countless other innocent people in the neighborhood.

Through information obtained from the FBI and the New York City Police Department, we learned that the group with whom we were dealing called itself "The Black Liberation Army." The BLA was an extremely violent and militant offshoot of the Black Panther Party, which originated in New York. The BLA broke away from Huey Newton's Black Panthers and became disciples of Eldridge Cleaver. He escaped to Algeria to avoid prosecution for his violent crimes in the US. Cleaver and his disciples were disgruntled by the fact that the Black Panther Party would not engage in the random assassination of police officers. The BLA had been identified in the assassination murders of four NYPD policemen and attacks on at least a half dozen others.

The first of these unprovoked attacks against the police in New York City came one evening when NYPD Officers Thomas Curry and Nicholas Binetti, both white, were in their patrol car, assigned to guard the home of Manhattan's District Attorney Morgenthau. Curry and Binetti were part of a twenty-four-hour guard for the DA because of recent threats on his life. Morgenthau's home was on Riverside Drive in upper Manhattan. The officers followed a car they observed slowly passing the house and pulled up alongside it. The occupants of the car, two black males, fired an automatic weapon and sped off. As the car sped away, the wounded cops got the license plate number, which was publicized in the media. Officers Curry and Binetti survived their wounds, but both were crippled for life.

Two days later, a package was received at the New York Times. In it was the license plate of the wanted car and a message.

"May 19, 1971
 All power to the people.
 Here are the license plates sort after by the
 Fascist state pig police. We send them in order
 To exhibit the potential power of oppressed peoples
 To acquire revolutionary justice. The armed goods
 Of this racist government will again meet the
 Guns of oppressed third world peoples as long
 As they occupy our community and murder our brothers
 And sisters in the name of American law and order.
 Just as the fascist marines and army occupy Vietnam
 In the name of democracy, and murder Vietnamese
 people in the name of American imperialism are confronted
 with the guns of the Vietnamese Liberation Army, the domestic
 armed forces of racism and
 Oppression will be confronted with the guns of
 The Black Liberation Army, who will mete out, in
 The tradition of Malcolm and all true revolutionaries,
 Real justice. We are revolutionary justice.
 All power to the people."

The night that package was received, NYPD Officers Waverly Jones and Joseph Piagentini, had responded to what they determined was a bogus call at a Harlem housing project (formerly the site of the New York Giants Polo Grounds). Returning to their car, they were shot at close range from behind. It seemed clear that the purpose of the call was to assassinate any officers who responded. Officer Jones was black. Piagentini was white. Both were killed.

The following day, another letter was received from the BLA, taking credit for the double assassination. The letter was determined to have been typed on the same typewriter as the previous letter.

Six months later, NYPD Officers Rocco Laurie and Gregory Foster, walking their beat during the evening on 11th Street and Avenue A on the Lower Eastside of Manhattan, were shot from behind. Both officers suffered multiple gunshot wounds. As they lay on the ground, the two young black males who had fired at them took their service revolvers. Officer Laurie, who was white, and Officer Foster, who was black, were both assassinated.

Three thousand miles away, in San Francisco, late one August night, came the first break in the New York police murders. A San Francisco police sergeant had stopped his patrol car for a traffic light when a car occupied by two black males pulled up alongside; one aimed a submachine gun out the window at the sergeant. The gun jammed. They sped off. The sergeant gave chase and put the call for backup on the air. Other units joined the chase, which stopped when the fleeing car became disabled in a wreck. Both occupants started shooting; the cops returned fire, wounding and arresting them.

Found in the wrecked car were two weapons that led to a break in the murders of the NYPD cops: one was the .38 caliber service revolver belonging to one of the murdered NYPD cops; the other was the .45 caliber semi-automatic pistol—the murder weapon of that cop.

The following day, three black males walked into a San Francisco police precinct. One pointed a shotgun at the desk sergeant and without a word, murdered him. Pellets from the blast also wounded a female clerk.

The evidence found in the wrecked car, plus a lot of intense work by San Francisco detectives, New York City detectives, and FBI agents, pointed at the killers of the cops in NYC, Atlanta, and now, San Francisco. The Black Liberation Army. Vicious fanatics, self-appointed revolutionaries, cold-blooded killers. They killed cops in New York

City, San Francisco, and Atlanta, where they felt it was safest to establish headquarters, primarily to hide Eldridge Cleaver when he sneaked back into the country from his self-imposed exile in Algeria.

John Thomas, Andrew Jackson, and Joanne Chesimard, the leaders of the BLA, were jammed into a van that arrived in Atlanta one night in the late summer of 1971, as well as Ronald Anderson, Samuel Cooper, Twyman Myers, and Freddie Hilton. Other BLA members followed by bus.

Joanne Chesimard, with John Thomas, were the heart and brains of the BLA. But Chesimard, it seemed, was who motivated and whet the homicidal appetites of her "colleagues."

Before the three escaped from the DeKalb County jail, I interviewed all members of the gang arrested on weapons violations, as part of my investigation for possible leads in the murder of Officer Greene. Four were responsive, although they gave up no meaningful information. One did not even acknowledge my presence. I was nothing more than another piece of furniture in the room. That was Joanne Chesimard.

Samuel Cooper, the BLA member arrested in Miami a year later, started talking "to make a deal," and told how Chesimard's hatred for police was her religion, and said she had sex with most of the leaders of the BLA, as well as others. Cooper went beyond that bit of gossip, divulging information that eventually led to many arrests and convictions. He gave police names of the BLA members who had committed crimes in various states, and described in detail what had happened in Atlanta. One story related directly to the investigation of the murder of Officer Greene.

Twyman Myers and Freddie Hilton, the two least experienced BLA members had screwed up their assignments on several jobs. John Thomas was getting on their asses about some of "the dumb shit they had done." Joanne Chesimard told them to "go out, find a pig, and off him," so as to satisfy Thomas that they could successfully do what was asked of them.

Myers and Hilton went out into the rainy, dark streets, looking for a cop to kill. They saw a policeman sitting alone in a paddy wagon parked at a closed gas station. They approached the wagon on the passenger's side, each with guns in held out of sight, opened the door, and asked for directions. Greene had just finished eating his sandwiches, was drinking what was left of his Coke, and had started to oblige, when explosions and flashes filled the interior of the wagon.

Greene slumped under the steering wheel, mortally wounded. The two BLA assassins grabbed his service revolver, holster, and gun belt, ripped his badge from his shirt, and ran back into the rainy darkness.

Twyman Myers and Freddie Hilton burst into the house where the others were waiting and threw the dead officer's gun and badge on the table, displaying their trophies for all to admire. "We did it! We did it!" Joanne Chesimard smiled approvingly. The two had redeemed themselves.

A month later, after Myers and Hilton killed Officer Greene, and the three escaped from DeKalb County, the BLA split up and went into hiding. They left Atlanta, leaving us with the unsolved murder of a police officer.

About a year later, we received a call from the Miami police department. "We've got a guy in our jail on an armed robbery charge. He says he knows something about an Atlanta police officer killing, and he wants to make a deal." That guy was BLA member Samuel Cooper. He told much more about the BLA.

Six months after Greene's murder, I was transferred from homicide to the Stakeout Squad. Twelve months after that murder, Cooper was arrested and talking. Because I was no longer in homicide, Sergeant Louis Graham and Detective DV Lee flew to Miami to interview Samuel Cooper. Graham and Lee returned with a thirty-five page written statement in which Cooper identified the leaders of the BLA and provided details of all of the BLA crimes he knew, including the assassination of Officer Greene.

Several months prior to the Cooper interview in Miami, Greene's service revolver was recovered from a pond in the southwest section of Atlanta. A woman, while fishing, found it submerged in shallow water near the bank. She gave it to the man in charge of the pond. He brought it to the APD and turned it over to me. The revolver was corroded with rust and appeared to have been in the water for some time, but the APD serial number was still legible. The state crime lab was able to restore the manufacturer's serial number, but could not provide any additional evidence. A diver searched the pond for Greene's belt, holster, and badge, but they were never found.

In the meantime, New York City police had placed nationwide lookouts for known members of the BLA, on charges stemming from the cop murders, as well numerous armed robberies, and attempts on the lives of other NYPD cops.

Five members of the BLA surfaced in St. Louis, where they engaged in a shootout with police; three were apprehended. Twyman Myers and Joanne Chesimard fled during that shootout.

The next time Joanne Chesimard was seen was in 1973, on the New Jersey Turnpike where a New Jersey State Police car stopped her for speeding. She pulled over, and as the trooper walked up to her car, she shot and killed him. When she was apprehended in New Jersey in 1977, she was tried and convicted for the murder of that trooper. She was sentenced to a life term at the New Jersey State Penitentiary. Two years later, she escaped with the help of four visitors who took a corrections officer hostage and commandeered his prison van as part of the getaway. Although she has since been on the FBI's ten most-wanted list, she is presently at large and reported to be living in Cuba, under the name of Assata Shakur.

In 1975, Freddie Hilton was apprehended in New York, unrelated to the police killings. He served time for robbery in the New York State Penitentiary.

From the early 1970s to the early 1980s, most of the BLA leaders and members were killed in shootouts, or caught and served, or are still serving various prison sentences. In 1974, Twyman Myers returned to New York City, hiding out in a rat-hole in the Bronx. The FBI and NYPD discovered where he was hiding, set up surveillance, and waited for him to come out. They wanted to take him on the street. Myers carelessly left his hiding place, and as soon as he was on the street, FBI agents and New York City detectives surrounded him. He pulled his gun. He probably did not have a chance to squeeze off a round because as soon as his weapon appeared, agents and detectives fired their shotguns, handguns, and automatic weapons at him. It was easy to imagine that his riddled body looked much as the bodies of Bonnie and Clyde did in the last scene of that film.

The night Twyman Myers' body, oozing blood from many gunshot wounds, lay on the garbage-littered street in the Bronx, I was on duty in Atlanta. I was on the roof of a two-story building with several other APD officers investigating a burglary. We were peering into a hole the burglars had cut, when over our radios came the voice of the dispatcher, announcing that Twyman Myers had been found, shot, and killed by FBI agents and detectives in New York City. We let out a cheer, and soon heard the sirens from patrol cars throughout the city, celebrating the delivery of justice to the BLA member who wantonly, senselessly killed Officer Greene.

Thirty years later, in 2001, Atlanta Homicide Detective Jim Rose, working cold cases, picked up the Greene file. He followed new leads, developed fresh information, and found several witnesses—former BLA members, who had served time, and were currently out of prison, working at regular jobs, and supporting families. They agreed to testify against Freddie Hilton for the murder of Greene.

Hilton had been out of prison and working for the telephone company in New York for nineteen years. Detective Rose had sufficient cause to have a warrant issued; Hilton was arrested by the NYPD, extradited to Georgia, and held in the Fulton County Jail. I was contacted by the Fulton County District Attorney's Office, and although I had retired, I was asked to testify as the lead detective at Hilton's trial.

In October 2003, thirty-two years after the crime, I had the bittersweet pleasure of looking Freddie Hilton in the eye and testifying against him. I got the satisfaction of being in the courtroom when his guilty verdict was announced by the jury foreperson; the judge sentenced him to three life sentences, without parole, for the assassination of Atlanta Police Office James Richard Greene.

Officer Ray Braswell

The Black Panther Party was a black militant group that advocated violence as a means of attaining the black man's proper place in society, although not to the extent of the BLA. The Black Panthers were more widely known than Eldridge Cleaver's Black Liberation Army.

There was a Black Panther presence in virtually every major US city. The Atlanta chapter's headquarters was in a small frame house in the Kirkwood Section, on Dunwoody Place. We knew they were there, but they kept a low profile. All of their activities—demonstrations, robberies, riots, intimidations—occurred at various locations around the city.

One night after midnight, in 1971, an Atlanta patrol car rode slowly by the house on Dunwoody Place. A shotgun blast of .00 buckshot came from within the patrol car, ripping through the front door of the house. The patrol car then sped away. A civilian witnessed the event.

A call came in reporting the shotgun blast. Several APD supervisors recognized the address and headed towards it to meet the responding patrol car. No one had been hit by the blast. Detectives were called in to investigate and establish a motive. The investigating detectives learned from the witness that while sitting on his front porch across the street from the Black Panther house, he saw an Atlanta patrol car come down the street and approach the house very slowly, nearly stopping in front. That's when he heard the blast. He said there were two policemen in the car. When asked how he could be sure that the two in the car were policemen, he said that as the car passed under the street light in front of his house, he saw the light reflect off their badges. He also saw shoulder patches on the sleeves of both men.

There were only two patrol cars that night with two officers assigned. Both were working beats on the south side. Both cars were occupied by white officers. One was the car that included Dunwoody Place on its beat. It was occupied by Officers Steve Mallory and LA Jones. The other car, which was three beats away from the Black Panther house, had assigned to it Officers Ray Braswell and LW Henslee. When the morning watch Captain, Claude Dixon, who was black, learned who was in the car, he didn't have to hear any more. He called Braswell and his partner to meet him at the police station.

As they gathered in his office, Captain Dixon didn't ask Braswell if he did it. He told him he did. Braswell and Henslee denied it, explaining they were nowhere near the Kirkwood area and didn't know about the shooting until they heard the call. Captain Dixon was determined; he said he would prove it, and when he did, he would have Braswell's badge, and might file criminal charges against him. Braswell continued to deny it, but knew there was no use protesting further. He told Dixon to do what he felt he had to do.

Later that morning, just before the morning watch was called in, Braswell and Henslee met with Mallory and Jones. Braswell told them, "I know you two did it; I got the blame for it." He looked Mallory in the eye and told him, "I'll take the heat this time, and not rat you out, but if you ever pull shit like that again, I'll not take another hit for you. The next time, I'll beat the shit out of both of you."

It was never proven who fired the shotgun blast at the house, and Captain Dixon's threats went unfulfilled. When the shit hit the fan, some people reflexively looked at Ray Braswell, people like Captain Dixon, who was just waiting to nail him.

Braswell acquired his reputation through some of the dumb shit he's pulled, such as the time in 1968, when Ray Braswell was working the four p.m. –midnight evening watch. It was a very busy shift, answering call after call until just after eleven p.m. Tired from working his extra job earlier in the day, Braswell parked his patrol car in a quiet place, hidden from view, to await the signal for the change of the watch. Almost immediately, Ray Braswell fell into a deep sleep.

The next thing he knew, morning watch Officer, Charlie James, was tapping on the patrol car window. It was 2:30 in the morning. The dispatcher had been calling him on the radio for the past two and a half hours. The whole morning watch was searching for him.

After the obligatory, "Holy shit," Braswell told James, "Charlie, you haven't seen me!" With that, Braswell drove very quickly to the police "city shop," parked the patrol car in an obscure spot on the lot, and loosened some wires under the hood of the car. He hitched a ride in a delivery truck back to the police station, got in his personal car, and drove home.

When he got home, Braswell's wife told him that someone from the APD had been calling to see if he had gotten home. Braswell called the police station and spoke with Morning Watch Lieutenant LC Williams. "Where in the hell have you been?" bellowed Williams. "The whole goddamn police department has been looking for you!"

"I had to shop my car right at watch change," explained Braswell innocently. "I got a ride back to the station, and by that time, everyone was gone." Lieutenant Williams didn't believe him, and told him so. Braswell didn't care and said, "Well, lieutenant, that's my story," then promptly hung up.

. The following day, Braswell found that most of the other superior officers didn't believe him, either. Everyone wearing gold took his turn chewing Braswell out. He insisted that what he told to Lieutenant Williams was the truth. When the patrol car was located parked at the city shop, it was discovered that some wires had indeed come loose. There was no way to disprove Braswell's story.

That's only one example of many over the years.

Several years after we both had retired, Ray Braswell confessed to me this incident, and others, where he bent the Rules. He therefore got a lot of the blame for things he wasn't guilty of doing. It's hard to live down a reputation.

I later heard through the grape vine that Mallory and Jones were, in fact, involved in the shooting, and had bragged about it. Captain Dixon and others like him still believe that Ray Braswell did it.

Because no one could prove it, the only thing Braswell suffered was another notch in his reputation; some of the notches were fair, and some, like this one, were not.

"Good morning, Chief"

In the spring of 1972, Police Chief Herbert T. Jenkins faced mandatory retirement after twenty-five years as Atlanta's police chief. In his tenure as chief, he ran the police department with a minimum of outside interference. He ruled with an iron fist. He was in charge; he was the boss!

A signal 10G (report to the chief's office) was a call no one wanted to receive. It usually meant one or two things—you were being promoted or you were being fired. Given that there were not many promotions made back then, anyone getting that radio call acknowledged it with a quiver in his voice.

Some policemen liked Chief Jenkins, some hated him. Most didn't know him, at least not personally. He kept his distance and remained aloof from his cops. I had personal contact with the chief only twice in my career, and on both occasions, he never spoke a word to me. The first time, we were in the elevator at police headquarters, just the two of us. "Good morning, Chief," I greeted him respectfully. He looked at me without acknowledging my presence, took a drag on his cigarette, and got off the elevator without speaking. The other time, I was in a patrol car, stopped for a downtown traffic light one night, when Jenkins pulled up alongside and stopped for that same traffic light. Once more, I said, "Hello," and again there was no response, only a blank look from behind a cloud of cigarette smoke. The light turned green, and he drove off.

"To the Victor belongs…" the APD

In the spring of 1972, the question we all were asking was who would be Jenkins' successor? The heir apparent was Assistant Chief Clinton Chafin, the chief of detectives. He had been groomed for years; he was a member of the inner circle of ranking police supervisors and part of the political clique. Chafin was experienced, competent, and highly qualified. He was liked and respected by the leaders in the business community.

All of that was rendered meaningless as politics interfered with the selection of the new APD chief. John Inman, a relatively obscure police lieutenant, started to challenge considerations favoring Chafin. He may have been obscure, but he was blessed with a "rabbi"—Howard Massell, the brother of Mayor Sam Massell.

Howard Massell was a shadowy, enigmatic character. He was very close to some of Atlanta's nightclub owners, who were being investigated for ties to organized crime, and he was a known gambler, which was illegal in Georgia. The precise nature of John Inman's relationship with Howard Massell was never determined, and speculation grew about Inman's rapid rise from lieutenant to assistant chief, just prior to Chief Jenkins' retirement. Not long after Inman was promoted to assistant chief, Howard Massell left Atlanta and relocated to Miami.

On the day of Jenkins' retirement, Mayor Sam Massell announced his decision. "The new chief of Atlanta's police is John Inman!"

Some in the APD were shocked. Others were pleased. We had been a racially divided department; now we were politically divided, as well.

There had been a bitter battle between Inman and Chafin, each making threats and accusations and slinging mud at each other. The hard feelings reached their respective supporters, even down to the rank and file cops. There were "Inman People" and "Chafin People" in the police department, although many cops remained neutral. The division made it difficult for the "neutral" cops to do their jobs.

Rather than make peace and repair the damage, Chief Inman "got even." Chafin was demoted to the rank of captain and banished to the Zone 2 precinct, out of the loop of decision-making at police headquarters; so were his loyal supporters. They were displaced, buried in the field, sent away from the nerve center of the police department. The opposition to Inman was gone, there were new faces in high places, and Chief Inman was in complete control.

At the time Inman took charge, his primary objective was to reduce a rapidly rising crime rate. The upswing in crime was a national trend, so the federal government, through the Law Enforcement Assistance Administration (LEAA), pumped money into American cities to deal with crime. Atlanta got twenty million dollars. Grants were applied for, new programs were initiated, additional police officers were hired, and new equipment was purchased. The APD felt like the winner of a sweepstakes, as if it had won the grand prize and a twenty million dollar shopping spree. We bought everything from Polaroid cameras to helicopters.

The Stakeout Squad—In the Beginning

One of Chief John Inman's first priorities was to address the increasing number of armed robberies in the city. Ironically, the most dangerous occupation in the city at that time was not a fireman, policeman, or an ironworker—it was a night clerk in a convenience store. On any night, the police radio on the evening watch dispatched police to three or four convenience store hold-ups.

In addition, many banks, restaurants, liquor stores, gas stations, and other types of businesses where there was cash on hand, were becoming victims of armed robberies. As the number of robberies increased, so did the shootings of storeowners, managers, and employees. Something had to be done.

Inman proposed the placement of cops inside businesses most susceptible to armed robbery. The cops would be hidden from view of anyone entering the premises, but where they could observe the cashier and everyone entering the store. The objective of this plan was to prevent, rather than respond to, armed robbery. The APD applied to the city for a share of the $20 million to fund a "stakeout squad," but it was months before the LEAA released the funds.

During those months, a small, temporary squad, consisting of two supervisors and a dozen patrolmen, was formed. Within a few days, the first positive results were seen. Officer DB Bowen, a SWAT officer, was staked out in a convenience store on the south side of the city. Two black males, each with a handgun, entered the store, pointed their pistols at the cashier, and demanded money. After they took the money, one of the robbers put his gun against the cashier's chest and pulled the trigger. Fortunately, for the cashier, the gun was a Rohm RG-10 .22 caliber, a cheap Saturday-night special, and it misfired. Bowen, armed with an M-2 Carbine on full automatic, with a thirty-round magazine, stepped out of the back room in full uniform, and challenged the robbers. They pointed their guns at him, and he fired a burst, killing both robbers instantly.

(The entire incident was recorded on videotape by the store's camera. It was used as a training film. Each time it was shown, it evoked spontaneous cheering from the cops viewing it.)

In another situation that proved the effectiveness of the stakeout squad, two white thugs walked into a DeKalb Avenue liquor store, ordering the elderly clerks, "Give it up, old men." The robbers stuck their guns into the faces of the two frightened clerks. After the clerks handed over money, the robbers took them to the back room and pistol-whipped them, leaving the clerks on the floor as they fled the store. Why beat up the clerks after they surrendered the money so easily? The speculation of the investigating police was that the robbers wanted to intimidate the clerks, to make it easy if and when they returned to hold up that same liquor store. For this reason, Inman's Stakeout Squad decided to stake out this same liquor store.

Exactly one week later, the same white thugs strolled into the liquor store, "Here we are; let's do it again—we want all the money." After the clerks handed over the money, the thugs announced, "It's party time again, only this time we're going to finish the job," as they marched them to the back room. Instead of the icy fingers of fear that had gripped the victims the week before, their blood was warm with anticipation of what was to come.

Stakeout Officers TJ "Banjo" Roberts and JF Smith, having observed and heard all of this through the one-way mirror, were waiting in the back room, both armed with shotguns. As the door to the back room was pushed open, the two clerks were shoved in, followed by the robbers. The room was cramped; there were six people jammed into a space big enough for four.

One of the robbers, recovering from his surprise, fired a shot at Roberts, just missing his head. "Banjo" returned fire with a deafening blast from his 12-gauge shotgun, hitting and killing one of the robbers. Unfortunately, one of the clerks caught part of the blast, which almost ripped off his arm. The surviving robber turned and ran through the store, heading for the front door. Smith fired a blast through the one-way mirror, killing the robber before he escaped.

I went to Grady Hospital and spoke with the wounded clerk as he was being prepared for the operating room. His arm was severely damaged, and he was in a great deal of pain, but he asked me to convey to both officers his profound gratitude and thanks. So far, the score was:

Stakeout Squad—4
Armed robbers—0

Part Three

Sergeant

E arly one afternoon, in 1972, I was taking a shower, getting ready to go to work on the evening watch. My wife, Betty, cracked open the bathroom door wide enough to stick her head through. She had received a call from Judy Fischel, the day watch homicide secretary. Judy had called Betty to let her know that my promotion to sergeant had been announced in the *Daily Bulletin*, an internal report of APD news. That's how I learned I had been promoted—from my wife, in my shower. In most police departments, promotions are recognized in an official ceremony, with family and department VIPs in attendance. Not so in my case. When I got to work that evening, I was instructed to go to the chief's office and turn in my detective's badge to personnel. A clerk handed me my sergeant's badge. So much for my sixty-second ceremony.

Stakeout/Decoy

My promotion to sergeant came just before Chief Jenkins' retirement, when I was still working homicide. It was a promotion "by selection"—not by test, not through competition. I was surprised; I had no mentor, no "rabbi." I did not politick for the promotion, and perhaps that is why I had been passed over while thirty or forty others were promoted. Nevertheless, someone eventually selected me for promotion.

I liked the concept of the stakeout squad, and I was convinced it was the most effective way to discourage attempts at armed robbery; I wanted to be part of it. Several months later, the federal grant was approved by the LEAA and the stakeout squad was expanded: one captain, one lieutenant, five sergeants, and fifty detectives; all handpicked volunteers. The revised squad had two functions: (1) staking out businesses for robberies and burglaries, and (2) utilizing decoy operations for street crime, such as muggings, rapes, and car break-ins, among others. I was one of the sergeants chosen; Wade Hagin was another.

Members of the Stakeout/Decoy Squad prepare for a nights work
(Sergeant H. B. Goldhagen far left)

"Drunk" Stakeout/Decoy Detectives W. R. King (left) and H.F. Pharr

"I'm going to sit there—watch your black ass get kicked!"

The stakeout squad received lots of publicity, mainly for two reasons. One was because of the early successes—four dead robbers in two attempted armed robberies. The other was the enormous expansion of the squad. The media gave us plenty of coverage, and we welcomed it. We wanted any thug thinking about committing an armed robbery to be fearful. We wanted them to know there were fifty detectives staking out businesses every night, all over the city. They knew we couldn't be everywhere, but they were never sure where we would be. We created a game of Russian roulette among would-be robbers; most did not want to play.

The curse of the stakeout detective was boredom. Hour after hour, night after night, sitting cramped in some back room—cold in winter, hot in summer. Sometimes the back rooms were dirty, foul smelling, and infested with roaches. Stakeout detectives sit; they wait. Nothing happens. Burnout occurred fast. To deter burnout and cope with the boredom, we devised a system for relief.

The stakeout squad was broken down into five units, with ten detectives in each, and a sergeant in charge. A team would be on stakeout duty for one week. The following week, the sergeant would take his team on the street and work street crime. The third week, they would work stakeout again. We alternated weeks this way, and it worked out well.

Working street crime, or "decoying," as it became known, was fun for the cops, whose gallows humor is not always appreciated or understood. We routinely used one of the members of the team as a decoy, whoever most closely fit the victim profile in a rash of similar crimes. We had several female detectives on the squad act as decoys if there was a string of purse snatchings or women kidnapped off the streets to be raped. The male cops took turns decoying as tourists, cab drivers, winos, businessmen, deliverymen, conventioneers, and such.

In the 1970s, Atlanta had become a major convention city. Unfortunately, this meant a higher incidence of crime—mainly against conventioneers. Occasionally, a visiting conventioneer would leave his downtown hotel at night and wander out of the safety of the hotel district. Such a wanderer often finds himself in isolated areas, susceptible to street crime—accosted, assaulted, robbed—some were even murdered.

Crime reports are reviewed and analyzed for trends or a series of similar incidents. If conventioneers were being victimized, and the muggings seemed to be connected, the sergeant would instruct one of his men to come "dressed up" as a conventioneer. The decoy conventioneer would wander around in a predetermined pattern so that the others in the team knew where he was and could cover him at all times. The cover team would blend into the area, as a priest, a telephone repair crew, a handicapped person in a wheelchair, a pair of lovers in a car or huddled in a doorway, or any of a dozen other disguises.

The "conventioneer" wore one of those little tags on the lapel of his suit—"Hello, my name is—" Some of the stakeout/decoy cops wore tags, too. Theirs read, "Hello asshole, my name is Jones, and I'm going to kick your ass." Or, "Hello, shithead, my name is Smith, and I'm going to blow your fucking brains out." We were quite effective, having arrested lots of muggers, robbers, rapists, and purse-snatchers. On several occasions, we witnessed attempts on a real victim, intervened, and prevented them from suffering the crime. On any given night, the areas around the bus stations were places we usually made an arrest. We would dispatch a "drunk" to stumble past the bus station. Before he got very far, a mugger would take the bait, hit our decoy, and we would nab him. We derived great satisfaction from seeing the look on the face of a mugger who couldn't believe he had been fooled by our tactics.

We were informed of a series of rapes in the Midtown area. White females were being abducted from the street by a black male, taken away, and raped.

In the heart of Midtown, on Juniper Street, between Sixth and Seventh Streets, was just a vacant field where old houses had long ago been torn down. All that remained were the overgrown stone steps that once led up to the front porches of the houses. The field was fifteen or twenty feet higher than street level, and featured a waist-high stone wall that extended about forty feet across, at the sidewalk.

We set up our operation to nab the rapist with Carla Waites, our female decoy, sitting on the stone wall. The cover team hid nearby in the vacant field, within striking distance. One member of the team was several blocks away in a chase car. Carla was blonde and flashy; we knew she would attract many men. Some, as we expected, offered her rides, trying to pick her up. Others mistook her for a prostitute, especially since many walked the streets nearby.

Earlier, I had instructed our decoy, "Carla, we're not interested in making vice cases by arresting 'Johns.' We don't want you to blow your cover by making a big deal over a guy wanting to give you a ride. If anyone offers you a ride or wants to get into a conversation, simply tell them, 'No, thank you, I'm waiting for my husband.' We are after a kidnapper, a rapist, and unless someone tries to force you into a car, we are not interested in him." I repeated these instructions several times, to be sure she understood how we needed to conduct the operation. "If you decline the offer of a ride, and the guy keeps coming on to you, ignore him." Carla was aggressive by nature, so her instructions had to be emphatic. After all, she was portraying the average, vulnerable woman waiting for her husband to pick her up, and could not appear to be a confident police officer backed up by ten armed cops.

Many cars stopped, many driven by "Johns." Some offered $10; some offered $100. Some simply wanted to offer a ride to wherever she was going; she declined; they moved on.

On one occasion, a black male circled the block and offered Carla a ride in his car. She declined. He left, but returned shortly. He again offered a ride, which Carla politely refused, although this time, he got a little nasty with her. He left and returned again. This time, she ignored him entirely, which caused him to be more abusive. "What's the matter, white girl? A black man not good enough for you? If I fucked you, you wouldn't go back to your honky old man." Carla continued to ignore him, and he grew increasingly abusive. Each of us in the cover team, hiding nearby and hearing everything he said, was getting angry with him. But based on the descriptions given by the rape victims, and the information from the detectives who worked the cases, we knew that this loudmouth was not the man we were looking for.

When he came back the fourth time, he was raving. "You mother-fucking white whore, when I stick a big, black dick in your ass, you're gonna show me some respect!" By this time, Carla had had enough. She casually left the wall and started walking up the steps leading to the vacant field. The guy got out of his car and followed her. She walked about fifty feet from the street into the desolate field, stopped, and turned to face him. He approached her, sneering, "What you gonna do now, white bitch?"

Carla responded by pointing to a nearby tree stump, and very calmly told him, "I'm going to sit over there and watch you get your black ass kicked!"

Ten pissed-off cops, black and white, came out of their hiding places, and pounced on him like a pack of wolves. There are those who might consider this police brutality; others would say it was street justice. Whatever it was, we left him on the ground, not moving. The decoy team got the hell out of there and heard no more about it. I don't know what that shithead thought happened to him, because we never identified our purpose or ourselves, and since both blacks and whites beat him, he probably never realized the police had got hold of him and kicked his ass.

Carla's "ride" never returned. We watched for reports from that zone for reports of anyone suffering a beating by a gang. Apparently, he made no report.

He Won't Kidnap, Won't Rape Again

The next night and every night for about a week, we set up for the kidnapper/rapist. Each night, Carla sat on the wall, the cover team nearby, hiding in the trees and bushes. After seven or eight days, a black male appeared at the Juniper Street lot. From the information we had, everyone in our decoy team knew that this guy was the guy we wanted. There had been about a hundred guys who stopped and engaged Carla in conversation, but none fit the profile we had been given. When this man offered Carla a ride, she politely declined, giving him the line about waiting for her husband. He said a few more words to her and then drove off, only to return a few minutes later. Returning was not unusual; many of the guys trying to pick her up returned for a second shot.

This guy returned a third time, stopped in the curb lane directly in front of where Carla sat on the wall. The cover team got tense when they heard him shout, "Get in the mother-fucking car bitch, or I'll blow your fucking brains all over the street." He was pointing a gun at her from his car window. Carla dove off the wall, running to her right in the direction of the rear of the car. He shot at her, missed, and put his car in reverse to follow her flight. I ran to look for Carla while everyone else fired their weapons at him and the car.

Juniper Street was a one-way street, four lanes wide. When the assailant put his car in reverse to follow Carla, it moved backward, under his control. But as the barrage of bullets pinged off and through the car, the car veered across the four lanes of one-way traffic—fortunately, there was no traffic during those few seconds—stopping only when the rear bumper hit a telephone pole on the opposite curb.

The first one to shoot was Ray Braswell, who was armed with a .30 caliber carbine. Carla fired both her guns in the direction of the car moving backwards alongside her as she ran.

Meanwhile, the police switchboard had lit up from people in the neighborhood reporting gunshots on the street. Some people thought they were witnessing a gang shootout. Three patrol cars were dispatched to the scene on a signal 25 (shots fired). By the time they arrived, however, it was long over.

The moment the car hit the telephone pole, eleven of us—Carla, me, the detective in the chase car, and the eight others in the cover team—raced toward it. Braswell, the first to reach the car, snatched open the door and grabbed the driver, intending to drag him out, restrain him, cuff him, and place him under arrest. None of this was necessary or possible—Braswell had a dead man in his grasp. Braswell dropped him, the dead man's head hitting the pavement with a thud, his legs still on the floorboard of the car. That's how the homicide detectives found him—half in the car, half out of the car.

The investigation confirmed that the guy killed by the decoy team on Juniper Street was indeed the serial kidnapper/ rapist we had been looking for. Three of his rape victims positively identified him at the county morgue.

Among the thirty plus bullet holes in the car, only two hit the dead guy. A .30 caliber carbine inflicted one of his wounds, and the other, a shotgun blast; either might have killed him. The rapist's gun was fired only once. Carla emptied both of her guns, five rounds in each. The result: one serial kidnapper/ rapist who will not kidnap or rape again.

Gin Rummy Was So Engrossing

Detectives Jackie Bolton and Doug Howell were staking out a convenience store on Glenwood Avenue in Southeast Atlanta. Both were veteran stakeout cops and had logged a lot of slow-ticking time in the back rooms of many various stores, waiting for something to happen. A deck of cards was standard equipment for them—a lively card game helped pass the time.

One night, Bolton and Howell were so engrossed in their card game that they did not observe what was going on beyond the one-way mirror. A robber entered the store, stuck his gun under the nose of the cashier, and demanded money. The cashier went through the motions, anticipating that at any moment, two heavily armed cops would suddenly appear to challenge the robber. The cashier was prepared to duck behind the counter, as instructed earlier, to be out of the line of fire should anyone start shooting. The gunman gathered up the money and walked out of the store. Nothing else happened!

Since the detectives did not appear out of the back room, the cashier assumed they had left the back room and were waiting outside for the robber, to take him down in the parking lot. Still, nothing happened. The cashier ran into the back room, interrupting the detectives' card game, blurting to them that he had just been robbed.

Score a "plus one" for the robber who got away, right under the gin rummy- playing noses of our two stakeout detectives. It was fortunate for the clerk, and for the detectives, that the robber took the money and left, and did not shoot the cashier after handing over the money.

All of us were embarrassed—Bolton and Howell, me as their sergeant, the stakeout squad, and the entire police department. We had been enjoying a lot of success, but we also suffered this and other losses. There were other incidents that wouldn't have made the publicity brochure (if we had one), both on the light and the dark side.

Ithaca Misadventures

Federal money, through the LEAA grant, made it possible to expand the stakeout squad and purchase new equipment, such as fifty Ithaca 12-gauge pump shotguns. Previously, members of the APD had used Remington or Winchester shotguns. The new Ithaca was different; it was designed and manufactured to "slam fire." Load it with five shells in the magazine, one in the chamber, press the trigger, and without releasing it, rack the pump mechanism to fire each shell. Racking the pump mechanism fired the shells, not pulling the trigger, so long as the trigger was depressed. Most Atlanta policemen were accustomed to using the Remingtons and Winchesters, and we now needed to learn to use and trust the new Ithacas. Unfortunately, not everyone learned.

One Ithaca misadventure: two detectives got in their car, headed for their stakeout. The one on the passenger side loaded his shotgun across his lap, in the direction of the driver. With his finger resting on the trigger, he racked one into the chamber. What followed was a deafening explosion inside the car as a rifle slug roared past the driver, ripping a ragged exit hole on the exterior sheet metal of the door beside him. Had the shell not been a rifle slug, but buckshot, the driver would have been wounded or killed.

Another: two detectives were unloading equipment from the trunk of their car as preparation to enter a stakeout in the back of a store.

186

Loading their shotgun at the opened trunk, they blew a hole in the trunk lid, forgetting they were dealing with an Ithaca and its deadly "slam fire."

One more: a hole was blown in the ceiling of a store's back room when a detective forgot he was loading his new Ithaca, not his Remington or Winchester.

Following every such misadventure, the detectives involved were required to return to the firing range, to re-qualify with the Ithaca shotgun.

"More exciting than bras and panties!"

After receiving authorization, civilians were allowed to "ride along" in APD units. I allowed civilians to ride with me many times. David Deutchman, a native New Yorker, married to my cousin, had just been transferred to Atlanta from Boston. He was a sales executive with the Maidenform Co., maker of women's lingerie. His evenings were spent, that first month or so, cooped up in his downtown hotel room. I looked in on him while his affairs were being wrapped up in Boston and preparations were being made to move his family to Atlanta. In the meantime, he was getting an acute case of cabin fever—urban style—complete with air conditioning, cable TV, and room service.

At that time, Wade and I were both sergeants working the stakeout squad. We invited Dave to ride along with us one evening, from six p.m. to two a.m. We had just gotten back in the car after eating a bite, when a signal 63 (officer needs help) was broadcast to cars in the downtown area. We were less than a dozen blocks from the call, and the first car to arrive. The location was a gas station; before Wade stopped the car, we saw two men in the office, one holding a handgun. An off-duty police officer, driving by a few moments earlier, had observed the same, and immediately called in for help. I instructed Dave to remain in the car as Wade and I approached the office. He remained, watching wide-eyed as Wade and I entered the office. Without any resistance, we disarmed the startled, scared man with the gun.

Due to the nature of the call, many police units were arriving. We cancelled the "help call," but more and more units continued came, and continued to come—APD units of every kind—patrol cars, detective cars, paddy wagons, motorcycles, and a helicopter. (A helicopter is usually in the air on patrol; whatever frequency their radio may be tuned to is overridden by a signal 63, which is broadcast citywide on all police frequencies.)

Dave was turned on. "This is a hell of a lot more exciting than bras and panties!" I could see amused disagreement in the faces of the cops who heard him.

Dave has ridden with me more than any other civilian has. He became familiar with the routine, the radio signals, and the different beats. He got to know some of the other cops, and they knew him. He always seemed to know what to do, and never got in the way. I always enjoyed his company.

Defend Yourself—Not Only Against the Bad Guys

Three hoods attacked a decoy. When they realized the cover team was moving toward them, the hoods ran away in different directions. Detectives HF Pharr and WR King, pistols in hand, chased and caught one who resisted. Pharr and King struggled with him. Pharr whacked the hood on the head once, but not hard enough to incapacitate him. Pharr continued to whack him in the same way in the same place, and his gun went off, the bullet hitting the hood in the head, killing him. After passing through the hood, the bullet continued, its path just missing Woody King's head. The homicide was later ruled justified, but accidental. Accidental or not, King wanted to kick Pharr's ass, but didn't.

In another case, Detective Bobby Durham was put out as a decoy in Plaza Park, a downtown hangout for winos, derelicts, and thugs. Durham was lying in a doorway, "passed out," and was being robbed by a lone thug. To make his portrayal convincing, Durham pretended to attempt to resist the theft. His portrayal was convincing enough that the thief felt he needed to hit Durham over the head with a bottle to get his money. Durham hollered, "Police!" identifying himself, as not the drunk he appeared to be. The robber started to flee, and Durham chased him.

Cover Detectives WJ Barnes and FH Sutton were not where they were supposed to be, leaving Durham on his own. In pursuit, Durham saw an object, which he believed to be a gun, in the robber's hand. The robber stopped running and turned around. Durham fired at him and killed him. There was no gun found on the robber, or anywhere in close proximity.

The media report generated a lot of controversy. Detective Durham was white; the dead robber was black. Ironically, the two most vocal critics of the shooting were Detectives Barnes and Sutton, both black—the same two who failed to do their jobs, which resulted in Durham chasing the robber without the backup they should have provided. They were the cover detectives closest to Durham when he was assaulted; they should have been on the heels of the robber.

To determine if the shooting was justified, Durham was subjected to investigations by homicide, by Internal Investigations, by the DA's office, and by the grand jury. All four investigations concluded it was "a good shooting," and he was exonerated.

One member of the cover team who was in a position to witness the chase, Detective JW Bailey (who was black), testified on behalf of Durham, refuting the testimony of Barnes and Sutton. Not long afterwards, Durham was removed from the stakeout squad and assigned to the field. Two years later, he again had to defend his actions, this time in federal court to determine if he violated the civil rights of a robber during his arrest. Again, Barnes and Sutton were the main witnesses against Durham, who was exonerated for the fifth time.

After his ordeal in federal court, Bobby Durham had had enough; he resigned from the APD, and went to work driving a bus for MARTA.

Besides testifying against Durham, Detectives Barnes and Sutton leveled serious racial charges against the white supervisors of the stakeout squad. None of their charges were ever substantiated. Each has since been involved in an incident that resulted in criminal charges against him. Sutton was fired. Barnes survived the charges against him, and was eventually promoted to sergeant.

Fired At, but Civilians Helped Apprehend

The Fox Theater in Midtown was showing the film version of William Shakespeare's *King Lear*. Lieutenant Richard Rambler and I were riding together one evening, paying close attention to the Midtown parking lots, where many armed robberies had recently taken place. Robbery Detectives Sam Guy and George Wade were riding in their car, doing the same. As they passed the Fox Theater, they observed two guys walking away from the theater's box office, one jamming a handgun into his jacket pocket, the other holding a brown paper bag. Handgun, brown paper bag, quick movement, added up to a need to investigate a possible armed robbery.

Sam Guy jumped out of the car, and the suspects took off running. George Wade, still in the car, immediately put out a lookout for the two on a possible robbery of the Fox Theater. The suspects were running through a parking lot where two civilians were just leaving their parked car. Detective Guy, still in chase, yelled to the civilians, "Police! Stop them." One of the civilians attempted to block their path. In response, one of the robbers pulled a gun, aimed it at the civilian, and pulled the trigger, but no bullet was discharged, just the sound of the trigger misfiring. There were three rapid clicks, meaning the robber tried three times to shoot the civilian. Fortunately for the intended victim, the gun was a cheap Saturday Night Special, a Rohm RG-10 .22 caliber. Despite the attempt on their lives, the civilians persisted, grabbing the would-be shooter and holding on to him until Guy caught up to them. The other robber kept running.

Rambler and I were driving southbound on Peachtree Street, approaching the Fox Theater, listening to all of this unfold on our police radio. I made a u-turn on busy Peachtree Street and turned onto 3rd Street, where we expected the fleeing robber would run. We guessed right. He darted out of an alley and ran between two parked cars. Rambler pointed a shotgun out of the car window, shouted "Police," and ordered him to halt. He continued running, as I chased him in our car, bumping him with the front fender. He went down and Rambler jumped out of the car, apprehending the robber who still clutched the paper bag. In it were $634 in cash and a handgun.

We turned him over to Detectives Guy and Wade, who arrested George Crawford, 18, a student at Clark College in Atlanta. Guy had already apprehended the would be shooter, Larry Harris, 19, a student at Morehouse College, also in Atlanta.

Reported in the *Atlanta Journal* the next day, "And the patrons inside, absorbed in Shakespeare's immortal classic, went to their homes when the show ended, unmindful of the drama that had unfolded about them." What made this arrest extraordinary were the civilians who "got involved."

About a year or so later, Detective Sam Guy was working an extra job as security at the Howard Johnson motel across from Atlanta-Fulton County Stadium, when he attempted to apprehend two men in the process of robbing the desk clerk. One of the robbers fired at Guy, shooting him in the thigh. The bullet struck the main artery in Guy's leg. Guy bled to death on the floor of the motel's reception area.

The Armed Robber Decides for Us When We Need to Shoot

Each time the Stakeout Squad killed an armed robber or rapist, the critics became more vocal—some referred to us as "The Execution Squad"—while our supporters continued to applaud our results.

I feel strongly that when an armed person confronts a stranger and tries to steal his money, the robber gives up his civil rights. It's the same for any person committing a violent felony, such as kidnap or rape. Why do I feel this way? One reason relates to a case I worked as a homicide detective:

There was an old Jewish man and his wife who owned a "Mom and Pop" grocery store in the high-crime area, a black neighborhood, of Atlanta's West Side. They owned and operated that little store for over forty years. As the population went from white to black, the couple continued to serve the community. Black teenagers regularly came into the store to shoplift and worse, the store was victim to armed robbery several times.

One day, in 1968, a robber entered the store with a sawed-off shotgun, demanding what was in the cash register. The old man's wife saw her husband boldly reach for the telephone in response to the robber's demand. The robber hit the old man with the barrel of the shotgun. It went off. There was nothing left of the old man from the neck up; scattered throughout the store were bits and pieces that were once his head. Investigating the scene later, I saw pieces of skull sticking to the glass on the meat display counter; I saw portions of brain matter mixed with flesh and blood oozing and dripping from canned goods on the shelves.

Four years later, when I was called to a business where a stakeout detective had just killed an armed robber, I looked at the shaken store owner or clerk, and down at the dead robber piece-of-shit on the floor, and wondered if that old Jewish man would be alive today if we'd had a stakeout squad back then. Those two old people have remained with me. I think about them whenever I hear or read that an armed robber's civil rights were violated.

We tried to let armed robbers know they should not enter a store or any business where stakeout cops might be ready for them. We tried to warn them. We came right out and told them we were there! We had one thousand 8x11–inch, bright orange, cardboard signs, printed with bold black lettering:

ROBBER/ BURGLAR NOTICE

THIS IS A

STAKEOUT LOCATION

When challenged by police,

Do not move or turn!

Drop your weapon immediately!

Raise your hands immediately!

ATLANTA POLICE
ANTI-ROBBERY/ BURGLARY TAC UNITS

These warnings were placed prominently in store windows and on doors all over Atlanta, in true stakeout locations, as well as locations that were not staked out. We figured that playing this "shell game," could dissuade robbers who could read and believed what they read, benefiting stores not really under stakeout.

ROBBER/BURGLAR NOTICE

THIS IS A
STAKEOUT LOCATION

When challenged by Police

Do not move or turn!

Drop your weapon immediately!

Raise your hands immediately!

And wave bye-bye !

ATLANTA POLICE
ANTI-ROBBERY/BURGLARY TAC UNITS

One of the thousand signs placed in windows and doors of convenience stores, liquor stores and other businesses around the city. An anonymous stakeout cop added a personal touch with some police gallows humors

We believed these signs would be a deterrent to some, maybe most, armed robbers. But we knew the hard-core robber, the career criminal, would come anyway. And they did!

We would have preferred to be able to arrest armed robbers without having to shoot or kill them. Some never let us exercise that preference; they left us no option but to shoot, to protect intended victims, to protect ourselves, to do our job. There were many instances:

Detective W. Mangrum was staked out in the back room of a liquor store on West Whitehall Street. A black male entered the store, grabbed the clerk by his shirt collar, stuck a pistol under his nose, and said he was going to kill him. Mangrum came out of the back room to challenge him. The robber turned and pointed his gun at Mangrum. Mangrum fired; the rifle slug from his 12-gauge shotgun killed the robber.

Detective KR Stripling was assigned to stake out a small food market on Lee Street. He observed a man in the store pull out a gun and point it at the clerk, demanding the store's cash. Stripling stepped out and challenged the gunman, who turned and pointed the gun in Stripling's direction. Stripling fired, killing the armed robber.

Detective LD Loy was on stakeout at a liquor store on West Peachtree Street, in Midtown, watching the activity in the store through the one-way mirror. One of the customers became a lone gunman when he pulled out his pistol, thrust it toward the clerk, and demanded all of the cash in the store. Since there were customers in the store, Loy was forced to confront the armed robber outside, after he got the cash and left the store.

Immediately following the armed robber to the parking lot, Loy announced, loudly and clearly, "Police officer! Drop your gun and raise your hands!" The response was a bullet that whistled past Loy's ear. Loy returned fire with his shotgun, and the armed robber started to run. Loy chased on foot, calling for assistance. The dispatcher, hearing Loy's huffing and puffing, realized it was a foot chase, and he heard the gunshots. Loy's panting and the gunshots made clear to the dispatcher what he needed to broadcast—the only information he needed from Loy was his location. "Any car near West Peachtree and Eighth Street, signal 36/63/25" (holdup in progress/officer needs help/shots fired). Loy fired his shotgun several more times, but the robber continued to flee, advancing half a block ahead of him. Loy pulled out his pistol, firing it several times, still running, aiming as best he could in the direction of the fleeing robber.

Patrol cars swarmed into the area. The robber seemed to have disappeared. The area was searched. He was discovered in a shed, dead, one bullet hole in his body. Autopsy revealed he was hit once with a .38 caliber bullet. Every shot from Loy's shotgun, fired from close range, missed the armed robber. It was a pistol shot fired at a dead run, from half a block away, that hit and killed him.

Detective DJ Rutledge and his partner spent the evening looking through a one-way mirror, pigging out on sausage and biscuits at Grandma's Biscuits on North Avenue, a fast food restaurant that had been robbed frequently. Their feast was interrupted when a young black man burst into the restaurant and pointed his gun at the manager.

"This is a hold-up, mother-fucker; give it all up, or I'll kill your goddamn ass," the gunman shouted, warning diners and employees. "Anyone move, and you're dead-fuckin'-meat!"

The manager complied, and the armed robber backed out of the restaurant, passing in front of the one-way mirror. From his side of the mirror, Rutledge pulled the trigger of his 12-gauge shotgun; the rifle slug shattered the glass, and then ripped through the side of the robber's neck, taking out half his throat. The slug continued across the dining room, through the door of the restroom, and lodged in the exterior wall. Bits and pieces of the robber's throat were deposited on the restroom door as the rifle slug pierced it, as well as within the wall where the slug finally ended its flight.

Wade and I arrived within moments and regarded the robber lying on the floor in a pool of blood, massive damage to his neck; we figured he was dead. Wade and I nearly clutched at each other, startled, when the "dead" bandit sat up and gurgled, "Mama." The slug hadn't killed him, but it did tear through his vocal cords. After the ambulance took him away, I looked at Wade. "If he survives and robs again, he'll have to write a note demanding the money!"

Because of this incident, all stakeout detectives were retrained and put on notice that, in the future, "There will be no shooting inside a business whenever customers are present."

Detective FC Allison and his partner were staked out at that same Grandma's Biscuits about a month later. Shortly before midnight, two armed thugs entered, demanded the cash in the register, got it, and started to leave. Allison and his partner had decided not to challenge them within the dining room, risking the possibility of shots, the robber's or theirs, going astray, harming or killing one of the diners.

They would take them in the parking lot. Allison and his partner followed them outside and confronted them; they responded by firing their guns. The two stakeout detectives returned fire as the armed robbers began to flee. Allison's partner gave chase, but Allison was down, shot.

Wade and I were cruising close by when the call came in. We had a passenger with us, Michael Elia, an editor with a large New York publishing company and a long-time friend. Mike was in Atlanta on business, but was with us this evening as a "ride along." Things had been quiet, uneventful, it was getting late; we were about to drop Mike off at his hotel when we heard, "Any car near Grandma's Biscuits on North Avenue, signal 63/50/4!"

We arrived within a minute or so and found Allison in the restaurant. A bullet had torn the fleshy part of his shoulder, but it was not a serious wound. His partner, still in a foot chase, did not reappear until later, after they eluded him. Cops in patrol cars, helicopters, motorcycles, detective cars, undercover cars, and vans converged on the scene. The wounded cop was transported by ambulance to Grady Hospital. The news media showed up and started filming the chaos of cops trying to figure out what had happened and how they could apprehend the robbers. Allison's partner was located; he was okay. The robbers were not located, but the hunt was on to find them.

Wade and I (with Mike sticking close to us) went to Grady Hospital to check on Allison. The bullet had gone through his shoulder without doing major damage. He was treated and released. The robbers eluded the dragnet that night, but robbery detectives picked them up several days later.

Mike returned to New York the next day, more anxious to tell his colleagues this "police story" than to talk about the work he did in Atlanta.

Affirmative Action Negated My Promotion—Again

Keeler McCartney, a newspaper reporter for the *Atlanta Constitution*, has worked the police beat longer than most policemen have been on the force. Veteran reporters like Keeler know their way around and make it their business to stay close to the nerve center of the APD. Because Keeler was very close to Chief Jenkins, and then to Chief Inman, he learned things that were going to happen before anyone else in the APD knew.

One evening in 1973, Keeler informed me that a new lieutenant was to be placed in charge of the homicide squad. He told me that two names were being tossed around as the front-runners; I was the primary candidate and Vice Squad Sergeant B.L. Neikirk was the other. Keeler said that if I were interested in getting the promotion, all I had to do was to say yes when asked.

I had worked homicide for five years and enjoyed a good reputation because of the work I did during those years. However, at the time, I was out of homicide, assigned to the stakeout squad, an assignment I enjoyed; I didn't want to return to homicide for three reasons.

One reason was the smell of rotting flesh. Seeing the blood, guts, and gore didn't bother me. It was the corpses, decomposing for days— in some cases, weeks. The stench of a rotting human being hung in my nostrils, seeped into the pores of my skin, and clung to my clothes. On more than one occasion, returning home after investigating a "ripe one," I undressed on my patio, tossed the clothes I wore that day into the garbage, and ran to the shower, letting the water run over me for a long time before dressing into fresh clean clothes, and only after all that did I move about the house. The shoes I worked in, I left outside; I never stepped with those shoes on any floor in my house. There were times I blew my nose into tissues so hard, attempting to rid my nostrils of the sickening stench of death, that blood appeared.

The second reason was the mission of the stakeout squad. I liked its proactive approach; I got satisfaction in preventing victims from being killed. Work in homicide was retroactive—investigating a murder, kidnap, or sex crime after it happened.

The third reason was that I had heard from the captain and the lieutenant in stakeout that an additional lieutenant was needed in the stakeout squad; I had the best shot at it.

I turned down the promotion from sergeant in stakeout to lieutenant in homicide, realizing that an offer like that does not come along every day. Neikirk accepted the offer.

When the other lieutenant's position opened in stakeout, I didn't get the job. GL Gamble, an obscure black sergeant from the field, was promoted to lieutenant and assigned to stakeout. I was told that the next lieutenant in stakeout had to be black. This was the second time the affirmative action monster had bitten me.

The hard lesson that I had learned, I often gave as advice to others throughout the rest of my career in the APD. "Don't ever turn down a promotion for an assignment."

You Do What You Must—You Get Scared After It's Over

Lieutenant Gamble rode with each of the stakeout sergeants at different times, learning his way around, and "getting his feet wet." He was riding with me one Friday night to look in on two of our stakeout detectives assigned to a "mom and pop" grocery store on Simpson Road on the West Side. Satisfied that things were okay, we returned to the car, where we heard the dispatcher announce, "Any car near Simpson and Lanier, signal 63/25" (officer needs help/shots fired). We were the first car to arrive, but found nothing. We reported to the dispatcher that we were at the location and asked if there was any other information. The dispatcher advised us to check down Lanier, a quiet, dark, residential street. About halfway down the block, we saw a patrol car pulled over, about three feet from the curb; the driver's door was open, headlights on, a police hat was in the street.

All was quiet. We jumped out of our car. I had a shotgun and quickly racked a round into the chamber. A female voice from the darkness of the porch of one of the houses shouted to us, "The po-lice ran down the street."

Gamble took off running, down Lanier Street. I remained at the patrol car, looking around. I heard a noise near the curb and discovered a black male hidden in the darkness, lying in a pool of blood. He was emitting what I had come to recognize as "the death rattle." I called for an ambulance, and continued to investigate. I found another black male beside a parked car, his torso on the curb with his legs under a car. He was dead, from what appeared to be a bullet hole in the middle of his forehead.

The sirens of patrol cars, responding from all directions, were getting louder and louder as they got nearer and nearer. I looked back at the first guy I found; his breath was no longer rattling. I put my finger to the carotid artery in his neck—no pulse; he was dead.

The police cars had not yet arrived. I stood in the dark, straining to see or hear anything from where Gamble had disappeared. After a few moments, I heard running footsteps. Then I saw someone running in the middle of the street in my direction. As he got closer, I recognized him as a policeman. When he saw me, he ran straight toward me, carrying an object that appeared the size and shape of a baseball bat. He reached it to the ground and slid it twirling across the pavement toward me. I stepped on it to stop it from going beyond me. It was a rifle—no stock—straps at the butt end.

He dropped to his knees directly in front of me. He was disheveled, sweating profusely, exuding a strong odor of fear. He was Officer BW Davis, the cop from the abandoned patrol car.

"Are you shot?"

"No, man!"

"Are you hurt?"

"No, man!"

"What's wrong with you?"

"I'm scared, man!"

Lieutenant Gamble returned as the cars started arriving. Where he was and what he did while he was gone, I did not ask, nor did I ever learn.

The quiet street came alive—sirens, blue lights, loud police radios, and louder policemen. Each new unit that arrived had the same question. "What the hell happened?" They kept coming, some in case help was still needed, some out of curiosity. The help call had been cancelled, no other assistance was needed, but that didn't stop them; most came to take a look. Although we were the first to arrive, neither Gamble nor I had any idea what had happened, and Davis didn't tell us.

The second wave to arrive included people essential to process the scene and clean up the mess—detectives, ID techs, the medical examiner, ambulances, the undertaker—naturally, the news media were there, too. All of this confusion happened under the watchful eye of a hovering police helicopter. After the scene was processed and the bodies removed, Gamble and I went to the homicide office to help them with the investigation.

Officer BW Davis, a black policeman assigned to the evening watch, worked a patrol car in the all-black Simpson Road section of northwest Atlanta. On this Friday evening, he noticed three black males on the corner of Simpson Road and Lanier Street. As he drove by, he saw them acting in a suspicious manner. His instincts as a police officer, and his experience from having worked that neighborhood, compelled Davis to circle the block and check the three men out. They were gone by the time he got back. He drove down Lanier Street and saw two of them walking down the sidewalk. He got out of the car and told them he wanted to talk to them. He asked one for identification; the guy just stood there with his hands in his pockets, staring directly at the officer.

"Man, take your hands out of your pockets. I'm talking to you," Davis told him.

The other guy walked up, assuring Davis, "Hey, man, take my word for it; he ain't got nothing."

Davis walked up and faced the first guy, pushing open the long coat the guy was wearing, revealing an ammunition clip sticking out from his pants pocket.

"Where's the other end of that?" Davis asked. The guy turned around and dramatically shrugged off his long coat, exposing a stockless M2 carbine attached to his shoulder with a harness. He raised his arm and pointed the weapon at the chest of the startled policeman.

Davis grabbed the muzzle and pushed it aside, away from his body, just as the guy fired a burst on full automatic. A dozen .30 caliber slugs ripped harmlessly through the empty space between the cop's chest and his outstretched arm. Davis drew his service revolver and fired twice into the guy's chest at point-blank range. The shooter fell backwards, the shoulder harness snapped, leaving Davis holding onto the muzzle of the carbine.

Out of the corner of his eye, Davis saw the second guy pointing a pistol at him from behind a parked car; two shots were fired toward Davis as he ran for cover. Davis returned the fire and continued running down the street, looking for concealment. He saw a woman on the front porch of a house and hollered to her to call the police and get him some help.

The woman on the porch had seen it all—the exchange of gunfire between Davis and the guy with the "machine gun," and the second guy with the pistol. When the policeman shot at each, both had gone down. She said that just before Gamble and I arrived, a third black male stood over the wounded man, who had originally had the machine gun, and shot him in the head three times. The third guy then walked off and disappeared into the darkness.

Autopsies revealed that the first guy was shot twice in the chest with Davis' service revolver, and three times in the head with a .357 Magnum. The second guy was shot once in the forehead with Davis' service revolver.

Several weeks earlier, the Detroit Police Department had sent out flyers nationwide for a couple of shooters. They were wanted for the murder of two Detroit police officers, plus the wounding of several others. Detroit was another city that had received federal money through LEAA grants. They had also formed a street crime unit similar to our stakeout squad and called it STRESS (Stop the Robberies Enjoy Safe Streets).

Brown, Boyd, and Bethune were three cop-hating Detroit hoods on an armed robbery spree. Each time there was a confrontation one or two STRESS cops went down. The trademark of these gangsters was the automatic weapon concealed in a shoulder harness. Brown was finally apprehended, and the other two left Detroit for places unknown.

The thug with the carbine, killed by Davis, was identified as John Percy Boyd, Jr., wanted by Detroit for aggravated assault, armed robbery, and the murder of Detroit STRESS cops. The second guy Davis killed was Boyd's cousin, a local Atlanta thug with a rap sheet for armed robbery and other violent crimes.

Within a couple of days, two Detroit homicide detectives arrived in Atlanta. Since Brown had been arrested, he'd been talking. According to the Detroit cops, Brown said that he, Boyd, and Bethune had made a pact that they would not be taken alive, and they would not go back to prison. Brown screwed up, and he got caught. The Detroit cops theorized that Bethune had finished off Boyd that night on Lanier Street. All we had to do was find Bethune.

We turned the heat up, and within a few days, Atlanta Detective Lieutenant Dyke Brown got a call from one of his informants. Bethune was trying to raise money to get out of town. He was supposed to meet a contact at the Atlanta University campus, a complex of Black colleges, where he would pick up the money he wanted.

Atlanta Detectives Frazer Bolton and Horace Walker, both black, were in the AU student lounge, the meeting place, among students and faculty. When Bethune walked in, he looked around, looked at Walker and Bolton, quickly left the lounge, and went upstairs, out onto a roof, followed by the two black detectives. On the roof, Detective Walker caught up with him. Bethune pointed his pistol at Walker; Walker fired, striking him in the heart. As the bullet from Walker's .45 caliber automatic slammed into his chest, Bethune's arms jerked back, causing his own gun to discharge, striking him under his chin. Either bullet would have killed him. The medical examiner's autopsy indicated that Bethune was probably dead before he shot himself.

The excitement of the chase through the school, and then the shooting, attracted a crowd of several hundred students. In the early seventies, police were not welcome on college campuses, regardless of why they were there. The students' mood turned ugly. All they knew was that the police had shot and killed some guy on the roof of the student center. Police reinforcements were called to the campus, holding the students in check until the scene was processed.

201

The decision was made to have the Atlanta Fire Department remove Bethune's body from the roof, lowering it down with ropes outside the building, rather than taking it down the stairs, through the building, past the students. The .357 Magnum found on Bethune matched the slugs taken out of Boyd's head. Officer BW Davis and Detective Horace Walker had to make a court appearance in Detroit at Brown's trial. They were given the red carpet treatment. The Detroit STRESS cops couldn't do enough for their two heroes.

He Ran 200 Feet with a .30 Caliber Bullet in His Heart

In 1973, there was a series of incidents, in which women had been kidnapped from bus stops in Midtown after dark. The kidnappers drove off with the women and raped them. The victims described the rapists as two white males in their late 20s, early 30s.

The bus stop at Piedmont Avenue and Fifth Street was dark and desolate, providing good concealment for our cover team, and it was right smack in the middle of Midtown. Behind it, on the southeast corner of the intersection, was an open, vacant lot. Detective Pat Beeland, an attractive brunette, looked like an ordinary wife; she was our decoy. Detective Beeland stood at the bus stop on the corner, under a streetlight, appearing to wait for a bus.

The biggest pain in a decoy operation's ass are all the guys stopping to offer a ride, trying to pick up our decoy, and the "Johns" offering, "Hey, baby, how about thirty dollars for a half and half?"

Pat knew the game and was good at it. She had an icy stare that easily turned off most of those guys and totally ignored the more persistent ones who eventually went away for easier game. My instructions to Pat were simple. "Stand at the bus stop and don't say anything to anyone. Do not, under any circumstances, get into a vehicle with anyone, and most importantly, should anyone pull a gun on you, drop to the ground immediately!"

Detective EH Frye was an avid hunter and expert marksman. Armed with a .30 caliber carbine, he was positioned on the ground in the vacant lot, hidden behind a bush. He was roughly fifty feet from the corner and had a clear, unobstructed view of Pat as she stood at the bus stop. Other members of the cover team were concealed in various spots around the intersection. One team member was in a chase car, parked several blocks away.

Of the many vehicles that stopped on the corner where Pat stood, we were suspicious about one in particular. In it were three white

202

males; they drove around the block once, slowed down, looked at her, drove around again, and after the third time around, the car went halfway down Fifth Street and parked. We watched from the darkness and saw one of the occupants get out of the car and walk back up Fifth Street toward Piedmont Avenue. The other two stayed in the parked car.

When he got to the bus stop, we saw that he was a young white male; he tried to make conversation with Pat. She ignored him. He stood there, saying nothing for a few moments, and then started again to try to make conversation. Again, she ignored him. They stood on that lonely corner, just the two of them. An alarm went off in my head, telling me that this guy was the rapist; it was as if he were wearing a sign, "I rape women that I pick up here!" Everything fit the information provided by victims and detectives. The only thing different was the car. My instincts had me wound tight; the hair rose on the back of my neck. We all froze, straining our eyes and ears through the darkness to hear what he was saying and see what he might do.

They stood in silence, neither saying anything, for about twenty minutes; luck was on our side—no bus stopped, obstructing our view, and causing Pat the problem of deciding whether to board it. Cars no longer stopped because she was not alone. She had her back to him, but she was watching his shadow on the ground, clearly visible from the streetlight. Abruptly, he walked towards her. When he was within two feet of her, she turned to face him. He was pointing a 9mm semi-automatic pistol at her.

She hollered, "Po—," flung herself to the ground, "—lice," completing the second syllable as she hit the ground. Frye fired, and the guy fell to the ground, but he bounced back up, running down Fifth Street where his buddies were waiting in the car. The corner came alive as the cover team converged on it. Piedmont Avenue and Fifth Street was the most dangerous place on earth in the thirty seconds that followed Frye's shot.

Everyone in the cover team was running, shooting, trying to stop the fleeing shadow from disappearing into the darkness of Fifth Street. I saw sparks as the police bullets ricocheted off the stone wall behind the running figure. I estimate thirty to fifty rounds were fired in those frantic thirty seconds. The suspect ran about a third of the way down the block, and then turned into the first alley, where we found him on the ground, dead.

We looked for his gun, but couldn't find it. Shit. Pat swore he had a gun, describing it as a dark semi-automatic handgun. After a desperate search, we found it; he had dropped it in the darkness as he ran alongside the stone wall.

We didn't want to believe the autopsy report. The rapist was shot only twice. He was hit in the heart with a .30 caliber round from Frye's carbine—Frye strutted and smiled a lot—and in the shoulder with one of the many .38 caliber bullets as he ran.

All wanted to know was, how the hell did the rapist get up and run that distance with a .30 caliber slug in his heart? And why, with all that shooting by this elite group of street cops, did only one bullet found its mark? (Many parked cars were killed that night on Fifth Street.)

One of the guys waiting in the car ran during the excitement and got away. The third guy was apprehended; he rolled over on his buddy to the homicide detectives. Both were in jail before daylight. The kidnappings and rapes stopped after that night.

Twenty-one months of the Stakeout Squad resulted in nineteen violent criminals dead and hundreds more in prison. Did we have an impact on the armed thugs that roamed the city? Damn right, we did. By the time we were through, a convenience store clerk was one of the safest jobs in the City of Atlanta.

Part Four

Lieutenant/Sergeant/Lieutenant

Thanks to the Federal Grant, Armed Robbers Knew Where to Go

E arly in December 1973, I was summoned to the office of Assistant Chief SL Salvant. He informed me that a federal grant had been approved for a special squad. He wanted me to be its commanding officer, and said the rank of lieutenant came with it. Promotions were being made by selection, rather than testing. I told him I was his man. I had learned my lesson, and was not going to be burned again, as when I turned down the rank of lieutenant to run the Homicide Squad.

I was promoted to lieutenant on Christmas Day, 1973. It was both Merry Christmas and Happy Chanukah for my family and me. Back then, marketers had not yet neutered greetings to the patronizing, "Happy Holidays!"

I was placed in charge of the newly formed Tactical Anti-Crime Unit (TAC), funded through another LEAA grant. Ray Braswell was promoted to sergeant and assigned to the TAC unit, along with two other newly promoted sergeants—Alan Laughin and Louis Coggins. We selected twenty-four patrolmen and one civilian statistician, as required by the grant. The grant required that patrolmen volunteer for the TAC unit; the sergeants and I selected the patrolmen we wanted.

Leslie Hale, among twelve others, applied for the statistician's job. She had a master's degree in mathematics and statistics. She was our choice, although we considered her over-qualified. I felt obligated to suggest she could become bored very quickly. She responded that she needed the job. I quickly returned, "Welcome aboard!"

Leslie kept the stats and developed the charts and graphs—whatever we needed to document our activity for the feds. She became a key member of the TAC unit. Want federal grant money? Be prepared to submit data, statistics, and more data and statistics, represented in various permutations on what seemed like endless paperwork, documenting every breath taken by everyone covered in the grant—in our case, the twenty-nine members of our TAC unit.

Our function was similar to that of the stakeout squad—to catch armed robbers in the act—but with one big difference. Instead of assigning officers inside stores and business establishments, we "wired" those places with portable alarms. We could wire up to twenty different businesses within a dozen square blocks. When any one of the alarms was triggered, it registered on the mobile console mounted within one of our cars. We would identify an area shown to be a high crime area, as required by the grant, saturate it with alarms in victimized stores, and then wait in our cars for an indication of a robbery in progress. When one of our alarms went off, the console car immediately notified the other TAC cars to respond to the location of the robbery in progress. Each TAC car had two uniformed TAC officers, both armed with Remington shotguns. Our response time was less than one minute, often within thirty seconds. When the TAC cars converged on a robbery was in progress, we brought plenty of firepower; most of the time, we didn't have to use it.

It didn't take long for the thugs to know we were there and not in other areas. They stopped robbing the area we covered and moved on to the areas we were not. Simple, right? They did not understand why we did not shift our coverage to other areas, but they didn't care why. We knew why we could not shift our coverage, and we did care.

We could not shift to another area because we were locked into the goddamn language of the goddamn grant—every goddamn syllable of every goddamn word of that goddamn grant! It allowed us no flexibility. If we wanted to operate in another area, we needed the approval of the Atlanta Regional Commission, the watchdog agency of all LEAA grants. But getting approval from the ARC for a change in the grant was a slow, tedious procedure, strangled in red tape, mired in bureaucratic glop.

It's supposed to be possible to have adjustments made to grants. Ha! I went personally to the ARC office to try to get adjustments made. I was bounced form one person to another, none of whom seemed to know anything about our TAC grant. But I persisted and finally located the person who administrated the TAC grant—a woman whose nose was stuck in a manual every minute of every hour of every working day. If it wasn't in that manual, it just wasn't! She seemed able to recite by heart what was in the manual, deducing what wasn't. "But lady," I implored, trying to remain composed and professional, "We need to be flexible; we need to move from place to place so we can be where the robberies occur." I explained the need for flexible mobility, the advantage of hopscotching over the city—here today, there tomorrow. I explained how the stakeout squad created the fear and uncertainty of "Russian roulette" in the minds of armed robbers.

None of what I said meant anything to her. "According to article this, section that, paragraph such-and-such, changes to the grant can only be made by submitting form XYZ in triplicate to the district office for review, where it will be forwarded to the regional office, to be studied by a committee, then to the director for a recommendation, and finally to God for approval!"

We changed locations only once that year. The armed robbers knew where we were and where we weren't; they stayed away from where we were, and did their looting and plundering around the rest of the city. The result was that the area covered by the TAC unit was robbery free, which made us look good on paper, even though we were not doing anything, just existing. Too bad the grant wasn't administrated by street cops, rather than a chain of bureaucrats who knew nothing and understood little about street crime.

Women Police Officers in the APD

If Equal Rights for Women started in the early 1900s like a ripple on a calm lake, then in the early 70s, it hit law enforcement like a tidal wave. As in just about every US community, women were recruited, trained, and fully integrated into every facet of the Atlanta Police Department. Women worked patrol cars, walked foot beats, rode motorcycles and horses, became detectives, worked SWAT, flew helicopters, and did whatever else the male police officers did. Women were assigned to high crime areas on all three watches, and like their male counterparts, some could handle it, some couldn't.

Male officers reacted in different ways to this revolution—women being allowed into what, historically, was their "men-only club." Some male officers resisted strongly, not wanting anything to do with the female officers. Some became overly protective; each time a female answered a call, several male cops showed up with her. Most male cops took a "wait and see" attitude; the women had to prove they were

207

capable of doing what any cop had to do. The skeptical cops needed to see how a female cop handled herself in a bar brawl, when physical force is required to bring things under control, or when responding to a domestic disturbance, where the husband had just beaten the shit out of his wife, and threatened to do the same to any cop who got in his way. Such situations would determine whether male cops could depend on female backup.

But that was not the worst of the male-female cop relationships. There were the male cops who thought they could "hit on" the young female cops and get away with it. Some did. But there were also women cops who knew how to "hit back," targeting supervisors who could grant choice assignments and good off days, for starters!

So there were male cops who were protective of women cops, male cops who would not accept female cops, no matter what, male cops who wanted to or were having sex with female cops, and female cops who were having sex with supervisors for favorable assignments. Add to that the normal tension between male cops and their wives or girlfriends (in some cases, both), as well as between female cops and their husbands or boyfriends (in some cases, both). Most cops' spouses did not like to think about them spending eight hours a night in a car with a cop of the opposite sex. In some cases, that made for trouble at home.

Fortunately, it was not all trouble and tension. With the introduction of women on the force came a new brand of humor, such as:

The first time rookie officer Mary Paulk put on her new uniform with the big, heavy, clunky shoes, she said she felt like a deep-sea diver. She said she thought she would have to use both hands to help lift her legs to get into the car.

Officer Nancy Stubbs was assigned to Zone-2 morning watch, under the command of Lieutenant DW Britt, who wasn't happy about women police officers.

"Stubbs, I guess I will have to give you a key to the precinct so you can get in during the night when you have to tinkle," Lieutenant Britt announced one night at roll call, generating snickering among the male officers. (The precinct is locked during the morning watch hours, when everyone is on the street.)

Stubbs looked Britt straight in the eyes. "No, Lieutenant, if the men don't need a key, then I don't need one, either." When she needed to get into the precinct, she used her credit card to unlock the door. Lieutenant Britt and some of those other oafs never caught on.

Officer Nancy Stubbs was married to Officer JR Stubbs, a motorcycle cop. Most of the male cops knew this and did not hit on her, out of respect. It did not stop all cops. Some risked their luck—Nancy was an attractive, street-wise, no-shit cop; she also knew how to put the more aggressive would-be hitter in their place. She told one obnoxious cop, "Look, I don't put out, I'm not a pimp (meaning snitch in police parlance); just keep me fed and watered, I'll be happy, and we'll get along." She had no more trouble with him.

Although I was reluctant to accept women police officers, I was one of those who took a "wait and see" attitude. I had never worked with a female partner; I was a supervisor by the time women were appointed police officers. As supervisor, I did have some women officers working for me. Most could handle the job fine. Some, like some of the men, were not cut out for police work.

A sad, painful example of one woman officer who was not cut out for the job came one evening at the West End Mall in the West End section of Atlanta. Sergeant WD Cameron and Officer Vanessa Hamilton were working extra jobs as security for the mall. They had received complaints of a man going around the mall harassing, threatening, and frightening people. When they saw him, the two officers confronted the man and ordered him out of the mall. He left without an argument. A short time later, the man was back again, behaving as before.

Sergeant Cameron and Officer Hamilton approached him again. This time, they saw that he had a gun in his hand, holding it against his leg, pointing toward the floor. They approached him with guns drawn; suddenly, he raised his gun, and without a word, shot Sergeant Cameron once in the face. Cameron went down and was probably dead when he hit the floor. Hamilton turned, fled to the security office, locked herself in, and did not come out until more police arrived. The responding officers shot and killed the man.

Officer Hamilton committed the most unforgivable act a police officer can—she ran out on her partner. She deserved to be fired. Instead, Officer Vanessa Hamilton was given paid off time because she was "traumatized," and then transferred to the airport detail, where she remained for what was left of her police career because no other cop would ever work on the street with her again.

The best of the female cops was Nancy Stubbs. She was mature, smart, dependable, and competent. She knew how to deal and talk with people, she knew when and with whom to empathize, she knew when not to take shit from thugs. She handled her calls, made her arrests, made her reports, never complained. She was a person who was a cop, not a woman who was a cop.

The resistance to women as police officers faded years ago, much as resistance to blacks as police officers, one-man patrol cars, types of ammunition, metal flashlights, or any other change in the Atlanta Police Department has long since gone.

"A rose by any other name—was no longer Police Chief"

The "second banana" in city government in the later part of 1973, was Vice Mayor Maynard Jackson. An articulate black attorney and eloquent speaker, Jackson was primarily a politician. The time was right for Atlanta to elect its first black mayor. The astute Mr. Jackson knew that if he could find a controversial issue, one hot enough to heat the passions of his constituency, he would be assured the top banana's spot, come Election Day.

Jackson didn't have far to look. John Inman was a strong "law and order" police chief, considered racist by most blacks in Atlanta. Inman was responsible for the stakeout squad and was a strong supporter of it. Maynard Jackson promised his constituents that if elected, the first thing he would do would be to fire John Inman and abolish the stakeout squad. His campaign was full of outrage over Atlanta's nineteen citizens, mostly black, murdered by John Inman's stakeout squad. His campaign speeches never mentioned that those nineteen citizens were thugs, robbers, murderers, and rapists. Nor did he mention what they did to their victims, who for the most part, were also Atlanta's citizens.

Maynard Jackson was elected mayor. What followed in Atlanta was bizarre, outrageous, unprecedented, and hard to believe. The year was 1974.

Lieutenant Emory F Sikes, commander of the elite, well-trained, highly disciplined SWAT team, was relaxing at home on Sunday, his day off, when his telephone rang.

"Emory, I want you and all of your men in the SWAT office tomorrow morning at eight o'clock." The caller was Major JR Spence, commanding officer of the special operations section.

"What's up, Major?" inquired Sikes with a certain amount of dread, thinking of a confidential conversation he'd had several days prior.

"Just have everyone there. I'll tell you about it in the morning." Spence hung up.

Monday morning, the team members crowded into the cramped SWAT office, which was located in the basement of police headquarters. No one knew why they were there; no one offered an explanation. The grumbling and bitching started. It was one thing to be called in on your off day for a tactical emergency, but quite another to come in on your own time only to sit around the office, not knowing what the hell was going on.

Lieutenant Sikes sat quietly. He knew what was coming. Major Spence appeared, instructing Sikes, "Empty the gun vault of all weapons, including shotguns, automatic weapons, rifles, and carbines. Get all the ammunition and tear gas. Have two of your men take it away from the police station and standby."

The major continued, "Lieutenant, you and the rest of your men report to the chief's office on the fourth floor in full gear, including shoulder weapons!"

Once in the chief's office, the SWAT team was briefed.

Newly elected Mayor Maynard Jackson had fired John Inman as police chief and named Captain Clinton Chafin as his successor. Chafin had arrived earlier and was occupying an adjoining office. He was going to take over the chief's office as soon as Inman vacated it. But John Inman's contract stated he could not be fired without cause, and therefore, he was still the chief. He was not about to give up his office to Chafin.

It was a showdown between two long-time antagonists, each proclaiming himself police chief, insisting the other leave. Each had his entourage, his close, loyal supporters—policemen of various ranks—all armed! Oh, shit!

They confronted each other in the large reception area adjacent to the chief's office. SWAT officers were posted throughout, including the entrance to the reception area, with orders not to let anyone enter without permission from Lieutenant Sikes. Loyalists to both camps pushed and shoved each other at the entrance as SWAT officers blocked them from the reception area. Tempers flared; threats were made.

SWAT Officer JW Powell had two tear gas canisters and instructions from Sikes that if even just one hothead drew weapons, he would pull the pins and roll the canisters to the middle of the reception area.

There was shouting, Chafin ordering Lieutenant Sikes and his men to leave the fourth floor, and then suspending them for not complying. Inman shouted that as Chafin was only a captain, he couldn't suspend anyone. Chafin screamed that he was the new police chief, on orders from the mayor. The SWAT guys were looking for instructions from Sikes, who was no longer sure whether he was demoted, suspended, or still an Atlanta policeman. In his frustration, he declared, "Look, I've been a policeman for seventeen years, and I can't jeopardize those years for a political power struggle. Both of you have been my friends, but it's my belief that John Inman is still the chief, so I will follow his orders."

Chafin turned to Major Spence, ordering him to remove the SWAT team. Spence stood with his arms folded, saying firmly, "The men will remain!" Chafin turned to the SWAT officers, ordering them to leave. When they didn't comply, he informed them that they were all fired. Lieutenant Sikes said that he didn't know if Chafin had the authority to fire anyone—Inman insisted that Chafin didn't. But Sikes wasn't going to risk the careers of his men, so he and the SWAT team withdrew to the SWAT office in the basement of the building.

All of this, every embarrassing, humiliating, bizarre, outrageous, unprecedented moment, was observed by the media, some scribbling swiftly with their pencils on their pads, others recording it under bright lights with their cameras and microphones. The public saw that its new mayor had incited the disorder in the APD, and our shame in letting it happen, on the six o'clock news on TV and read about it on front pages of the morning newspapers.

The pushing, shoving, and glaring eventually shifted to grumpiness and murmurings. Inman sat in his office; Chafin sat in the adjoining office. A stalemate. Inman's attorney went to court and got an injunction restraining the City from taking further action in removing Inman as police chief, until the dispute could be resolved by the courts. John Inman had won round one.

Maynard Jackson was furious. He was the mayor! He was determined not to let John Inman beat him. But John Inman did beat him. The court ruled that Inman's contract was legal and binding, and he should remain the police chief for another four years. That's when Maynard Jackson did something stupid, the dumbest thing ever done in the history of the Atlanta Police Department. He brought A. Reginald Eaves to Atlanta.

Jackson and his cronies had rammed through the legislative process a new City Charter, which reorganized the city government. It created a Department of Public Safety, and with it, a higher level of bureaucracy with a higher-level commissioner at the helm. The new Department of

Public Safety would oversee four bureaus—police, fire, corrections, and civil defense. The Atlanta Police Department was to be known as "The Atlanta Bureau of Police Services." The police chief was "director of police," and assistant chiefs of police became "deputy directors of police." Unlike Shakespeare's "A rose by any other name, would smell as sweet," Mayor Jackson worked it out so that "a police chief by any other name was no longer a police chief."

Da-Da Reginald Eaves, Public Safety Commission for Life

A. Reginald Eaves and Maynard Jackson had been college classmates. Eaves was currently working for the City of Boston, running their city jail. Jackson announced that he was going to scour the country to find the most qualified person to fill the position of Commissioner of Public Safety, a position already dubbed "Super Chief" by the media. Among the two hundred and fifty million Americans, several thousand might have qualified for that job. If Mayor Jackson had searched for "the most qualified person in the country" it's amazing that his search led to his old school chum, A. Reginald Eaves. All that "scouring" and "searching," when he simply could have picked up the phone, called Eaves, and said, "I was going to search the country for the most qualified person for a new job here in Atlanta, but I know, I just know, that you are the most qualified!"

Reginald Eaves became the Commissioner of Public Safety, but that didn't change the court's ruling that John Inman could not be fired or demoted, and was still, officially, the Director of the Bureau of Police Services.

The mayor moved Inman out of the police headquarters into a small, closet-like office at the old municipal auditorium, where the police personnel section had some office space. Inman had no authority, no responsibility, no function, and no purpose. When the mayor and city council created the Department of Public Safety and a Commissioner of Public Safety—A. Reginald Eaves—they affectively neutered Chief Inman's office and title to Director Inman. Undermining the chief's authority gave Eaves direct control of the day-to-day operations of the APD. The court did not reject that. It simply ruled that Inman could not be fired from the remainder of his contract, except for just cause. Inman reported each morning to his cubbyhole, checked his mail, read the newspaper, hung around for a while, and then went home. Doing nothing else, Inman was drawing his full salary.

Eaves occupied the chief's office on the fourth floor of the headquarters building, where he ran the day-to-day operations of the police bureau. He needed help and advice due to his lack of knowledge and inexperience with Atlanta police operations. The obvious sources of help were the deputy directors. Eaves, however, chose to surround himself with a small group of black police officers who formed the leadership of the black police organization, the Afro-American Patrolman's League (AAPL).

This group of AAPL officials became Eaves' aides, bodyguards, and drivers. He even broke from the tradition of the Ford Crown Victoria --in which previous chiefs had driven themselves -- and ordered a limousine. He went around the city accompanied by his entourage. It was amusing to observe them—scrambling out of the limo, in each other's way to ensure that it was safe for Eaves to make his appearance. "Reggie" would exit the limo regally, sort of like, "Da-Da! Reginald Eaves, Public Safety Commissioner for life." Then he was whisked into a building by his "secret service." This cast of circus performers included Patrolman Beverly Harvard, who eventually scaled the supervisory heights of the APD.

It was frightening to police officers, detectives, and superior officers, who had worked their way through the APD, that this "Idi Amin" clone, this black racist demagogue, was in charge of the entire Atlanta PD. He had the power, and he pulled the strings. Reginald Eaves had colossal ego and arrogance, and he was corrupt—character traits that would ultimately lead to his downfall.

Starting at the Top—Nowhere to Go but Down, Fast

Eaves' downfall in Atlanta started before he left Boston. He had lived in a city-owned house while he was the Boston jailer. When he moved out of that house to meet his destiny in Atlanta, he brought with him the furniture—furniture that was not his. It was the property of the City of Boston. Boston officials tried to communicate with Eaves about it. Never receiving any response from Eaves, they initiated legal action against him. When Eaves realized the Boston action was not going to go away, he sent the City of Boston a check for seven hundred and fifty dollars. Boston settled for it. Atlanta's "Super Chief" was not a thief—was he? A series of other acts, professional and personal, followed, surrounding Reggie with questions and controversy.

One had to do with his nephew, hired through a local poverty program, to work in the Commissioner's Office, where he had access to

214

all police files. That was no big deal, until it was learned that the nephew had a criminal record. This caused the Atlanta Police Bureau to be expelled from the Georgia State police intelligence network.

Another was the time Reggie ordered two plainclothes policemen (Ray Braswell was one) to pick up his girlfriend from her apartment, in the middle of the night, and transport her across the city to Reggie, at his home. These two cops were commandeered from their assigned burglary detail duties and occupied for two hours, wasting time on the taxpayers' bill.

"Don't call him a nigger—just start shooting"

There were many other incidents—the kind that happen when little men find themselves in positions of power and abuse it—like Reggie's chosen band of henchmen, the power-hungry leadership of the AAPL. Most black policeman did not support the AAPL, and in fact, disavowed it, because it did not have the best interests of all of Atlanta's black policemen at heart. They knew the AAPL for the self-serving organization that it was. (Many white policemen felt the same way about the predominantly white Fraternal Order of Police (FOP), which was the AAPL counterpart.)

Under the Jackson/Eaves administration, white police officers who violated rules and regulations were disciplined to the fullest extent allowed, while blacks had their wrists slapped. The most glaring example of blatant racism during Reggie's reign of terror started with a racial slur uttered by a white cop:

Officer CB Blore received a call to handle an automobile accident on the freeway one rainy night. On the rain-slicked interstate, Blore had his hands full tending to the injured and trying get an ambulance, the fire department, wreckers, and another patrol car to the scene, besides keeping the fast moving traffic away from the scene. His only link to the assistance he needed was through the APB dispatcher in communications. There had recently been a large influx of black female civilians hired as radio dispatchers in the APB. At the other end of Blore's radio was an inexperienced, poorly trained dispatcher.

Dealing with the many things that had to be attended to, Blore was becoming increasingly exasperated with the incompetence of the dispatcher. In his frustration, Blore muttered, to no one in particular, "That stupid, goddamn nigger!" A white woman who had been involved in the wreck was standing nearby; she overheard the comment, and was offended by it. She reported it the next day.

Blore was summoned to Reginald Eaves' office, where the commissioner expressed his outrage, suspending Blore for ten working days, without pay. Many white cops thought the punishment excessive.

Ironically, a short time later, a black employee of the APD was reported for making the same sort of remark to a white cop. A white communications sergeant got into an argument with a black male civilian dispatcher who called the sergeant a "white motherfucker." The sergeant filed a complaint. When the complaint got to the commissioner's office for final disposition, Reggie downplayed the whole incident, explaining that the expression was part of the black man's cultural heritage, and he didn't mean anything by it. The black dispatcher walked away with a reprimand.

Blacks had been treated badly in Atlanta, as in other cities and towns. White policemen generally treated blacks with disrespect, and the word "nigger" was as much a part of their vocabulary as "good morning." Every reasonable person, white and black, realized it was time for this to end. It had to change, but it would not change overnight. A ship at sea required time and distance to negotiate a change in direction—so it was with this cultural ship. Reginald Eaves wanted to change the ship's direction on a dime, despite the laws of physics. He intended to teach these white boys—white cops—a lesson. Blore's racial slur gave Reggie his opportunity. He came down hard, which might have been acceptable had he been consistent. Reggie not only showed his blatant racism, but also poor judgment and weakness under the prodding of his AAPL advisors.

In the same police department *Daily Bulletin,* announcing Blore's ten-day suspension for a racial slur, was an announcement of another suspension—this one of a black police officer. WM Taylor, while off duty, became involved in a conflict with a black civilian, which led to Taylor's shooting out the tires of the civilian's car. Taylor was found to not have violated any laws. Taylor, a black officer, was suspended for three days. Echoing throughout Atlanta's police precincts for a long time after that bulletin was, "The next time someone gives you shit, don't call him a 'nigger,' if he is black—just start shooting!"

Top Heavy With Brass, so Mass Demotions of Superior Officers

It was announced that all superior officers who did not have at least twelve months in grade were to be demoted back to the next lower rank. There were two classifications in each rank—"permanent" and "acting." Those in permanent positions were building tenure and being paid for that rank. Those in acting positions were not. It was assumed that those holding acting positions would be the ones demoted. Not so! When word came down that the wholesale demotions would include all with less then twelve months in grade, even those already classified as permanent, we couldn't believe it. We were about to get a lesson in how "justice" and "politics" can work, for or against you, depending on who you were.

The purge was on; it started with the assistant chiefs and worked its way down. Each week, career police officers trudged to Reggie's office and emerged one rank lower than when they went in. The reason given for the mass demotions was that the police bureau was top-heavy with brass. That was bullshit. Everyone knew it was bullshit—even those who could put a stop to what Eaves was doing. When it was over, almost one hundred police officers had been demoted!

In September 1974, I was demoted back to sergeant, as were nineteen other lieutenants. One was Jesse Pitts, a policeman almost as long as I was, and who had held the rank of lieutenant as long as I had. We were permanent, not acting, lieutenants. Jesse Pitts was a good street cop, a more than competent superior officer. Any police department in any city would have benefited from having Jesse Pitts as a superior officer. Jesse Pitts was black.

Shortly after his demotion, Jesse Pitts went to the commissioner's office and confronted Eaves. "Commissioner, I want to know why I was demoted!"

Eaves sat back on his "throne" as Pitts continued, "I've been with the city for seventeen years, and I earned my position. I was in a paid position, and I've always thought that when you were getting paid for a particular rank, that rank was permanent." He informed Eaves that his was not an acting position; he held the permanent rank of lieutenant.

Eaves stammered, "Wait a minute, hold on a second—what do you mean 'getting paid'?" Eaves turned to Deputy Director Eldrin Bell, who was present in the room. "Eldrin, what's this all about? I thought we were just demoting acting positions."

Bell told Eaves, "Pitts was one of those that got bumped." Eaves told Pitts not to worry. He assured Pitts that because of his good performance record he would get his rank back. Did Eaves know that permanent, as well as acting positions were affected? Was it Eaves' intention to demote all positions held less than twelve months? Did

217

Eaves blatantly lie to those who questioned it? Was Eaves unaware of what was being done by his "close advisors"? If so, why didn't Eaves correct the situation when Jesse Pitts made him aware of it? Was Eaves dominated and controlled by the AAPL?

These questions were never answered, and the situation was never corrected. The demotions stood. Jesse Pitts, Ray Braswell, and others never got their rank back. It was eight years before I regained mine.

...Followed by Promotions to Fill the Vacancies

Eaves supposedly demoted the superior officers because the department was "top-heavy" with brass. At the end of 1974, Eaves initiated a promotional process to fill the vacancies created by the demotions.

The sergeant's exam was the first step in the process. When the results were in, the list was brought to the commissioner's office for Eaves to review. The list was overwhelmingly white; few blacks had passed. Eaves told his aides that because there were not enough blacks on the list, it could not be used. He suggested another list be made up, one favoring blacks. The episode might have gone unknown, were it not for Captain KE Burnette, who was sitting in the commissioner's office at the time.

Ken Burnette and I went through the police academy together; we have maintained a strong friendship since. Ken Burnette was a rising star in the Atlanta Police Department towards the end of the 1960's. He has been called competent and conscientious, among many other favorable superlatives; anyone who knew Ken and got to work with him recognized his honesty and integrity.

At the time, Burnette was the commander of the Intelligence Unit. He was responsible for getting the APB reinstated to the state intelligence network, after the fiasco with Reggie's nephew. The intelligence commander reported directly to the commissioner, so Burnette was in the commissioner's office on a regular basis.

During one of those visits, Deputy Director Clinton Chafin and Major RJ Davis brought the results of the sergeant's exam, informing Eaves, "We've got a problem—not enough blacks!" They went on to explain the racial breakdown of the list. (We had been told that the identities of the applicants were to be kept secret; they would be known only by their social security numbers, to insure the secrecy and fairness of appointments.) Burnette witnessed this on a Friday afternoon.

On Monday morning, after spending a weekend concerned about the likelihood of Eaves altering the test results, Ken Burnette camped outside the commissioner's office.

"Commissioner Eaves, I have a problem. Friday, I heard the conversation about the results of the sergeant's exam." Burnette had to get it off his chest. "Give me the latitude to express my true feelings to you." Eaves told him to continue.

Burnette went on to tell Eaves that he was concerned something wrong was about to be done with the list of sergeant applicants. "You said this would be a fair test, that race would play no part. It looks now like some of the white applicants are going to be bumped and replaced by blacks."

Eaves confided to Burnette that he had made a commitment to the black community that a certain number of blacks would be promoted to sergeant, and there was tremendous pressure that would be put on him if it didn't happen. Eaves confessed, "Captain, if I don't honor that commitment, I will be in trouble politically."

Captain Burnette never blinked, "Commissioner, I can't forget it. If that list is altered, I will make a public statement." The list came out in its original form, and twenty-one new sergeants were made. Reggie lost that one; he would have to be more careful next time.

Burnette Told the Truth, Eaves Lied, Burnette was "Buried"

A short time later, the president and secretary of the Fraternal Order of Police, John Wooten and Donna Starnes, appeared before a department disciplinary trial board. They were charged with making false accusations against Reginald Eaves and with distributing copies of the accusations at a city council meeting. Included in these accusations was an account of Eaves' unfair, racially motivated promotional policies, with specific reference to the sergeant's exam.

Eaves was testifying under oath and being questioned by the FOP attorney, John Nuckles, representing Wooten and Starnes. Ken Burnette was coming down a back staircase in the police headquarters building, past a partially opened rear door to the committee room where the hearing was being held. He saw Eaves on the stand and paused to listen to his testimony.

"Commissioner Eaves, when you learned there were only a few blacks on the list of candidates for sergeant, did you ever consider any action to alter these results?" asked Nuckles, getting right to the point. Eaves replied with startled innocence that he had not.

Burnette was thunderstruck. Two police officers were on trial for being untruthful, and the commissioner, under oath, lied. Burnette had another wrestling match with his conscience. He called John Nuckles and told him that Eaves had lied. It made no difference, Wooten and Starnes were fired.

Several months later, during an appeal hearing before the Civil Service Board, Eaves was asked once again if he considered altering test results. This time, he was confronted with the conversation that took place in his office when the results first came out. Reggie stuck to his denial and convinced the board he was telling the truth. Wooten's and Stames' dismissals were upheld.

Burnette got a call from Major Davis, who was really pissed. "Ken, the commissioner is all over my ass. He thinks I blew the whistle on him. Don't worry; I'm taking the heat for you."

Burnette replied, "Look, no one has to take the heat for me. Meet me in the commissioner's office."

Later, the two were granted an audience with a highly agitated Reginald Eaves. As soon as Burnette set the record straight, Davis was dismissed from the meeting. Eaves started ranting and raving at Burnette, "Report to Chafin; you won't be talking to me anymore." Slamming his fist on the desk, he threatened Burnette. "I'm going to bury you!" A hysterical phone call to Chafin and a stroke of Eaves' pen, and Burnette was buried.

Deputy Director Chafin passed the buck, sending Burnette to Deputy Director Childers. Childers instructed Burnette to report to the basement of the headquarters building, where Lieutenant Herring was set up in a cubbyhole office. Lieutenant Herring administered the motor pool, the police fleet of rolling stock.

"Find yourself a place to hang your hat in Herring's office, but have nothing to do with him. You will supervise no one!" Burnette's assignment was, "See if you can straighten out the mess in the detective parking lot."

Burnette scrounged up an old, three-legged desk and a broken chair from a very uncooperative and reluctant Property Section. They knew Burnette was in Reggie's dog house, and in disfavor with the deputy directors. They were reluctant to give him decent furniture.

Captain KE Burnette was launched on a new career—from commander of the Intelligence Unit one day, to parking lot and car wash attendant the next. In his new assignment, he arrived at four a.m., then ferried detective cars back and forth from the city shop. At the shop, he ran them through the car wash and filled the gas tanks, both usually done by the detectives assigned to the cars. It was common knowledge that he was being punished and publicly humiliated for challenging King Reggie.

Ken Burnette handled the punishment well. Instead of being bitter, or developing a chip on his shoulder, he smiled a lot and had a good word for everyone. He accepted this do-nothing assignment and went to work. By the time he was through, the mess with the cars in the detective lot was straightened out.

"Not even cops who were borderline psychos"

I was an outspoken critic of Reginald Eaves; I didn't care who knew it. Because of my criticism, I became a marked man. I was transferred from zone to zone and systematically harassed. After settling in an assignment in one zone, I was uprooted and transferred to another, and uprooted again after two months or so. Going from watch to watch not only keeps you out of sync physically, but the regular change in schedule screwed up the opportunity to work an extra job, which most cops need. It also hampered going to school part time, or sharing babysitting chores with a working wife.

I got the full treatment from Eaves and his deputies. What the dumb bastards didn't realize was that although most would succumb to this kind of pressure, some wouldn't. The harder they leaned on me, the tougher I got, just as I did when I was in the US Army. These guys were amateurs, incapable of intimidating me.

I reacted to the way I was treated differently than Ken Burnette. He was a very religious person, with a deeply rooted Christian ethic. "Turn the other cheek," was a natural reaction for him. I subscribed to "An eye for an eye," but I wasn't satisfied with an eye. I wanted the entire head.

I developed a tremendous hatred for A. Reginald Eaves, pondering ways to get his head for my eye. I even considered violence. What deterred me was not the violence I might inflict on him, but the risk of being caught. My career would be ruined, my family devastated—and spending time in prison for doing violence was not worth it.

Other cops contemplated killing him. None attempted it, not even those who were borderline psycho.

Twenty-one of Twenty-eight Sergeants—Black; Seven of Nine Captains—Black. Any cheating?

Mayor Jackson and Commissioner Eaves were determined to promote more blacks, one way, or another. In 1975, they made plans to administer promotional exams to fill vacancies in the ranks of sergeant and captain, resulting from the mass demotions less than a year earlier.

The promotional process that followed came to be known as the "Cheating Scandal!" Officer WM Taylor, an obscure black patrolman with five years of service, was selected and instructed by Commissioner Eaves to develop promotional examinations for the ranks of sergeant and captain. When Eaves selected him, Taylor was assigned to the crime analysis team and had some prior experience in the planning and research section.

The promotions that resulted from Taylor's tests—twenty-eight new sergeants of which twenty-one were black, and nine new captains, seven of which were black. Reggie and Maynard were more than pleased with these ratios.

That something was wrong was immediately obvious. Few black police officers knew what was behind these promotions. It wasn't until two years later that four black officers came forward to reveal to Mayor Jackson that Eaves had permitted cheating on the sergeant and captain tests. Each of the four officers had his own motivation for divulging his knowledge of the cover up.

The Administration Allowed Cheating Because it Achieved Affirmative Action

It was 1977, an election year for the office of Mayor of Atlanta. A police sergeant, two detectives, and a patrolman, all black, arrived at city hall, requesting a meeting with Mayor Maynard Jackson. They were told the mayor was too busy; he was engaged in the mayoral campaign. However, the chief administrative officer and the chief of staff granted them an audience. Sergeant JW Bailey, Detectives SC Dorsey and JL Manning, and Patrolman WM Taylor rocked city hall with what they revealed.

They reported systematic, widespread cheating on the 1975 promotional exams for sergeant and captain. They accused Public Safety Commissioner A. Reginald Eaves and his AAPL cronies of masterminding, executing, and covering up the cheating.

Mayor Maynard Jackson was convinced these allegations were made to embarrass his administration and damage his chances for re-election. He ordered the city attorney to investigate, and mandated that the investigation be concluded prior to the election. Once the city attorney's office realized the enormity of the case, they knew that it could not be resolved in the time frame imposed by the mayor. Therefore, the mayor ruled that the investigation into the allegations of cheating was incomplete and inconclusive. The mayor asked the city council, which was comprised entirely of politicians, to investigate the allegations. The city council voted by a large majority not to investigate because it was too politically sensitive. Here's the truth of what was "too politically sensitive":

Eaves instructed Taylor to develop promotional tests for sergeant and captain. Eaves ordered Taylor to turn copies over to Sergeant TN Walton, president of the Afro-American Patrolmen's League. The AAPL drew up a list of "favored" candidates that the AAPL wanted to be promoted.

Taylor testified later that Eaves told him, "I want these AAPL people to score high enough that I will have no problems promoting them. You get with Walton and work it out. I don't want to know anything about it." Eaves told Walton to hold "study sessions" with those on the list, but to do it verbally because, "I don't want any copies floating around." Lieutenant Dyke Brown was told to do the same.

These sessions were held in the homes of favored candidates, as well as Walton and Brown's homes. Some of the AAPL guys were so stupid they didn't pass the test even though they were "tutored"—given the answers to questions on the test. The promotions were made shortly after tests were given. Word leaked out among black cops. Those not among the "favored" were angry enough to want to go public about what they had learned. But threats and intimidation from the AAPL leadership, high ranking black police brass, and Eaves himself kept them from revealing what they knew.

The four accusers who came forward two years later were:

* Sergeant JW Bailey — At the time of the testing, he was vice president of the Policemen's Benevolent Association. He had gotten hold of a copy of the test answers before the promotions were made and confronted Eaves and several members of the AAPL. Eaves said Bailey tried to blackmail him into a promotion and verbally abused and threatened him. Bailey smoldered for two years until he got support from the other three.

* Detective SC Dorsey — At the time of the testing, he was the president of the PBA. He said they waited for two years to accumulate enough proof to support their accusations.
* Detective JL Manning — A member of the AAPL, and on the "favored list." He was tutored at Sgt. Walton's house, where he was verbally given the answers to questions on the test. Manning made notes, but said he was not given all of the answers. He did not pass the test. He held that against Walton and the AAPL.
* Officer WM Taylor — Stated that he had finally concluded that it was in the best interest of the APD to make known the cheating and cover-up. He further stated that he was in the process of leaving the APD.

Between the four of them, they made the case against A. Reginald Eaves and the Afro-American Patrolmen's League.

Although politicians in the city council considered the allegations too politically sensitive, the media kept the pressure on Maynard Jackson. The public demanded answers. The accusations of cheating were not going to fade away or be forgotten. Jackson had to do something. The mayor announced the appointment of two prominent lawyers, one white, and one black, to act as co-counsel and thoroughly investigate the accusations of cheating, which became known as the "Cheating Scandal." During the announcement the mayor said, "Let the chips fall where they may," which he would later regret.

Attorneys Randolph Thrower and Felker Ward set up shop and went to work. They were granted subpoena power and conducted their investigation thoroughly and fairly. They investigated, interviewed, examined, deposed, researched, evaluated, and spoke with ninety-three people related to the cover-up.

The investigators used the polygraph examination extensively in their quest for the truth. When Eaves was notified to report for his polygraph examination, he checked himself into a hospital, where he remained for several days. He was hiding from the same machine that he had ordered many of his subordinates to submit to during his three-and-a-half-year reign of terror.

In the weeks that followed, many attempts were made to get Eaves to come in for his polygraph test. Reggie, realizing that he could not hide indefinitely, finally came in, accompanied by Sergeant C. Whitehead. The sergeant had recently been to school to become a polygraph examiner. Eaves and Whitehead reviewed the questions to be asked; they altered some of them. When Eaves was finally hooked up to the machine, he squirmed, fidgeted, held his breath, tensed and flexed his muscles, and wiggled his fingers—all things that would cause a polygraph examination to go haywire. Whitehead, a student of the polygraph, was aware of these disruptive techniques; he was serving his master well.

Almost an hour later, after several charts had been run, Eaves moaned weakly that he was exhausted and could not continue. Co-counsel pointed out to Eaves that because of his disruptive actions during the examinations, the results were incomplete and inconclusive. Co-counsel advised that it would be in Eaves' best interests to return later to be re-examined. After repeated efforts to get him back to the polygraph examiner failed, Eaves advised co-counsel that he would not submit to further testing. Eaves had suspended police officers, without pay, and threatened them with dismissal, for refusing to take the same test he was now refusing to take.

Many months later, the Thrower-Ward investigation was complete; they submitted their report to the mayor. Maynard nearly choked on the "chips," which fell with the force of a giant Sequoia right across "the most qualified person in the country"—his pal, A. Reginald Eaves.

Maynard Jackson implored Reggie to submit his resignation, to bow out as gracefully as possible; sparing those involved the pain associated with dismissal. The egotistical, arrogant Mr. Eaves refused, insisting he had done no wrong. The mayor was forced to fire his buddy and lock him out of the police chief's office. There were dismissals, demotions, and suspensions for most of those involved in the cheating. Some slipped through the cracks and escaped punishment. The majority of the guilty parties were the inner circle of the Afro-American Patrolman's League. They defended the cheating as necessary to achieve affirmative action.

Some Hated Him, but Would Shake His Hand; I Would Not

During the two years between the promotions and the discovery of cheating, I had not been reinstated to lieutenant. I was still being punished for my criticism of Eaves, and I was still being shifted from assignment to assignment. One of those assignments was Zone 5, evening watch. The building that housed the Zone 5 Precinct was an old, decaying storefront crawling with vermin. City officials realized

225

new quarters were needed for the Zone 5 Precinct, but not only was there little money in the police budget, what there was, was being wasted by Reginald Eaves for his limousine, his personal entourage, and a private shower in his office, among many other such perks he felt he warranted.

The decision was made to move the Zone 5 Precinct into one of the larger fire stations. It was to be an experiment, and if successful, would cause other police precincts around the city to do the same.

After a few days in our new quarters at the fire station, Eaves decided to dedicate the new Zone 5 Precinct at a news conference. He called for it to be held at three p.m., during watch change. The day watch was to be held over and instructed to fall in with the evening watch for roll call, creating the illusion of twice the number of police officers going on duty to impress the TV audience.

As sergeant, I would be standing roll call. I pictured what was about to happen. Eaves and all the police brass would appear; Eaves would go down the ranks shaking hands, and everyone would smile as TV cameras showed Atlanta's finest greeting their commissioner. The truth was that most police officers, black and white, disliked him; a few hated him as much as I did. But everyone would shake his hand without displaying displeasure. I would not shake Eaves' hand!

In walked Deputy Director George Napper, a black, followed by two white Deputy Directors, Chafin and Childers. I had not met Napper before and didn't know much about him. He was from California and had been in his position for only a short time. I had decided not to shake anyone's hand that day, to justify not shaking Reggie's hand. As Napper approached me with his hand extended, I declined. I said I had injured my hand and could not shake hands. He eyed me suspiciously, as did the other deputy directors. They all knew it was bullshit, but there was no way for them to do anything about it.

Eaves never showed up that day. The taxi drivers, protesting some issue with the mayor, demonstrated by circling city hall, disrupting traffic. Reggie rushed to city hall to protect the mayor from the cab drivers. Had I known Eaves was not going to show up, I would have shook hands with the three deputy directors, keeping them and the other brass that learned about my behavior, from being pissed off at me.

Britt, Me, and the Munchkins

In 1976 the merry-go-round stopped, leaving me at Zone 2, where I was put on the morning watch, and where I remained buried for the next several years.

The morning watch commander in Zone 2 was Lieutenant Dennis W. Britt. I liked him; I called him Archie because he said things Archie Bunker (from the 70's TV show, *All in the Family*) might have said. Britt had been around for about thirty-five years, working the streets in uniform, most of it on the morning watch, which was his preference. He chose to stay on the morning watch, away from the big brass, out of the mainstream.

"Daddy" Britt, as many affectionately referred to him, was an anachronism. Things were simple. "If it was good enough thirty-five years ago, it's good enough now!" Good policing had nothing to do with the academics with their MAs, PhDs, new management techniques, or psychological reasons for crime. "Policing is just a matter of good common horse sense." It all boiled down to "the good guys" and "the bad guys."

Lieutenant Britt had a big heart and a narrow mind. The things he said to me could have offended me, but he said them out of ignorance, not malice, like the time I told him I'd been in the army as an infantry grunt. He replied, "All the Jews were in the quartermaster (supply) you know, like running a clothing store. Just like all the niggers in the army drove trucks!" Lieutenant Britt left the precinct every night after roll call, heading straight for the all-night donut shop.

Stop by a twenty-four-hour donut shop in any city in the country, and chances are there will be one or more patrol cars parked in front, especially at night. The coffee is usually free, and more than likely the donuts are, too. The donut shops are an oasis for the cops, a pit stop, and a place to take a break, use the bathroom, and make a call on the telephone. Cops meet there to talk during lulls in the action, to fight off the boredom of a slow night. For a donut shop, this is the best and cheapest security to be had. For the price of several dozen cups of coffee and donuts, the police cars coming and going is one hell of a deterrent to would-be robbers and drunks that might hassle the lone employee.

After Lucy, the woman who ran the donut shop by herself during the wee hours, had served him several cups of coffee, Britt began his nightly quest for burglars through the dark streets and alleys. At about five a.m., when the morning editions of the newspaper were being delivered to the paper boxes throughout the city, he would "appropriate" one from a delivery truck. He always returned to the donut shop as his last stop for the night. Before he climbed onto his favorite stool at the end of the counter, there was a cup of coffee waiting for him. The place was usually crowded with early morning regulars grabbing a quick coffee and donut before hurrying off to work.

"Lucy, run some hot water through those dirty socks again and let me have another one," he'd say, or tap the empty cup with a spoon to get Lucy's attention.

One morning, as I was about to join him for a cup of coffee, I deposited a quarter in the paper box and took a fresh morning edition of the newspaper.

"Goldie, any policeman who buys a newspaper ought to be horsewhipped!" he said. He explained that with so many newspaper delivery trucks violating traffic ordinances, such as stopping on the wrong side of the street to make deliveries, all you had to do was call their attention to it, and you were ensured a free paper each morning. "There's nothing wrong with that; why, with policeman's salaries so pitifully low, it was always standard practice, and used to even include the milk truck and the bread truck."

The donut shop ran promotions every now and then. A card was given with each purchase. Scratch off a portion from the card, and it would reveal the prize, such as free coffee and donuts, or one dozen donuts, or two dozen "munchkins." Munchkins were about the size of a golf ball, the part punched out of the center of the donut to make the hole. They were packaged in brightly colored, little kiddie boxes, with pictures of elephants, giraffes, kangaroos, and teddy bears, and a handle at the top so it could be carried like a lunch pail.

One morning, Britt was scratching a stack of the cards and he said, "Let's see what you won this morning, Goldie." Then he called out, "Lucy, the sergeant is a winner; fill up a box with a couple dozen munchkins for him to bring home to his kids." Britt and I had our usual aimless conversation, about such things as the dumbasses running the police bureau. Conversation and coffee finished, I left, leaving my prize, the box of munchkins, on the counter.

Later, I heard a call reporting a prowler in the rear of a house on Monroe Drive. I was headed for the precinct; the location of call was on the way, so I decided to back up the responding patrol car. Other cops were drifting towards the precinct; they wanted to get off on time and not be caught in morning rush-hour traffic. As I pulled to the curb at the call, several other patrol cars arrived from both directions. Monroe Drive is a main thoroughfare for surface street traffic and has two lanes in each direction. The several patrol cars, and a paddy wagon, blocked the curb lanes on either side of the street, causing traffic to merge into a center lane in each direction.

The prowler turned out to be a wandering drunk and was loaded into the wagon. Before any of us left, another patrol car approach, horn blowing insistently, grabbing everyone's attention—cops and onlookers. It was Lieutenant Britt. He stopped in the center lane, halting all southbound traffic. He stuck his head out and hollered, "Hey, Goldie! Come here! You forgot your munchkins!" He handed me the cute little box and drove off.

I was trapped in the middle of the street, a slow, steady stream of traffic in both directions passing me, a uniformed police sergeant, balanced like a statue on the yellow line, holding a brightly colored kiddie box covered with elephants, giraffes, kangaroos, and teddy bears.

Exasperating; He Was Exasperating

Carl Pyrdum was a young, skinny, blond-headed patrolman with eyeglasses. I first met him when I was a sergeant assigned to morning watch, Zone 2. He knew everything and wouldn't listen to anyone—not his peers, not his supervisors. In a squeaky voice, he would reply to a motorist who asked why he was stopped, "Well, it wasn't just for shits and giggles," or "Well, you might have passed the written test, but you failed the driving test!"

He was eager for a chase—so eager he might initiate it. On calls that did not require a "code 3" response, he would drive at warp speed, resulting in quite a few wrecked patrol cars. He was lucky; he was never seriously injured in any of them.

One February night, Lieutenant Britt advised us at roll call that freezing rain was predicted for the next several hours. He told us to go to our beats, and once ice glazed the streets, to park somewhere "centrally located." Pyrdum and several others went to Futo's Wrecker Service, off Cheshire Bridge Road, to wait out the weather.

Later that night, the ice hit, creating a solid glaze. There were dozens of wrecks, mostly fender benders. People were told to exchange information, and come in and file an official report the following day. Patrol cars were only dispatched for emergencies, and they were cautioned to proceed slowly. A call came in to check on a prowler in the rear of a closed business. It wasn't urgent, but it had to be answered. Pyrdum took off, fishtailing out of Futo's lot. On Cheshire Bridge Road, trying to control his car over the ice, he lost. The ice won on a downgrade, and his car spun through an empty parking lot, crashed through an iron railing, and plunged twenty feet to an adjacent parking lot below. The car landed on all four wheels, totaled. Officer Carl Pyrdum, once again, was not hurt. A second patrol car was dispatched to handle the original call.

Some months later, my brother Glenn was in Atlanta, on a ride along with me one night. The city sanitation workers had been on strike, and the different zones had police officers detailed to the various Department of Sanitation facilities around the city to deter vandalism. One of these facilities was in Zone 2, off Cheshire Bridge Road, across from Futo's Wrecker lot. Officers Carl Pyrdum and Pat Keeney were assigned there in separate cars. Glenn and I stopped by, chatted with them, and left.

We were on Cheshire Bridge Road, approaching Piedmont Road, when we heard over the radio that a patrol car was in a chase—the patrol car that covers the northernmost beat in the city, headed away from the city, several miles north of Zone 2. The dispatcher notified Fulton County PD and the Georgia State Patrol for assistance. I got on the radio to advise all other APD cars to disregard the chase.

However, I knew Carl Pyrdum! I told Glenn that we were between the chase and Pyrdum, so it would be smart for us to pull into the closed gas station on the corner of Cheshirebridge and Piedmont. I knew what was going to be coming up behind us. We stopped in the darkened lot and heard Pyrdum coming. He was traveling too fast to take the ninety-degree turn onto Piedmont Road, so he cut through the gas station lot, where his car almost collided with ours. The wake of his car caused ours to rock. The chase ended a few minutes later when Fulton County stopped the car. I confronted Pyrdum later, privately, and chewed out his ass for his unnecessary risk-taking. But I knew he would do something like that again, no matter what I said. He was frustrating to supervise.

At about five a.m., Officers Carl Pyrdum and Pat Keeney, and my brother and I, met for brunch at the IHOP. Pyrdum was eating a stack of pancakes oversaturated in syrup and jabbering, trying to justify his actions in past incidents. His knife slipped from his hand into his plate, drenching the handle with syrup. He picked it up, not skipping a beat and continued eating, syrup dripping from his hand. I finally asked him why he didn't go wash his hands and ask for a clean knife. He put his hand out, palm down. The dried syrup acted like an adhesive, keeping the knife from falling. He said, "Hey, boss, this way you don't drop your knife!" Exasperating, he was!

Pyrdum was called to the office of Deputy Chief Clinton Chafin, who told the officer he had cost the city more money in damage to police vehicles than anyone else in the history of the Atlanta Police Department. Chafin told Pyrdum he was being transferred to the Atlanta airport precinct, with orders that he not be assigned to a vehicle. Deputy Chief Chafin said that as long as he was with the Atlanta Police Department, Officer Carl Pyrdum would never get behind the wheel of another city vehicle.

Several years passed; Chafin was no longer with the APD, having left to become the police chief of the Fulton County PD. Pyrdum wrangled a transfer out of Purgatory to Zone 5. He was assigned to a large, downtown foot beat, and the beat included a little three-wheel Cushman scooter, similar to those used by Meter Maids. Within a week of his new assignment, he attempted to chase a car on his scooter. Yes, he wrecked the scooter.

However, it wasn't all "shits and giggles" with Officer Carl Pyrdum. After a year or so, he was back working a car again. One night, he got behind a stolen car, and as he followed, he called for backup. Officer David Lieber fell in behind; they stopped the car in a parking lot. There was one subject in the car. As Pyrdum was getting out of his car, he was shot twice in the stomach. Lieber shot and killed the shooter immediately. Pyrdum recovered and was back on the job within a year. Lieber was suspended for five days, without pay, for using "unauthorized ammunition."

The APD had always issued round ball ammunition, the projectile a solid piece of lead. Another type of ammunition is "hollow point." Its projectile is not solid, but hollow at the point. The hollow point has more stopping power; it causes more internal damage as it enters the body because it expands upon entry. The round ball enters and exits the body more cleanly.

Instead of the issued round ball, many APD cops used hollow points because of its stopping power. Before it was officially authorized, cops paid for hollow points out of their own pockets, a practice largely ignored by APD bosses.

When Reginald Eaves took over, he began to receive complaints from the black community about the hollow points. Most victims of police shootings in Atlanta were black males; these victims would have had a better chance of survival with the round ball ammunition.

Eaves initiated a new ammunition policy, in which APD cops could use only approved ammunition. Maximum grams of weight and grains of gun powder where mandated; it was tantamount to anemic ammunition, and became known throughout the APD as "Reggie pellets." There were incidents where violent people were shot with the Reggie pellets, but they didn't go down. This craven, political policy placated members of the black community, but made our jobs that much more hazardous and difficult.

The policy continued long after Eaves was gone. It wasn't until the late 1980s that the policy was changed and hollow points were authorized. There were several studies made (one by the FBI) showing that in an urban area, round ball ammunition was unsafe for the public. There were incidents documented around the country where round ball went through the target person's body and struck a third party.

FBI Agents Did Not Tell the Whole Story—the Real Story

After Ray Braswell lost his stripes in the mass demotions of 1974, he was assigned to the burglary squad as a detective. Herbert Lamar Myers, a/k/a "Lemo," was a career criminal. He'd been in and out of prison for most of his life. He'd commit a burglary, be arrested, go to prison, be paroled, commit a burglary, be arrested, again and again.

Braswell was working several burglary cases he felt had the unmistakable signature of "Lemo." Through fingerprints and other evidence, Braswell concluded that Herbert Lamar Myers was the perpetrator and obtained the required search and arrest warrants.

Braswell found Lemo at home at an old, small frame house on Juniper Street in Midtown, where Lemo Myers lived with his mother and seven-year-old daughter, and arrested him for a series of burglaries. A search of the house found property taken in several of the burglaries. On the way to the city jail, Lemo said that the timing of his arrest couldn't have been worse. There were no groceries in the house, and his mother had only a few dollars.

After depositing Lemo, Braswell went back to the house on Juniper Street. He drove the mother and daughter to the AandP grocery store on N. Highland Avenue in his detective car. They had less than twenty dollars. He chipped in twenty dollars of his own so they could buy what they needed.

Two years later, Herbert Lamar Myers was out of prison and on parole. Ray Braswell was back in uniform and working the evening watch. He received a call from the police switchboard operator, giving him a telephone number left by a man who wouldn't leave his name.

Braswell called; Lemo answered. Lemo gave Braswell information on four men who had just escaped from prison. They overpowered two US marshals, took their guns, and left each handcuffed to a tree in the woods. Lemo said, "The four are sitting in the rear corner of Ray Lee's Blue Lantern," a bar on Ponce de Leon Avenue. He cautioned Braswell that they still had the marshals' guns.

Braswell contacted the FBI, who confirmed that they were indeed looking for the escapees. They had just found out about the marshals. He was surprised the four had been located so fast. Braswell told the FBI agent to have several agents meet him at a location several blocks from the Blue Lantern. Armed with more than a good description from Lemo, and knowing where the four were sitting, Braswell went through the front door; the agents went through the rear. The four escapees surrendered without a fight, and were hauled off by the FBI.

Afterwards, Lemo Myers approached Braswell on the street and said he appreciated what Braswell had done for his mother and daughter the night he was arrested. He added, "We'll call it even now."

The next day, in the newspaper, there was an item about how the FBI had apprehended four armed and dangerous prison escapees. It praised the agents' quick action in locating them so soon after the escape, and so on—all about the FBI—not a syllable about Officer Ray Braswell, or the APD, or how and why Braswell got the information, which was not only the real story, it was a story the newspaper would loved to print.

What US Justice Didn't Do, the APD Cheating Scandal Did

During the four years (1974-78) that A. Reginald Eaves was police commissioner, he and his AAPL pals were in complete control of the APD and ruled it with reckless abandon. Throughout the police bureau, there was an undercurrent, a rumble of wrongdoing by Eaves and the AAPL—mutterings in patrol cars, behind closed doors, and in police precincts, as well as at police headquarters.

I was frustrated, sometimes depressed, because there was no relief in sight. Eaves had strong support and backing from the mayor's office, the city council and the majority of the electorate. Several of us were outspoken critics of Eaves. When we ranted and raved, most policemen kept their distance from us; they didn't want to be too close when Reggie came down on us. Our complaints, our criticisms, and our charges of what was going on, meant nothing to anyone who had the power to do something. No one was going to take on Reginald Eaves, Maynard Jackson, and the City of Atlanta. We were a small group of disgruntled policemen; our pleas were dismissed and forgotten.

My spirits were lifted one night when a colleague called, asking me to meet him later that night. The caller was Sergeant Ray Appling, who worked in the zone adjacent to mine, also on the morning watch. He had had a meeting several days before with an FBI agent brought from Los Angeles to Atlanta. The agent specialized in investigating political corruption. Appling met him through a friend in the district attorney's office. The agent was looking for someone with whom he could work in confidence, someone who would point him in the right direction. Appling suggested he contact me because of my reputation (good or bad, depending on whom you talked to) and the contacts I could establish for him.

Two days later, I met with FBI Special Agent Bill Whitley. He said there were strong reasons to believe that corruption and illegal activity had infiltrated city government, specifically, the police bureau, and went all the way to the top. His job was to go through all the smoke and see if there was any fire.

Yes. I was his man. Yes!

The relationship started slowly. I, like most policemen soon after being appointed, had developed paranoia, and it stuck. Most cops have dealt with FBI agents before and didn't trust them; justified or not, that's the way it was. I used my influence on cops who knew me; I was able to convince most to come forward and give Whitley the information he needed.

Many mornings after getting off duty, I met Whitley for breakfast, where we reviewed the information he had compiled. I would give him insight into the people whose names were cropping up, suggest other people to interview, and discuss strategies and options. This continued for over a year; Whitley was overwhelmed by the number of people wanting to give him information on corruption in the Atlanta government and the APD.

It was becoming clear that policeman of all ranks were involved in illegal activities. It wasn't only in the police bureau; the same suspicions hung over city hall. Glaringly obvious from the information sources had given to Whitley was that the majority of those being looked at in his investigation were black and that directly or indirectly, the worst culprit was A. Reginald Eaves.

"Okay, Bill, now that you have it, what are you going to do with it?" I asked Whitley one morning, when I knew my involvement had ended. He told me he still had a few loose ends to tie up, some blanks to fill in, and then he would go to the US attorney for final review.

"Goldie, when I go to arrest Eaves, I'll call you so you can be present to see me put handcuffs on him. That's a promise!" Special Agent Bill Whitley never kept that promise. He didn't arrest Eaves or anyone else he investigated.

The US attorney for the Northern District of Georgia was the key player in that decision. Maybe the results of Whitley's investigation weren't strong enough to present to a grand jury. Possibly the US attorney was reluctant to take on black officialdom in Atlanta, due to political ties between the City of Atlanta and the Carter administration.

I never found out why nothing happened. Whitley never contacted me with an explanation. I really didn't expect that consideration; I had dealt with the feds before.

What the United States Justice Department couldn't, or wouldn't do, the Cheating Scandal did. The Atlanta Police Bureau got rid of A. Reginald Eaves. In 1978, Mayor Maynard Jackson fired his old school chum, the "most qualified person in the country." But he landed his ass on one of the seats of the Fulton County Commission, the county that encompasses Atlanta, where he ran for and was elected Fulton County commissioner in a district that is largely poor and black. To this electorate, Reggie can do no wrong.

But he could, and did. Again.

Ultimately, the feds nailed him for extortion. He was convicted on three counts of accepting money for his favorable vote on zoning matters. He was sentenced to six years in the federal penitentiary and fined $25,000. It took until the mid-1980s, but he ended up where he should have been long before.

These two facts will never change:

I will always be a well-respected and honored retired Atlanta Police Captain.

A. Reginald Eaves will always be a criminal and an ex-convict.

The last laugh is not only the best laugh, it's orgasmic.

I Let My Weaknesses Follow the Path to Peer Acceptance

In early 1979, I suffered an acute case of lower back pain. I was at Piedmont Hospital, visiting my father, who was recovering from a car accident. Standing at his beside, my back gradually gave way, and I could no longer stand. After sitting a while, I got up and hobbled to my car. When I got home, I barely made it from the carport into the house.

I was flat on my back, in bed, unable to stand or walk, for the following six weeks. I was taken to the hospital for all the prescribed tests, such as myelograms and electro-myelograms. I had to be transported by ambulance. The doctors recommended back surgery or prolonged bed rest. Neither guaranteed a cure. I opted not to have the surgery, and lay around on my dead ass, consuming a steady diet of muscle relaxers and pain pills.

I did a lot of reading during that time. Always a voracious reader, it has been one of my main pleasures in life. During that period I read just about everything James A. Michener had written.

I also did a lot of thinking. Somehow, the Michener books triggered a reevaluation—perhaps I was evaluating for the first time—my feelings on the race issue. The emotions that surfaced as I lay there, day after day, week after week, caused me to ponder why I harbored such resentment and negativity against blacks. Was it hate? Fear? Insecurity? Did I share the colonial mentality of superiority?

I decided it must have been peer pressure—that force that drives one to illogical and unreasonable limits. I had been willing to "go with the flow," to be accepted by colleagues, friends, family, whomever. It didn't make sense to me that I would dislike an entire class of people because of their racial or cultural differences. After all, wasn't I a member of persecuted minority? My culture was the original persecuted minority—a persecution that had lasted for over five thousand years and reached every corner of the world.

I began to understand that my weakness took me down the path of least resistance. I let my need to be "one of the boys" control my thinking and suppress my sense of right and wrong.

I didn't then, and I don't now, accept affirmative action, or racial quotas. I don't favor anything that advocates placing incompetent or unqualified people in unearned positions for the sake of racial, ethnic, or gender parity. I realized that because I believed that, because I would not accept what affirmative action was about, didn't mean I was the racial bigot I thought I had become. It was time for me to follow my conscience, instead of the mainstream majority.

We Both Had Disdain for A. Reginald Eaves

After a couple of months, my back healed enough that I was able to return to work. After several days, I was required to attend a two-day race relations seminar. It was held at Pascalls restaurant/motel on ML King Drive, the center of civil rights activity during the 1950s and 1960s. The seminar was conducted by Dr. Charles King, a very large black man. It was mandatory for all APD sworn personnel. There were twenty-five of us in the class—five from the APD, the rest from different government agencies and the private sector.

When I had something to say in class about race, I said what I believed. Dr. King was confrontational in the way he conducted the class. He was intimidating, arrogant, and argumentative. He declared war. I held to what I believed.

Things got heated when he compared me to Adolph Hitler. I was enraged. We were in each other's faces, yelling, cursing—well beyond the bounds of a spirited debate—stopping just short of physical violence. The other twenty-four people in the class, none of whom felt the wrath of the blustering Dr. King, witnessed all of this.

That was the first day of the seminar.

At the end of class on the second day, Dr. King asked me to stick around. He was very sorry for the "Hitler" comment, and he apologized to me. He said that he always picked out a "live one" to create conflict and controversy in class. He broke out a bottle of wine, and we sat around for a couple of hours talking, one on one, quietly, calmly, rationally. By the time I left, we had found that we were on common ground—we both had a disdain for A. Reginald Eaves.

I had come to grips with the racial issue. I judge people on an individual basis, instead of lumping them together in a particular class. To this day, I still have utter contempt for any "bad guy," regardless of race, and feel an equal opportunity hatred for a bully. Race is a non-issue for me now. I regret that I hadn't been aware, or stronger, for so long, and that I let peer pressure suppress the rational feelings I believe were inside me all that time.

My Back Came Back

It was good to get back to work after lying around for two months. I had to wear a back brace and could not stand for more than thirty minutes at a time, but at least I was out on the streets, functioning to some extent. The moment I returned to work, I was concerned about how my back would hold up during a physical confrontation. The answer came within three weeks.

One of the cars in my sector received a call at about four a.m.; a woman was screaming in a house. I was two blocks away, and as I pulled up, I saw the back door wide open; I could hear screaming. I charged up ten steps leading to the open door and followed the screams through the house to the front room. I saw a young woman in a nightgown crouched behind an easy chair in the corner of the living room; a black male was standing over her, trying to drag her out of the corner.

I grabbed him from behind and spun him around; while still in my grasp, he started to run across the living room. I was directly behind him. He stumbled, but I held him up as our momentum thrust us back toward the couch across the room. I steered his head into the heavy, wooden arm of the couch, stunning him enough to take most of the fight out of him. Still, he resisted as I nudged him through the house to the back door. Officers LS Moore and DL Overstreet had arrived and were approaching the foot of the stairs. I launched the intruder head first, down the stairs, special delivery, to two very surprised cops.

The victim was a flight attendant for Eastern Airlines. She shared the apartment with one roommate. They were asleep, awakened by the noise of the back door being forced open. When the intruder got in, he spotted one girl and chased her through the house, where he attacked her. The roommate locked herself in her bedroom and called the police. The intruder was arrested and charged with burglary and attempted rape.

My back? I never thought about it during the incident, nor did it prohibit me from doing what I did. It ached some afterward, but didn't cause any additional problems. I knew then that my back had come back; I was going to be okay!

Our Dark, Gallows Humor

Police officers are a strange species. For the most part, we are the average guy next door. Yet, we experience things he never does. In our working lives, we see the worst in people, the underbelly of society. We live with violence, grief, carnage, tragedy, fear, pain, brutality, horror, sorrow, and despair. We are exposed to all of this and more, day and night, month after month, and year after year. It is difficult to witness the burdens and suffering of these unfortunate people. It's emotionally draining and mentally unhealthy, and often leads to alcoholism, drug addiction, divorce, and sometimes suicide. It has ended many careers.

In the early 1980s, the city made available a staff of psychologists to combat these issues. When symptoms of stress were noticed and reported, usually by a supervisor, you were invited to have a "talk" with the psychologists. Most of the time, this invitation was declined, or strenuously resisted. There was a stigma attached to visiting a "shrink"; we "macho men" could handle things ourselves, or so we believed! We built up defense mechanisms, a moat surrounding the brain. In some cases, this mechanism was dark, gallows humor.

Working Zone 2, morning watch as a sector sergeant, I monitored a call received by one of the cars in my sector. "Car 3207, at Juniper and 10th Streets, signal 50 and 4." (Person shot, ambulance on the way.) It was shortly after midnight. Several patrol cars were already there when I arrived. Lying in the middle of the intersection was the victim, shot several times, still alive, but laboring to breathe.

We recognized him as a local thug; most of us had encountered him at one time or another. He'd been arrested numerous times for a variety of street crimes, and we'd had to chase and fight him some of those times. None of us rushed to administer CPR. A crowd of nearly a hundred people had gathered. We kept them on the sidewalks and blocked off the intersection to traffic. By this time, six patrol cars had arrived. We stood in the middle of the intersection, waiting for the ambulance.

Within a few minutes, the thug stopped rattling; clearly, he was dead. I grabbed the radio microphone from my shoulder and without keying it, said loudly, in my best stage voice, "Cancel the ambulance, and start a garbage truck!" All the cops thought that was amusing; laughing, they "high-fived" each other.

Someone in the crowd didn't think it was amusing. She was offended by our crude, insensitive conduct and made a complaint. A couple of days later, I was in the chief's office, getting a scalding ass chewing. My up-coming transfer to the day watch was cancelled, and my off days were changed—there went the extra job I had lined up. My big mouth got me into hot water once again.

Atlanta's "Missing and Murdered Children"

As the 70s were ending, I was still in political exile, banished to the hinterlands, doing penance. This was during Atlanta's "missing and murdered children" cases.

Within a two-year period, from late 1979 through 1981, the bodies of twenty-nine black children, teenagers, and young adults were found murdered in the Atlanta area. The victims, most of whom were male, were discovered several days, in some cases weeks, after first being reported missing. The city was under siege; parents (notably black parents) were frantic, afraid to let their children out of their sight. It had been determined that a serial killer was responsible for these crimes, and a special homicide task force was formed by order of Atlanta Police Commissioner Lee P. Brown.

Atlanta Homicide Detectives Sidney Dorsey and Louis Graham were the original lead investigators. As more victims were found, other law enforcement agencies joined the task force. Dekalb County police got involved (several victims were found in their jurisdiction), as did the Georgia Bureau of Investigation. The families of some of the victims hired private investigators. The United States attorney general ordered the FBI into the case. As the task force expanded, some bizarre types offered their services—people on the fringe—including one clairvoyant. President Ronald Reagan authorized federal funding to assist the investigation. Several celebrities contributed large sums of money to create an award fund.

Conspiracy theories and rumors were widespread, from the Ku Klux Klan, to "snuff" filmmakers, to "mad scientists" engaged in mysterious medical experiments. Each day seemed to produce yet another theory. The local media were frenzied, and eventually the story gained national media attention, as well.

All leads were followed up on, but the mystery (and the discovery of bodies) continued. Finally, one night, during the ongoing police stakeouts at the Chattahoochee River, an Atlanta police officer stationed on the riverbank heard a splash in the water under a small bridge. He radioed this information to Atlanta Police Officer Carl Holden, who was standing by in a patrol car several blocks away as part of that stakeout. Holden stopped the only vehicle coming off the bridge.

The driver of that vehicle was twenty-three-year-old Wayne Williams, a mild-mannered black man who lived with his parents in a middle-class Atlanta neighborhood. Williams was a part-time free-lance photographer, with hopes of a future in the entertainment industry, particularly radio broadcasting.

FBI agents appeared on the scene, relieved Holden of his suspect, and took credit for the arrest. Soon after, the body of Nathaniel Cater, a twenty-six-year-old black man, was recovered from the river near the same bridge.

After additional investigative work and extensive legal maneuvering, Wayne Williams was indicted, tried, and convicted of the two most recent murders. Ironically (as "missing and murdered children" had become a household phrase in Atlanta), the victims of the last two murders were not children, but grown men in their twenties. Authorities announced that Wayne Williams was responsible for the deaths of the other twenty-seven murders, and cleared those cases, as well. Currently, Williams is serving two life sentences in prison for the last two murders.

During this time, the question was repeatedly asked: "Where are Hagin and Goldhagen, the two hot-shot homicide detectives?" We had no answer. We were never told why we weren't assigned to the homicide task force, and we didn't ask.

Years later, the two lead detectives, Sidney Dorsey and Louis Graham, stated that in their opinions, Wayne Williams did not murder all of the other victims. However, law enforcement authorities took no further action.

Hostage Negotiations, the Beginning

During the early 1970s, several violent incidents occurred in different parts of the world; incidents that ended disastrously:

*The 1971 takeover of the maximum security prison at Attica, in upstate New York, where inmates rioted and took corrections officers hostage. After a five-day standoff, the New York State Police took the prison by force, killing thirty-nine inmates and hostages.

*The 1972 Summer Olympic Games in Munich, Germany, where members of the Black September faction of the Palestine Liberation Organization took Israeli athletes and coaches hostage. Several hostages were killed in their quarters at the Olympic Village. The rest were taken by helicopter to the airport to be transferred to a plane and flown to an unknown destination. The German police were set up for a rescue attempt at the airport, it did not succeed, and all of the hostage athletes and most of the terrorists were killed.

*John and Al's Sporting Goods in Brooklyn, NY was the scene of an armed robbery. A silent alarm was activated, and police arrived before the four robbers had a chance to leave. One of the responding officers was killed. Several customers and employees were held hostage, and the standoff began. The long siege ended forty-seven hours later, when the hostages escaped by kicking a hole in the wall of the room they were locked in and making their way to the roof, where they were met by police. The robbers surrendered shortly after.

These and similar incidents made it necessary for police officials to look for a better way to handle hostage situations, to minimize, if not eliminate, violence. After the "John and Al's" incident, New York City Police Detective Sergeant Frank Bolz and Detective/Psychologist Harvey Schlossberg examined the issue. They created a new philosophy for dealing with hostage takers and developed strategies and tactics for "hostage negotiations." During the mid-70s, hostage negotiation tactics were employed by law enforcement organizations throughout the United States.

Atlanta started its first hostage negotiations team in 1976 with thirty-five members. I declined the invitation to join; I believed the team was too large, and most were there for the wrong reasons—such as being in on the action, and getting their names in the paper, or faces on TV. The majority of the team eventually lost interest and dropped out. In 1978, after the initial furor had died down, I joined the hostage negotiating team, whose numbers had dwindled to less than ten.

Hostage negotiators are trained in the principles of hostage negotiation and dedicated to the preservation of life through peaceful resolution. I bought into the concept that negotiation was the way to go in these situations.

Members of the hostage negotiation team are police officers of various ranks, from many different functions within the police department. We carried out our day-to-day assignments, and only when called upon to handle a hostage crisis did we leave our regular assignment and form a negotiation team.

Negotiators handle hostage situations, barricaded gunmen, and suicide attempts. I was involved in many negotiations during my fourteen years as a team member, and later team leader/coordinator. Our team negotiated the release of hostages, while convincing the barricaded gunman to surrender without having to use force. The team has also talked many suicidal persons out of jumping or into surrendering a weapon.

The use of physical force is a last resort, an indication that negotiations aren't going forward, and disaster is imminent; then we deploy SWAT. That is a difficult determination to make because we know that the potential for injury and death is very high for all involved.

Our success rate was outstanding—about 95%. High-ranking officials in the APD and city government recognized from the data and coverage in the media, that negotiation was a strategy that was working. Therefore, it became official policy that same year.

Unfortunately, there were times we lost a hostage or suicidal person. When that happened, it deeply affected every team member, leaving psychological scars that lasted a long time.

APD Hostage Negotiators on FBI Turf

In 1980, the United States federal office building in downtown Atlanta was at the corner of Peachtree and Baker Streets. The Atlanta field office of the FBI made its home on the ninth and tenth floors. Since then, a new federal building, the Richard Russell Building (named in honor of United States senator Richard Russell of Georgia, who spent a lifetime serving in the US Senate), was built at Spring and Mitchell Streets, also in downtown. The FBI field office did not relocate to the new federal building; instead, they fled the city and set up an office building in suburban DeKalb County.

One Sunday morning in 1980, I was working a plain clothes detail out of Zone 2. At about ten a.m., a Zone 5 car called for the special operations response team to the federal building at Peachtree and Baker Streets for a hostage situation. I responded immediately and met with FBI Special Agent-in-Charge, John Glover, in the lobby of the building. APD hostage negotiator Frank McClure arrived minutes behind me. Glover briefed us:

On Sundays, the federal building was closed, including the FBI offices in the building. But this Sunday, there were eight civilian employees installing new computer systems on the ninth-floor office of the FBI. There was a lone uniformed security guard in the lobby. A man carrying a large canvas bag knocked on the glass front door, indicating that he wanted to enter. The guard told him the building was closed, and he should come back the next day. The man pulled out a handgun, pointed it through the glass at the guard, and demanded he open the door. Once inside, the gunman disarmed the guard and said he wanted to go up to the FBI office.

When they got to the ninth floor, the gunman herded everyone into one office. They convinced him they were not FBI agents. The gunman sent the guard back downstairs with instructions to get an FBI agent to come to the office. The guard called 911 and the FBI emergency number.

All available local FBI agents, FBI negotiators, and the FBI SWAT team were notified. Special Agent-in-Charge Glover didn't want to wait until they arrived. He knew McClure and I were APD hostage negotiators. He took us to a telephone in an office off the lobby and asked us to try to make contact with the gunman.

Frank made the call. A hysterical woman answered; he assured her that everything would be okay and asked her to put the gunman on the phone. A male voice got on, said he was armed with several guns, and warned that if he saw any police he would shoot the people he had taken hostage.

The security guard was interviewed, and he confirmed that the gunman had two handguns—one taken from him—a shotgun, an automatic shoulder weapon, hundreds of rounds of various types of ammunition, and a hunting knife.

McClure started a dialog with the gunman, who wouldn't reveal his name. He told Frank to call him "Friend."

As McClure tried to get his new "friend" to tell more about himself, FBI agents and Atlanta police swarmed into the lobby. The FBI negotiators arrived and started breathing down our necks. Glover pulled them back, telling McClure and me to keep at it. The only demand that Friend gave us was to find the psychiatrist who had treated him at one of the mental health facilities in the past and bring him to the ninth floor, in exchange for all the hostages. While procedure would not allow this to happen, there was no reason to admit this to Friend. Teams of detectives were sent to locate the psychiatrist and bring him to the scene as a source of intelligence that might help in the negotiations.

Meanwhile, Atlanta Police Chief, George Napper, arrived and conferred with FBI SAC John Glover. They agreed that McClure and I would continue the negotiations. They paired up their SWAT teams, one FBI SWAT agent with one APD SWAT officer.

The building engineer, who was called in on this Sunday morning, produced blueprints of the building. The prints showed ventilation ducts running parallel to the main corridors on each floor. The ducts were big enough for someone crouching to move within. One SWAT pair was put into the vent on the ninth floor.

It had been three hours since the hostages were taken captive; they began to complain that they needed to use the restrooms, which were at the end of the main corridor. Friend marched the hostages down the corridor, his automatic weapon pointed at their backs. The louvers on the wall separating the corridor from the vent were angled, which made it possible for the SWAT officers to peer into the corridor, but no one in the corridor could see them. They saw the hostages pass by, and although they had the green light to take a shot at the gunman, they held their fire, afraid if they did shoot him, his reflexes might cause him to pull the trigger of his automatic weapon.

As he herded the group back from the restrooms, he held his automatic weapon towards the ceiling. When the group passed out of view of the two SWAT officers, and Friend came into view, they opened fire. He was hit almost thirty times, and our concerns were realized; the gunman did reflexively fire several rounds, fortunately up into the ceiling, hitting no one. Several of the hostages were cut with flying glass and debris, but none were seriously hurt.

The psychiatrist was not located until the following day. I wondered if he knew he was wanted at the FBI offices and made himself scarce. We never learned why Friend demanded the psychiatrist's presence, but surmised that he wanted to harm him. We later learned that he had a long history of mental illness.

Frank McClure did a good job. He was able to keep Friend calm and talking, possibly preventing the slaughter of his hostages. Some of the FBI hostage negotiators were displeased that local negotiators were the focus of media attention.

When the police kill someone, a top police official, usually dripping with regrets about having to use deadly force, blah, blah, gives a statement. Not this time. Agent Glover gave the interview. "We had a heavily armed subject threatening the lives of eight people. He was terminated!" End of statement. Glover walked away. FBI SAC John Glover became my hero.

I Got My Rank Back

The lawsuit that arose from the mass demotions engineered by A. Reginald Eaves in 1974, and the charges of cheating in subsequent promotions, was still tied up in federal court in 1979. Germane to the demotions and cheating were several other lawsuits brought by individuals and groups claiming discrimination and reverse discrimination. Federal Judge Charles A. Moye, whose court was assigned these litigations, put pressure on all parties to get together and reach an agreement.

To comply with Judge Moye's mandate, the parties met at city hall in the summer of 1979. Mayor Maynard Jackson, Public Safety Commissioner Lee Brown, and Assistant City Attorney Roy Mayes, represented the city. Jimmy Richardson, WD Cameron, and Buck Moore represented the Afro-American Patrolmen's League (AAPL), along with their attorney, Antonio Thomas. I was heavily involved with the Fraternal Order of Police (FOP) and was present as one of their negotiators, along with FOP president, Mike Maloof, and our attorney, John Nuckles. Floyd Reeves, who had filed the original lawsuit, charging the city with racial discrimination, and his attorney, Robert Stroup, were also present.

Mayor Jackson started the meeting by extolling the virtues of affirmative action. It was immediately obvious that these negotiations were not going to work, and within thirty minutes, the meeting ended.

Two months later, in the fall of 1979, the parties tried again, this time with the help of the US Justice Department. Federal mediators were there to conduct and facilitate the negotiations and assist the parties through any impasses. There were many. The mediators stayed neutral on all the issues during the negotiations, neither lobbying for nor favoring any position. Samuel Hider, the director of the City Labor Relations Board, replaced Mayor Jackson. All the other players remained the same.

I didn't want to participate on the second go-round and promptly declined. I viewed my involvement in the negotiations as a conflict of interest. I had been one of those reduced in rank during the mass demotions. There were re-instatement and back pay issues, and I didn't want to be perceived as looking out for my own interests. Nuckles and Maloof insisted I be a member of their negotiating team; Commissioner Brown ordered me to attend.

For the next five weeks, we were at it day and night, five days a week. At times, things got hot and heavy. On two occasions, Nuckles, Maloof and I walked out. We were being "tripled teamed" by the city, the AAPL, and Reeves. They took the same position on most of the issues. It became racial! No one was listening. We would not have returned, had it not been for Commissioner Brown's diplomacy. He assured us the racial rhetoric would be toned down. He also reminded us of Judge Moye's instructions that we reach agreement on a consent decree.

Another time, after a sixteen-hour session, Maloof and I almost came to physical blows with members of the AAPL team. We were all very tired, and our tolerance levels had plummeted to new lows. We got into an intense argument centered on race. We stood, shouting in each other's faces. The others had to restrain us from attacking each other.

Finally, the five weeks ended with a consent decree. It was a bittersweet agreement; most police officers were left out and did not like it. The consent degree was lengthy and complex; it resolved a number of issues and separated the people it covered into different classes. It favored members of both police organizations, the FOP and AAPL, at the expense of cops, black and white, who were not members of either group.

For the blacks, the consent degree weighed heavily on affirmative action in the sense that it addressed issues of past discrimination, favoring black officers who had been with the APD prior to 1971.

For those officers, black and white, who were in paid positions, yet were demoted by Eaves' mass demotions, there were back pay and seniority entitlements. They would be reinstated to their former ranks, providing they passed the next promotional exam (taken on a pass/fail basis).

For police officers of any rank who had been sworn members of the police bureau prior to 1971, the consent decree permitted them to take any of the next promotional exams, up to the rank of captain. The police officers who were not members of either group were less favorably considered in the consent decree. They had no vote and therefore no say in whether or not to accept the consent decree.

I was not happy with the consent decree because I saw it as divvying up the "spoils," and leaving out the majority of non-aligned police officers. The only issue I lobbied hard for was to get FOP members John Wooten and Donna Starnes re-instated to the APD after their firing, several years prior, for being untruthful. The draft consent decree included their reinstatement.

When the five-member FOP executive board met to vote on its acceptance, I was the lone dissenting vote. The rest of the FOP membership, by majority vote, accepted it, as did the AAPL. Judge Moye signed the consent decree into law, and that was that.

A large number of cops felt left out, those who did not meet the criteria specified in the consent decree—those who were not members of either the FOP or AAPL, had not been reduced in rank from a paid position in the 1974 demotions, or were not on the APD prior to 1971.

Some cops accused me of looking out for my own interest and selling them out. I sat on the FOP executive board and was one of the negotiators for the consent decree. I had a lot to gain with the passage of it—primarily, my rank and back pay. I told everyone that I had voted against accepting it. Several cops, some who never bothered to discuss it with me, were so angry they chose not to believe me, or anyone else who tried to tell them the same thing. A few have not spoken to me since.

I was reinstated to the rank of lieutenant after I took the exam. Although it was a pass/fail test, as mandated in the consent decree, I was fifth highest on the list. That was 1982—eight years after I was demoted.

Doing Three Jobs for the Pay of One

When I was promoted back to lieutenant, I was transferred back to the Criminal Investigation Division as commander of the Auto Theft Squad. I hated it.

I was confined to the office—a desk job. Whenever I thought I had the attention of my boss, Captain Jim Oliver, I lobbied for a transfer. After months of bitching and moaning, I finally got my transfer, but there were strings attached. Captain Oliver and I were summoned to the office of the chief of detectives, Deputy Chief Eldrin Bell. Oliver and Bell proposed a deal; to get out of auto theft, I take over the Vice Squad, the Fugitive Squad, and the newly formed, experimental, Major Offenders Squad. Despite my eagerness to transfer out of auto theft, I had to consider two issues.

One, I didn't want to work vice; no one wants to work vice. It's dirty, slimy work. You coexist with the dirtiest and slimiest of criminal society. Working in the larceny, burglary, or robbery squads, you investigate crimes, work normal hours, and lead a more normal life than is possible working vice.

Two, the span of command and control had always been one lieutenant, one squad. I was being asked to take three squads for the price—the pay—of one. It took me less than five minutes to accept. Anything to get back on the streets.

It's very simple; as long as there is demand for something, it will be supplied. Nothing can prevent the supply, if there is demand. No law, no law enforcement, no preaching—nothing will stop supply in the face of demand. Let's see if I can provide a simple, clear example.

Prostitution. Demand. Supply. Prostitution. The only way to stop it is to eliminate the demand. Hasn't happened in thousands of years, it's not happening now, and doesn't look like it ever will.

In law enforcement, the best we can do is arrest the supply—the prostitutes and pimps—and only sometimes can we arrest the demand—the customers, the "Johns." On the supply side, it's circular. We see the same pimps and prostitutes, over and over, again and again. And it's not going to change.

The value the vice squad is able to achieve can be measured in two ways: one, favorable PR, which comes from the perception that the APD is doing something to make prostitution go away; and two, the side benefit of information about other criminal activity that can be obtained from the prostitutes and pimps, which is much more important. Developing informants within this subculture solves crimes and locates wanted persons. In years past, all new detectives were assigned directly to vice for this reason.

She Supplied Herself to Others, to Us She Supplied Information

A well-known prostitute was arrested one night for soliciting. I was working the streets along with other vice cops, but something about me caused her to solicit me. (I made the case.) When she learned I was the lieutenant in charge of the vice squad, she said she wanted to speak to me privately and make a deal; she knew four men who were regularly burglarizing houses and where they were fencing what they stole. I gave her a "copy of charges"—similar to a traffic ticket—instead of putting her in jail and set a date for her to appear to answer those charges. I wanted time to see if her information was any good. If it was, we would take care of her, and if it was not, she would go to jail.

I turned the information she gave me over to the burglary squad detectives. The four burglars and their fence were arrested, and a ton of stolen property was recovered and returned to the owners of the dozens of houses that had been burglarized. I had her case dismissed. I instructed her not to come to court, to prevent anyone from seeing her and wondering about her dismissal and the arrests of the burglars. I felt the precaution was justified.

Because her information was good, I told her I was also in charge of the fugitive squad, and we wanted some very bad people. I showed her mug shots, gave her the names and the street names of fugitives that might appear in her part of the city.

She became my best informant. No one ever provided nearly as much useful information. She helped us for nearly three years. The various squads were able to clear many felony cases with the information she provided. The fugitive squad located and apprehended felons wanted for some time.

It was a win-win situation for her and us. She got a free ride. She had my business card and instructions to use it whenever she was picked up. I would get a call from the arresting officer, and if he had her on a straight soliciting case, I asked the officer to issue a copy of charges. When the charges came up in court, I was there, and with the approval and consent of the city solicitor and the arresting officer, the case would be dismissed. I thought it was a great trade-off. She came through for me many times, and I always kept my word to her.

In subsequent years, moving from vice/fugitive and working other assignments, I lost track of her. I never knew what became of her. Such is the nature of "subterranean" society.

"When the dick gets hard, the brain goes soft"

The intended function of the Major Offenders Squad never materialized. It was subsumed by the Larceny Squad, which handled major fraud cases. For the three years that I had responsibility for the vice and fugitive squads, I worked various hours so I could spend time with both watches of each squad. It was never dull.

For instance, to make a case for soliciting for prostitution, we had to play the "word game." By law, we needed the prostitute to state her price and the sex act she would perform for that price. Otherwise, the case would be dismissed as "entrapment" and thrown out of court.

We kept the pressure on the prostitutes, letting them know we were there so that they couldn't take over the streets. When we let up pressure anywhere, the prostitutes immediately appeared, and not long afterwards, phones started ringing at the mayor's office and the chief's office. That's when I got the heat. It was in my best interest to keep the pressure on as much as possible.

Arresting the girls gave us no satisfaction; but arresting pimps did. Pimps were bullies with everyone, especially the girls, but when they had to deal with the police, they were cowards.

In one incident on the Stewart Avenue corridor, two vice detectives and I heard yelling and screaming behind an old abandoned gas station. The source of the noise was a man and woman. He held her against the back of the building by her hair, alternately slapping her in the face and punching her in the stomach. We recognized both of them. She was a prostitute we had arrested many times, and he was her pimp. We grabbed the pimp, put him on the ground, and proceeded to do to him what we had just seen him do to her, but we did better than slapping. He begged us not to hurt him—crying, sobbing, and pleading for us to stop. Bullies are tough with women, but not so tough when they're on the receiving end.

The woman told us he beat her and several other prostitutes in his "stable" when they didn't bring in enough money. She said all the prostitutes were terrified of him. We arrested him for aggravated assault. She declined to prosecute, but it didn't matter because we witnessed it. We testified to it in court. He served less than six months and was right back on Stewart Avenue. Our victim was again turning tricks for him.

Male hustlers, like female prostitutes, were also a problem, sometimes worse. They loitered on Cypress Street in Midtown, trolling for homosexual men to pick them up. A male hustler would sometimes rob a pickup—physically assault him, or worse. When a vice cop posing as a homosexual heard enough for a legitimate case of soliciting sex and "badged" the hustler, more often than not, the hustler tried to run away. In one incident, Officer JD Underwood was "trolling" for male hustlers on Cypress Street, when he came upon one who had just robbed and beaten up a middle-aged man. JD intervened, and the hustler ran. JD chased him for five or six blocks until at, Spring and 10th Street, the hustler ran into a dark parking lot. Underwood was right behind him, closing fast. The hustler jumped over a four-foot brick wall in his attempt to get away. On the other side of the wall was a twenty-foot drop to the concrete sidewalk. JD almost followed him over, but stopped just in time, remembering where he was. The hustler suffered serious injuries from his fall. I remember seeing the broken leg bone protruding through the skin.

The "john" operation was different. We detailed a few female police officers to pose as street prostitutes, dressed accordingly, including shoulder handbags.

Our favorite location for conducting these operations was an open parking lot at the corner of Juniper and Eight Streets in Midtown. We operated mostly at night, set up in the dark corner of the lot. We put our "prostitutes" out on the sidewalk. The cover cops stayed as close to the women as they could without revealing they were there or were cover cops—trying to blend into the cityscape.

One problem with a john operation was that it often attracted patrol cars that should not have been there. Cops who knew our policewomen were working as decoys wanted to stop and look at the women they had only seen in uniform dressed as babes and check out their tits and asses. I spent a lot of time chasing them away. Too much police activity would undermine our operation.

When a vehicle stopped for one of our "hookers," the driver would engage her in conversation. The word game had to be played, but because our prostitutes were female police officers, it had to be played in reverse. The female officer had to wait until the john described the sex act he wanted and what he would pay. When he verbalized both clearly, she could make her case. The female cop would switch her handbag from one shoulder to the other, the signal for the cover cops to move in and make the arrest.

There were a few cardinal rules that had to be followed.

For the policewomen:

- Never get into a vehicle.
- If threatened with a weapon, back away from the vehicle slowly.

For the cover cops:

- When the female officer gives the signal to move in, walk; do not run to the vehicle.
- Have your badge out, clearly visible, when you get there.
- Announce, clearly and distinctly, "Police!"

The arrests didn't always go as planned. Sometimes "Murphy's Law" prevailed—anything that could go wrong usually did! On one occasion, one of our "prostitutes" gave the signal for cover cops to make the arrest. The cover team approached the truck, but when one cop reached in to remove the keys from the ignition, the driver decided to leave—in a hurry. There was a tussle inside the cab of the truck, with our guy half in, half out. The truck traveled down the street, picked up speed, jumped the curb, and hit a light pole.

The cop and driver were taken to the hospital, treated, and released. The cop went home; the john went to jail. The remainder of the operation was cancelled for the night.

During these operations, there was a lot of activity in our corner of the parking lot. Marked police paddy wagons came and went, taking the arrested to the city jail, and auto-wreckers were in and out with the johns' impounded vehicles. Our police "hookers" followed their arrests and sat in cars, under dome lights, completing paperwork. Superior officers stood around supervising.

Despite the activity, the johns continued to arrive, oblivious to everything going on. They were focused on our role-playing prostitute on the sidewalk outside the lot. "When the dick gets hard, the brain goes soft," vice cops say to describe behavior that leads to such easy arrests. It was not unusual to arrest thirty or forty johns—from "men of the cloth" to career sexual offenders and everything in between—in a single operation. We identified dozens of "wanted persons," most for minor crimes. On occasion, we got lucky and arrested a serious felon, like the time our National Crime Information Center (NCIC) check identified one of our johns as wanted for a series of armed robberies in Mississippi, Louisiana, and Texas.

The john operations were held once every two or three months. It was a break in the routine and took on a carnival-like atmosphere that we all enjoyed.

Dr. Jekyll, John Presley, and Mr. Hyde

John Presley was a friend. We were both sergeants and for a couple of years worked together in Zone 2. John was someone you liked being around, a good, nice-looking guy, bright, friendly, soft spoken, helpful—socially and professionally—and he did his job. However, John Presley was an alcoholic, a drunk!

Some years before we worked together, I was working homicide; Presley was a burglary detective. He had screwed up a case he was working and had been called into the office of the chief of detectives.

The detective department was located on the third floor of police headquarters. The detective squad rooms were located off a large open area. Presley was in Superintendent Chaffin's office, next to this open area. Although Chafin's door was closed, everyone on the third floor heard the chief of detectives rant and rave. (I have never known anyone who could deliver an ass chewing as effectively as Chafin. He could terrify and intimidate the toughest detectives.) The verbal abuse continued for fifteen minutes, and then the door opened, and out came John Presley, red-faced and defeated. From within his office, Chafin slammed the door shut behind Presley. Everything got quiet in the open area; nobody was moving. John was halfway toward the burglary squad room, still in the middle of the big open area, when Chafin's door opened again, and Chafin came out, bellowing, "And furthermore, Presley, when anyone calls you 'Detective,' you correct them!"

Fast forward to Zone 2, morning watch. Presley and I worked alternate off days on the morning watch. People said about him, "If you can't get along with Presley, you can't get along with anyone." But that was his Dr. Jekyll; he had a dark side, his Mr. Hyde.

He was single and lived alone in an apartment in the city. While he was on duty, he was straight as an arrow. I worked with John quite a bit; never did alcohol affect his behavior, and I never smelled it on his breath. It was different when he was off duty.

His passion and his weakness was beer. On off days or off nights, he drank it by the case. He would start drinking at home during an off day, but Presley was not content to drink at home. He liked to party and go out in the evening after drinking all day. That's when trouble started. He would get falling down drunk somewhere and the police would be called. The cops answering the call would recognize Presley, but they didn't always know what to do with him. Presley would mutter something about "calling Sergeant Goldhagen," which they did—anything to get him off their hands. It was easy to find me because when Presley was off, I was usually working. When I arrived, the responding cops and I would put him in the back seat of my patrol car, and I would take him home. I had to nudge, push, pull, and carry him up the flight of stairs and then put him to bed. This routine occurred more often than I'd like to admit. I was putting my job, or at least my stripes, in jeopardy, but he was my friend.

On one occasion, after I had started my watch, my patrol car was having problems, so I took it to the city shop and rode for the rest of the watch with another Zone 2 supervisor, Sergeant Oz Adams. I received a call to meet an officer at the El Morocco Club in Midtown. An off-duty detective, working an extra job at the club, had a very drunk John Presley on his hands. When Oz and I arrived in the lobby, we saw Presley run into a closet and lock the door. After asking Presley several times to unlock and open the door, I kicked it open, and found myself looking down the barrel of his gun. Oz and I froze until he lowered the gun. He was ready to go home; we were his taxi.

There were times when he would take off his usual work night, coinciding with my usual off night and call and wake me in the early morning hours, babbling drunk. A couple of times, I got out of bed and went to get him, knowing I was saving his job. Looking back, I don't know that I did him any favors. As time went on, John continued his downward spiral, getting into situations where I was not able to help. He lost his stripes and was demoted back to patrolman.

When I left Zone 2, I had been reinstated to the rank of lieutenant, working auto theft. One night, when I was at home and asleep, at about three a.m., my phone rang; it was John Presley. I immediately started cursing, threatening to cut him off, but he sounded different—not babbling, not drunk.

He said he had just committed armed robbery and wanted to turn himself in to me. I started sputtering into the phone that this had gone far enough and that the next time I saw his drunken ass, I was going to kick it. He assured me he had not been drinking, and as I became more awake, and listened more intently, realized that he did sound sober. He said it was no joke. He had just gone into a convenience store and robbed it at gunpoint. He asked me to meet him at police headquarters. He wanted to surrender to me. I told him I'd be there in thirty minutes. I called my boss, Captain Jim Oliver, and let him know what was up. He said that he would meet us there, also.

Captain Oliver and I were in Oliver's office when John walked in, accompanied by his brother. He looked as bad as I've ever seen him. He handed me his gun and badge without a word, then sat down and cried. We confirmed that there had been an armed robbery earlier at the convenience store at Piedmont and Pharr Roads. We requested a copy of the report and everything matched—John Presley had held up the store.

The rest of the morning was taken up with all of the administrative things that needed to be done for a situation like this. By then, the place was buzzing, and the news media was salivating. I wanted to spare John further humiliation. I requested permission to drive him to the city jail myself. I suggested a paddy wagon act as a decoy in the driveway in front of the building, where all the TV cameras were waiting.

The brass reluctantly agreed; John would be handcuffed and Sergeant Carlos Banda, his immediate supervisor, would go with us. We went down a back elevator, where I removed the handcuffs and led him quietly out a side door. We drove out of the detective lot in my car, just three guys on assignment. No one gave us a tumble.

We didn't say much on the way to the city jail. When we got there, we told the medical staff what had happened and they asked us to take him to the psychiatric ward at Grady Hospital, where he could be evaluated. We did and as we were about to leave him on the eighth floor of Grady, he looked at me and whispered, "Thanks."

When Atlanta Police transfer an arrested person to the city jail, to the detention area of Grady Hospital, or to the psychiatric ward of Grady Hospital, the arresting or transporting officer turns the prisoner over to the corrections officer at the intake portal. The arrest ticket and any other paper work are handed from officer to officer. I gave John his arrest ticket, and he handed it himself to the officer as he walked through the intake door. It was a shitty day.

Several months later, I drove down to visit John at the Georgia State Prison, in Ware County. It was a four-hour drive from Atlanta to South Georgia. I brought his girlfriend along, the one he was dating at the time of the robbery. We were in the big day room with lots of tables and chairs filled with inmates and families; it was visiting day. There wasn't much to say. I left John and his girlfriend alone for a long time. I walked outside trying to figure out why John did what he did. I never did come up with an answer.

"I know what I am going to do"

It was a perfect day, sunny and mild, but it would not last. The dark clouds of insanity would eclipse the bright sun. The call came requesting the Special Operations Section Response Team. A hostage situation!

The hostages were brothers, ages two and four. The hostage taker was their father, who was divorced from their mother. He was threatening to kill them and then himself. Frank McClure and I were to handle the negotiations.

Before they divorced, father, mother, and their boys had lived in Dallas, Texas. Following the divorce, the mother took the boys with her to Atlanta to live with her sister. Leaving the children with a neighbor, the sisters went out for several hours, job hunting. The father came to Atlanta to locate the boys. After a brief search, he located his ex-wife's sister's apartment and then the neighbor's apartment, where the boys were. He took the boys by force, then broke into the sister's apartment and waited.

The neighbor called 911, specifying where the father was. In response to the police officer's knock on the door, the father shouted that he would shoot the children if anyone tried to enter the apartment. The cop backed off and the SOS Response Team called. Upon the arrival of additional police, perimeters were set up, residents of the complex evacuated, and non-essential movement was restricted within the area. When the mother arrived, she was met at the outer perimeter and escorted to the command post, where she was informed of the situation.

The hostage negotiators set up in the neighbor's apartment. The mother was kept away to avoid distractions or interference. We made contact with the father over the telephone.

"She took my boys away from me—her and that damn judge," he screamed at us over the speakerphone. "But I'm gonna overrule that fuckin judge. If I can't have them, she's not gonna have them, either! I'll kill them before I let her have them!" We could hear the kids crying in the background.

The delicate negotiations began: calm him down, keep him calm, and keep him talking, and say whatever we think will establish a rapport and trust. Slow it down; time usually works against the hostage taker.

The SWAT team was in place, ready for a tactical forced entry and rescue operation, but they were kept at bay by his threats to shoot the children if anyone tried to come in. Getting those kids released was up to us.

For several hours, we listened to the father swing from enraged to calm and rational. Any conversation was good; as long as he was talking, he wasn't hurting the kids. We were willing to listen as long as he was talking.

We were using our special hostage telephone—a direct line between both ends. Unlike typical phone calls, our conversation had down time and breaks in dialogue. We explained, "All you have to do is pick up the receiver; we're here."

I introduced myself as Harry, the name I always used in crises situations. He said to call him Joseph; he didn't like being called Joe.

"Joseph, you really don't want to kill your boys," I pleaded. "Think of all the things you'll miss—their first days of school, tossing a baseball, helping each one break in a new baseball glove, teaching them to ride their bicycles, to swim."

"How am I going to do that, Harry, when that fuckin' whore has them all the time and keeps my boys away from me?" he replied, anger in his voice.

We knew the conditions of the divorce decree. "Listen Joseph, you have liberal visitation rights," I said, desperately trying to calm him. "Use that precious time to do those things and more. Priceless memories are made between a father and his sons, and strong bonds are formed, love that will stay with them as they grow into manhood."

"Yeah, easy for you to say, Harry, you don't know that goddamn bitch like I do. She ain't never gonna let that happen. She's gonna take my boys and keep runnin' and hidin'!

"I gotta think, Harry, gotta clear my head. I'll think about what you said, and I'll call you back in fifteen minutes!"

When he got loud, the kids cried harder. Hearing their cries, I smelled the smoke, felt the heat, and heard the screams of two little girls lost in the fire when I was a rookie cop. I had to take a break, get away from the speakerphone. I went outside, hoping I could regain my composure. That didn't happen.

Someone pointed me out to the boys' mother, identifying me as the negotiator talking to her ex-husband. She ran to me, dropped to her knees, and grabbed my legs as tightly as she could. She looked up into my face, pleading, "Don't let him hurt my babies—please, oh, God, please!" What she said and the way she said it, has not been easy to forget, no matter how much I try not to remember.

McClure and I had been back and forth on the phone all day and were into the eighth hour, when he called again. He was no longer yelling, ranting, raving, cursing, and threatening. He spoke quietly, in a low voice.

"I know what I'm going to do. I hope that bitch is near the phone so she hears the sounds of her children dying. I want her to know she caused it, and I want her to always remember it!" The message was frighteningly clear.

Immediately, the SWAT team commander gave the order to move to the forward position and get ready for entry.

McClure never lost his cool. "Listen Joseph, she's not worth your two boys dying over. Don't do anything that you'll regret for the rest of your life. We'll speak to that judge on your behalf and tell him what she is doing." Joseph didn't say anything, there was no dialogue, just the sounds of the children crying and screaming in the background.

When Joseph didn't reply, Frank continued. "Joseph, come outside and talk to me, or let me or Harry come inside"-- nothing, just the crying. It lasted less than a minute, but it seemed more like an hour. We held our breath for that minute. Finally, the silence was broken by the faint, deflated voice of Joseph, "Okay Frank, I'll meet you outside."

Just like that, it was over!

I have been involved in many hostage situations, enough to know that you cannot second-guess yourself if things go wrong. It serves no purpose. Nevertheless, I would not have been able to overcome the guilt, blaming myself had those children been killed. Living with that would have been hard.

Something inside me replays the helplessness in the mother's eyes, begging me to get her boys back into her arms. No matter how hard I try to resist that replay, it happens when I least expect it, most often when driving alone. My nostrils fill up with the smoke of the burning shack where two little girls had been left alone. I have to pull off the road until I stop sobbing.

I Agreed to Have a Beer With Her, so She Would Give Me Her Gun

As a hostage negotiator, I enjoyed many successes and suffered occasional failures. Many situations creep out of my memory, flickering through my consciousness. The following incident doesn't flicker; it rather simmers continually on the back burner of my mind.

I was at home one evening when notified by communications to respond to a hostage situation in a middle-class neighborhood of Atlanta. When I pulled up at the scene, I saw most of the Special Operations Response Team, consisting of SWAT, the hostage negotiating team, and the special operations section commander, who would direct operations as the on-scene commander. A city psychologist, in the capacity as advisor, was also on hand. The rest of the group that was off-duty had to be called in from home. They arrived at the same time I did.

The location was a residence belonging to a couple in their mid-thirties, parents of a newborn baby. The wife was a counselor with the Georgia Regional Mental Health facility. She was currently on maternity leave; having given birth a few weeks earlier. Other counselors were handling her caseload until she returned to work. One of her patients, a very disturbed woman, was not happy about that. She had somehow obtained the home address of her counselor and showed up at her doorstep.

The patient was armed with a revolver and forced her way into the house. She was angry about not seeing her counselor during the regular sessions. She focused on the new baby as the cause of it all. She asked the counselor where the baby was and when told it was upstairs in the nursery, she went upstairs. She warned the couple to stay downstairs, or she would shoot the baby.

They called 911. When the responding officer arrived and entered the house, the woman took a shot at him, and then ran back upstairs to the sleeping baby. When the sector sergeant arrived, he called for special operations.

The residence was a modest two-story house, bedrooms upstairs, common areas on the main level. An enclosed stairway from the living/dining room led to the upstairs rooms. I took my position, out of her sight, at the base of the stairs, and established "voice to voice" contact with the woman, out of sight, at the top of the stairs. We caught glimpses of each other when we each peeked out from the walls behind which we hid. The first thing she said to me was that if anyone attempted to come up the stairs, she would shoot the baby. It was not a great way to start, but at least it established dialogue between us.

She and I talked on and off for over an hour. When we weren't talking, she would leave the top of the stairs for a few minutes and then return. At one point during our conversations, she left abruptly. I heard her shout, indistinctly, and then I heard a gunshot. My blood froze. I had failed. She had shot the baby, I thought.

What actually happened was that the SWAT team, with the approval of the on-scene commander, put in motion a rescue attempt. The crib was located next to the window in the nursery. It was a mild spring evening, the window was open, and across it was a flimsy aluminum screen. The SWAT plan was to rappel two of their team down from the roof, remove the screen, and take the baby from the crib, out the window.

The SWAT plan unraveled when, while talking to me, she heard an unfamiliar sound from the nursery. She ran into the nursery where she saw a boot and leg outside the window. She fired a shot into the window space; her shot went astray, hitting no one. The woman was screaming at the two would-be rescuers who scampered back up to the roof. The parents were screaming and crying, fearing the worst had happened. I was yelling for someone to tell me what the hell had just happened. I had not been told about the SWAT plan, and when I learned about it, after the fact, I was pissed at everyone. Had I known, I would have made every attempt to keep her at the top of the stairs, focusing her attention away from the nursery. (We never determined where that bullet ended up; there were no reports.)

When the situation settled down enough that I thought I could get a sensible response from her, I asked about the baby in a way I hoped would convince her that both she and I should be concerned about it. She said the baby was okay and still asleep. Believing her, I allayed any anxieties I was feeling about the shot, calmed myself down, and tried do the same for her. I needed to reestablish communication with her, creating a "one-on-one" dialogue, develop a rapport, leading to the ultimate objective—the trust a negotiator needs to convince a hostage taker that the best thing for her or him is to release the hostage unharmed.

Whatever rapport and trust I had established during the hour or so prior to the SWAT team's appearance at the nursery window was gone. To rebuild that rapport and trust, I had to convince her I had no knowledge of what happened, and had I known I would have stopped it, or let her know I was trying to stop it.

After everyone had calmed down, and things were quiet, it took an hour to get her to agree that she would let me arrange for her to speak to a doctor, but only if I gave my word that no one would go near her. At that point, I knew I would be able to resolve the hostage situation. (I would have strangled the on-scene commander if, at that point, he or any member of the SWAT team tried another stupid stunt!)

She and I made a deal. We agreed to meet on the stairs, she halfway down, I halfway up, where she would hand me the gun, butt first. Then we would go to the dining room table, sit down together, and drink a beer. After that, she would then be driven to the Georgia Regional Mental Health facility and turned over to the staff. Criminal charges would come later. Everything happened as agreed.

After she was taken away, the on-scene commander gave an interview to the media, the SWAT team packed up their gear, and the patrol cars went back in service. I walked down the street to my car, thinking to myself: the baby slept through it all.

Before I got to my car, a familiar voice called out, asking if I'd like to go somewhere to have some coffee. It was Trudy Boyce, one of the city psychologists who had been with me, in my ear, throughout the entire incident. We went to an all-night diner, had coffee, then more coffee, and finally breakfast, daylight barely appearing when we left and went our separate ways.

Ordinarily, when these situations were over, I would go straight home to where my wife and kids were deep asleep. My wife had a job to go to, my kids had school; I could not wake them to talk. I had no one to talk to about what had just happened, about anything. I never could go straight to bed; I was always hyped, my adrenalin not yet normal. I couldn't read a newspaper, magazine, or a book; I was not able to concentrate on what I read, and television annoyed me. Instead, I paced back and forth through the quiet house, reliving incidents over and over in my mind, beating myself up for the things I should or should not have said or done; it was worse when the outcome was not successful.

The time spent talking with Trudy Boyce after the baby incident made me realize how important it was for a negotiator to talk to someone after a hostage situation. Of course, we talked about the incident, but it wasn't what was said, but the opportunity to vent and rehash it—to have someone acknowledge a job well done, or to be reassured when it did not turn out well that you did your best and nothing else could have been done differently to change the outcome. De-briefs go a long way to eliminate the emotional and psychological baggage a negotiator carries over time

Tear Gas Induced Flames, Like in Waco

Georgia Power Company workers were going door-to-door in a quiet residential neighborhood one morning, advising residents that their power would be shut off just long enough to do some work on the power lines. At one house, a man with a shotgun met the workers. He threatened to shoot them if they messed with his power. They left and called the police. Patrol cars arrived, and two officers knocked on the front door. When the door opened, the man fired a shotgun blast, hitting both officers. One officer drew his weapon and got off a round as he went down. A third officer who was behind the first two dove sideways off the steps onto the ground, not shot, but injured in the fall. The man retreated into the house, slamming the door behind him. "Signal 63" was broadcast, officers responded from everywhere, and the three injured cops were taken by ambulance to Grady Hospital.

The Special Operations Response Team was called, and began arriving shortly. The long siege began. A neighbor was gracious enough to let us use her dining room as a command post. Lieutenant Wesley Derrick and I tried to communicate with the man by telephone, but all we got when he answered was a few seconds of babbling. Over the next seven hours, each time we called him, he answered the phone, muttered the same senseless babble, and then hung up. During those hours, he fired the shotgun intermittently from within the house.

Dr. Lloyd Bacchus, a psychiatric adviser for our hostage negotiating team, managed to stay on the phone long enough with the man to identify himself as a doctor. Bacchus said it might be a good idea if they were to meet in the front yard of the house, where they could talk about the situation. The man agreed.

I borrowed a white jacket and stethoscope from one of the EMTs who was with the ambulance standing by, and we also borrowed the ambulance. One of the other negotiators drove, and I rode in the back. The plan was that as the gunman approached within reach, I would take him to the ground, assisted by other cops nearby. When we pulled in front of the house, I stuck my head out of the back of the ambulance, and in a loud voice shouted that I was Dr. Bacchus, ready to step into the center of the yard.

Major Holley came over the radio, instructing the driver to leave the front of the house immediately. We left as instructed. The man's family was down the street, observing what was going on. An officer heard the man's son call him from a payphone and warn his father that it was two policemen, not a doctor and his driver, in the ambulance.

After seven hours without any sensible communication, just a shotgun blast every now and then, Major Holley made a decision. He authorized the SWAT team to fire a tear gas canister into the house. They did. Instead of the man exiting the premises, we saw flames. The house was on fire.

The fire truck standing by around the corner was called to put out the fire. They said, "Hell, no! You got two cops with shotgun wounds in the hospital. This guy has been shooting out of his house all day, and now you want us to pull up in front? Hell, no!" It didn't take long for the house to become fully involved in flames. It didn't take much longer for us to realize that no one was alive in the inferno and that the houses on either side had to be protected. The fire department lieutenant reluctantly agreed to bring his trucks around the corner, with a SWAT escort, to put water on the adjacent houses. That was done, there was no damage to those houses, and the house engulfed just burned to the ground.

The following day, when it had cooled down enough for investigators to enter the house, they found the dead gunman, who was burned badly. It was determined that he had suffered one gunshot wound, probably from the shots fired by the wounded policeman as he fell, as no one else fired into the house. Both wounded officers recovered. The man was shooting birdshot, which saved the two officers from being more seriously injured or killed. The third officer hurt his back when he dove to the ground. He was out for several months, but ultimately recovered.

Breaking Hostage Negotiation's First Commandment Could Be the Last Ever Broken

Not fully awake, guiding my hand in the dark to the phone, I picked up before the third ring, one eye opened toward the night table clock. It was nearly two a.m. I groaned, realizing I had to get out of bed, as I was the hostage negotiator on call that month. The Atlanta police dispatcher advised me that there was a suicide attempt in the lobby of the Hyatt Regency Hotel downtown. The rest of the Special Operations Response Team had been notified and were on the way.

I arrived twenty minutes after my phone rang, running into a din of police activity at the front entrance of the hotel. Major Holley, the on-scene commander and Captain Spence, the SWAT commander, briefed me.

An APD 911 operator had received a call from a male who told her he was in the lobby of the Hyatt Regency Hotel, he had a gun, and he was going to shoot himself. He then hung up, saying nothing more. When the responding officer walked into the lobby, he found a man with a gun standing at the bank of pay phones in the rear of the lobby. The man threatened to shoot himself if the officer or anyone else came near him. That's when special operations was notified.

Two SWAT officers escorted me to the rear of the lobby, where I positioned myself behind a wall for cover, close enough to communicate with the man with the gun. Covering me were two sniper/observer teams positioned on the balconies overlooking the lobby. One of the teams, SWAT officers Carlos Serrano/ Leroy Bullard, were concealed on the third floor balcony. Carlos Serrano was the best I'd ever seen with a sniper rifle. There was also a SWAT assault team not far from my location, out of sight. The lobby had been cleared and the elevators shut down, which didn't matter much as there were few guests around; it was 2:30 in the morning.

The man with the gun was white and in his mid-twenties. We started talking "voice to voice" at a distance of about forty feet. I was behind the wall with my head and shoulders exposed. He was out in the open, still beside the phone bank. We were really shouting at each other to be heard. I learned that his wife had left him and taken their two small children. He attempted to get his family back—by persuasion, threatening, and finally begging. His wife would not change her mind. He didn't want to live without his children and his wife.

We shouted back and forth for thirty minutes. But shouting wasn't going to develop the trust needed to get a subject to yield. Despite the shouting, I was able to establish a first-name rapport. His name was John. I needed quieter, more intimate conversation to resolve the situation without harm to anyone.

One of the basic rules of hostage negotiations is that a negotiator should only engage a subject "face-to-face" when all other means of communications have been exhausted, and then only with the approval of the on-scene commander and the concurrence of the SWAT commander. A negotiator should never go face to face with a person armed with a gun—that's the first and the last commandment of negotiating.

There are three motives why someone like John gets in this situation. One is a cry for help—he wants to talk to someone, to vent, and does not intend to kill himself; he wants someone's attention. Another is that he does intend to kill himself, but wants an audience, perhaps for the media to observe and report; he wants someone, such as the wife, to live with the guilt of "look what you forced me to do." Finally, he wants to kill himself, but cannot do it himself, so he will force the police to do it for him. He'll take a shot at the police, knowing they will return the fire—"Victim precipitated homicide," or "suicide by cop." With all this in mind, I took note of the layout of the hotel lobby.

There was a comfortable seating area adjacent to the phone bank— three upholstered armchairs, equally spaced around a coffee table. I asked John to sit with me so that we could talk without shouting. He agreed, but I explained that before I could sit with him, I needed the permission of "my boss," who would let me do it only if John promised he would not hurt me in any way. This is a very calculated, psychological step. John must verbalize aloud, "I promise I will not hurt you"—a very powerful statement.

He did, and then we moved to the chairs. We sat across from each other, the coffee table, a large chunk of granite, between us. He still had in his hand the gun, which looked like a .32 caliber revolver. He had not threatened me or anyone else. He had kept us at bay by threatening to shoot himself if we came hear him.

I was breaking two rules of negotiation—sitting face to face with someone who has a gun in view without asking permission from the on-scene commander. He would not have granted it. I knew Major Holley would be upset with me on several levels. I had my back to Holley, so we could not communicate with each other, which was just as well for me, as he had to stay where he was, fuming. I knew I would feel his wrath later. I also knew that Serrano had John in the cross hairs of his riflescope, the tension on the trigger halfway back. If, at any time during our conversation John pointed his gun at me, two things were going to happen. I would dive to the floor behind the coffee table, and both snipers would take their shots. And I knew they would not miss.

We talked for a couple of hours, and John decided not to kill himself. I emphasized with him and his situation. That seemed to work. We made a deal: he would put his gun on the coffee table, and then he and I would walk to the front of the lobby. I told him he would be arrested, searched, and handcuffed. He would not be taken to jail, but to the eighth floor of Grady Hospital, the psychiatric ward, to talk with the doctors. I agreed to ride with him in the back of the patrol car to Grady Hospital. I tossed my car keys to another police officer, asking that he drive my car to Grady.

I was able to avoid Major Holley since I had to leave immediately with the prisoner. But the next day, privately in his office, he chewed—no, he gnawed me out, threatening to have me tortured the next time I pulled a dumb stunt like that.

When I got home, Betty was getting ready for work. She asked, as she always did, if anything interesting happened during the incident. As I always did, I told her the basic facts. And as I always did not do, I left out the part that would have upset her worse than the major—breaking the two commandments of negotiation.

For six years after I retired from the APD, I instructed a two-week course six to eight times a year in hostage negotiations, now called crisis negotiations, for the US Army Military Police School in Ft. McClellan, Alabama, and Ft. Leonard Wood, Missouri. This course, which required two instructors, was designed by Dennis Zakrewski, referred to by all as "Zak," a retired twenty-five-year veteran of the US Army. Early in those years, I realized that Zak was the best of the best instructors in all the training classes I attended in my long career. Zak taught me not only how to instruct, but a few things about hostage negotiations.

Running a close second to Zak was Harry O'Reilly, a retired New York City police detective. I attended many of his courses in plainclothes street crime and undercover operations.

J. Edgar Hoover Died. I Became Eligible to Attend the FBI Academy

The goal of most career police officers in the United States and other countries around the world is to attend the FBI National Academy, at Quantico, Virginia. It is an honor; it is prestigious and respected throughout the law enforcement community. In addition to the knowledge gained, it provides a network of law enforcement contacts throughout the United States. It also looks great on a resume. The flow of Atlanta police officers going to Quantico was halted for a decade in the mid-1960s.

In the middle of the Civil Rights era, when segregation vs. integration in the South was the major domestic issue, passions ran deep on both sides. FBI Director J. Edgar Hoover telephoned Atlanta Police Chief, Herbert Jenkins, with a personal request. Hoover asked Jenkins to "keep an eye" on Martin Luther King, Jr. because, said Hoover, "He is a trouble maker."

Chief Jenkins had a strong relationship with King's father, Reverend Martin Luther King, Sr., and contacted "Daddy King" to tell him of Hoover's call and the FBI's interest in King, Jr. The King families' phones had been tapped by the FBI, and word of the phone call got back to Hoover. The FBI director again called Chief Jenkins.

Among other things, Hoover vowed that as long as he, J. Edgar Hoover was the director of the FBI, no Atlanta police officer would attend the FBI National Academy, and none did. After Hoover's death in 1972, Atlanta police officers once again became eligible to attend the academy in Quantico. My opportunity came in 1984.

I was in my office one afternoon when my phone rang. It was Police Chief Morris Redding. "Goldhagen, do you still want to go to the FBI Academy?" "Yes, sir," was out of my mouth before I could even think about it. I had applied several years before and had almost given up on the idea.

The chief of police must nominate an officer, who must go to the local FBI field office to be interviewed, investigated, and approved or

267

not, for acceptance at the academy. Redding did his part, and I was accepted. The year was 1984; I was admitted to the fall session. Up to two hundred and fifty law enforcement personnel from all over the United States and some foreign countries attend each session.

The FBI Academy, adjacent to the US Marine base, is an imposing complex dominated by two large dormitories that house the attendees, and the FBI new agents class. Essentially, it is a police academy for FBI recruits. We shared the dormitory buildings with the new agents, but trained separately.

The fixed rule in The FBI National Academy was that no two attendees from the same state could share a room or suite. I was assigned to a room with David Fromader from the Fort Atkinson, Wisconsin PD. The other two in the adjoining room were Barry Hart from the Evansville, Indiana PD, and Art Herrman, a federal agent from Phoenix, Arizona. None of us knew each other before the academy. We lived together for three months and got to know each other pretty well. We formed strong bonds that grew into lasting friendships.

From the curriculum offered, each attendee chose the courses he/she wanted to take. Five courses were required, plus the two mandatory physical training and firearms training courses. The attendees were diverse. We were a kaleidoscope of ethnic, racial, and religious groups—both male and female were represented—and we were split into five sections of fifty each. Barry, Art, Dave, and I were assigned to section five. It was a long three months; everyone missed home and family. Most of us were able to get home over the Thanksgiving Day holiday. A couple of weekends, Betty met me in Greensboro, NC, halfway between Atlanta and Quantico.

I learned a lot from courses such as Constitutional Criminal Procedure, Interpersonal Violence, Theory and Practice of Terrorism, Mass Media and the Police, and Police Labor Relations. I finished with three As and two Bs, better than most of my colleagues from the Atlanta Police Department who were at the academy before me.

I even had some fun visiting Washington, DC some weekends, and exploring northern Virginia and the Chesapeake Bay area in Maryland. And as required by tradition, all of us went to the "Love Boat," a restaurant/bar on a boat moored permanently on the water just outside of Quantico. All the new guys at the academy went to check out the local babes. Everyone had to go at least once.

In the meantime, I had re-injured my back. I believed it was from tossing the medicine ball in the gym during physical training. Dave, Barry, and Art insisted it was a result of those weekends in Greensboro. Each evening after class, I lay on my bed, trying to mend.

I made Dave and Barry swear a blood oath that, come graduation day, they would assist me across that stage to receive my diploma, even if they had to carry me. Fortunately, there was no need; I walked across on my own.

Graduation was a formal affair, a big deal for the entire group. The three months away from home and loved ones was over. No matter the politics back at the APD, this one thing could not be taken from me. FBI director William Webster presented us with our diplomas. All the wives, husbands, and significant others attended proudly. The celebration following the graduation ceremonies was like a prom for the graduating class of "Hoover High." I was then, I am now, and forever I will be, a graduate of the 139th session of the FBI National Academy.

Dave and Linda Fromader, Barry and Barbara Hart, and Betty and I have stayed in touch over the years. We meet every year or so in Fort Atkinson, Evansville, or Atlanta. Next year I will host our twenty-second-year reunion in the charming city of Savannah. It's always fun. (Art dropped out of our group after the first few years.)

139th Session, F.B.I. National Academy
F.B.I. Academy, Quantico, Virginia
September 30, 1984 - December 14, 1984
Graduation diploma presented by F.B.I. Director, William H. Webster

Lieutenant H. B. Goldhagen graduating
from the FBI National Academy

To Dilute an Award for Achieving Results, Give the Same Award to Someone Who Did Nothing to Achieve Those Results

Back in Atlanta, after graduation, I resumed my duties as commander of the Vice Squad and the Fugitive squad, both in the Criminal Investigations Division. Meanwhile, in the Field Operations Division, Deputy Chief WJ Taylor and Major WW Holley were lobbying Chief Redding to transfer me to the Special Operations Section, in the Field Operations Division. I did not want a change; I liked working for Jim Oliver, who in the meantime had become a major. He supported my decision.

One night, around 1:30 a.m., during a vice operation, Chief Taylor showed up looking for me. He pulled me aside, telling me that the plain-clothes street crime unit (TAC) had not been accomplishing its mission. He told me he and Major Holley had just come from a late night, unannounced visit, and found the lieutenant sitting in the precinct reading a magazine, the officers in his command riding around aimlessly, without purpose or direction.

He said that the personnel in the unit were willing and able officers, including the two sergeants, and that there was lack of leadership from the lieutenant. Chief Taylor looked me in the eye and said he wanted a hands-on commander (like me) to marshal the TAC unit into doing what it had been commissioned to do. He wanted me to transfer to the Special Operations Section and take over the street crime unit. Once again, I declined. Taylor turned and left the scene, obviously not happy with me. A few days later, Deputy Chief Beverly Harvard was transferred to the Criminal Investigations Division as the chief of detectives! Ugh.

This was the same Beverly Harvard who had "played nice-nice" with A. Reginald Eaves when he was chief of the APD and she was only a rookie. He transferred her to his office after she had been a cop on the street for just a few months. Eaves created a new position for her, the affirmative action officer. She controlled all transfers and assignments, making sure the correct number of white, black, male, and female police officers were in place to meet the goals of the affirmative action policy.

When Eaves was fired, Harvard resigned from the APD. She surfaced several years later as a civilian, working in the Personnel Section, drawing a major's pay, with strong support from influential members in the black community. Within a year, she became a sworn officer with the rank of deputy chief. With a little more than a stroke of the pen, she became the commanding officer of the Administrative Services Division. With yet another bold pen stroke, Beverly Harvard, who had never made a felony arrest or investigated a crime, was the chief of detectives.

The moment my head cleared, I contacted Major Holley to tell him I was ready to move to special operations, away from Beverly Harvard. The next day, I got a call from Chief Redding, who said he was getting one story from Major Holly and another from Major Oliver. I explained that I now wanted a transfer, he said okay, and I was on the next order.

On the first night of my arrival at the APD TAC unit, we gathered around the Special Operations Section (SOS) precinct in a relaxed, informal manner. I purposely did not give them the "there's a new sheriff in town, and here's how we are now going to do things" routine. But I did lay out the following ground rules:

- The entire unit, all eighteen of us, would work six p.m. to two a.m., with everyone off on Sunday and Monday, including me.
- We would work city-wide, in assigned teams of three, on a routine basis, concentrating on downtown and midtown, for general street crimes.
- If there should be an epidemic problem anywhere in the city, and Major Holley wanted it addressed, that would be our mission until it was resolved.

The two TAC sergeants, Jessie Pitts (the same Jesse Pitts that lost his rank during the mass demotions by Eaves) and Doug Overstreet, were highly motivated, very competent, conscientious officers. Each was responsible for half the unit, and it didn't take long for their motivation to filter down to the TAC cops themselves.

The first major assignment occurred in late January, within a week of my arrival. Major Holley and I were ordered to report to Chief Redding's office at police headquarters. When we arrived, there were approximately twenty people sitting around a large conference table. Chief Redding presided. Among the others were deputy chiefs, a couple of majors, the sex crimes squad lieutenant, and several of his detectives; also present were detectives from the Fulton County police and the East Point police, as well as staff members who worked for the big brass. I looked around at everyone at the table. It took a few minutes to realize that they were all looking at me; I was going to be the star of this show.

Chief Redding started by briefing everyone on an on-going problem. For the past year, a serial rapist had been operating along the Campbellton Road corridor. The rapes occurred within the jurisdictions of Atlanta, East Point, and unincorporated Fulton County. Twenty-four rapes had been reported during those twelve months, apparently committed by the same man. Detectives had not come up with a suspect.

Chief Redding ordered Major Holley and me to eliminate this problem. What's more, we had two weeks to find and apprehend the rapist before he went public with the announcement of a serial rapist. Once these crimes hit the media, our chances of catching him by covert means, that is, by putting out female decoys as bait, would sharply diminish. Chief Redding made it clear to the senior officials that I was to be provided whatever resources I requested—I felt I had won the lottery.

For the next several nights, I huddled with Sergeants Jesse Pitts and Doug Overstreet, to decide on a strategy and develop tactics. I learned that six months prior, during the summer, the TAC unit had attempted to catch what appeared to be the same rapist. They didn't have a strategy and had made many tactical mistakes. The Campbellton Road area was all black. The entire TAC unit, both black and white cops, rode up and down Campbellton Road in the same vehicles, night after night. They went into the same restaurants and donut shops, talking to everyone. Everyone, including the rapist, knew the cops were there and why.

I wasn't going to repeat those mistakes. White TAC officers were excluded from this detail. They continued to operate in the downtown and midtown areas, concentrating on routine street crime under the direct supervision of Sergeant Overstreet, a white officer.

For the Campbellton Road area, I chose Sergeant Pitts, a black officer, and the rest of the black TAC officers, supplemented with a few black detectives borrowed from the Vice Squad. I was with them, but remained out of sight, directing operations from a stationary motor home.

All the rape victims were black females. They were attacked in the dark after getting off MARTA buses somewhere along Campbellton Road, walking the dark, lonely streets to their homes. An analysis of the attacks showed that two of the twenty-four victims had gotten off the bus at the intersection of Campbellton and Mt. Gilead Roads. They'd had to walk along Mt. Gilead Road for several blocks to an apartment house complex. The road was dark and heavily wooded on both sides.

Campbellton Road runs for miles, so we couldn't cover all of it at all times. We had to choose a place to set up our decoy operation. The choice of location was a crapshoot, a roll of the dice. We decided on Campbellton and Mt. Gilead Roads because at least two of the twenty-four rapes occurred near that intersection; the other rapes had occurred in random locations along Campellton Road. We decided, largely on instinct, that Campbellton and Mt. Gilead would be the location of the next rape.

Our decoys were two black female officers in the TAC unit, Sheila Bell and Phyllis Hayes, plus two black female officers I borrowed from Zone 4. These four female officers would be our bait. The plan was for them to arrive individually at the MARTA station, separately board successive buses at fifteen-minute intervals, starting at the Oakland City MARTA Rail Station, which was the beginning of Campbellton Road, and ride on the Campbellton Road route to Mt. Gilead Road, where they would leave the bus. Each decoy wore a "body bug," so we could monitor her conversations.

One of the TAC cops knew the manager of the apartments at the end of Mt. Gilead Road. He commandeered a vacant apartment with a clear view of the entrance from Mt. Gilead Road. Because we felt it would have been disadvantageous to our mission to divulge the reason we needed the apartment, we led the manager to understand the apartment was being used for a drug sting.

The critical part of the operation was to position the cover cops so that there would be no blind spots. It was critical that the decoy always be in full view of at least one of the cover cops. Mt. Gilead Road was very curvy for the entire four blocks from the bus stop on Campbellton Road to the apartments. Sergeant Pitts placed each of the TAC and vice cops so that when one cover officer watched the decoy walk past his view and out of his line of sight, she would immediately come into full view of the next cover cop. Cover cops were positioned in the woods, alternately, on both sides of the road. Once in place, they stayed put for the duration of the shift.

During this assignment, we ate our dinners immediately after roll call each night, and then went out to Campbellton Road. All of the rapes had occurred after ten p.m., so we slipped into our positions quietly and set up early each evening. Once at the location, there was no going off for a coffee break; there were no bathroom breaks—well, not in a regular bathroom—there was to be no movement, no noise. As if these circumstances were not bad enough, it was bitter cold in Atlanta at this time of year. Some of the cover cops brought blankets for extra warmth; some sipped coffee from thermoses brought from home. Every cover cop was out in the cold for six continuous hours. I was hidden in an innocuous looking motor home parked in the lot of a tire store on the corner of Campbellton and Mt. Gilead Roads. But I wasn't any warmer then the troops; I couldn't keep the engine running, for obvious reasons, so it was as cold inside as the cold outside.

For the duration of our operation, each decoy officer exited the bus at Campbellton and Mt. Gilead, walked down Mt. Gilead Road to the apartment complex, went into the vacant apartment where a TAC officer was waiting, warmed up for a short time, then walked back to Campbellton Road, crossed the street, and caught a bus going back to the Oakland City Station. They continued this circuit for six hours every night. We got an added bonus whenever a civilian female got off the bus and walked Mt. Gilead Road to the apartments. When that happened, our decoys were instructed to keep a distance from the civilian females, so that each walked far apart from the other, both observed by cover. The civilian females were never aware that they were being covered in the same way as our decoys.

I was in the motor home, on the corner, where I could see the bus stop, to alert the cover team whenever any female, our decoy or not, got off and started walking down Mt. Gilead Road. Two SWAT cars assigned to this detail were standing by about ten blocks away in either direction. The Zone 4 cars were advised to stay away from Campbellton and Mt. Gilead unless we called them for back up. They were aware of our operation and listened for any activity from us. The helicopter unit stayed on normal patrol, but was on notice to respond immediately if we needed their assistance. For two weeks, this was our routine, and we stuck to it, cold night after cold night.

On the last night, the fourteenth night of our mandate, it happened. Officer Sheila Bell left the bus, walked to the vacant apartment, remained for a short while to warm up, and then left, walking along Mt. Gilead Road back towards Campbellton Road. It was late, about 11:30 p.m.; she was the only person on the road. She noticed a man walking toward her and mumbled something about him into her body bug; what she said came through garbled. One of the cover cops also saw him and advised the rest of us that he had the man in view. The man and Sheila passed each other; he continued about ten feet beyond her, then turned, rushed back toward her, grabbed her from behind, and hurled her to the ground. Sheila was simultaneously tried to protect herself and hold onto him. The cover cops left their locations and rushed toward them. The attacker looked up, saw them coming, got off Sheila, and ran for the woods. He dove down a steep embankment, heavy with bushes and brambles, and disappeared into the rectangular thicket, which was about the size of a city block.

Promptly, the TAC officers were on foot, the SWAT units moved in, and Zone 4 responded with six patrol cars, all searching for the rapist. The helicopter hovered over us, its powerful searchlight playing on the dense jungle-like cover, unable to penetrate it.

The wooded area was cordoned off immediately after he disappeared. We were convinced he was still in there. I gave instructions for the cars to hold their positions while we continued the search. The helicopter hovered overhead, trying to place its light just ahead of where one group was searching, then ahead of another group's search. I decided if we did not find the suspect soon, we would wait until daylight, bring in reinforcements to help search, and heavy machines to clear the brush.

None of that was necessary. SWAT Sergeant Calvin Wardlaw and TAC Officer Benjamin Lucas saw some movement under the brush. They jumped down, found the attacker, and brought him back to street level, where Officer Sheila Bell identified him. He was advised of his Miranda rights at the scene, and then transported by one of the SWAT cars to the special operations precinct.

I instructed SWAT Officers Travis Harvey and Dan DeVita to take the suspect to my office and wait there with him until I arrived. They were told not to have any conversation with him. I instructed the second SWAT car to follow them and stand guard outside the closed door of my office, not letting anyone enter until I arrived. I instructed communications to notify the sex crime detectives and have them to respond to the special operations precinct. My immediate supervisors, Captain Eugene Robinson and Major WW Holley were also notified.

When the detectives arrived, we turned over our prisoner to them. He was identified as twenty-four-year-old Alvin Lee Johnson, of 1224 Fairburn Road SW, Atlanta. He had a lengthy arrest record for violent crimes. With a search warrant, they went to his house in daylight, where they found coats, handbags, jewelry, underwear, and other items belonging to some of the twenty-four rape victims. Victims who had seen his face during the attack identified him in a lineup.

He would grab his victims from behind and drag them into the woods, as he tried to do to Sheila Bell. Other times, he would take them behind a building or garbage dumpster, and force them at knife point to lie on their stomachs so they could not look at him, then he'd remove their clothing and rape them. He denied it all.

Two weeks after the arrest, the TAC unit was summoned to city hall and was presented with a proclamation by the mayor and city council, for outstanding police work, et cetera, alluding to our work in capturing the rapist. Someone else was presented with a proclamation for outstanding et cetera, et cetera, et cetera. Guess whom. Yep, it was Deputy Chief Beverly Harvard and the Criminal Investigations Division. Her band of merry men couldn't find a bleeding elephant in the snow. I started to say something about it, to protest to those assembled. I wanted to say, "Hey, wait a minute, CID had nothing to do with the apprehension of the Campbellton road rapist." I didn't. I whispered to Major Holley, "Don't let them get away with this." He told me to be quiet and keep my seat. I whispered the same to Deputy Chief Taylor, who was next to me on the other side. He ignored me. Both Holley and Taylor sat there, mute, letting people who accomplished nothing in two years take credit for the apprehension of the serial rapist.

I thought of the bitter cold nights and the cops who had the commitment, motivation, and discipline to remain quite, unmoving for hours on each of those nights. I thought of the decoys and the risks they took, night after night. I sat there and got very angry. Listening to praise being heaped on those others, I kept my mouth shut; I said nothing.

Harvard's award adorns the wall of her private office. That award diluted the award to the TAC unit. It's simple arithmetic—add a minus one to a plus one, and you get zero, which is how most of us felt about our award after hers was announced. On the other hand, the only things Officer Sheila Bell received were scratches, bumps, and bruises.

CITY OF ATLANTA

120 RALPH McGILL BOULEVARD, N.E. ATLANTA, GEORGIA 30303
404 • 658-7845

ANDREW YOUNG
MAYOR

GEORGE NAPPER
Public Safety Commissioner

April 14, 1986

Lieutenant H. B. Goldhagen
Bureau of Police Services
Special Operations Section

Dear Lieutenant Goldhagen:

I want to personally express my thanks and appreciation for the solid police work and sustained effort you put forth in the investigation, pursuit and apprehension of the Campbellton/Mt. Gilead area rapist, culminating in the arrest of a suspect on February 4, 1986. This kind of work you did in this case is exemplary of the high standards and dedication your unit members demonstrate.

I am proud of your work and pleased that it has resulted in removing a dangerous and fear inducing person from the community at large. You have made a real contribution to the greater safety of our city, and I commend you.

I am directing that a copy of this letter be placed in your permanent record.

Sincerely,

George Napper

GN:bh

cc: Chief Morris G. Redding

Letter from Police Commissioner George Napper commending the TAC Unit for apprehending the "Campbellton Road Rapist"

"Wonderful! Just wonderful! Absolutely wonderful!"

The Special Operations Section (SOS) is subordinate to the Field Operations Division and commanded by a major, as are the six zones commonly referred to as precincts in other city police departments. The difference between zones and SOS is that SOS operates citywide, without geographical boundaries. It is home to many of the special units and responsible for many functions—traffic, motorcycles, hit and run, parking enforcement, SWAT, TAC, mounted patrol, helicopters, and hostage negotiators.

Special operations handles all major events where large crowds gather and traffic is a concern—parades, road races, festivals, demonstrations, presidential visits, VIP visits, major sporting events (such as the World Series, the Super Bowl, the All-Star Game), and all other special events. Members of the TAC unit work in uniform for these events.

Most events are routine after a while because they occur repeatedly. There were, however, those that were not routine and became memorable events. The special events coordinator of the city's Bureau of Cultural Affairs, Ms. Holly Mull, got the bright idea to have a giant block party right in the middle of downtown Atlanta. It would be held on a Saturday, from mid-morning until after dark, in July, when it doesn't get dark until after nine p.m. Traffic would be restricted for six square city blocks, centered on Woodruff Park. This memorable event was known as "Light up Atlanta."

The first "Light up Atlanta" went off without disaster. There were no tragedies, despite a lack of provisions made for emergency vehicles, should they have been needed, to get through the enormous crowd. After that first "Light up Atlanta," the police and fire departments advised city officials not to hold such an event again, due to the potential for disaster. These warnings were ignored.

The entire special operations section was detailed for the second event, along with many other police officers from the city. About twenty police officers were assigned to me; our sector was on the Peachtree Street side of Woodruff Park. As the day wore on, the crowds increased so that it became difficult to move. It was a very hot, humid day, with people pressing on people to get into restaurants for food, water, and restrooms. The geniuses at city hall did not think to bring out portable restrooms. Tempers flared, and we had to separate people to keep them from getting physically abusive. The office buildings in the area were closed for the weekend, but security guards admitted cops to use the restrooms and get drinks of much needed water.

When it got dark, things worsened. The city officials, including Holly Mull and the VIPs, left "Light up Atlanta," just before Atlanta "lit up." They likely had retreated to their air-conditioned houses or condos, downing cold beers or sipping cocktails. While they did, gangs of black male teenagers started assaulting the crowd, knocking people down, groping women, beating, and robbing. Where they struck, we went after them. We tried to catch up to them, but the large crowds made it impossible. As we pursued one gang, another attacked people in the place we had just left. We were chasing our tails.

We decided that our best strategy was to remain at one location, where we were expecting the return of a large gang that had been there previously. We had been on our feet in the heat since morning, without a break, and we were exhausted. When a gang of approximately one hundred teenagers broke through the crowd, it became "stick time." There was no asking a mob to "be nice." Officer Ray Braswell had been assigned to my detail; we were together, side by side, all day. Now we were back to back, swinging our clubs to protect the crowd from them, adrenalin pumping—the fuel that energized us, kept us going.

I'm not sure how much longer we could have continued flailing, but we didn't have to. Braswell and I were grateful to see the Mounted Patrol coming our way down Peachtree Street, through the parting crowd. About twenty horses, shoulder to shoulder, across from curb to curb, clearing everything in their way—the cavalry to the rescue, sans bugler! Behind them followed about fifty motorcycle cops in four waves—moving whatever the horses had not.

We were relieved, thinking the worst was over. It wasn't. Gunshots were reported from two blocks away at the MARTA Five Points station. The horses continued at a gallop down Peachtree Street to that location. The SWAT team working that sector engaged with another gang of thugs. A horse went down; a mounted cop was injured.

Order was not fully restored until midnight. The crowds were gone; the thugs in the gangs either were in jail or had faded into the night. Several people were shot or stabbed, hundreds were assaulted, scores injured and robbed, and several police officers injured. Dozens of patrol cars were damaged.

Resting at home the next day, my day off, I saw Holly Mull interviewed on the local news. When asked how she thought "Light up Atlanta" had gone, she said, "Wonderful! Just wonderful! Absolutely wonderful!" That was the last "Light up Atlanta."

The Loudmouth Cop, the Young Cop, the Injury, the Disability Letter

Weeks turned into months, winter turned to spring, then came summer. The TAC unit was on the streets night after night, and because of our presence, we had the thugs looking over their shoulders. We were kickin' ass, figuratively and literally, putting up respectable numbers, arresting a lot of these thugs and bullies, administering some street justice along the way. But just like the mule you have to hit in the head with a two-by-four to get his attention, these "tough" guys only understood superior force. The revolving doors at the jailhouse didn't mean much to them. Further recognition came from top brass, who noticed our numbers!

The size of the TAC unit was increased temporarily for the summer months, according to the following plan: police officers from the six zones were allowed to volunteer to work one of their off days, in plain clothes, to make overtime pay. The number of undercover cars and vans available, as well as the span of control, limited the number of volunteers each night.

Officer RP Miniatis, a Zone 3 officer, showed up each week for his overtime tour. We were working our usual three-person teams, no special assignments. The TAC supervisors were getting complaints about Miniatis from the regular members of the unit. The gist was that Miniatis had a negative attitude. Apparently, Miniatis was going on and on about how zone policing was "real policing" and saying that all TAC did was drive around, drink coffee, and waste time. These remarks would make any of the TAC unit cops not want to work with him; they requested he not be assigned with them in the future.

TAC Officers JD Underwood, Dan Devita, and Sheila Bell, two white males and a black female, made up one of our teams for some time. They did a good job, handled their assignments well, made arrests where appropriate, completed their paperwork, and did not generate any complaints from the public. They liked working together, but Devita had just transferred to the SWAT team. The remaining two needed a partner, and it was Miniatis' overtime night.

I called Underwood and Bell into my office and told them I was going to assign Miniatis with them. We agreed that he needed an attitude adjustment. The plan was for them to leave the precinct immediately after roll call, skip dinner until later, and make cases, non-stop—even petty violations. This might convince the big mouth that we were not the donut patrol.

JD Underwood was a young police officer—small, youthful looking, easily passing for a high school senior. He was very fast and deceptively strong. (He reminded me of myself when I was a young cop, years before.)

The undercover trio's first activity occurred at Spring Street and West Peachtree Place, where two thugs who offered to sell them drugs approached them. The deal was made, the drugs were exchanged for cash, and Underwood badged them. Then it happened.

One of the dealers was carrying a full can of Coca-Cola in a tee shirt—two simple items—each harmless by themselves, but place the can in the center of the shirt, grab the shirt by its four corners, twist the end of the shirt loaded with the weight of the can, and swing it, and it becomes a weapon. In a desperate attempt to avoid being arrested, the seller swung that weapon at Underwood, hitting him on the side of his head. Underwood went down, and his attacker started to flee. Underwood bounced up and started a chase on foot. While that happened, the other seller punched Miniatis square in his face, knocking him stupid. Sheila Bell drew her weapon and put the guy on the ground. Underwood caught up to the fleeing thug, subdued him, and put handcuffs on him, leading him by the cuffs like you would a horse by its bridle, back to Bell and Miniatis, then collapsed. Sheila got on the radio, called for assistance and an ambulance (signal 63/4—officer needs help/ambulance on the way), the signal that always draws a crowd.

I was a few blocks away when the call came in. I was the first car to arrive. When I got out of my car I observed JD Underwood and a black male lying side by side on their backs, JD staring up at the sky, not saying anything. The black male beside him, handcuffed, was bleeding from the head. Sheila Bell was holding a pistol on the second black male who was lying face down; Miniatis was sitting on the ground, propped against a car, and appeared to not know where the hell he was—he was unhurt, though momentarily stunned.

When the ambulance arrived, Underwood and the guy with the bloody head were loaded and taken to Grady Hospital. Officer Dan Devita, who had just joined SWAT, and his SWAT partner, Travis

Harvey, arrived at the scene. I asked Devita to ride in the ambulance and Harvey to follow in the patrol car. I told them to stay with Underwood until I got to the hospital.

During the hour or so before I arrived at the Grady Hospital ER, Devita and Harvey were with Underwood as a young intern examined him. JD's vital signs were monitored for a short time, and then he was released. The intern said Underwood would have a headache for a day or so and authorized a few days of "injured off" time. Underwood got off the stretcher and immediately collapsed onto the floor. Devita and Harvey had just collected Underwood from the floor and put him back on the stretcher when I arrived.

We raised enough hell in the ER that a neurosurgeon came down, and upon cursory examination determined that Underwood's injury was more serious than first diagnosed. He was admitted to the hospital for further evaluation.

His inner ear had been damaged, upsetting his equilibrium. He was out "injured off" for three months. During that time, several neurologists and ear specialists examined him. His symptoms were regularly occurring nausea, similar to sea-sickness; loss of balance, so that the only way he could walk was close beside a wall, touching the wall every few steps; the appearance of a staggering drunkard; and hearing loss that required him to wear hearing aids. They could do nothing for his "condition." He would have to learn to live with it.

He returned to work on "light duty" status in the precinct, doing office work. There were times he was so sick he couldn't complete the watch and had to be taken home. As time went on, his condition worsened. We knew he couldn't continue to work and would soon have to apply for a disability pension.

I have never gotten over what happened that night. I had set things in motion to prove to a loudmouth cop that we were better cops than he thought we were. If I hadn't encouraged Underwood and Sheila to teach Miniatis a lesson, maybe they would have had dinner right after roll call, as most of us did, and not run into those thugs. I've carried a lot of guilt through the years because of that. I knew how much Underwood wanted to be a cop, and he was a good one. Those who knew Underwood and worked with him have often wondered how he was so severely injured, yet able to chase the thug, catch up to him, subdue and handcuff him, and drag him back, yet could not stand up without toppling over. I guess it's not how big you are, but what you've got inside your chest.

As his commanding officer, I had to write the letter requesting Underwood be placed on a disability pension. I put it off as long as I could. As I wrote, my mind flashed back to Underwood before going on watch, seeing him on the street staring up at the sky, and seeing him on the stretcher at Grady. I saw him at the precinct on light duty trying to make his eight hours, so sick he was incapacitated. It took me a long time to write that letter. It was very difficult. I was alone in the precinct, and everyone had gone for the night. I locked up at 3:30 a.m., went to my car, sat for a few minutes, and cried.

Cuban Detainees, Federal Prisoners, FBI Negotiators, and Us

In 1980, Cuba's Fidel Castro emptied his country's prisons and mental institutions. He sent the criminals and mentally ill, about 100,000 in all, from the port of Mariel, Cuba to the United States. This became known as the Mariel Boat Lift and the refugees, the "Mariellitos." The Carter administration authorized them to disembark in Miami, Florida, where they were detained until the US government could decide what to do with them. Some criminals were sent to prisons in various states, most to the federal penitentiary, in Atlanta, Georgia. They were officially designated "detainees." They had not violated any US law, yet they could not be released into our society. They were dangerous people. What should be done with them? No one seemed to know, so they sat in prison for several years, their future uncertain.

In the fall of 1987, rumors began circulating that a deal had been worked out between the US government and Castro to return the Mariellitos to Cuba. This was not what the Mariellitos wanted.

The federal penitentiary in Oakdale, Louisiana also housed many detainees. The rumors created anxieties that smoldered, flaring into a full-scale riot. The Cubans took prison guards hostage, they began rampaging, burning, and vandalizing. The FBI was called in and their hostage rescue team was dispatched from Quantico, Virginia.

It made national news, and when it reached the Mariellitos in the Atlanta Federal Penitentiary, the Cuban detainees told their prison guards that they had better lock it down—lock all inmates, US federal prisoners and Cuban detainees, in their cells—no mess hall, no exercise yard, no day room, no privileges, no work. Some of the Cuban detainees warned that the same thing was about to happen in the Atlanta Federal Penitentiary. Prison officials took no action; three days later, it happened. Several hundred Cuban detainees took one hundred

283

prison guards and civilian employees hostage (a lot more than in Oakdale), and began rioting, burning, and looting federal buildings within the penitentiary. If there was any good news, it was that in both the Oakdale and Atlanta riots, the hostages were not being hurt or mistreated. The Cubans kept the US prisoners away from the hostages, to protect them.

I was home when I got the call. The APD operator told me there was a riot and hostage situation at the Atlanta Federal Penitentiary, similar to what had been happening in Oakdale, Louisiana. The operator said that the special operations response team members who were on duty were already at the scene, the rest were en route.

On my way to the federal penitentiary, I tried to understand why the Atlanta Police had been called. Although the prison is within the City of Atlanta, the entire square block, and the penitentiary that sits on it, is federal property, under federal jurisdiction. When I arrived, it was evident why we were called. The FBI had jurisdiction, but the Atlanta Field Office of the FBI had not gotten itself organized to deal with the riots. They had to round up their SWAT team agents and break out their SWAT gear. We needed to keep things from getting worse until the FBI could organize. The FBI hostage rescue team was busy in Oakdale, so FBI SWAT teams were being flown to Atlanta from six different field offices around the country.

We had our act together quickly—we do this all the time. Our hostage phone was made available to the FBI; it was a special piece of equipment—portable, controlled from our end, one of the several features that make our phone invaluable to us. Using our phone, FBI special agent Dee Rosario, a Spanish-speaking negotiator from the Atlanta field office, made contact with one of the Cubans. He confirmed that everyone was all right, no one was hurt; the Cubans did not intend to hurt anyone and no US inmate would go near them.

A large office, just inside the federal penitentiary administration building was set up to be used by the hostage negotiators. A similar office across the hall was set up to serve as the command post for all the brass. By early morning, the FBI SWAT and hostage negotiating teams started arriving. A team of FBI hostage negotiators, most of them Spanish-speaking, was brought down from Quantico.

By midday, the basic command center had been organized. The Federal Bureau of Prisons had relinquished control and authority to the FBI. All involved federal personnel went on twelve-hour shifts, eight a.m. to eight p.m. and eight p.m. to eight a.m. I wondered why four Atlanta Police Department hostage negotiators were still on the scene. The room was full of FBI negotiators, most of them Spanish-speaking, with more FBI negotiators on the way. There were many federal personnel, so why were four APD negotiators, Frank McClure, Gerry Sanchez, Bernadette Hernandez, and I still around?

We eventually learned that we were there because Atlanta Police Chief George Napper and the special agent-in-charge of the Atlanta field office, Wendal Kennedy, had agreed that one APD negotiator be part of the negotiations team. The agreement made little operational sense to me; it must have been made for political purposes—likely a little interagency jealousy, or guarding one's turf. I suggested that if one of us had to be on each twelve-hour shift, it would make good sense to have Sanchez and Hernandez on each shift since they spoke Spanish; furthermore, Gerry Sanchez was Cuban. What made sense to me made no sense to the brass. They wanted Frank and me to do it because we were the senior negotiators. Frank McClure had always been well connected with the bureau, and I suspect some of the "good ol' boy" networking came into play. I was sure of that when Frank was assigned to day shift, and I got stuck on the graveyard shift.

Rioters vandalized the hostage side of our phone within those first few hours, but the FBI hostage phone had become available, so the negotiators were using the FBI hostage phone. (The bureau later replaced the damaged parts of our phone.) Atlanta Police established an outer perimeter, where they were responsible for crowd and traffic control on the streets surrounding the prison. I went up in an APD helicopter to observe the open compound. There were several buildings; the largest had been burned and was still smoldering. The other buildings were looted, and there was lots of debris all over the compound. There were hundreds of people milling around within the compound.

The situation had settled down somewhat. Dialogue, all in Spanish, was going on over the phone between the FBI negotiators and the Cubans. The FBI negotiators wanted the Cubans to release all hostages and end their takeover. The Cubans wanted a guarantee from the FBI that they would not be sent back to Cuba. When asked about any sick or injured, the Cubans replied that one of the older hostages was complaining of chest pains. The Cubans released that hostage, and he was taken to the hospital, where his condition was determined not to be serious. FBI personnel later interviewed him, and he provided them with valuable intelligence. He said that no one was being mistreated, and there was no contact with any of the US inmates. The attitude of the Cubans toward the hostages was civil, even amiable.

The FBI negotiators told the Cubans that as long as they kept talking and no one was being mistreated or harmed, federal personnel would not attempt to enter the compound. Otherwise, they would enter and use force, if necessary. This theme continued for several days; we were all hoping that the powers in Washington would not take much longer to work out whatever was needed to meet the Cubans' demands.

Everyone in the FBI negotiation room heard both sides of the phone conversation, because it came through open speakers in the room. The dialogue had become slow, dull, and boring, and remained that way for a long time, too long to expect that any good for anyone would result. One night, around midnight, the volume and tempo of the dialogue suddenly picked up; the Cubans were saying they wanted to release someone—not a hostage, but a federal prisoner.

Early on, in any hostage situation, there is a plan developed, and agreed to by all parties as to how anyone is to be released. Details include where the exit point will be, the actions of the released person, hands empty, showing, walk straight ahead, walk to the right, walk to the left, until met by police—or any other process—based on the situation. The release plan was put into motion. The Cubans opened the gate at the barricade and shoved into the "no man's land" a white male, handcuffed, and in leg irons. A couple of SWAT guys approached to retrieve him. They had to help him walk, as he was rubber-legged.

The released prisoner was Silverstein, a white supremacist (despite his Jewish-sounding name), who had been serving time in the federal penitentiary at Marion, Illinois for bank robbery. While at Marion, he killed his cellmate and was transferred to the federal prison in Atlanta. He was confined to a maximum-security cell, isolated from the rest of the prison population. He was considered extremely dangerous. The Cubans told us later that during the rioting Silverstein was released from his cell. Whether he was deliberately released or some rioter pushed the wrong button remains unknown. The Cubans said they were concerned he would go on a murderous rampage against the prison guards. When the rioters broke into the pharmacy, they looted various drugs, and later slipped a hefty dose of a powerful tranquilizer into something Silverstein drank. That morning, after daylight, US marshals took him to the Fulton County Airport and flew him to the federal penitentiary at Leavenworth, Kansas. The release of Silverstein was a dramatic moment and had everyone on his or her toes because prison officials, knowing his history, were concerned he would be the one to turn things violent. But it was tempered with humor when the Cubans called and asked for the return of their handcuffs and leg irons.

Gary LeShaw, the attorney representing the detainees before the takeover, was allowed to meet with them; after all, they were his clients. He met with them each day and assured us that everyone was doing fine. Food was sent for everyone each mealtime. Edwin Meese, the US attorney general at the time, came down from Washington, stayed for a few hours, and then flew back to DC. As we could not discern that his presence affected forward motion in the negotiations, we decided he came for a photo-op.

We were into the second week when Bishop Desmond Tutu of South Africa arrived at the prison. He and Gary LeShaw had a series of meetings with the Cubans. The Cubans said they trusted Tutu and LeShaw. They said that if Tutu and LeShaw could get a written agreement from the US government specifying that 1) they would not be sent back to Cuba, and 2) each Cuban's confinement would be reviewed on a case by case basis, they would release all of the hostages unharmed, and surrender.

The Cubans also wanted a TV reporter present to witness and report the particulars of the final agreement, and the hostage release. FBI SAC Kennedy asked McClure and me to go outside and select a local TV reporter, one that we knew to be fair and objective. The media was lined up across from the prison; TV, radio, and the print media, maybe one hundred in all, local, national and international. Frank and I agreed on Marc Pickard, from one of the local TV stations. We had worked with him in the past. He was to be the representative of the media pool. We made his day.

On the twelfth day, it happened. The deal was made. Afterwards, released hostages confirmed that they were treated well and that the Cubans kept the other prisoners away from them. The agreement in Atlanta included the Cubans in Oakland, and both incidents ended without anyone getting hurt.

Hostage negotiator, FBI Special Agent Dee Rosario did an excellent job in keeping the lid on the situation, talking to, and bonding with, each of the different Cubans who got on the phone. He talked for long hours over twelve straight days. Dee Rosario deserved much of the credit for the outcome.

	U.S. Department of Justice
	Federal Bureau of Prisons
	U.S. Penitentiary

601 McDonough Blvd., S.E.
Atlanta, GA 30315-4423

December 21, 1987

Lt. H. B. Goldhagan
Atlanta Police Department
175 Decatur Street, S. E.
Atlanta, Georgia 30335

Dear Lt. Goldhagan:

I would like to take this opportunity to express my sincere appreciation for your assistance during the recent disturbance at the United States Penitentiary, Atlanta, Georgia.

Throughout this crisis, you, along with several others, spent many long hours negotiating with the hostage-takers. This is a very difficult and demanding job that you performed in an outstanding manner. The teamwork, responsiveness and cooperation that you displayed are commendable.

You can take pride in the fact that your efforts contributed to the peaceful conclusion and release of all hostages, unharmed.

Again, thank you for the help and support.

Sincerely,

J. S. Petrovsky
Warden

Letter from the Warden of the Atlanta Federal Penitentiary after the Cuban detainees uprising and hostage taking

Everybody Hates a Quota—Except the Quota Maker

For promotions, assignments and transfers, the performance of every City of Atlanta police officer must be evaluated on a regular basis. There is usually a formal annual performance evaluation given by a police officer's immediate supervisor. Two methods have evolved over time, neither of which is without its flaws.

One method is entirely subjective, which makes the evaluation as variable as the evaluator's human nature—experiences, preferences, impressions (whether founded or not), and peculiarities. Given the same police officer, under the same circumstances, during any given period, one evaluator might give glowing, generous, forgiving appraisals across the board, while another evaluator, for whatever reasons, might nit-pick an officer's recent performance, down to the smallest, insignificant detail. Conversely, the same officer, having performed identically, could suffer or benefit from a different evaluator, depending on his or her disposition, whims, attitudes, likes, dislikes, and biases. This method is flawed by its nature.

The other method is an objective evaluation. For instance, the number of arrests made in a certain period may be used to compare an officer's effectiveness relative to the entire police department. Is this an accurate representation of the performance of an officer, a unit, or the department as a whole? Or does the arrest data fill an upper level supervisor's mandate—that is, a quota? This method is flawed by its objective.

The quota. Hated by the public, detested by police officers, it is food for the media to chew and spit back. Police departments justify their existence by numbers; they live or die by numbers. The TAC unit also had a body count—the number of perpetrators arrested in the act of committing a crime. We did not inflate these numbers.

The terms "arrests" and "cases" are used interchangeably. When a person is arrested and charged with four different violations, it should be counted as one arrest, four cases. Some units log it in as four arrests, which looks good on paper to someone who doesn't know what's going on. They are playing a numbers game, which he or she usually wins—until someone who does know what is going on discovers it. TAC correctly distinguished between arrests and cases, accurately identifying each. Each person ("body," in police gallows humor jargon) counted as one arrest, regardless of the number of cases (violations).

In spite of the fact that TAC reported its numbers and statistics accurately and legitimately, while other units throughout the APD "cooked their books," the bosses recognized TAC's achievements on two separate occasions, creating "overtime details" to supplement the unit with additional manpower for its proven results.

I Never Again Said, "Bring me some bodies!"

Officers Benjamin Lucas, Herman Glass, and Phyllis Hayes, two black males and a black female, comprised one of our three-person TAC teams. They hadn't made an arrest in a couple of nights, so it was time for me to juice them up. One night, right after roll call, as they were headed out the door with the rest of the cops, I called out, "Lucas, bring me some bodies!"

A few hours later—"Any car near Echo and Dalvigney Streets, signal 63/50/4." Damn those signals; it was the worst of all calls—officer needs help, person shot, ambulance on the way. "Who was shot? An officer? Someone else?" Like a jolt of electricity, those questions run through the mind of every cop who heard those signals. Phyllis Hayes came on the air; she said Lucas and another person had been shot. Responding units put their vehicles in overdrive. We found Lucas with a gunshot wound to his arm; the other person shot was DOS—dead on the scene.

Lucas was taken to Grady Hospital; the medical examiner arrived at the scene for the dead guy. Homicide detectives were also on the scene; they took TAC Officers Glass and Hayes to the homicide office for written statements. All witnesses were interviewed; any evidence, including the guns discharged, were collected to be analyzed. Internal Affairs detectives also arrived at the scene, to interview Officers Glass and Hayes, but they had to wait until the homicide detectives finished their interviews.

Most of us working the six p.m. to two a.m. watch, had dinner shortly after roll call, to get it out of the way. Most of our activity occurred later in the evening. At about ten p.m., our three-person teams were in different parts of the city, the Lucas-Glass-Hayes team was near Bankhead Highway and Ashby Street. They were cruising the small, dark streets for drug activity. Sitting in their car at the corner of Dalvigney and Echo Streets, they were approached by a black male who asked if they wanted to buy some "rock," street jargon for crack cocaine. They said they would. The guy told them to stay where they were; he would be right back with it.

The three got out of the car and waited. When the guy returned, he wanted to see the money. They flashed the money; the exchange was made. They badged the guy and announced, "Police." He stepped back, surprised. He pulled out a gun; Officer Herman Glass was alert for that possibility and was immediately on top of him, they both went down.

The drug seller started shooting as he went down, hitting Lucas in the arm. Lucas and Hayes had their guns out, but could not shoot because Glass was locked onto him. Lucas shouted for Glass to get off him, and the guy continued to fire. Glass rolled off and away, and Lucas shot the guy, killing him. Later, after all that was over, five bullet holes were found in the tail of the coat Lucas was wearing; there had been no bullet holes in it at the start of his watch that evening.

Local black activist, Hosea Williams, who was to Atlanta what Al Sharpton was to New York City, started to raise hell, before the drug seller's body was cold. He said the black community was tired of white police murdering black men. His remarks appeared in the morning paper. When it was revealed that the three officers involved were black, we heard nothing more out of Hosea.

The incident was investigated, first by the Atlanta Police Homicide Squad, then by the APD Internal Affairs Unit, and finally by the Fulton County District Attorney's Office. All conclude that the shooting was justified—"a good shooting" is the common phrase, though it makes some people wince.

Lucas's luck went from bad to worse that night. His wife was notified that he was hurt, and she was brought to Grady Hospital. A short time later, his girlfriend showed up. They created a pretty good disturbance right in the ER. Things settled down when the girlfriend was escorted out of the hospital. Lucas was lucky he was shot only once that night.

Although it probably had nothing to do with what happened that night, I never again instructed any police officer to, "Bring me some bodies!"

Despite official confirmation that the three cops were black, it was suggested that there was a "white wash"—a cover up. The case was turned over to the civilian review board. Lucas, Glass, and Hayes were the only three subpoenaed. I attended the interviews as their commanding officer and sat to the side during their interrogations. When the members finished questioning the three officers, I requested permission to address the board. I had Lucas' raincoat with me—I had checked it out of Property—I put it on, walked in front of the members of the board, and asked them to look at the tail of the coat. I lifted and spread the tail so they could see the five bullet holes. One picture was worth a thousand words. Case closed.

Harold B. Goldhagen

He Was There When We Weren't, but He Was Caught Anyway

Two years after we caught the Campbellton Road rapist, we were called upon to covertly do the same for another series of rapes. Six women had been sexually assaulted in the Courtland Street area of downtown over three months, in the winter of 1987. The victims, all white females, described the rapist as a black male in his 20s or 30s.

The details of each of the six rapes were similar: the victim left work from one of the downtown office buildings later than the normal five p.m. quitting time. She walked to one of the ground level parking lots or to a multi-story parking deck. She was grabbed from behind as she got into her car, shoved inside, and raped inside her car, still parked in the lot.

The rapes were happening in December, January, and February, when it got dark early, and the streets were deserted. It was unusually cold, so cold that one of the victims was treated at the hospital for mild frostbite to her toes. The rapist kept the victims in their cars, partially undressed for long periods without the heater on; he did not want the engine running. All six victims emphasized the stench of his body.

We used a different strategy than we used at Campbellton Road. We did not use female police officers as decoys. There were enough females walking into dark, lonely parking lots, all potential victims. We just had to watch them very carefully, so they would not actually become victims. Surveillance was conducted from undercover vehicles, as well as by spotters on the roofs of a few parking decks. From their positions, the spotters, equipped with binoculars, had a good view of the streets leading to the parking lots. All personnel from the TAC unit, black, white, male, and female, were used in the operation. Two patrol cars from Zone 5 were used as chase cars—Officer Ray Braswell in one, and Officer Bob Visk in the other. They were to stand by, out of sight, at either end of the target area, and were not to receive any other calls. The surveillance vehicles were placed at strategic locations, watching the parking lots and the decks of the multilevel parking lots. Whenever any one of us spotted a lone female walking towards a parking lot, every one on our team was notified, and we went on high alert until she was safely in her car and drove out of the lot.

We persisted with this strategy for almost four weeks, night after night, except on our off nights. During those weeks, there were no sexual assaults in that area, which was good news for the community; however, it was not good news for us because not only had we not glimpsed a likely suspect, we appeared to be the reason there were no rapes or attempted rapes.

292

At about eight p.m. on Monday night of the fourth week, someone called 911 to report a woman screaming in the parking lot at Courtland Street and Ralph McGill Boulevard. Zone 5 police responded quickly and flooded the area. They located a hysterical victim number seven and carefully coaxed from her a description of her attacker. The description matched, and the manhunt was on.

Our unit worked that location on Tuesday through Saturday nights—five nights every week. Sunday and Monday nights were our nights off. I was called at home and immediately went to the scene. More resources were deployed. After an hour of searching, Officer Ray Braswell, who always seemed to be where he was needed, along with Officer Jerry McCrary, pulled a guy out of a dumpster in the parking lot of the Travel Lodge Motel at Courtland and Baker Streets. Also found in the dumpster was the victim's handbag, containing all of her identification. The suspect was turned over to the sex crimes detectives.

We learned later that he, a homeless man, was the serial rapist. He lived in the bowels of a vacant building under Courtland Street, near Houston Street. He told the detectives he knew our unit was out there, watching and waiting for him to strike. He knew where we were set up and the vehicles we were in when we were there. He eventually recognized that we were there Tuesday through Saturday nights, but not Sunday and Monday nights. On Sundays, the downtown office buildings were closed; therefore, there were no potential victims. Once he figured that out, he hit that Monday night, when he saw that we were not around.

In the Campbellton Road operation, we had gotten away with all of us taking the same off days, on Courtland Street it was a different story. The perpetrator lived right under our noses, watching our every move. The hunted became the hunter; at least to the extent that we gave him the opportunity to decide when it was safe to strike.

We learned a valuable lesson; although Sundays and Mondays are the sequential days with the least criminal activity, we had better jumble those days every now and then to keep the bad guys off balance.

Terrorism, When it Was Over There, and Not Yet Here

In the past several decades, there have been many acts of terror around the world, mainly in the Middle East, Europe, and Latin America. International terrorism was not then a daily topic in the United States. Some of us were aware of it, but weren't concerned about it; most just ignored it. I was aware of international terrorism, concerned about it, and became a student of it. I kept up with what was going on, and I soon realized that the United States was not as insulated from terrorism as was widely believed.

In 1982, I sent a memo to Atlanta Police Chief Morris Redding, expressing my concern that it would not be long before what was happening in other parts of the world would be happening here in the US. I informed him of a counter-terrorism training seminar to be conducted in Israel by well-known experts in the field. Who better to teach the course than the Israelis? After all, they wrote the book on counter-terrorism. I didn't want to appear self-serving, so I recommended Redding send anyone from the APD, not necessarily me, to attend the seminar. My memo was ignored; no one was sent.

In the mid-80s, there was deadly violence almost daily in Israel and Northern Ireland. Atlanta had a number of foreign consulates, including those of Israel and Great Britain. No one from the APD was in contact with any of the many foreign consulates. The more I thought about it, the more convinced I was that some type of contact should be initiated.

I went to my boss, Major WW Holley, commander of the Special Operations Section, and expressed my concerns. Should anything happen at one of these consulates, the APD, and more specifically, Special Operations, would be the first responders. I suggested that someone from Special Operations visit each foreign consulate, become familiar with the facility, and establish a contact person so that we would be prepared in advance. Holley agreed, and I was given the assignment.

My first visit to the British consulate in the Peachtree Center complex downtown went smoothly enough. The consul general received me. I explained the purpose for my visit. He seemed pleased, was cordial, showed me around, and introduced me to a contact person. When I left, they thanked me for the interest and concern of the APD.

However, my introductory visit to the Israeli consulate was different, vastly different. The consulate itself was located in Midtown, at Peachtree and Fifth Streets (it has since moved to Spring and 16th Streets), and was on the fifth floor of an old five-story office building. A video camera was mounted on the wall and trained on the door. There was an intercom on the wall near the door. I pushed the button, and a voice asked who I was and what I wanted. I was in uniform; I introduced myself and asked to see the consul general. I was "buzzed in" and entered what was more a chamber than a entrance foyer; there was no furniture, just four walls with a glass partition in one wall, a floor and ceiling, and of course, the door in front and the door behind me. When the door closed behind me, it locked automatically, much like what happens when entering a maximum-security prison. The door in front of me was locked. A man behind the glass partition asked me a few more questions. When he was satisfied that I was not Yassar Arafat, or any other security threat, he buzzed me through the second door. (I learned later that both doors and walls were made of steel; the glass partition was bulletproof.)

I was led to a small office, where we sat and talked. As I explained the purpose for my visit, he offered me coffee. To be polite, I accepted, but on my first swallow, I wished I hadn't. The coffee was a Middle Eastern brew, dark, bitter, thick as sludge. I let the rest sit and get cold. The man was a member of Shin Bet, an Israeli law enforcement agency, a combination of our FBI and Secret Service. After several minutes of questioning, the agent took me to a larger office to introduce me to the consul general. After explaining the purpose of my visit, to coordinate any emergency response by Atlanta Police to the Israeli Consulate, they asked me to return and encouraged me to stay in touch.

Special Agent Harry Jones, with the US State Department Protective Services Division (similar to the Secret Service), had been trying to establish contact with the Israeli Consulate for a long time, but kept getting the cold shoulder.

"Harry, I'm in," I told him on the phone.

"Get me in, and I'll buy you lunch," responded a surprised Harry Jones. I did, and he did.

Harry accompanied me on my second visit a few days later. I introduced him first to Shin Bet agent Eli Yitzak within the confines of the steel-lined outer chamber. Then, in a conference room, introductions were made to the consul general and the vice-consul. Coffee was served, and this time I declined. I noticed the "God, what is this shit?" look on Harry's face at his first swallow of their coffee. Harry survived, and we kept a close relationship with the Israeli Consulate, I more often than Harry Jones.

The Shin Bet agents rotated in and out of the Israeli Consulate, one agent at a time, for approximately two years. Then they were replaced by a successor. Over six or seven years, I got to know three agents pretty well.

The first one, Eli Yitzak, was very young. He had planned a weekend trip to Disney world in Orlando, Florida. He had his airline tickets, hotel reservations, and auto rental, and was looking forward to a fun weekend with his girlfriend. But that was same weekend the consul general was to attend a formal function on a Saturday night at a downtown Atlanta hotel, where he would be the featured speaker. A Shin Bet agent always accompanies the consul general whenever and wherever he goes.

Eli was supposed to accompany him. I was not scheduled to work that night, so Eli asked if I would cover for him and go with the consul general in his place. I agreed, glad to help; I liked him, and it was a good way for the two of us to start working together. Dressed in a suit, I was the consul general's bodyguard for the evening. Everything went well; there were no incidents, no problems.

Unfortunately, there were problems for Eli. The word got back to Shin Bet headquarters in Tel Aviv that Eli had asked me to replace him. Eli was recalled immediately. I learned later from his replacement, Zruya Avishai, that Eli had been assigned to a dreary outpost in the Negev Desert. Zruya said Eli was lucky he hadn't been kicked out of the service because not doing what he was assigned to do was a dereliction of duty.

Zruya Avishai was in Atlanta for a very quiet two years. Nothing much happened that was of concern for either the APD or the Israeli Consulate. During those two years, Zruva and I just kept in touch from time to time. We got together socially once, when he and his family came to my house for dinner.

When Zruya's assignment was finished, he went back to Israel. His replacement was Shraga Karyan, a colonel in the Shin Bet. Shraga was a bit older than Zruva; he had a lot more "juice," due to his rank, his longevity, and his experience. Shraga and I hit it off right away. I think it surprised him to find a Jewish policeman in Atlanta, Georgia with a little "juice" in his own right. In our first few meetings, we talked a lot about international terrorism. He was surprised and delighted that I was so knowledgeable on the subject.

Throughout the 1980s and into the early 1990s, there were more and more terrorist incidents against Israeli and Jewish targets around the world. Synagogues, consulates, and embassies were being attacked in Europe, Africa, and the Middle East. Every Israeli embassy and consulate was on high alert.

All Shin Bet agents were required to qualify with their weapons regularly and pass certain physical fitness tests. Shraga was looking for a pistol range to do his required shooting; it had to be more than just a regular pistol range. From his description, I thought the APD SWAT range would serve his needs. I introduced him to SWAT Commander Captain Julian Spence. The three of us went out to look it over, and Shraga said it was perfect. Captain Spence got the okay from Major Holley.

When the Shin Bet trainer came down from New York to qualify Shraga, he liked our APD swat range so much, that after we received the required authorizations, all Shin Bet agents stationed in the United States were trained and qualified on our range in Atlanta.

Shraga and I became good friends, visiting each other's homes with our families. We went to baseball games together. He loved baseball and became an Atlanta Braves fan. One evening, when the Shin Bet trainer was in town, the three of us went out to dinner. Our steaks had just been served when Shraga's pager beeped. (This was during the first Gulf War, and cell phones were not yet as efficient, inexpensive, or available and popular as they are now.) When he returned to the table after making his call, he grimly said, "Iraq has just bombed Israel with a number of scud missiles." They dropped money on the table and were gone. I settled the bill, leaving three perfectly good, uneaten steak dinners on the table. (Betty wanted to know why I didn't put them in takeout boxes and bring them home with me. I guess I was excited and wanted to get home to turn on CNN.)

The Israeli Consulate in Atlanta stayed on high alert due to bomb threats from anonymous telephone callers and demonstrations in front of the building, with forty to fifty people chanting and shouting, carrying signs and banners proclaiming, "Death to Israel" and "Jews out of Palestine." Threatening phone calls—"We will finish what Hitler started"—suspicious people in the lobby of the building, and things of that nature.

With Major Holley's approval, and help from Captain Spence, I coordinated extra security measures for the consulate. The APD assigned manpower and resources when deemed appropriate. We had high visibility, such as frequent drive-bys of patrol cars and marked patrol cars sitting parked on different sides of the building at scattered intervals; SWAT officers in the lobby and corridor outside of the consulate office. I dropped in and said hello to Shraga at least once a day. Nothing of any consequence happened.

Shraga Karyan returned to Israel at about the same time I took my retirement in 1992.

It was ironic that, after my retirement, law enforcement officials from Metro-Atlanta went to Israel to be briefed on terrorism, in cooperation with the Israeli government. It wasn't long after that law enforcement personnel from around the state, as well as Atlanta, began making regular trips to Israel. These trips became so popular that certain politicians from the City of Atlanta and the State of Georgia took advantage of a free "junket" to visit the Middle East—state legislators, county commissioners, city council members, even some of the power brokers from downtown boardrooms, politicians, and businessmen—none of whom knew or cared anything about international terrorism. Most didn't know terrorism from needlepoint.

Nevertheless, it was good that awareness of international terrorism had developed, as well as plans for how to root it out before it could occur locally. But what burns my ass about it is that I was the guy who initiated the original contact with the Israeli government. I was the person who established a working relationship with the Shin Bet. I was the guy who predicted terrorism was going to be a major concern in the United States. I was the person who was concerned about terrorism long before it became the "word" on TV, radio, and politicians' lips, and in the newspapers every day and night. I was the guy who tried to convince my chief to take advantage of what was being offered. Ultimately, I was the guy who didn't get to participate when it really happened.

The Cover Team Accused Me of Stalling Before Giving the Signal to Come in for the Arrest

The Tactical Anti-Crime , the TAC unit of the late 1980s was exactly like the Decoy Squad of the early 1970s. The TAC unit was a plainclothes, street crime unit that handled the many street crimes that came its way. It was put on special assignment when needed. Atlanta had grown from a charming, big southern town to a vibrant, bustling, major city with professional sports, headline entertainment, excellent restaurants, first class hotels, and big conventions.

This explosive growth placed an additional burden on the Atlanta Police Department, specifically on the Special Operations Section. The table of organization within the APD was divided into four divisions. The Field Operations Division (FOD), the largest of the four, included uniform personnel commanded by a deputy chief. All six zones (precincts) in the city, and the Special Operations Section, were subordinate to the FOD and commanded by majors. Within the Special Operations Section are the different specialized units with lieutenants in charge—tactical anti-crime is one of them.

SOS was charged with keeping citizens and visitors safe, including crowd control, traffic control, and the constantly increasing crime rate. The more Atlanta boomed, the more it became a haven for criminals of every kind.

Since the mid-70s, most of Atlanta's street crime occurred in the hotel district in the downtown area. No one felt safe in the streets after five p.m., unlike the downtown areas of New York City, Chicago, and other major cities, where there was a pulsating city life, regardless of the time of day. The only life in downtown Atlanta in the evenings belonged to the homeless, the predators, and the thugs. When the visiting businessperson or conventioneer left the hotel for an evening stroll, he or she became a target for the ever present, watchful predator, waiting for the right conditions to strike his prey.

We, as a plainclothes, street crime unit, addressed this ongoing problem regularly. We analyzed the crime reports and concluded that the victim profile of street robbery in that area was a white male between thirty-five and fifty-five years old. We needed a decoy to fit those parameters. I looked around the squad room and saw black officers, female officers, and young white male officers; none fit the profile. I became aware that everyone in the room was looking at someone who could be our decoy. They were all looking at me—not too big, bald, eyeglasses—no one said a word; after all, I was the lieutenant, the unit commander, the boss! I expected anyone in my command to do what he or she had to do to get the job done; and so I had to do what I had to do. I volunteered myself, to everyone's delight, to be the pigeon.

Numerous complaints came in that conventioneers and businessmen were being accosted and robbed on the hotel district streets in the evenings. All victims were white males walking alone; the culprits were two black females.

The two would engage the victim in conversation, deliberately distract him, and then casually walk away. Later, the victim discovered his money or his wallet, or both, was not in his pocket and his watch was no longer on his wrist. None of the victims described how they were so distracted that they were unaware anything was taken from them. I soon learned.

Every night I strolled where most of the robberies were reported; I did all the things I shouldn't have done, such as isolate myself in desolate places. It was like throwing a worm into a fishpond. I wore a sport jacket, dress pants, dress shoes, dress shirt, open collar, no tie, and as clearly as shouting, from the label of my jacket, my name tag read, "Hello, my name is——from——."

Walking up Baker Street, toward Peachtree Street, alongside the Hyatt Regency, I was approached by two black females, who ran up to me from across the street. One took my hand and placed it under her blouse on her bare breast. The other one had her hand in my front pants pocket, fondling me. I had marked money in my pocket, and as soon as she removed her hand, I grabbed her wrist and gave the arranged signal to the cover team. They were very close; they moved in and made the arrests. They were not women at all, but a couple of transvestites.

I confess that I have felt a few breasts in my lifetime—and these felt as good as any. I don't know how they do it. The cover team accused me of stalling and enjoying the moment before giving the signal. No further robberies by black women were reported in the hotel area after they were arrested.

I Was a Police Lieutenant, and the Most Mugged Man in All of Atlanta

The street robberies and muggings continued. There were always conventioneers and tourists downtown, so we continued our tactics. I was still the decoy. Sergeant Pitts had to keep reminding me to adjust my body language, to walk like the non-threatening accountant or pharmacist I might have been, to stop walking in a defensive posture, not to look like I was ready for a fight, not to look like I was prepared to protect myself.

I did as Pitts suggested; apparently, I did it well because there were times I was knocked to the ground and got some scratches, bumps, and bruises, although I never was seriously hurt. When I was knocked down, the cover team exacted from the perpetrator a "pound of flesh" on my behalf. A little street justice. We violated rules and regulations, as well as the law. But that's the way it was. We were a tight-knit group. The officers in the cover team realized that because of my rank, I didn't have to be the decoy. They all appreciated that I did what I didn't have to do, to get the job done, and they respected me for it. I doubt if there are records to cite otherwise, but I was the most mugged man in the City of Atlanta during that time, perhaps ever.

Red Dog

Towards the spring of 1988, Major Holley and I were summoned once again to the chief's office. Present at the meeting were Deputy Chief WJ Taylor, Chief Morris Redding, and Police Commissioner George Napper. We were given a bunch of happy talk about the performance of the TAC unit, getting the job done on the various difficult missions that had been assigned to us, and so on and so forth. The compliments were their way of leading into yet another change in direction for the TAC unit.

This time change pointed us in the direction of drug trafficking, which had reached crisis proportions in the city. Street level drugs were accompanied by street level violence, which can be ugly and fierce. The TAC unit was assigned to combat this problem, and only this problem. Most of the drug activity occurred in the thirty-two public housing projects in the city, as well as in private apartment complexes, on street corners, and down dark alleys.

Additional personnel were needed to bolster the TAC unit so that we might be able to undertake this massive problem and hopefully have some success in reducing it. The overtime program was revived; zone officers were permitted to work one of their off days. We went operational the evening following that meeting. We kept to our six p.m. to two a.m. schedule.

We had to learn by experience in dealing with the drug problem, as there was no precedent for this in the City of Atlanta, no guidelines to follow. It would be trial and error—on the job training.

We targeted the lowest level of the drug trade—the thugs that deal "dime bags" of crack cocaine on the streets. They had formed gangs to guard against anyone who tried to sell on their turf. There had been turf wars with other drug-dealing gangs, drive-by shootings, and violent shootouts in the streets, where they usually killed each other—which was okay with us. Unfortunately, innocent people, too many of them children, were killed in the crossfire—which was not okay.

The Atlanta Police Narcotics Squad, the county and state narcotics squads, and the DEA all concentrated on suppliers at different levels; they pretty much ignored the street-level dealers. The APD beat cars

301

usually responded to one call and then another. It was too overwhelming for a single patrol car to cope with drug-related activities and shootings. There was no shortage of "customers" for us because they had operated openly and brazenly, unchallenged, for so long.

Officially, we were known as the "Overtime Drug Detail." We were in full uniform, drove marked and unmarked cars and vans—four to a car, six or more to a van. We arrived at a predetermined target area, chosen from a long list of drug-infested locations. We had many to choose from; all we had to do was pick one. We struck in force— suddenly, unannounced—overwhelming the dealers. We made mass arrests and confiscated lots of crack cocaine, guns, and cash. The media loved to report all that, so we got lots of attention from many people.

Police Commissioner Napper was ecstatic. This was his baby; it was working and getting good press. He doubled the size of the TAC unit and made permanent all the members of TAC. I was able to pick and choose from the pool of volunteers, and there were plenty. This was where the action was. We were authorized two more sergeants, so in addition to Sergeants Jesse Pitts and Doug Overstreet, we added Sergeants Gerry Sanchez and Bernadette Hernandez. I was the lieutenant and commander of the unit.

The Overtime Drug Detail just didn't sound proper to Commissioner Napper. He wanted a name that reflected the personality of the unit. Our tactics were very aggressive when we raided a location. We used the elements of surprise, speed, and force. He chose the name "Red Dog," a popular football term meaning to go after the quarterback by any means—up, over, through, or around—to tackle him before he could pass off or throw the football. Napper was convinced that Red Dog propagated the macho image. It dripped with testosterone.

At the end of the watch, our first night out with our new identity, Sergeant Pitts called in all members. "2711, Give all Red Dog units a signal 16G." (Go to the precinct.) Immediately following that transmission, we heard barking over the radio from other units; it persisted for ten minutes. The barking continued every night at the end of our watch, but as the weeks went on it diminished, until it finally stopped. Our brothers in the APD, those clowns who barked, either got used to our name, or tired of barking.

We operated mostly at night, six p.m. to two a.m.—the most productive hours. We kept our Sunday and Monday off days, it was required that our off days be consecutive. The least active night was

Sunday, so that meant our second night off had to be Monday, because Saturday night was certainly not inactive. Nevertheless, we occasionally changed hours and off days because we had learned from the Courtland Street rapist that it was the way to keep the bad guys from figuring out when and where we might be.

We did not "go by the book" because there was no book in the APD for the kind of work we did. We did it by trial and error—adapting and adjusting, adapting and adjusting, over and over.

We confiscated automatic weapons several times, so a SWAT team was attached to us for cover. They carried shoulder weapons, providing additional firepower should we be met with automatic weapons. We coordinated with the air unit—the APD helicopter. It came in after we hit a location and lit it up for us.

Several Red Dog officers in plainclothes scouted locations to verify that drug activity was occurring and identify the individuals involved. This gave us advanced intelligence, which we sincerely appreciated, because without it, we went in blind.

When we hit a location, we froze everyone we discovered there until we were sure we knew who was who. We made sure "Grandma" and young children were gotten out of the way quickly and safely. There was usually a foot chase each time we hit a location. We kept some officers on the perimeter of the location to cut off escape.

Everyone fitting the profile—young black males in their teens to mid-20s, hanging out in areas known for street drug activity and gang violence—was put on the ground and searched. We almost always found drugs, money, and guns. With few and rare exceptions, the drug dealers and gang members we arrested were young black males.

That was our mission—the streets. The Narcotics Squad handled the sophisticated dealers operating in secret. We checked the city in all four directions and found only young black males that were selling drugs out in the open. Every now and then, we caught in our net a car with young white males and females who had come from the suburbs to buy drugs in the city. If we found drugs on them, we arrested them, making them the lucky ones—more fortunate than the white kids who weren't caught by us. Other white kids who came to these areas were usually robbed, shot, raped, or killed.

The Red Dog unit continued to operate night after night after night in the drug and gang-infested areas of the city. We made many arrests and confiscated a considerable amount of drugs, money, guns. Did our work make any difference? Did it stop the flow of drugs? Did it break up the gangs? Did it stop the violence in the poverty-stricken areas? I have no reason to believe that it did.

It was simple supply and demand, the first chapter in any introductory level college textbook on economics. As long as there is demand, there will be supply. In drugs, there will be teenagers and young men to distribute it on the streets for the suppliers. Working for the suppliers, they make the kind of money that buys the most expensive cars, jewelry, and clothes. They get paid in cash, and they buy with cash.

The Trojan Horse

The Red Dog Unit had raided the Bowen Homes housing project on Bankhead Highway again and again, with the same results we were getting from other known drug locations in the city: mass arrests of "drug thugs," in addition to the confiscation of their drugs, money, and guns. However, as the days and then the weeks went on, each time we rolled into Bowen Homes there was no drug activity; all was quiet. Bowen Homes was unique in that there was only one way in and one way out. It was like a giant cul-de-sac, with hundreds of two-story brick apartment buildings on acres upon acres, with streets connecting them all. These streets led to a feeder road, which intersected at the entrance with Bankhead Highway, a main thoroughfare. The drug dealers and their thugs had placed lookouts, equipped with walkie-talkies, at the entrance to Bowen Homes. As we turned in off Bankhead Highway, onto the feeder road, the words "Fire in the Hole" and "Red Dog" was quickly relayed to the dealers, who then disappeared. The drug dealers had set up an early warning system.

One evening, just before roll call, Officer Ray Braswell asked me to step outside to the parking lot; he had something to show me. It was parked in the rear of the precinct—a 27-foot U-Haul truck. He had borrowed it for the evening from an acquaintance who owned a truck rental agency.

Braswell had figured out how we could get into Bowen Homes unannounced. Plans were hastily made. Sergeant Jesse Pitts, a large black male in his late forties, in plain clothes, drove the truck. Red Dog and SWAT officers were jammed into the rear compartment, which would have ordinarily carried freight without the power of arrest.

Later that evening, the truck turned off Bankhead Highway into the Bowen Homes entrance; the ever present lookouts paid it no attention.

Pitts drove the truck into the center of drug activity. No sooner had he parked, than several dealers were at the driver's side of the cab, trying to sell Pitts crack cocaine.

At the same time, at back of the truck, thugs attempted to open the rear door, to see what they could steal. The cops held the door down from the inside. As more and more thugs came to assist lifting the door, a pre-arranged signal from Sergeant Pitts signaled the cops inside to let go of the door. Out came the "Dogs." That night in Bowen Homes, approximately thirty drug dealers were arrested, and large amounts of crack cocaine and money were seized, as well as an assortment of weapons, small caliber handguns to automatic weapons.

Sometimes all that's needed is a little imagination, or remembering what the Greeks did with the Trojan horse. Thanks to Ray Braswell, Atlanta did the same two thousand years later. I had never realized that Ray Braswell was an ancient history buff!

Red Dog Commander Lieutenant Goldhagen (left) briefing Police Commissioner George Napper (center) and Special Operations Major W.W. Holly (right) before a raid in a drug and gang infested housing project. Motorcycle Lt. W.A. Mock in far right of photo

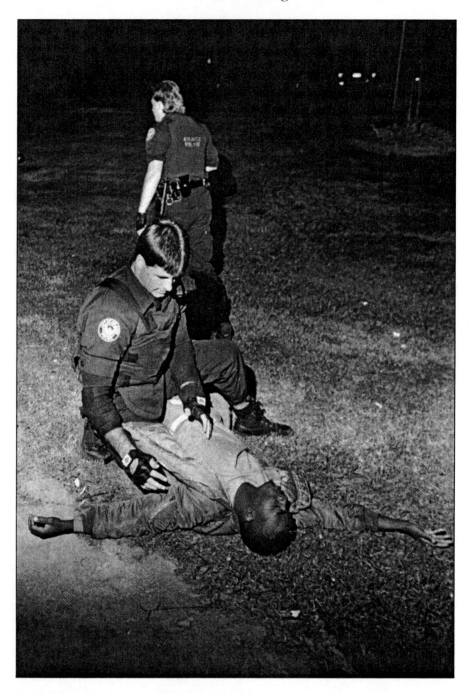

SWAT Officer Tony Volkadav (kneeling) and Red Dog Officer Rick Chambers subdue a drug dealing gang member who chose to fight

*Red Dog officers have drug dealing gang
members secure and under control*

Red Dog officers heading for the second raid of the night

307

Undone by Our Success

The Red Dog unit was getting a lot of publicity. We were high profile. Our success eventually was our undoing. Major Eldrin Bell, the Zone 3 commander, a controversial and political figure, had been up and down like a yo-yo in the ranks of the APD during his career. During his last controversy, he was demoted from deputy chief to his permanent rank of lieutenant. He had been caught up in an FBI sting, targeting organized crime figures. Bell was having dinner at the restaurant with some of those people when the FBI raided it.

Mayor Maynard Jackson had always been Eldrin Bell's power—his mentor, his "rabbi," but because of all the negative publicity, and the media clamoring for Bell's head, Jackson couldn't keep Bell from taking the fall. However, within a year, Bell was appointed to the rank of major, and placed in command of the Zone 3 precinct.

Zone 3 was tough—lots of crime and violence—dubbed "The Combat Zone" by the media. But it wasn't enough for Bell; he needed more. He was looking for a way to climb back up. His ladder was Red Dog.

Bell had other sources of power—some black members of the city council and Atlanta's black elite, including the clergy. Eldrin Bell had enough "juice," to have the Red Dog unit removed from the Special Operations Section. Red Dog had tripled in size and was changed from a unit to a section. A lieutenant commands a unit or squad, whereas a section or zone has as its commanding officer a major. It was now designated the Red Dog Section, commanded by Major Eldrin Bell. He had found his way back into the limelight. (He eventually went on to become chief of police.)

I had command of Red Dog for a year. When Bell took it over, I remained in Special Operations to run the TAC unit. All of the original TAC officers were given the choice: remain in Red Dog or return to the TAC unit. Every one chose TAC; the familiar faces were together again. During the year I was in command of Red Dog, one of the "Dogs" was shot, not seriously, and several injured. Considering what we did, night after night, we were very lucky that none of us were seriously hurt, or killed.

On December 19, 1988, Betty and I planned to celebrate our twenty-ninth wedding anniversary with a romantic dinner at a nice restaurant. I was scheduled to take the night off. That same week, my good friend Michael Elia from New York was in Atlanta, attending a conference of economists, economics teachers, and publishers of books on economics. Mike was an editor with The McGraw Hill College Textbook division. He called, inviting Betty and I to join him, several McGraw Hill managers, and two key economics textbook authors, for dinner at the Mansion, a pricey restaurant located at Piedmont and North Avenues. This was the same night Betty and I had planned to dine alone. But dinner with a good friend, and some of his business friends, with McGraw Hill picking up the check? Why not?

On our way to meet Mike and his group for dinner, I stopped by the precinct during roll call, to take care of some business. I was in my best suit; Betty looked like a movie star. All the troops wanted to know what was up with the threads. I admitted it was our anniversary; we'd been invited out to dinner.

We met Mike and his group at the restaurant. Everyone was seated at a long table. There were about a dozen of us. We had just given the waiter the order for our meals, when conversation at the other tables ceased; there was quiet. The clinking of silverware and glasses stopped, the waiters stopped hustling and bustling. Then I saw six Red Dog officers—big, fierce-looking, black, white, Latino—in black fatigues and boots, wearing all their gear, marching through the restaurant, tromping single file towards me.

I froze. I didn't know what they were going to do—maybe snatch me up, cuff me, drag me out of the restaurant, hopefully release me in the parking lot, embarrassing the hell out of me. This is cop humor, esprit de corps, and all that.

But, the lead guy, Officer Gregory Ragsdale, a huge bear of a man, was holding a string of balloons that read, "Happy Anniversary" in bright colors. I was relieved; no cops with decorative balloons bobbing over their heads would fake an arrest of their boss. Sergeant Gerry Sanchez had a box, gift-wrapped in silver paper. They presented the balloons to me; to Betty they presented the box, which contained a bottle of champagne and two champagne glasses, along with an anniversary card signed by all the Red Dogs. After some congratulatory handshakes and hugs, they turned and marched back out the way they came.

After the shock wore off, and the restaurant was back to the normal din, I apologized to the McGraw Hill bunch. They thought it was great. They had never witnessed anything like that. Two different worlds.

My birthday, December 28, follows our wedding anniversary by a week. For police officers, that's when crime activity, low during the Christmas holidays, gets back in gear. We're back to kicking ass, night after night, and we have the evening watch SWAT unit and the helicopter unit attached to us.

I was at the precinct after roll call that night, planning the night raids, when I received a call on the radio from Major Holley, who wanted me to meet him at the SWAT hut. The SWAT hut is where the SWAT team is housed—a small concrete block building on the corner of Peachtree Street and Memorial Drive. When I pulled up, I saw Major Holley standing outside the front door. His car was the only one parked along side the building. The hut was dark, which meant all the SWAT officers were on the street, where they should have been. Major Holley unlocked the door and walked in; I was right behind him. As I entered, I noticed movement at my right. I reached toward my gun, then all the lights went on, and thirty people shouted "surprise" to an astonished Red Dog commander. I damn near shot the helicopter pilot!

My eyes focused on two people in the center of this group. My still startled brain could not figure out what my wife, Betty, and my daughter, Kris, were doing in this setting. They surprised me with a birthday party with the blessings of Major Holley and Captain Spence, in the most unlikely place.

The tables were full, loaded with tons of food that Betty and Kris had made and brought from home. There was a big homemade cake, inscribed with, "Happy Birthday, Top Dog." We ate until we were stuffed. Later on, some of us were not as fleet of foot during the inevitable foot chases.

From the beginning, it was TAC, then Red Dog, and finally TAC again. We were a tight, close-knit group, all of us—black, white, Latino, male and female. Our nightly assignments with their inherent danger, forged friendships and cemented bonds. We depended on each other for survival, not unlike soldiers in combat. We became family.

Occasionally, before the Christmas holidays, I hosted a get-together at my home for all members of the group—wives, husbands, and significant others included. As their commander, I wanted to show my sincere appreciation to these dedicated, highly motivated police officers. I didn't want to give speeches with the standard clichés, or the usual bunch of happy talk. That was about the most the cops around the APD got, if that, from their bosses.

Betty and my daughter Kris did all the work, preparing the tons of food consumed by this ravenous bunch—shrimp, chicken wings, crabmeat, tuna and macaroni salads, dips, cheese and crackers, etc.

There was beer and soft drinks to wash it all down, and for those who still had room, lots of homemade desserts and the police officer's best friend—home brewed coffee. The next day, there was not enough food left over for me to have a decent snack.

Jesse Pitts, Gregory Ragsdale, and I have recently discussed doing it again, to recreate that feeling of camaraderie. The original players are scattered throughout the APD, but with some effort, we think we can pull it off. Betty and Kris are standing by in the kitchen. They enjoyed it as much as we did.

Red Dog and SWAT officers gather at the "SWAT Hut"

*Red Dog Commander Goldhagen at the "SWAT Hut" during his
surprise birthday party with daughter Kris (left) and wife Betty*

Everyone, Even Assholes, Must be Protected to Speak Freely

The Ku Klux Klan, White Supremacists, and Neo-Nazis are small
groups that assemble and express themselves in our society, although
most of us would like to think they don't exist anymore. They are a
fishbone caught in society's throat; they just will not go away. They are
an embarrassment to anyone with an IQ over 60. They show up now
and then, here and there, in different parts of the country. Simply
announcing a planned rally, they get a lot of attention from the media.
The problem for law enforcement is not policing them—that's easy.
The real difficulty is policing the multitude of people that come to
protest these rallies.

In 1989, the Southern White Knights of the Ku Klux Klan applied for a permit to hold a rally on the steps of the state capitol, and then to march through downtown Atlanta. The City of Atlanta and the State of Georgia both denied permits. The KKK took it to court; the court ruled they had a constitutional right to peaceful demonstration, forcing the city and the state to grant the permits.

City and state law enforcement officials, from past experience, realized what was coming, so they prepared for the worst. The following are approximate numbers of law enforcement personnel assigned to the rally:

Georgia National Guard	2,000
Atlanta Police Department	800
Georgia State Patrol	500
Georgia Bureau of Investigation	100
Georgia Department of Corrections	50
Georgia Department of Natural Resources	50

(To put this in proper perspective, a presidential visit to Atlanta requires approximately two to three hundred Atlanta police officers, and twenty to thirty Georgia State Troopers.)

The rally was to be held in mid-May on a Saturday morning, beginning at ten a.m., on the front steps of the state capitol building. Metal barricades were set up blocking all streets leading to the capitol building, with a two-block buffer zone. All 3,500 law enforcement personnel and National Guard troops were in full riot gear.

Right on time, at ten a.m., two pickup trucks pulled up in front of the capital building; from out of the pickups came five Neanderthals in white robes, dunce caps on their dumb heads, carrying bullhorns. Five! That's right, five KKK nitwits!

They gave their hate-filled, bigoted, racist, anti-Semitic speeches from the steps of the state capitol to the cops and the media, because they were the only ones who could hear the bullhorns. The crowd of citizens could not hear it because they were kept beyond a perimeter two blocks away in all directions. Had the five morons in white packed up and left after their speeches, that would have been that, and everyone would have gone home, or gone for coffee or a burger.

Unfortunately, these five intellectually deprived KKK members had a permit to march through downtown Atlanta, and that's just what they were going to do. We in the Atlanta PD knew what was going to happen next.

The five robed idiots "marched" out of the cordoned-off area, protected within a moving pocket, insulated by two thousand National Guard troops. The police were on the outer perimeter of the massive group of troops. Our job was to repel any attempt by the anti-demonstrators to break through and get to the Klansmen. And (albeit reluctantly) we had to do our job as our sworn duty and responsibility. The crowd was estimated at between 30,000 and 50,000.

The paltry procession of white marched up Central Avenue, approaching Decatur Street. Some of the crowd breached a four-foot wall around a construction site, where they found bricks, rocks, bottles, and chunks of concrete, the stuff of urban artillery, using it to bombard the procession. I went over the wall with a group of Atlanta police officers led by Captain Spence, commander of the SWAT team. After a short battle, we drove them out, and the bombardment stopped. Several skirmishes between anti-demonstrators and the police broke out throughout the length of the march. The crowd never got close to the Klansmen.

Two hours after the march started, it was over. We were back at the state capitol, where it began. The State Patrol escorted the two pickup trucks out of the area through a back street. The National Guard loaded their gear and personnel into their trucks and returned to their posts. All personnel from the state's law enforcement agencies returned to the Georgia hinterlands, from whence they came. Their departures left Atlanta police officers as the only remaining law enforcement presence. That seemed to be okay because the crowd had dispersed, and calm and order was restored in downtown.

We were wrong about that.

The vacuum was quickly filled with roving gangs of young thugs. These same ones showed up at every downtown event. They had been on the fringe of the crowd all day. There were no longer the massive law enforcement personnel present as earlier in the day. Most of the Atlanta police officers had gone back to their precincts, remaining available to downtown were some of the Special Operations Section cops and some Zone 5 cops. In all, we were only about twenty cops.

There were over a hundred thugs running wild through the downtown streets, breaking out store windows and vandalizing cars,

314

among miscellaneous wanton damage. We were being pelted with rocks, bottles, anything the thugs found convenient to hurl in our direction. The cops were exhausted; the thugs were having a good time. It was hit and run, crash and run, hide and seek. We were all over the place, chasing them from block to block. No arrests were made during this melee. But justice was delivered immediately, right on the spot, to those we did catch. Order was finally restored at about ten p.m.

The totals for the entire day:

- Dozens of anti-demonstrators arrested, no information on how many injured
- Several dozen police and guard personnel injured, suffering mostly cuts, bumps and bruises; the most seriously injured was a guardsman hit by a chunk of concrete, breaking his leg
- The Southern White Knights of the Ku Klux Klan were entirely unharmed—not a scratch anywhere on any of them. Their freedom to speak here in the United States was protected.

Lt. Goldhagen (front) commands a quick reaction team during the 1988 Democratic National Convention

*Lt. Goldhagen with Sgt. Hernandez standing
by at an abortion clinic*

The TAC Unit of the Special Operations Section.
Police Chief Morris Redding (rear row far left)

My Fourth of July Bowl of Soup

The Fourth of July is an American holiday: cookouts, fireworks, family and friends, some fun, some relaxation. But not for me back in 1980, when it started out as just another day of work.

At that time, I was the sergeant of a plainclothes detail working Zone 2, day watch, with Officers Gene Lassiter and W. Goldwire. The three of us worked as a team, concentrating on the illegal drug activities occurring in the Kirkwood area of the city.

We were cruising around, looking for the usual suspects, when we spotted a black male in his twenties walking down the street, carrying a brown paper bag. In many places, a brown paper bag might have in it a quart of milk, a couple of apples, or a homemade sandwich to be eaten during a lunch break. But there are places where the likelihood is that the person carrying that brown paper bag is transporting bad stuff. For those of us who worked drugs in the area, a brown paper bag was what we refer to as an "indicator."

317

We drove slowly alongside him—two white males and a black male in an unmarked car. He gave us furtive glances, another indicator, and then broke into a run. Goldwire jumped out of the back seat and chased him on foot. They turned the corner, and Lassiter, who was driving, sped around the corner to head him off. The suspect had reached an empty parking lot, running faster, widening the gap between them.

We caught up to him with the car and brushed him with the right front fender, knocking him down. He bounced up. I jumped out of the car while it was still moving. The suspect ran back toward the street, where Goldwire was blocking the way. I was now in pursuit of the suspect as he ran right over Goldwire. I narrowed the distance between us, close enough for me to tackle him.

Lassiter left the car and joined the foot chase directly behind me. He attempted to tackle the bad guy at the moment we went to the ground, so Lassiter tackled only the air above us, and did a belly flop skid across the concrete, skinning himself badly. (Lassiter later told me that he thought I would not be able to bring the suspect down by myself because of the way he ran right through Goldwire, and how unfazed he was when he was hit by the car.)

Goldwire was still laid out, hurt from the force of the impact when the suspect ran over him. The bad guy and I were struggling with each other on the ground. I got him in a headlock just as Lassiter; his clothes tattered, bleeding from the scraping, got to us. Pissed at the bad guy, Lassiter started pistol-whipping him in the head, but because his head and mine were so close, both of us were pistol-whipped. The two of us finally got the bad guy under control. He had dropped the brown paper bag when I tackled him. Lassiter picked it up. In it was a heroin package the size of a brick.

During our struggle to contain him, a large crowd had gathered, witnessed what happened, and become hostile. We put in a call for help and an ambulance. Within a few minutes, a dozen patrol cars arrived and dispersed the crowd. Sergeant Rufus Shepherd, a colleague from Zone 2, was among the responding units. He had been eating his annual Fourth of July barbecued spareribs at his favorite rib shack—sauce on his fingers, lips, chin—when he received the signal 63. He confessed that he had to think for a moment whether to stay with the ribs or to respond to the help call.

Goldwire had a concussion; Lassiter was bleeding from his hands, elbows, and knees. The bad guy had head injuries; I had head injuries—my jaw knocked out of line, a hole in my ear, and a black eye—all my injuries administered by Officer Gene Lassiter. At the precinct, bloodied and battered, after being treated at Grady Hospital, we were razzed by the other cops about "the Fourth of July Massacre." I got most of the ribbing because mine came from a subordinate officer. "Your men dislike you so much, they just wait for an opportunity to beat the shit out of you!"

When I got home that evening, instead of barbecue ribs with all the trimmings, I had a bowl of soup—my Fourth of July bowl of soup.

Part Five

Captain

No One Notices, No One Cares, but Everyone Gets Home Safely

The Fourth of July had always been a big day for me, personally and professionally, because it was always an intense work day—though rarely as punishing as the day of "the Massacre," a decade before. Several major events took place throughout the day, from early morning until late at night. It began at seven a.m. with the Peachtree Road Race, a 10K race, with 55,000 runners, starting at Lenox Square Shopping Center in Buckhead, and ending in Piedmont Park in Midtown. That was followed by the Fourth of July "Salute to America" parade, starting at noon in downtown Atlanta, along Peachtree Street. The Atlanta Braves usually played at home every July 4 evening to a sellout crowd, and there were fireworks in the stadium at the end of the game. There were also several other large fireworks displays from different locations within the city later at night.

It's a fun day for the public—attending or participating in the day-long events. The responsibility of handling it properly, smoothly and safely, falls on the Atlanta Police Department. It is a daunting and overwhelming mission. The logistics, the nuts and bolts of putting it together, are managed by the Special Operations Section. The many functions, the size and duration of the operation, require additional manpower, so police officers from all over the city are detailed to SOS on July 4.

As a lieutenant, and later as a captain, my Fourth of July usually started at two a.m., when my bedside alarm went off. I was at the SOS precinct before three a.m. Roll call was at five a.m. (Even though assignment rosters were made up several days prior, there were always last minute changes and adjustments.) Major Holley and Captain Spence usually gave me the task of announcing everyone's

320

assignments. I did this from the podium, up on a platform, looking out over a huge assembly room filled with four hundred or so pissed off, surly cops who didn't want to be there. For most of them it was a legal holiday, their off day. They preferred to be home, in their backyards, grilling hamburgers, eating ribs, drinking beer, relaxing.

As I called names, I gave each cop two assignments—one for the road race and one for the parade. Before I started, I told them to write them down as I called them out. Most had a bad attitude, ignoring their assignments. Roll call lasted an hour. When I had finished, I asked if there were any questions.

"Captain, which one was for the race and which for the parade?"

"Sir, could you repeat my assignments?"

The questions were rarely amusing, and most indicated a bad attitude.

In preparation for the day's first event, MARTA buses were parked outside to take everyone to their posts along the race route. A sergeant was on board each bus with a roster sheet, to supervise the drop-offs. All traffic was restricted along the route; the shutdown had been announced weeks in advance. Everyone—newspapers, television and radio—was put on notice. We sent motorcycle sergeants the entire distance to make sure every intersection and driveway entering Peachtree Road was covered, preventing any traffic from entering Peachtree Road or crossing it.

The wheelchair race started at seven a.m., on the same route as the foot race. After the forty to fifty wheelchairs came 55,000 runners. Somehow, despite the bad attitudes, we were always ready. The races ran without a hitch.

At noon, we re-grouped for the parade downtown. Due largely to the efforts of sergeants and lieutenants, all the cops (even the stragglers), were in their assigned positions on schedule. By this time, we were feeling the heat and humidity. The sun was blazing, soaking our dark blue uniforms, bulletproof vests, hats, and hard uniform shoes.

After the parade, most of the extra cops were allowed to go back to their precincts. SOS personnel handled the Braves game and the fireworks afterwards. The other fireworks displays were handled by the respective zones, along with motorcycle cops from Special Operations.

I had to wait at the precinct until everyone was accounted for, which meant I was the last one out the door. On July 4, I usually got home at two a.m., twenty-four hours after being wakened by my alarm.

My feet hurt so badly, I had to soak them before I was able to go to bed. It was a stressful and exhausting day for all the cops—a day that required lots of planning before and perfect execution during, so that everything ran smoothly for the public, who probably did not notice or care. But, as cops, we knew many thousands of people got home safely that night.

I retired from the APD in June 1992. A few weeks later, on the Fourth of July, I slept in during the Peachtree Road Race and watched the "Salute to America Parade" on TV in the air-conditioned comfort of my home. After a relaxing afternoon of barbecue and beer with family and friends, I watched the Braves game and fireworks on TV. It was the first Fourth of July in a long time that my feet didn't hurt.

Extra Jobs: I Hated Having to Do Extra Jobs—Except One

Extra jobs are a fact for most police officers. In police departments around the country, they are referred to as "second jobs," "off-duty jobs," "moonlighting"—in Atlanta, they are called "extra jobs." Some police departments prohibit them as a matter of policy, and some have rules and regulations to control them, but largely, most police officers work extra jobs. It's not what we want to do, it's what we have to do; it's a matter of economics. In Atlanta, cops need authorization, and except for a few restrictions and stipulations, they are usually approved to do extra work. Over the years, I've had many extra jobs, from one-time jobs to regular, steady extra jobs. They were varied—too many to remember, or too bad to want to. I never liked having to work any extra job, except one.

Every city that had a major league baseball team also had a "security representative"—retired FBI agents who lived in that city. Their role was ill defined and loosely organized. Sometimes they showed up at the ballpark—most of the time they didn't. There was little or no accountability, and the baseball commissioner's office was dissatisfied with this "security."

In 1987, Kevin Hallinan, a recently retired lieutenant with the New York City Police Department, proposed a deal to the baseball commissioner: hire him, put him in charge of Major League Baseball security, and he would replace the inefficient ex-FBI guys with active police officers in each major league city.

Hallinan searched the directories of FBI National Academy graduates in each city for quality police officers. He believed in the quality of police officers around the country, who were sent by their respective agencies to attend the FBI National Academy. He thought them special. For the most part, he was right, with some notable exceptions—such as Atlanta's Beverly Harvard, who sent herself to Quantico. Not knowing anyone personally, Hallinan needed a starting point and chose one from each major league city—a roll of the dice. He found Major Lee New for Atlanta. After a series of interviews with candidates from each city, Kevin Hallinan had assembled his first group of resident security agents.

Lee worked this security position for that first season under Hallinan, but was not satisfied. He was not particularly interested in baseball, and the time spent at the ballpark conflicted with personal and family issues. He worked the first season in 1987, but did not want to continue into 1988.

Lee and I had known each other, personally and professionally, for many years, and he knew I liked baseball. He also knew I had attended the FBI National Academy, which at the time was a pre-requisite for Hallinan. Lee asked if I were interested, I told him I was, and he recommended me as his replacement. After an interview with Kevin Hallinan, I became the new Major League Baseball resident security agent for the Atlanta Braves for 1988 season. It was an approved extra job.

As a resident security agent, I was the eyes and ears for the commissioner's office—the liaison between Atlanta and Major League Baseball in New York. At a minimum, I was required to attend one game, preferably the first, of each series of three visiting team games (visiting teams usually are in town for three games). Most games start at 7:35 p.m.; I had to get to the ballpark at about 6:15 p.m., which required a quick change and quick commute because I was working for the APD ten a.m. to six p.m. My "uniform" as a resident security agent was a business suit, shirt, and tie, even in the heat of July and August.

Before each game, I was required to visit with the managers, traveling secretaries of both teams, and the new crew of umpires. (The umpire crews rotate from city to city for each three-game series.) I also stayed in contact with the director of stadium operations, the chief of stadium security, and the off-duty APD police detail. The teams and umpires knew I was there to deal with any problems or concerns they had. These were many and varied.

I was working a game one evening, when I was notified to meet the director of stadium operations. When I arrived at the office, there were two detectives from the APD Sex Crimes Squad. They had an arrest warrant for one of the umpires, who at the moment was calling balls and strikes behind home plate. The charge was rape.

They were about to arrest him in the middle of the game—taking him off the field. I suggested that the arrest could be made just as easily after the game. After a lengthy conversation, I assured them that the crew of umpires was going to be in Atlanta for the next three days and that they could execute the warrant at any time during those three days or nights. I told them the name of the hotel where the umpires were staying.

The following day, I met with the detectives and their supervisors at the Sex Crimes Squad. I learned that the case for rape was not a slam-dunk. There were some inconsistencies in the story told by the alleged victim. I could not interfere, but I lobbied hard that she be given a polygraph test before executing the warrant. The woman failed the polygraph and later admitted that the sex had been consensual; she had made up the rape story to extort some money from the umpire.

Other issues had to be addressed, although none quite as dramatic. Was the integrity of both clubhouses and the umpire's room adhered to, according to the rules mandated by the commissioner of baseball? This concerned unauthorized visitors entering the clubhouses, also the times the media (with media credentials) could be in the clubhouses to interview players. Another was keeping unauthorized people off the field and away from the players during batting practice. And were the vendors throughout the ballpark cutting off beer sales at a certain time during the game? Ticket scalpers were a headache that never went away, as was the sale of counterfeit merchandise.

On occasion, a player or players would get into an altercation at one of the many nightclubs or bars. The resident security agent had to investigate these incidents and forward a report to Kevin Hallinan at the baseball commissioner's office in New York. Any contact of a known gambler or drug dealer with a player or umpire required an immediate phone call to Hallinan at anytime, night or day.

I made it clear to the Braves players and coaches from the beginning that I was not there to take care of their traffic tickets. I didn't get buddy-buddy with the players, never went through the clubhouse backslapping or high-fiving. I was friendly, but distant. I was a representative of the commissioner of baseball, and an Atlanta police lieutenant, and maintained the same professional posture with the

Atlanta Braves as all the cops I worked with. I had a lot of latitude. There was no place in the ballpark that was restricted or off limits to me—not even second base during a game, should I be so inclined. (If I had done that or anything else equally as stupid and arrogant, I would have been immediately fired by Kevin Hallinan).

In 1989, I was flown to California with several other resident security agents to work the Oakland Athletics/San Francisco Giants World Series. I was in Candlestick Park in San Francisco, sitting on a chair outside of the Giants' clubhouse, when an earthquake hit. It was measured at 7.1 on the Richter scale—a very powerful quake; it knocked me off the chair. I've been in many dangerous situations during my long career, but that massive earthquake was the most scared I've been. Panic was averted by the quick actions of Major League Baseball security, Candlestick Park management, San Francisco Police, and the California Highway Patrol. Fifty-five thousand fans filed calmly out of the ballpark. There were no casualties!

The first two games of that series were played in Oakland at the Oakland Alameda Coliseum. On Monday, we shifted to San Francisco, where game 3 was to be played on Tuesday. Early on Monday, everyone—the baseball teams, umpires, and all levels of security—drove down Interstate 880, the Nimitz Freeway in Oakland and across the Oakland Bay Bridge. When the earthquake hit the next day, sections of both Interstate 880 and the Bay Bridge collapsed.

Several weeks prior to the World Series, I took the test for captain. When I checked into the Fairmont Hotel in San Francisco, there was a message from Betty. I had placed seventh on the captain's test from a pool of fifty.

It was a dream extra job. In 1991, the Braves went "from worst to first." The Braves management asked me to travel with the team during the playoffs and World Series to handle security issues. I informed Kevin Hallinan, he thought it was a good idea. It was the first time a resident security agent traveled with his team. In later years, all RSAs traveled with their teams through the post season. I had plenty of vacation and comp time—enough to be gone for all post-season playoff games. Traveling with the team meant riding on team buses, flying on team charter flights, and staying at the team hotel. The Braves furnished all that, and per diem money—the same as the players and coaches received.

In subsequent years, when traveling with the Braves in the post season, I was allowed to take Betty with me at the team's expense. The players and coach's wives go also. To my utter delight, Major League Baseball insisted on paying me for going. I had the best of both worlds.

The 1991, the World Series was between the Atlanta Braves and the Minnesota Twins. The series went the full seven games—the seventh and final game at the Metrodome in Minneapolis. The Braves lost that game in ten innings, in what baseball people around the country said was the best World Series ever.

Flying home on the team charter that night, Manager Bobby Cox had gotten an Atlanta Journal newspaper. He called my attention to an item about a parade planned to honor the Braves in downtown a couple of days after returning home. I read the article and looked at the map with the proposed parade route. I told Bobby I thought it was all wrong. I've worked many parades and sporting events in Atlanta and understood the dynamics of spectators and rabid fans.

The first thing wrong was the parade route itself; it was too short. It would wind through the streets of downtown, making stops at the state capitol, where politicians would make some speeches, then on to city hall, for more politicians and more speeches. My second concern was the open convertibles, two players or a player and his wife, sitting in the rear of an open convertible. My final concern was the size of the crowd; 100,000 people were expected.

Baseball excitement had erupted in Metro-Atlanta in 1991 like never before. I saw it at the ballpark during the playoffs and World Series games played at home. I saw it from the team buses traveling to and from the ballpark and the airport; thousands of fans lined the route, doing the "tomahawk chop" as the buses rode by. I saw it at the airport, where a thousand fans crowded the gate, giving the team a send off. I saw the fans in the middle of the night, waiting to greet the team at the airport returning from post-season play in Pittsburgh and Minneapolis.

I was working my extra job with the team in Minneapolis. I was not working with the APD in Atlanta planning the parade. I tried to tell my bosses my concerns, but they weren't listening. My biggest concern was the crowd size. I tried to tell them that the expected 100,000 was much too low. Plans were made and fixed; there would be no changes.

On parade day, people started lining up along the route very early in the morning; as morning went on more fans arrived. As morning went to midmorning, still more arrived, the crowd thickening by noon to what was later estimated at 750,000. Everywhere along the parade route, the crowd spilled off the sidewalk into the street. Had the parade route been planned to cover a longer distance, the crowd would have distributed itself along the route, meaning fewer people on the sidewalks, and no spilling into the street.

This crowd was in the street, uncontained, all over the convertibles. Fans reached into the convertibles, snatching caps, sunglasses, whatever they could grab from the players—their wives jostled, mauled, by outstretched arms reaching to touch the players. Police officers tried linking arms to hold back the crowd, but it did no good; the crowd was too large. I was in the street outside city hall, linking arms with Chief Eldrin Bell on one side and Deputy Chief Julius Derico on the other. The crowd surged; we were pushed to the ground. When the convertibles reached city hall, we had to rescue the players, coaches, and wives, taking them out of the cars and bringing them into city hall. The parade was clearly over at that point, and the crowd dissipated. The parade and everything about it was an embarrassment to the city and the police department. Disaster was averted because it was an adoring crowd; but it was an uncontained adoring crowd.

When the World Series games were played in Atlanta, I was still off APD duty. My assignment for Major League Baseball was to escort and provide security for the commissioner of baseball, meet his private jet at the Fulton County Airport, take him downtown to his hotel, and escort him to the ballpark, where he watched the game from the owner's box on the field. I sat directly behind him, the second best seat in the house, and was paid to do it.

I served under four Baseball Commissioners; Peter Uberoff, Bart Giamatti, Fay Vincent and Bud Selig.

Baseball Commissioner Fay Vincent and Resident Security Agent
Harold Goldhagen at Atlanta – Fulton County Stadium. "Best extra
job, ever!"

The Stretch Limo Peeled Off from the Motorcade; Thirty Cars Followed

The United States Secret Service is the law enforcement agency responsible for the protection of the president and vice president of the United States and their families; former presidents, and presidential and vice presidential candidates during an election year. An additional mandate for the Secret Service is to protect visiting foreign heads of state while on US soil.

The Protective Services Division of the US State Department is another law enforcement agency with similar responsibilities. Its subjects are VIPs within the state department: the secretary of state, all assistant secretaries, under secretaries, and all US ambassadors throughout the world. The Protective Services Division also provides protection for certain visiting foreign dignitaries not heads of state, such as the Pope, the secretary general of the United Nations, the Dali Lama, and the shah of Iran (after he was deposed), among others.

When Nelson Mandela was released after more than twenty years in a South African prison, he became the symbol of the end of apartheid in that country and was immediately thrust upon the world stage. He began a world tour, which included a half-dozen cities in the United States, among them Atlanta, Georgia.

With the assassinations of President John F. Kennedy, Robert Kennedy, Martin Luther King, Jr., Anwar Sadat, Yitzak Rabin, and the attempts on President Ronald Reagan and the Pope, no world figure is immune. Nelson Mandela was no exception, and the duty to protect him was clear to all law enforcement agencies in cities on Mandela's tour. The primary responsibility rested with the US state department's Protective Services Division.

US State Department Special Agent Harry Jones was the agent in charge of the Atlanta office. Harry and I knew each other and we got along well. Plans had to be made; this visit would be a major event. The initial planning meeting was not held at Atlanta police headquarters or the offices of the US state department. The King family is a very powerful force in Atlanta; they insisted the planning be held at the King Center, the site of the Martin Luther King, Jr. tomb. The black elite agreed, comparing Nelson Mandela's struggle against apartheid to Martin Luther King's struggle in the civil rights movement. No one argued.

Present were Special Agent Harry Jones, representing the United States government, Atlanta Police Chief Eldrin Bell, and several deputy chiefs and majors. I was a captain, the lowest ranked among the police brass there. In addition, there was the King family and other members of Atlanta's black elite, some of whom I didn't recognize. Everyone who was "someone" in the Atlanta black community was present, although there were those who were "someone" only unto themselves.

There were only two white faces at that meeting—Harry's and mine. The plans, the event, and the execution were going to be entirely in civilian hands. The police chief and other top brass were not going to challenge the King family, Reverend Joseph Lowery of the Southern Christian Leadership Conference (SCLS), or any of the other black clergy at that meeting. Anything Harry Jones attempted to discuss was shouted down; I was virtually ignored.

Harry Jones was required to be at that meeting; it was his job to be there. My presence meant nothing to anyone. I was completely immaterial to the planning. I tried to beg off attending subsequent meetings. Major Holley would not let me off the hook. I was the commanding officer of all traffic related functions in the city, and traffic issues would be a major component of this visit. I had to attend all meetings at the King Center, despite not being permitted any input.

There were moments at the meetings that were laughable. For example, it seemed like everyone wanted to ride in the same limo with Mandela—a Greyhound bus would not have been big enough! Each wanted Mandela to visit their church, their school, their home, their place of business, or some other facility of theirs. Some took issue with a rally and speech to be held in the football stadium at Georgia Tech. "Why does he have to go to a mostly white college? We have black colleges in Atlanta!"

The most outlandish objection was when someone proposed no police presence, because "Mandela might be uncomfortable and offended by the uniforms!" When we heard things like this, Harry and I would look at each other, roll our eyes, shake our heads, and look down at our hands, wanting to be where we could do what we were trained to do, what our experience told us we should do.

In these meetings, everyone thought he was more important than anyone else was; what he had to say was more important than what anyone else was trying to say. The King family dominated, but others had to have their say. Reverend Joseph Lowery of the SCLC had to be heard; that prompted other prominent clergy members to say what they felt had to be heard. The city politicians were not to be out done—huge egos clashed.

For law enforcement, the logistics of an operation of this magnitude are enormous. It calls for dedicated, experienced people who know what they are doing because the success of such an event, from beginning to end, depends on the details. Fortunately, the SOS lieutenants and sergeants had lots of experience handling these types of events; they did it often, and they handled all presidential visits to the Atlanta.

After many meetings at the King Center, Mandela's itinerary and the venues he would visit was finally decided. Given that we had no input, we accepted those as constraints; Harry and I went to work. We hunkered down at the SOS precinct, without any outside interference or distractions, with the special operations staff, and we hammered out a plan.

I don't know if running a VIP motorcade is a science, an art, or neither, but I do know it better be done right. It is purposely structured, with good reasons for the position and path of every vehicle. (I had previously been to the US Secret Service Training Center in Washington D.C. for a week, and all we did that entire week was run motorcades). The first thing we needed to know from the King Center chiefs was how many vehicles would be in the motorcade. Every day, the King Center called to advise us of an increase in the number of vehicles. We had no control and received no help in that regard; my bosses stood on the sidelines and let it all happen. We ended up with about fifty vehicles in the Mandela motorcade; it looked more like a funeral procession. (Most presidential motorcades consist of fifteen to twenty vehicles, not counting motorcycles.)

The charter flight carrying Nelson Mandela arrived near a private hanger at Hartsfield International Airport. The massive motorcade was lined up; no one was in the cars because they were on the tarmac to greet him when he came down the steps of the plane. After a good bit of hand shaking, hugging, backslapping, and picture taking, we got everyone back in their vehicles.

The motorcade started to move with the Atlanta police motorcycle escort—twelve motorcycles, paired as usual, leading the way. I was in the lead APD patrol car. Harry was in an unmarked state department car directly behind the limousine Mandela was in. We followed I-75/85 toward the city. The first stop was to be Bobby Dodd Stadium at Georgia Tech, where Nelson Mandela would address a packed football stadium of 50,000 spectators.

Reverend Joseph Lowrey of the SCLC was in his stretch limo about a third of the way down from the front of the motorcade. As the motorcade was proceeding along the downtown connector, which is I-75/85, Lowrey decided to stop at the SCLC office on Auburn Avenue. His limo exited the freeway, and thirty vehicles followed. The last three vehicles were an ambulance, an APD patrol car, and a Georgia State patrol car. I got a frantic radio call from our tail car wanting to know what the hell was going on. The state trooper was also barking his frustration over his radio. I told them to contact the ambulance and catch up with the motorcade. The rest of the cars would simply have to get to Bobby Dodd Stadium on their own.

Georgia Tech campus police chief, Jack Vickery, had the underground parking garage below the stadium sealed off and cleared of parked cars. The motorcade, minus the thirty wayward cars, pulled into the garage and parked in this secure location. Nelson Mandela was well into his speech when the rest of the original motorcade straggled in, one by one. Some few were allowed into the garage; the rest had to park wherever they could and walk several blocks. Mandela was well received; there were no further problems.

The next stop was Morehouse College, part of the black Atlanta University system, comprised of four colleges. Nelson Mandela spoke in a large auditorium to an overflow crowd, many watching on closed circuit TV throughout the campus.

A day or two before an operation of this size takes place, we make a dry run along the route to check out the plans—what the organizers intend to happen—against what we expect could happen from what we observe during the run. Because we had checked out the route, the APD motorcycle escort, the pilot car (State Patrol), and the lead car (APD, the car I was in) all knew our stopping points. This included the one where the Mandela limo, which would be several cars behind me, was supposed to stop exactly adjacent to the walkway leading to the steps of the auditorium, the crowd held back by metal barricades along the walkway from the street to the steps. That's what was supposed to happen if we had total control over the details. What happened on the day of the event, however, was somewhat different.

As we approached the stop at the walkway, we saw one of Mandela's staff standing in the street. We quickly tried to get him out of our way by beeping the car horns; we opened the windows, trying to shout him out of our way. We even tried to nudge him out of the way by moving our vehicle slowly against his body, but he stood firm. Because we did not run him over, we could not pull past the walkway with the metal barriers. We stopped rolling forward. The moment we stopped, all the cars behind us stopped, car doors started to swing open, and occupants exited, falling over themselves. Nelson Mandela had to walk half a block through the crowd.

My frustration level was on the rise, not just because of the antics of morons like that staffer who would not budge, but because of local black community "big shots" who didn't cooperate, simply because they wanted to assert themselves. I knew what had to be done to keep things orderly and on track, but I was stymied by these big shots; most were nitwits. My superiors stood mute, not supporting me at all.

The third stop was the King Center, where Mandela placed a wreath on the Martin Luther King Jr. gravesite and attended a service at the Ebenezer Baptist Church, followed by a reception inside the King Center.

We made it through the day, despite last minute changes, without any serious harm. Harry Jones was on the verge of breakdown. He and I suffered the same frustrations, aggravated by moronic antics and super egos. At the end of the day, we got Nelson Mandela, safely and soundly, back to the airport on his way to the next city on his tour. At the end of the day, Harry and I were pissed off, beaten down, and worn out.

"Air Force One, wheels up!" Then I Breathed a Little Easier

A presidential visit is very different from a foreign dignitary visit. Wherever the visit, the United States Secret Service handles it with military precision, yielding control to no one, but asking the help of all. The Atlanta field office of the Secret Service notifies local law enforcement agencies to expect to be involved. A meeting is scheduled, inviting those who will take part in ensuring the security of the president. An advance team of agents from the president's detail in Washington, DC conducts the meeting, along with the special agent-in-charge (the SAC) of the local office.

In preparation for the visit of the president to Atlanta, the local law enforcement superiors involved were given a thorough briefing on the itinerary and identity of the venues the president would be visiting. We then separated into groups with our counterparts: Secret Service, Atlanta police, Georgia State Patrol, Cobb County police, and US Air

Force security personnel. I was the APD traffic captain, so my responsibility was the motorcade. My group planned for what we knew we had to do. The other groups met, each going over its respective responsibilities, such as venue security, intersection control, and bridge and overpass security.

In one capacity or another, I had been involved in a number of presidential visits over the years, starting with President Richard Nixon. As a patrolman, I guarded a stairway in a hotel, worked traffic at an intersection along the route, or secured a bridge or overpass when the motorcade passed beneath. As a sergeant, I supervised police officers doing those things. As a lieutenant, I was usually responsible for securing a venue. I had worked visits for Presidents Gerald Ford, Jimmy Carter, and Ronald Reagan. The last presidential visit I worked before retiring was President George H. Bush (the elder). I worked a visit for Bill Clinton when he was a candidate for president.

My responsibility for the motorcade included control of the intersections along the route, which I delegated to traffic lieutenants and sergeants. The president usually flew into Dobbins Air Force Base in Marietta, GA, in Cobb County, twenty miles north of Atlanta. All the motorcade counterparts made a couple of dry runs from there to each of the stopping points in Atlanta; Air Force personnel don't leave the base, so they only participate in dry runs within the confines of the base.

The day before the visit, two US Air Force cargo planes arrived at Dobbins with equipment and hordes of national media. The equipment included two presidential limousines. Both are in the motorcade, one behind the other. (One is a decoy for potential assassins—which limo with dark tinted windows contains the president? The shell game.) Also, to prepare for "Murphy's Law", should one develop car trouble.

The presidential limousines may look like wedding or prom limos, but are actually tanks—custom built, armor plated all around (including the undercarriage), with two-inch-thick bulletproof glass, bullet resistant tires, and more. There is a reinforced firewall between the passenger compartment and the gas tank, should it explode. The passenger compartment is as secure as a bank vault.

Also included are two or three Suburban SUV's for Secret Service personnel, heavily armed tactical teams. The basic standard operating procedure is, should there be an attack, the president would immediately be removed from the point of attack by the president's detail, and the tactical teams would stand and repel the attack.

The day the president arrives, the motorcade is lined up on the tarmac, all vehicles in the proper order. When the very impressive Air Force One touches down at Dobbins and taxis to the spot where we are all waiting, the president de-planes and is greeted by the welcoming committee.

I am usually crammed into the lead car with my motorcade counterparts—Secret Service, Georgia State Patrol, and Cobb County police, plus a driver. We chatter away on our individual radios and to each other, all at the same time, always in communication with our agency dispatchers. Georgia State Troopers block every entrance to the freeway on the route. The state patrol has several cars in the rear of the motorcade, forming a rolling roadblock so no vehicles can overtake the motorcade.

As soon as we enter the Atlanta city limits from Cobb County, the motorcade becomes my responsibility. I continually give our location, which alerts police officers on the bridges and overpasses. As we approach, all vehicle and pedestrian traffic is frozen until the motorcade passes. Part of my responsibility is to know the location and quickest route to the nearest Trauma One center hospital wherever we are along the route. I also have to know alternate surface street routes to the venue(s), should the freeway be blocked for any reason.

When the motorcade exits the freeway for the surface streets, the police officers assigned to the intersections along the route close down those intersections. When we arrive at the intended venue, it is expected that it will have already been secured—swept by bomb sniffing dogs—every doorway, every hallway, every stairway, guarded by a police officer. Sniper/observer teams will be on some of the rooftops, and all traffic will be stopped.

When the visit is over, the procedure for the motorcade is reversed to take the president back to Dobbins. On the tarmac, before he embarks, the president usually comes over and personally thanks the uniformed police officers present. All of us stay put until the departure. Everyone monitoring the APD radio breathes a little easier when they hear my voice broadcast, "Air Force One is wheels up!" I breathe a little easier, too

CITY OF ATLANTA
ATLANTA POLICE DEPARTMENT
ELDRIN BELL
CHIEF OF POLICE

June 25, 1992

Mr. Harold B. Goldhagen
Captain, Retired
Atlanta Police Department
6866 Kingsboro Drive
Lithia Springs, Georgia 30057

Dear Captain Goldhagen:

On behalf of the City of Atlanta Police Department, I want to take this opportunity to personally **COMMEND** you on thirty years of dedicated service and to **CONGRATULATE** you on your recent retirement.

The Atlanta Police Department will truly miss you and your commitment to the citizens of this city. Your professionalism, dedication, and commitment exemplified the type of commander we needed in law enforcement services.

We wish you the best in your future endeavors and ask that you keep us in your thoughts and your prayers. **Again, CONGRATULATIONS!**

Sincerely,

Eldrin Bell
Chief of Police

EAB:ml

Retirement letter from Police Chief Eldrin Bell

Declaration of Gratitude

The Consulate General of Israel in Atlanta wishes to express its gratitude to Captain H. B. Goldhagen, upon his retirement, for his ongoing support of many years. Captain Goldhagen made us all feel secure and relaxed and was always ready and willing to help when needed, especially during hard times such as the Gulf War. He is an example of an excellent civil servant who frequently went above and beyond the call of duty.

The Consulate General of Israel wishes Captain Goldhagen good luck in his new undertakings.

Dr. Alon Liel
Consul General
25 August 1992

Declaration of Gratitude from the Israeli Consul General .

Epilogue

A nd so it went.

Day and night, months turned into years, years into decades. Before I knew it, thirty years had gone by. Thirty years.

How could that have happened so quickly? My two children grew up in a blink of an eye. My son, Alex, my daughter, Kris, were babies, then school children, teenagers, young adults before I realized it. They grew up while I worked crazy hours, spent long hours in court, worked a variety of extra jobs, and tried to get some sleep in between.

As a young police officer, I often heard some of the older policemen talk about retirement. Some of them couldn't wait to get their time in and go. That was hard for me to understand. The thought of my own retirement someday, saddened me. I loved this job and never wanted to leave it. "Someday" snuck up on me.

Police work is a young person's profession. I no longer belonged on the street. It wouldn't be fair to me (for my own safety), to my fellow police officers, who depended on me for backup, or to the people I was sworn to protect. I could have gotten an inside job, a safe, administrative desk job, as others had done before me. I saw them trudge in every morning, go through the motions, read the newspaper, answer the telephone, shuffle papers, hang around, take long lunches, then leave for home before the traffic got bad. Some of these guys stuck around until they became pitiful old men. That was not for me.

My last three years as a captain took its toll on me. I had a huge responsibility for every special event in the city, and there were plenty such events—parades, festivals, road races, walk-a-thons, VIP visits, bicycle races, protests, escorts, demonstrations, major conventions, disasters, major sporting events, and all the incidents that shut down freeways and major arteries, and caused traffic to be re-routed.

In my last three years, I was the hostage negotiation team leader, on call twenty-four hours a day, seven days a week. For the first time in my career, I was on the day watch, with weekends off. It didn't matter! The hostage calls came mostly after midnight, usually on cold nights when it was raining. Many nights, I would be awakened by the dreadful sound of the telephone. I had to drag myself out of my nice warm bed, from beside my nice warm wife, to go out into the cold and wet miserable night. I went. I was just about burned out.

It was time to go. The day I put in my retirement papers, I had such mixed emotions that I had to force myself to sign my name. The reality set in when I attended staff meetings for the planning of the next special event, and I wasn't involved. I was left out—the lame duck.

I spent my last day cleaning out my desk, gathering up the stuff I had collected over the years. I made several trips out to my car. The people in the precinct saw me coming with empty arms and going back out with another box; they knew what was happening. They left me alone; they sensed I was in a funk. Only one more box, nothing more to do, I put my keys on my desk—the next time I walked out the door, they would no longer be "my" keys; it would no longer be "my" desk—I looked around, took a deep breath, and carried the last box to the car. I should have gone back in and said my goodbyes, but I couldn't trust my emotions. I didn't want to embarrass myself.

As I drove away from the precinct that last time, the Rodney King riots had been going on in Los Angeles, and rioting was spreading to other major cities. Driving south on Spring Street, crossing Mitchell Street, I saw them coming, hundreds of them from the Atlanta University Complex, once students, now rioters, headed for the State Capitol Building and downtown. The usual suspects, the regular thugs, were right behind. They were breaking out windows, turning over cars. I heard the sirens of the police response. My instincts pulled me one-way, common sense the other. Common sense won; I headed for I-20, and home.

When I arrived, I stopped off in the kitchen on my way to the bedroom to change clothes. I stood there for a moment and said to Betty that this was the last time she would see me in my uniform. What I was most proud of was not the captain's bars on my collar, but the six hash marks on my sleeve, each representing five years of service. There I stood—a high school dropout without a complete formal education. After thirty years as an Atlanta police officer, I had earned the equivalent of a master's degree in life, maybe even a PhD.

As you enter the Atlanta Police Department Headquarters building at 165 Decatur Street, you will see a glass-enclosed display case hanging on one of the walls in the lobby, a memorial to the dozens of Atlanta police officers killed in the line of duty over the years. In it are individual rectangular brass plaques, each engraved with the name of the police officer, the date of his death, and the manner in which he was killed. Among them are plaques bearing the names of Officers James R. Greene, Charles R. Dickson, and Donald D. Baty. There are far too many more.

As I look back at the close calls, the near misses, and "what-ifs," I consider myself fortunate and truly grateful that there is no brass plaque with my name on it. Whenever I've walked through the lobby and seen another plaque had been added, I've been struck by how damn lucky I've been.

It's been thirteen years since I retired; my uniform still hangs in the closet. If I could pass on words of wisdom to young police recruits ready to embark on their careers, I would repeat the words of a wise sergeant who said to me on my first day at the Police Academy:

"Use common sense and good judgment, and don't take yourself too seriously. Whenever you can, apply 'the spirit of the law,' rather than 'the letter of the law.' Always remember common sense and good judgment!"

If they can accept and apply that simple philosophy, they will be a credit to their uniforms and badges during and after their careers.

About the Author

Harold B. Goldhagen is a retired captain and thirty-year veteran of the Atlanta Police Department. Since retirement he has been a licensed private investigator. He instructed in hostage negotiations for the United States Army, and served as a liaison for Major League Baseball between the Baseball Commissioner's Office and the Atlanta Braves. He lives in suburban Atlanta with his wife and family.

CPSIA information can be obtained at www.ICGtesting.com
Printed in the USA
LVOW11s1814131215

466484LV00003B/665/P